NIGHTMARE

Blood was everywhere. Spattered across the walls and floor, pooling on the counter, in the sink, dripping down from the ceiling and across the frosted shower stall. Blood that erupted into infinity in the splintered shards that mesmerized her by its crimson brightness in the all-white room.

She stared at herself, nude, one hand raised, and beyond her own reflection, in the bathtub, Kasey saw a bare, blood-streaked arm sticking straight up against the tiles.

She dropped the glass, heard it shatter in the basin. Without moving her feet, she twisted around, stared disbelieving at the bathtub. A naked woman lay sprawled in a thickening pool of blood.

Above the body, scrawled in blood across the tiles, were the words, YOU'RE NEXT.

* * *

"Leaves readers screaming for more."
—*Nevada* Magazine

Books by Carol Davis Luce

SKIN DEEP
NIGHT STALKER
NIGHT PREY
NIGHT PASSAGE
NIGHT GAME

NIGHT GAME

CAROL DAVIS LUCE

ZEBRA BOOKS
KENSINGTON PUBLISHING CORP.

ZEBRA BOOKS are published by

Kensington Publishing Corp.
850 Third Avenue
New York, NY 10022

First Printing: April, 1996
10 9 8 7 6 5 4 3 2 1

Printed in the United States of America

*For my brothers Harry L. Davis and
Alan (Crazy) Christian,
and for the newest additions to the Luce clan,
sweet little Jacob and Jessica.*

Acknowledgments

I wish to thank the following people for their contribution to this novel:

These people gave me an inside glimpse into the hotel and casino business: Jim Crane, Jeri Coppa Knudson, Bill Knudson, and Ted Benture.

Thanks to supportive friends, family, and readers JoAnn Wendt, Kay Fahey, Patricia Wallace Estrada, Cathy Pierce, Patti and Michael Specchio, and Alonna Shaw.

Special thanks to Priscilla Walden.

One

The blue-white incandescence of the King's Club marquee spilling through a narrow slit in the blackout drapes provided the man in the hotel room the additional light he needed to do what he had come to do. The air conditioner whirred softly. In the bed behind him, a lone occupant lay sleeping. The Monk listened to the old woman's light snores as he stood at the dresser and rummaged through her fat handbag.

Usually he worked silently, coming and going without making a sound. But not tonight. The old woman was deaf. He had found her hearing aid, looking like a wad of pink bubble gum, on the nightstand. And if that weren't enough, the sounds of her own snoring would mask any noise he might make.

The Monk opened another compartment in her purse. He pointed the beam of the penlight inside, illuminating vial upon vial of tablets and capsules, boxes of lozenges and suppositories, both prescription and over-the-counter—a regular pharmacy housed within cheap imitation alligator. He scanned the labels, found what he was looking for, popped the lid and poured the pink-and-blue capsules into the pocket of his windbreaker. He returned the empty vial to the purse and moved on. The next compartment was crammed with coupon books, casino circulars, and a dozen slot tokens—*funny money* embossed with the hotel name, *KING'S CLUB,* Sparks, Nevada.

He hefted the bag. A good ten pounds, maybe fifteen, even. It never ceased to amaze him how these old gals managed to tote so much weight around for hours on end. And that was just the half of it. To get to gaming paradise they rode all day on a crowded, noxious bus, then shuffled through one line after another with fistfuls of promotion packets to redeem casino freebies, stayed up around the clock pulling slot handles or staring at bingo or keno boards, and still they found time and energy to slip in a little sightseeing before boarding the same noxious bus again forty-eight hours later. The gambling junkie; no hardier creature existed.

Tucked away in a blue corduroy pouch he found cash, credit cards, traveler's checks, and jewelry. He pocketed a few bills, spilled the jewelry onto the dresser top, and sorted through it with a leather-gloved hand. Most of the pieces were bulky and old-fashioned: brooches, clip earrings, and bracelets—nothing that interested him, too easily identifiable. He returned the jewelry to the pouch.

Behind him he heard a faint sound, like a snort, then all was quiet. He turned his head slowly, saw the old lady sitting straight up in bed. She stared at him, her eyes enormous in her pale, thin face. From across the room he could see in her expression confusion, disbelief, and fear. The fear was unmistakable. It was that particular raw fear that he could see and sometimes smell, that gave him a delicious sense of superiority, a sense of power.

If he decided to walk out of this room right now, in all likelihood he would get away scot-free. Although their paths had crossed earlier in the day when she had asked him to direct her to her room, it was doubtful she had yet made the connection.

Carefully replacing the jewelry pouch in the purse, the Monk turned slowly and moved toward the bed. Her wide-eyed gaze did not leave his until he reached her side, at which time she glanced askew at something on the nightstand.

The thin beam of his penlight crawled over the objects there. Hearing aid, eyeglasses, an open pill vial, and the telephone. He lifted the vial. A dozen tiny white pills. Nitroglycerin? He closed his fingers around the vial, looked at her.

One puffy-veined hand went to her chest and the other instinctively reached for her medication. Recognition suddenly sprang into her eyes and her hand froze in midair. *He was no longer a stranger to her.*

He waited for her to make the first move.

For an old woman with a bum heart and bad eyesight she surprised him with the swiftness in which she left the bed and darted across the room toward the door. He should have known better than to underestimate a gambling junkie, he thought as he lunged after her.

He caught her at the door, pulling her away as she clawed at the handle. Her body was light and as fragile as a sparrow's. As she struggled against him, he hoped her bones weren't as brittle as they felt, that they wouldn't snap under the slightest pressure, that she didn't bruise easily. This death, he decided, would have to look natural.

In the closet area behind her he spotted a clear dry cleaner bag covering a garment. Ripping off the plastic, he worked it over her head and wound the edge around her neck, careful not to pull too tight. His intention was not to strangle her, but to let the plastic do the work. He wanted no marks.

As she bucked and twisted, the thin plastic, like a clinging membrane, drew in and out over her nostrils and mouth. He carried her thrashing body back to the bed and held her down. For several minutes he watched her, back arched, eyes and mouth open wide. The bony fingers of one hand clutched the sleeve of his windbreaker; the other hand clutched at her heaving chest, over her heart. Pain replaced the fear in her eyes.

He relaxed his hold, pulled the plastic away.

She sucked in air, or tried to. Her hand, reaching for the medication that had been on the nightstand, flailed helplessly in the air. He sat back. Waited. Watched. Within minutes she lay still, eyes open, no movement. He listened for and was rewarded with a final exhalation of breath. The death rattle.

He pried her hands away and, inside the rigid claw of her palm, forced the vial of nitroglycerin. In the pale light he caught the glinting of a large diamond on her finger. The stone was at least two carats. Even in the dim lighting he sensed by the many brilliant facets that it was a quality-cut stone. A solitaire with a plain setting, not likely to be as traceable as the gaudy pieces in the jewelry bag. He pulled at it, felt its resistance, pulled and twisted until the ring finally came free. He dropped it into the pocket of his windbreaker.

He rolled the plastic cleaner bag into a ball and stuffed it into the other pocket to be disposed of later. Slowly coming to his feet, he surveyed the room. Satisfied that there was nothing to incriminate him, the Monk quietly let himself out.

Before he left, he hung the "Do Not Disturb" sign on the knob.

Seven miles away in the neighboring city of Reno, at the *Silverbar,* unobserved and sitting quietly in the dark, Kasey Atwood had a clear view, a bird's-eye view, of the subjects below.

Kasey stared at an old woman with a dowager hump, concentrating on her mouth. The woman lifted her pointy chin to the man facing her and, with a certain daring in her piercing eyes, formed the words, *"Hit me."*

He did.

"Again," the old lady mouthed, doggedly.

He hit her again.

The woman stiffened, pounded a fist on the green felt, and flung her cards across the table, hitting the blackjack dealer in the chest with them.

Without a word, his face expressionless, using the cards from her "busted" hand to scoop up her bet, he dropped the chips in the tray in front of him and moved on.

On a black-and-white monitor in the tiny room known as the "eye in the sky," a room filled with TV screens that monitored the casino gaming Kasey continued to watch the action. Four of them sat at the "21" table—a mixed bag of age, intellect, and breeding: the dowager-humped woman, a Paiute Indian with a straw hat, a ponytailed young man in denim with silver rings on his fingers and gold hoops in one earlobe, a conventioneer with a lopsided name tag pinned to the lapel of his jacket. All were poised for battle, win or lose, squared off against the tall, grim-faced man with manicured fingernails.

She noted that the dealer's *up* card was a queen.

The Indian hit and busted. The young man in denim stayed. At the last hole at the table, the man in a gray wool-blend jacket with suede patches at the elbows, a man of average appearance wearing a crooked name tag, hesitated a moment before sliding his cards under his bet.

Kasey nudged the surveillance man sitting beside her and tapped the screen. He turned a knob on the monitor. The camera zoomed in to the end seat, to the anchorman's bet and cards. The top chip read *SILVERBAR,* Reno, Nevada. Five dollar chips. Four bet. She counted twice to be sure.

"How many, Joe?" she asked.

"Four."

The dealer played out his hand, took a hit on sixteen, and busted. He began to pay the winners.

Kasey noticed the anchorman had stayed on fourteen. She leaned in closer to the screen to watch the dealer pay off. A moment later she exchanged glances with the beefy man at her side, then smiled. The player's bet had mysteriously increased by two.

She lifted the receiver and punched several numbers. One floor up, in the executive office, a phone rang. It was late, nearing the end of the swing shift. The raspy voice of the casino manager answered.

"Ward, it's Kasey. I'm in the eye. Check out the action on BJ seven."

She heard his desk chair squeak and groan and pictured him leaning across his desk to the monitor, a monitor identical to those surrounding her. She gave him a moment to channel in on the blackjack table that she was watching.

"Yeah, got it," Ward Bellini said.

"Seems the guy at third base has a favorite dealer."

"Dumping out?" he asked.

"Yeah. Crossroaders. I've been watching that pit and that dealer for three nights. I'm pretty sure the same guy's been playing, following the dealer from table to table. Tonight he's dressed like a conventioneer, last night it was western wear, and the night before it was tourist casuals. Fortunately for us, he has a habit of snapping his watchband. Those little quirks always get them. The dealer has a few quirks, too."

"Signaling?"

"Among other things."

"Are you sure?"

"Got it on tape. Dealer's hot this shift, so signaling alone isn't enough. There's a lot of pressing going on." In her many years of surveillance, Kasey knew this common form of cheating was probably one of the hardest to detect. The dealer and player worked as a team. A set of signals clued the player to the denomination of the dealer's hole card. Once the player had that information, he had an added advantage. To further sweeten the take, the dealer might cap or press his "buddy's" original bet at the pay-off. Teams like that could take in two to three hundred bucks a night, seven nights a week, and not get caught—unless they got greedy. They always got greedy.

"Good work, Kasey. Who's in the eye with you?"

Kasey looked over at the burly man with the perpetual scowl, a man of few words with whom she'd spent the past three nights. He was removing the incriminating cassette. "Jolly Joe."

Without taking his eyes from the monitor, the man allowed himself a half-smile.

"Tell him to take care of that lousy sonofabitch and his sidekick. He knows what to do. I'll put in a call to the Gaming Board."

"Will do." She nodded to Joe.

"You think that's it?" Bellini asked. "Anything else?"

"That's all I spotted. 'Course with these two it was easy. Greedy guts got 'em. Our dealer's so damn hot that even with signals the percentages stayed in favor of the house, so instead of calling it a night like any pro-team with an ounce of brains would do, they tried making it up on the payoffs." From the corner of her eye she saw Joe leave the room. Within fifteen minutes he, with the aid of two security officers, would detain both dealer and "buddy" in a holding room until an agent from the Gaming Control Board showed up to take over. She added, "When word gets out about these two, if anyone else is dumping out, they'll cool it for a while. Give me a call if the tables should turn unlucky again."

Kasey checked her watch. Midnight. Joe still had a couple hours on his shift, but she had accomplished what she had been hired to do—spot a cheat. Self-employed, she punched no time clock.

She stood, stretched. If she went straight home to bed, she'd be lucky to get six hours sleep before Artie Brown cranked up the mower and weedmuncher, the Saturday-morning ritual. Kasey needed her beauty sleep tonight; she was going to an elaborate wedding the next day. She had never met the two intended—the invitation came from the guardians of the bride, a couple she hadn't seen in ages. Although it was both business and pleasure, it was the first social event she'd made time for in months. After the bombshell her mother had dropped on her that afternoon, she needed a big job and she needed it bad.

When Joe returned, Kasey said good night, left the dim, quiet room, and made her way down an even-dimmer catwalk and a steep flight of stairs. She pushed open a door and stepped into the bright, noisy casino with its flashing lights and ringing bells.

She blinked, paused until her eyes became accustomed to the brightness. Straight ahead on the stage in the small cabaret, an Elvis impersonator wearing Ray Bans belted out "All Shook Up." Heavy in the air was the aroma of tomato sauce and garlic from the Friday night all-you-can-eat spaghetti feed in the Silverdollar Diner. A typical weekend in July. The house was packed.

On her way out, weaving through the gaming tables and slot machines, she felt a surge of cool air from the overhead vents. The oxygen, a wake-up call supplied by the casino, kept drooping players going a little longer. Mesmerized by spinning reels and wheels, rolling dice and fast-dealt cards, without windows or clocks and with the glass doors tinted dark, twelve midnight could be twelve noon for all it mattered to those psyched with gaming fever.

At the back door she dropped three quarters into a triple 7 machine, pulled the handle, backed up, watching until the first two reels clunked to a stop without a match, then turned around and kept on going.

The Monk disposed of the plastic dry cleaner bag in a large green Dumpster at the rear of the hotel, shoving it deep into the raw kitchen-garbage. A cool breeze lifted the fine, sparse hairs on the top of his head. One thing he liked about this area was the cool evenings. Sleep was easier when it wasn't so hot. The scent of rotten meat and fish sent him back a step.

He glanced around, thrust his hands into his pockets, and quickly walked away. As he headed for the employee lot across the street, he worked his fingers around the capsules and felt the smooth metal of the diamond ring. If the diamond were real, it would be worth a buck or two. Of course, he'd have to hock it, and that might be a bad idea just now, especially if the cops were to get suspicious. Hey, no hurry. He wasn't pressed for bread. He'd just tuck the ring away for the time being; and maybe one day, if things ever got tight again, he'd head to Vegas and pawn it there.

The Monk didn't expect things to get tight for a while. It was good now. Really good. He had a real sweet deal going for himself, and he was going to play it for all it was worth.

The deal of a lifetime. It was definitely going to be worth plenty—and not just in cash.

In the parking lot, as he opened the door to his black Camaro, he glanced up at the eighth floor of the King's Club. He had killed the old woman in 814 tonight. It wasn't the first time he had killed. There had been at least two others, not counting Jimmy Sue. He couldn't count her because he'd never found out if she'd lived or died. There was something about not knowing that titillated him. Killing was not something he did for kicks, not like those serial killers who snuffed people because they liked it, or because God or Satan told them to. Nuts like that usually ended up a slave to their own whacked-out chemistry, pathetic and out of control. No, he didn't get any real kick out of it; it just seemed to happen.

What he did get a kick out of was brawling, using his fists, feeling his knuckles driving into flesh and bone. The dying came as a result . . . an end to a means. His fists, his temper, and his obsession for retaliation had gotten him into a shitload of trouble throughout forty volatile years.

From his shirt pocket he brought out a bottle of antihistamine, squeezed off a shot in each nostril, and sniffed, waiting impatiently for his blocked sinuses to clear. He cursed his allergies and the dry air of Nevada. Years ago he'd become hooked on the antihistamine. Forced to use it daily in order to breathe.

He climbed into the car, reached under the seat, and pulled up a pint bottle. He popped one of the capsules into his mouth and washed it down with a shot of tequila. The drug he had taken from the old woman's purse wouldn't alter or enhance his mind. These shiny pink-and-blue babies would do their miracle work undetected.

He turned the key and smiled when the engine immediately caught, the loud roar reverberating throughout the parking lot. He revved it several times, getting a natural high on the powerful sound, the acrid smell of high-octane gas and exhaust, the solid mass of vibrating steel surrounding him.

All he needed now to make him feel complete was the uniform. The stiff blues, badge, radio, keys, utility belt. But most specifically, the commanding weight of the gun at his hip.

Two

The old carriage house, no longer used for carriages or automobiles, had been converted into living and office quarters five years ago when Kasey moved back home. Her bungalow, a miniature replica of the main house, stood like a proud offspring in the cool shadows of the white, two-story woodframe structure with its green shingled roof and shutters. Both structures were enveloped in a jungle of wild gooseberry and lilac bushes, shasta daisies, bluebeard, English lavender; and along the western boundary of the four-acre parcel, towering sycamores lined up like sentries to buffer the late-afternoon winds. A grand weeping willow stood in the front yard, its thirsty roots taking moisture from a nearby stream; and in the rear beyond the vegetable garden, extended an apple and peach orchard, the branches of the peach trees now heavy with ripening fruit.

More than a half-century ago, the five-bedroom house and what was then fifteen acres, had served as a productive, operating dude ranch for Kasey's widowed grandmother. Cassie Bane and her daughter, Marianne, had once catered year-round to a succession of prominent women. Movie stars; socialites; the wives of producers, directors, and tycoons from California resided under her roof for a minimum of six weeks. Contingent upon the weather, they rode horses, tended the gardens and orchard, played endless games of canasta and contract bridge, skied on the nearby slopes, or took long contemplative walks.

As diversified as they were, all had one thing in common: divorce. And there was never a shortage of guests.

All that had changed years before. Times got tough for the Banes, and most of the surrounding acres had to be sold. Again times got tough. To pay off the Atwood debts, they were forced to borrow against the house. The boarders, once prominent, were now just plain folk and fewer in number. Then, in the spring of the present year, after long-suffering with cancer and a series of strokes, Grandma Bane, at the age of ninety-one, mercifully succumbed.

Early that Saturday morning, the ringing of the telephone in the small bungalow bounced off the high-beamed ceiling and cedar paneling of the loft where Kasey Atwood slept to sharply jar her sleep-numbed brain.

Moving only her arm, she knocked the receiver off the cradle and onto the floor. One eye opened to peek at the clock: 7:28.

She buried her face in the pillow and moaned. She'd scarcely closed her eyes. Instead of falling right to sleep the night before, Kasey had lain awake thinking about the latest wrinkle in the life of the Atwoods. Kasey's mother, not one to bring up bad news until the twelfth hour in the event some miracle should occur to save the day, had informed her that not only was their savings all but gone, eaten away by Grandma Bane's medical bills and the funeral costs, but the house and property were on the line as well.

Kasey's mother had always been close-mouthed about personal finances. Whenever Kasey had asked, Marianne's stock answer was, "The stars will provide. They always have."

Well, the stars had come up short this time.

But they would pull through this. No way in the world would Kasey allow their homestead to be stripped from them. Not without a fight. If she had to beg, borrow, or steal, she'd get them back on their feet. The house had sheltered three generations of Bane women. They had a problem, yes, but nothing that a steady income couldn't fix—which at the moment was not in the stars. Kasey's consultant jobs were usually based on a flat fee: a retainer upon taking the job, the balance rendered when the job was done. She figured just one long-term, high-paying job would do the trick. That, or the big payoff on the *Megabucks;* and since gambling for her consisted of a few coins dropped into a machine on her way out the casino door, it had to be the job.

She stretched, making a groaning sound deep in her throat, then slowly sat up. Downstairs in the kitchen she heard water running through the coffee maker. In a moment she'd be able to smell it. She rose, took two steps, and tripped on the phone cord. Disgruntled, she hauled the receiver up by the cord and was about to hang it up when she heard the voice. Amazed by the caller's tenacity, she asked, "You still there?"

"Hello? Kasey Atwood? Are you Kasey Atwood?"

"Maybe." She sat on the edge of the bed. "Who's this?"

"Look, I got your name from the guy who delivers my booze. He said you might be able to help me."

"Help in what way?"

"He said you were a—what do you call it?—a spotter."

"A consultant, actually. Who's the guy who delivers your booze?" Kasey didn't advertise. All her business came from word of mouth, friends referring her to other friends and associates. At one time she had considered having cards made, putting an ad in the yellow pages, and maybe even ordering stationery with a logo—something plain and simple like *Eyespot* or *Eyewitness*—but business had been steady without it. Also, the fewer people who knew what she did for a living, the better off she was. When asked her occupation, she said telemarketing. End of inquiry.

"Sonny Kubbet," he said.

Sonny was a friend of hers. A driver for a local beer distributor, his *mouth* was one of those whose *word* made the rounds, and to the right people. "Where does he deliver?"

"Well, hell, how should I know? All over town. Hey, you want the business or not?"

Curb that wicked tongue, she told herself. She needed the work, in fact, all the work she could get. Lack of sleep was no excuse to be surly to a prospective client. "Sorry, what I meant was who are you and how do you know Sonny?"

"The name's Leroy Tate. I own Clementine's in the mall."

Kasey knew it well. Clementine's was a going concern, a new bar and restaurant near Meadowood. By day, it catered to hordes of shoppers; and by night, with the live music, dance floor, barrel-sized drinks, and young, good-looking personnel—where flowing hair and exposed skin seemed the chief criteria—it rocked to a beat of a different kind. And Kasey knew that wherever business was good, really good, there was someone with a hand in the till.

"Go on."

"Business is booming, but you wouldn't know it by the night receipts."

"Do you work out of the bar, Mr. Tate?"

"Yeah, sure. I'm here most nights. We're closed Sundays."

Kasey quoted her fee and the terms, said she would come out one night during the week to watch the action, then give him a report the following day.

"What night you coming?" he asked.

"I think it's best if no one has that information, not even you, Mr. Tate."

"Tonight?"

"Sorry, I have plans." She thought of the wedding at the Kings' that afternoon. "Next week."

"Yeah. Okay."

"I'll be in touch." She hung up, stood, and sluggishly followed the aroma of brewing coffee down the spiral staircase to the kitchen.

Kasey closed the front door of her bungalow, being careful to make no noise. As usual she didn't bother to lock it. No one would mess with anything. She quickly crossed the yard to the back door of her mother's rooming house, climbed the steps, and almost made it inside before the dog rounded the side of the house and made a lunge for her.

"Down, Snickers, *down!*" she said gruffly to the six-month-old Saint Bernard who every morning greeted her by jumping up, his sopping tongue attempting to lick the blush right off her cheeks. She pushed at the dog, trying to keep dusty paws the size of baseball mitts off her new dress. "I swear to God, Snick, you're heading for obedience school. Down! Get dowwww—*Ma!*"

In an instant, Marianne Atwood had the door open. She held a spray bottle, the one she used to mist the indoor plants. "Out of the way, Kasey. Andy said this would calm him down." Andy was the mailman on their rural route. Her mother began to squirt the dog in the face.

Snickers turned toward the water. Instead of discouraging him, the dog opened its mouth and lapped at the shooting stream happily, only to shake his head and send water flying. Kasey hurried inside, leaving her mother to handle the situation.

A moment later, Marianne was back, empty-handed. As she closed the door, she looked out, shaking her head. "Well, there goes my good watering bottle. Dumb animal, dumb, dumb." She slammed the door, turned, and marched to the sink. "You know what he did this morning? He pulled up one of my new rose bushes, roots and all. Never saw anything like it, a dog who likes to chew on thorns. How'd we get stuck with such a dumb-dumb?"

There was no point in reminding her mother that everyone in the area knew what a sucker Marianne was for stray animals. One way or another, God's creatures found their way to her door. Four months ago, the puppy had been left on the back porch in an empty Snickers box.

"My, you look nice," Marianne said. "It's about time you did something fun for a change. Who knows, maybe you'll meet someone."

"I'll try to catch the bouquet."

Her mother got that serious look. Oh-oh, Kasey thought, here it comes again.

"Kasey, honey, Kevin has been dead eleven years. It certainly wouldn't be disrespectful to his memory if you married again."

"I married again. And divorced. Remember?"

"That one didn't count," she said brusquely. "Whose wedding did you say you were going to?"

"The niece of an old friend. Actually it's an interview for a new assignment. Wish me luck. It could be just the job to get us out of the hole."

"Oh, Kasey, it shouldn't be up to you to fix this. I could go to work. Lord knows, I've had plenty experience cooking, cleaning, and waiting on people."

The thought of her mother looking for a job outside the home at her age made Kasey ill. Not that she wasn't as strong as an ox and couldn't do the work of two people, but her mother loved the ranch, loved tending to it and to the four boarders who resided there.

"No, absolutely not," Kasey said, giving her mother a reassuring hug. "We'll be just fine. Don't you worry about a thing. I'm getting some really good vibes about this job offer."

Three

At the top of the hill, above the golf course in north Sparks, the sister city to The Biggest Little City In The World, a hot July breeze softly caressed the yards of white streamers, floral bouquets, and elaborate bows, wedding decorations carefully arranged over the lavishly landscaped rear yard of the King residence. At two o'clock the wedding reception was well under way. The outdoor ceremony, with the bride and groom exchanging vows under a white lattice arch between the waterfall and the natural-rock swimming pool, had gone beautifully, as well as the sit-down brunch for two hundred. Guests were scattered all about the sprawling grounds. The young revelers, those who weren't dancing, playing tennis, or swimming, hung out at the portable bars, fast getting bombed on top-quality booze.

Kasey Atwood joined a small group at the edge of the pool. At the center of the group, looking aristocratic in a chic silk dress and wide-brimmed hat that shaded smoky gray eyes, stood the hostess, Dianne King. Kasey had to admire Dianne. She was a clever, determined woman who knew what she wanted and knew how to go after it. Although Dianne certainly looked the part, her highborn manner was acquired, not inbred, and no one knew it better than Kasey. When in their early twenties, Kasey and her pal Dianne had run cocktails at King's Club.

Kasey let her gaze sweep over the grounds and the house. It was really something, all right. Opulent. Pricy. Yet, Kasey felt no envy. She was content with what she had. She, along with Dianne, had achieved her goal. Dianne had married the owner of King's Club and assumed his social status, and Kasey ran her own consultant business.

Over the gurgle of the waterfall, Dianne went on about one community event after another. Unable to keep her mind on the conversation, Kasey found her attention drifting. Instead of relaxing and enjoying herself, she watched, especially the help—mentally working. Which was one reason Kasey was here today. Earlier in the week Dianne had called to discuss an assignment at the club. The wedding invitation was something of an afterthought. Kasey, needing a break from the business and curious to see the King estate, accepted. Now, after an afternoon of being social, of eating, drinking, smiling, and chatting with strangers, she was eager to get back to work. And, she told herself, more than a little intrigued at the prospect of working at King's Club again.

It had been there in the Sutro Bar eleven years ago that Kasey first became interested in the business of "spotting" as a profession; sexual harassment had been the catalyst. Her supervisor, Buddy Walker, and the bartender, Leonard Smart, had made Kasey's working hours sheer hell. It began innocently enough with jokes, then moved on to sexual innuendos, propositions, and ultimately assault.

Kasey had been on her own. Rumor had it Dianne was involved with the owner's son, and Walker and Smart had enough sense to lay off. The day Walker trapped Kasey in the supply room and shoved a sweaty hand up the short skirt of her uniform was the day Kasey went to Ralph King, Jay's father, who had listened patiently to her complaint, sympathized with her grievance, then informed her that the accused were two of his best employees, therefore too valuable to risk losing. When she told him they were stealing him blind, he asked for proof. Two weeks later, she had enough concrete evidence to take back to King. King fired both men on the spot, then further surprised her by offering her the supervisor position.

Kasey finished her champagne and moved away from the group. Dianne caught her eye, nodded when Kasey pointed to her empty glass.

"Ten minutes? Jay's office?" Dianne said. "Do you know the way?"

"I'll find it."

As she moved toward the nearest bar, Kasey had observed that all afternoon the bartenders, two to each portable bar, four bars in all, shamelessly hustled tips and that occasionally one disappeared and stayed gone longer than she considered customary.

Instead of stopping at the bar, she put down the empty glass and walked on by, heading toward the lot where the caterers and domestic help parked their cars. A bartender had gone this way a few minutes earlier for a second time. Just before rounding the corner of the house, she heard the soft thunk of a car trunk closing.

Footsteps sounded behind her.

Kasey ducked into the shadows of a deep arch at a side door. A moment later, one of the white-gloved servers, wearing a cardigan with the front crossed snugly over her protruding abdomen, passed. By the size and shape, Kasey suspected that what she cradled to her bosom like a tender babe was a prime rib roast. The woman hurried past, heading down the incline to a row of parked cars.

Kasey followed, staying close to the house, out of sight. The parking area was tiered. She stopped behind a van on the tier above and watched the woman approach the bartender at the rear of a brown Ford Escort. The trunk opened, a mesh bag went inside. From where Kasey stood, she could see down into the trunk. It was filled with booty, enough food and booze to cater another wedding party.

The woman got into the car and quickly drove away, incriminating evidence gone with her.

Kasey automatically registered the license plate number before ducking back behind the van to wait for the bartender to return to the house. Several moments later, she heard his footsteps heading her way.

Suddenly someone had her by the arm. She spun around, drove her hand straight down, knocking the hand away, then backed up, out of reach.

"Oww! Goddammit, that hurt!" he said, rubbing his arm.

Expecting the bartender, Kasey was surprised to see a man in his mid-twenties. A man who looked vaguely familiar. Beneath neatly trimmed dark hair, a sharp-planed jaw gave him a seasoned look, and if not for a certain innocence in his soft brown eyes and full lips, he would have looked much older. He was dressed in a tux, the jacket now missing, the bow tie undone. The best man.

"What do you want?" she said.

"What do *I* want? I'm the one who should be asking that question. These are my wheels," he said, running a loving hand over the side mirror. "This happens to be my van you were trying to break into."

"Trying to break in—*Oh, come on!* Do I look like someone who'd break into your van? Or anyone's van?"

"So what are doing here?" When she didn't answer, he grinned and said, "You're waiting for someone. Right? A guy. A boyfriend. The bartender! Shit, you came out here to meet that bartender?"

She tried to push past him.

"You missed him, honey. Your friend went back to the house."

"Thank you." She tried to go the other way.

"Hey, look, how about me? How about I buy you a drink? Champagne? I can get us a bottle. Two bottles. A case of the best. We can go for a ride."

She pushed him aside.

"Maybe later, huh? A dance? Save me a dance." As she

hurried back to the house, he called out, "Hey, what's your name?"

A housekeeper led Kasey through the large house of Grecian design in shades of white, pale pink, and Windsor blue to a wing far removed from the pool and the noisy wedding reception. At a closed door at the end of the hallway she tapped lightly. "Come in," a male voice called out.

Kasey opened the door and stepped into a spacious room of dark wood accented by tones of hunter green, deep gold, and garnet, a sharp but pleasant contrast to the washed-out interior of the rest of the house. A soft light, which filtered through the wood-shuttered windows, gave the office a rich, glowing ambience, as warm and welcome as a blazing fire in an open hearth on a chilly day. Today the room was cool, compliments of central air, but the pleasing glow prevailed.

Kasey closed the door, stood with her back to it. The oxblood leather wing chair behind the walnut desk was empty.

"It's good to see you again, Kasey," Jay King said from across the room. After slipping out of his tuxedo jacket and draping it over the back of a chair, he turned to her. "What's it been? Seven years?"

She smiled. "Something like that."

"At the open house?"

She shook her head. "I couldn't make it that night. Something came up." What came up was a divorce from her second husband. The final papers had arrived the day of the Kings' house warming and she had been in no mood to celebrate that evening, or even to be civil. So Kasey had called Dianne to cancel. Jay and Dianne had officially taken over the late Ralph King's home, a move Dianne had eagerly anticipated since her marriage to Jay two years earlier. She remembered Dianne had become angry, accusing her of being jealous and spiteful. "I counted on your being here," Dianne had complained. "You know I don't know half these people."

Most of "these people" were now outside having a good time. Dianne now knew them all. It was Kasey whom Dianne did not know.

"You're looking very well," he said in his quiet, low-pitched voice. "In fact, you're looking—is it permissible for a man who is about to offer a woman an assignment to say that she's looking quite lovely? It's hard to know what to say these days."

"Since I haven't accepted your offer yet, I'll take it as the compliment it was meant to be. Thank you. You're looking very well yourself."

And she meant it. At forty-two, Jay King was tall and trim, in good shape—his once-black hair now streaked with silver, his blue eyes as clear and bright as she remembered. He had a face that had matured early in life, held, and would probably continue to hold for many years to come, merely becoming more distinguished with age. His eyes and mouth were his best features. A crooked eyebrow and his nose, a fraction off-center (probably from being broken years ago), added enough character to categorize him as ruggedly handsome. Today, in the tux, he looked incredibly debonair. Years ago, Kasey had had a crush on Jay, but of course he had never noticed her because he had been too dazzled by Dianne and her charms. Seeing him again after all these years made her feel a strange tugging deep inside. She realized she was still attracted to him, and she wondered if that would in any way influence her work performance should she accept his offer. She decided to adopt an attitude of wait and see.

He gave her a small smile, looked away. "Dianne should be along soon. Something about a crisis in the kitchen."

Kasey wondered if she should tell her host about the trunkload of his food and drink that was on its way to places unknown. This meeting today was to discuss a prospective job at the club and had nothing to do with his home and the hired help. He might consider it meddling if she brought it up. She had dealt with all kinds, and she knew that not everyone was eager to learn they'd been deceived or cheated, especially by employees whom they liked and trusted.

"How is business?" he asked.

"Busy. I've had to take on help for the smaller jobs."

"You like your work?" He went to the window.

"Very much."

"Do you ever just relax and let go?" He stood looking out. He motioned to her to join him. When she did, he said, "When you're at a party or a wedding reception, is it possible for you to dissociate yourself from your job?"

She followed his gaze. To the extreme left she saw the parking area where she had followed the bartender and maid. She turned to him. "You saw?"

He nodded. "I know a little something about spotting, too. I've been gouged more times than I care to admit. At shindigs like this in particular. Those two were pretty damn sloppy. They think because of the number of people, the confusion, the drinking, no one will notice."

"And they're right," she said. "Most employers are too trusting or they close their eyes to a little pilfering, thinking that if they lower the boom they're going to be ripped off big time."

He smiled, nodded. "True. How true. Dianne says you're very good, and after today I have to agree. We could use you at the club."

"In what capacity?"

"Showing my nephew the ropes. The spy business, as it were."

"Your nephew?"

"Dianne told you we took in my niece and nephew last year when my brother died of cancer, didn't she?"

"No. No, she didn't. She just said that your niece was getting married . . . here, at the house."

He nodded, looked outside again. "They're really a couple of great kids. Well, not kids anymore. Their mother died when they were small and their father, my brother, raised them. Did a fine job. They used to spend their summers here when my dad was alive. They stopped coming after Dianne and I took over the place. Dianne . . . well, as you know, Dianne has never had much patience for kids."

How well Kasey knew. After Dianne's divorce from her first husband, she had given him full custody of their two-year-old son. Once she confessed to Kasey that although she loved her son with all her heart, she just wasn't cut out to be a mother.

"I'm going to miss Brenda," Jay was saying. "After their honeymoon in Egypt, they'll be moving to Chicago."

"And your nephew?"

"Next month, he'll begin his final year at the university. After graduation, he'll come into the business with me. He's been working at the club summers and breaks for years now, so he knows a little about the industry. He's not as mature as his sister. But he's a quick study."

They were interrupted by the door's opening. Dianne entered, and with her was the young man from the van.

Kasey was taken aback by his appearance. Wearing his tuxedo jacket, his black tie in place again, for just a moment there he looked like Kevin. Kevin in his tuxedo on their wedding day. She felt a wrenching deep inside.

Jay turned. "Ah, there you two are. Brad, have you met Kasey Atwood yet?"

"Not officially," he said. He quickly crossed the room and took her hand. It felt more like an embrace than a greeting. "It's my pleasure, Miss Atwood."

Kasey smiled, gently pulled her hand away.

Jay moved around the desk and joined Dianne. He closed the doors. "Kasey, it was Dianne's idea to ask for your help."

"Oh?"

"Guilty as charged," Dianne said. "Jay and I discussed it, and you were the logical person," she continued. "He prefers to run everything himself, doesn't trust many people, but he's been so busy lately with the plans for the expansion that he really doesn't have the time to take on any additional tasks." She linked his arm with hers. "I don't see him enough as it is. You'll be doing both of us a favor. Say you'll do it, Kasey. Please?"

"Well, I do have several other commitments—" *Don't blow this. Remember, the ol' homestead is at stake.*

"Dianne discussed the fee with you?" Jay asked.

"Yes. It's a very generous offer. Much more than I'm used to getting." Why don't I just cut my own throat? she asked herself. "An offer I can't refuse."

"Good. You choose the hours," Jay said. "Brad is flexible. Right, Brad?"

"I'm all yours. Whenever."

Kasey turned to Brad. "Your uncle says you're a quick study, so it shouldn't take us too long. A couple of weeks, maybe. We'll start with the day shift in the hotel. When you're ready for the casino operation, we'll switch to swing. That's the busiest shift. You'll see and learn more then."

"I have a feeling I'm going to learn plenty," Brad said, grinning.

Jay gave his nephew a long, cool look. A look that wiped the foolish smile from the young man's face. Before anyone could fill the uncomfortable void, the phone rang.

Jay answered. He listened for several moments. His expression went from passive to grave. "Go ahead. Call the police. I'll be there in ten minutes." He hung up, quickly crossed to the chair, grabbed his jacket, and put it on.

"Oh, Jay," Dianne said, "you're not going to the club today of all days. What in God's name could be that important?"

"That was Epson, the hotel manager. Housekeeping found a body in one of the rooms. They called me before the police. I should be there."

"Natural causes, Jay?" Kasey asked.

"Sounds like it. Elderly woman found dead in bed, no sign of a struggle. It happens. And a little too frequently, if you ask me."

Kasey had to agree. She'd seen her share. Mostly the elderly or the infirm, those with high blood pressure, diabetes, or heart problems. These people came from a lower elevation, sea level cities, to the high altitude of Reno and Tahoe. Aside from the climate change and thinner air, their daily routines were radically thrown out of kilter—long, late hours; crowded casinos; too much alcohol and too little food—adverse conditions which could unbalance even the hardiest of troopers.

"Let Epson handle it. That's what he gets paid for."

"Dianne, if it's not handled right, the reputation of the hotel could suffer."

Kasey saw a look pass between husband and wife. It was obvious this was an ongoing argument.

"Should I go with you?" Brad asked his uncle.

"No. Stay. Enjoy your sister's big day." Jay reached for his wife; but before he could touch her, she turned away. The hand dropped.

"We'll talk Monday morning, Kasey. Nine, my office," he said. Then he was gone.

"Brad, dear, would you excuse us, please. I'd like a word with Kasey in private."

After Brad had gone, Dianne strode to a bar built into the bookshelves. "Drink?"

Kasey declined.

"Do you have a cigarette?" Dianne asked.

"Sorry, don't smoke."

"That's right, you quit. Oh, it's just as well, Jay hates when I stink up his study." She fixed herself a scotch on the rocks, then sat on the arm of the wing chair. "Jay's quite dedicated to the club."

"I noticed."

"He'd live there if I'd let him."

Kasey watched Dianne's frosted pink lips narrow to a hard line. Dianne's dream had come true when she married Jay—the wife of a club owner, the big house and expensive cars. But at what price?

"What's going on?" Kasey asked.

Dianne turned to look at Kasey. She raised a questioning eyebrow.

"Jay is hiring me to do a job any surveillance man can do. I can always use the work, but we both know the club has qualified personnel on staff for that sort of thing. So what's going on?"

"You're right, of course. You're very perceptive, and that's exactly why I suggested you to Jay. At this point, he's only doing it to humor me." Dianne stood. "Just what did he tell you?"

"Only that he wanted me to train Brad."

"Nothing about threats or harassment?"

Kasey shook her head.

"Isn't that just like a man." She sipped her drink. "The past couple of weeks there've been some strange things going on at the club. Jay is concerned, but he won't admit it. *'Adverse publicity could hurt business,'* blah blah. Of course, with one of the biggest weeks of the year coming up, followed by the balloon and air races, he has good reason to be concerned."

"What's happened so far?"

Dianne went back to the bar, slid the mirrored panel to the side to reveal a wall safe, and opened it. She handed Kasey a business-size envelope with the King's Club logo, stationery supplied by the hotel and found in every room. Inside was a yellowed photograph cut from a newspaper. Las Vegas, MGM Grand Hotel. Clouds of black, billowing smoke poured out of the windows of the super structure. Caption: *MGM Grand Burns: Death toll mounts.*

"Just the photo, no note or message?"

"No, but it's certainly self-explanatory."

"Are there others?"

"Yes and no. Others came before this one. However, Jay didn't take them seriously and tossed them. This is the first one he saved. They were all news clippings and all had something to do with crime or violence. He took notice of this one because of the hotel. I suppose because it indirectly involves the love of his life."

"Do the police know about any of this?"

"God, are you kidding? As I said, Jay is scared to death the media will get hold of this and turn it into a three-ring circus. Violence, especially threats of a hotel disaster, tend to be bad for business."

"Threatening phone calls?"

"I don't think so. At least Jay hasn't said anything about it."

"You want me to look around, see if I can find out anything?"

"If you would."

"I'm not a private investigator, Dianne."

"I know that. But you see things that others don't. You have this built-in radar, this . . . this innate ability to uncover things. It may be nothing," she added. "A sore loser. Someone Jay blackballed. I may bitch about Jay's time spent at the club, but I wouldn't want anything to happen to it. He'd be lost without that damn place. It's like a mistress, taking all his time and energy." She laughed sarcastically. "At times I wish it was a mistress. Another woman can be challenged. How does one challenge a dream?"

Both were silent for several long moments. Kasey sighed. "Okay. I'll do what I can."

"Thanks, you're a true friend." Dianne finished her drink, rose. "Well, I'd better get back to the guests. Even today, that flashy, concrete bitch has managed to lure my husband away."

They returned outdoors to the reception. A five-piece band set up in the gazebo played rock music, and dancers filled the three-tiered deck.

At the edge of the pool, Brad King came up behind Kasey and pulled her into his arms. "You promised me a dance, remember?"

"I was about to leave."

"Not until we have that dance."

She gave in. "One, then I have to go."

"Do you always play this hard-to-get?"

"I'm not playing anything, Brad."

He pressed his hand to her lower back. "C'mon, lighten up. It's a party. You're tighter than a clock mainspring. I get this feeling you're going to just snap and go shooting off across the lawn."

The image made her laugh softly. She forced herself to relax.

"Yeah, there, that's much better. The armor is falling away; I can feel it."

His fingers probed, massaged her lower back. It felt nice and she let him.

He pulled her close. "Ummm, you smell good. You know, Kasey, you're just the kind of woman I've been looking for. Bright, attractive, mature. I've always had a thing for older women."

"Really." That morning her mother had read her horoscope from the newspaper. It said: "Keep an open mind for today true love is near." As her young partner nuzzled her ear, she thought, *Yeah. Right.*

When his hand slid down to cup her buttock, she covered his hand with hers, pulled back, looked him in the eyes, and—with a sweet smile—said, "That was your token feel, Mr. King. From now on, especially on the job, don't waste my time with this crap." At which point she bent his pinkie finger back until his knees buckled. He groaned, then quickly released her.

She walked away. Before she rounded the corner of the house, she glanced back to see him standing on the deck, flexing his fingers and staring after her with that damn smile still in place. *Great,* she thought, *he's into pain.*

Four

Jay King drove south on I-80. He thought of his meeting with Kasey Atwood only minutes earlier and for some reason it gave him a good feeling. He had always liked Kasey. Of all of Dianne's friends, Kasey had been the most down-to-earth, the most sincere. She was intelligent and very attractive, yet didn't seem completely absorbed with herself like many of his wife's current acquaintances. Until she had walked through the door of his den, he had forgotten just how disarming she could be.

Disarming? Odd choice of a word, he told himself.

He had no time to dwell on it, however, for as he approached downtown Sparks, the sight of King's Club straight ahead swept all else from his mind. The twelve-story structure never failed to fill him with pride and a sense of accomplishment.

Not a large establishment by Reno or Vegas standards, but one of the larger in Sparks. In two years, if everything went according to plan, King's Club would be the biggest, finest hotel casino in the area. At present it had 750 rooms, four restaurants, an indoor pool, three cocktail lounges plus cabaret, convention, and banquet facilities. Much of its current technology was antiquated—the phone, computer, and surveillance systems in general—but with the completion of the approved expansion and renovation, it would rank up there with the best.

In 1958 Jay's father, Ralph King, opened the doors of a bar and grill on B Street—renamed Victorian Avenue in the early nineties. He began with limited gaming, a few payoff pinball machines, one-armed bandits, and a basement bingo parlor. Within ten years he was owner/operator of a full-facility gaming and hotel establishment to equal any in the Rail City of sixty thousand.

Jay exited the freeway, drove two blocks to the entrance to the club, parked his silver Lexus in his private parking space on the second floor of the garage, and entered the hotel through a private entrance. Minutes later, he was in the elevator on his way to the eighth floor and what he hoped to God was a routine death.

A uniformed officer stood outside the open door of 814. Jay King identified himself and warily stepped into the room. The coroner was bent over a body in the bed. Two attendants stood by with a gurney. Jay's stomach knotted when he spotted his friend, Detective Frank Loweman, talking with the hotel manager, Mark Epson. The detective's presence meant bad news.

Loweman nodded at Jay, moved away from Epson, and approached him. Loweman wore the darker of his two gray suits. He wore only gray. Someone had once told him gray brought out the blue-gray of his eyes. But the main reason, he said, was that it cut down on accessories. He needed only one pair of shoes—black—white shirts, and three neckties—a couple of blue ones for everyday and a red one for festive occasions. Today he wore the blue striped tie.

"Nice of you to dress for the occasion, Jay," Loweman said of the tuxedo, "though somehow I think the gesture will be lost on our guest of honor."

"Tell me it was natural causes. Tell me her last wish was to come to Sparks to die in bed in my hotel."

"Her last wish was to die in bed at the King's Club."

"Thanks," Jay said.

A passing couple slowed, craned their necks to see into the

room. The uniformed cop waved them on. "Please move along, folks. Official business. Nothing that concerns you."

Loweman buried his right hand into his pants pocket and jingled the change there. "The lady was seventy-something and had a heart condition. Died clutching her nitro. No one on either side heard anything, and nothing looks disturbed. She's been dead awhile. Rigor mortis is complete and showing signs of resolving. Dr. Wing puts the estimated time of death around midnight or a little before."

Although sorry the woman was dead, Jay felt tremendous relief. If Loweman were correct, her death was unavoidable; no blame could be placed on the hotel or its management. An elderly woman with a weak heart had died while on a weekend jaunt, doing what she liked to do.

"How long have you been here?" Jay asked.

"Since it came through on the radio. I was in the neighborhood. If there's something going on at my good buddy's place, I'm gonna look into it."

"She have family?" Jay asked.

"Two daughters down in Southern California. The deceased . . ." He consulted his notes, ". . . one Louise Steiner, came up on a bus, one of those golden tour packages. She left her friends around ten last night to turn in. The group had a sightseeing tour to Virginia City and Lake Tahoe planned, but she bowed out, saying she wanted to sleep late. According to the floor maid, the 'Do not Disturb' sign was on the door when she made up the other rooms this afternoon."

"Who found her?" Jay asked.

"Mrs. Curtis, over there." He nodded toward the door where an elderly woman stood in the corridor wringing her hands. "After the tour she returned to the hotel. Got concerned when she couldn't get her friend to respond to calls and knocks, so she contacted the hotel manager. Together they went in. Manager said the rooms have memory locks. He's gonna check it out."

Jay and Loweman moved aside to allow the gurney through.

Dr. Wing, jacket open, sauntered toward them, pulling off surgical gloves. He nodded at Jay, turned to Loweman. "Happened pretty fast, I'd say. Doesn't look like she had time to take a pill or make a call." He stared at the sheet-shrouded form going by. "However, there's a slight redness on her neck. It's probably nothing, but I think it should be looked into."

"You want us to treat this as a crime scene?" Loweman asked.

The doctor hesitated, glanced around. "Lock it up for now. We can always come back in. Like I said, it's probably nothing."

"I'll alert the front desk, have them pin the room," Jay said. "Nobody will disturb a thing."

"Okay. That'll do." Loweman turned to the woman standing in the doorway. She had stopped wringing her hands and was now twisting a ring on her thin, bony finger. She looked lost, confused as to what she was to do now that the body was being taken away. "Mrs. Curtis?"

She turned quickly, eyebrows rising as she looked from Jay to Loweman.

"Mrs. Curtis, I'm Det. Loweman, Sparks Police. I understand the deceased was a good friend of yours."

"Yes, yes of course. LuLu and me, we go way back. Oh dear . . ." Tears sprang to her eyes. Realization was overtaking the shock. "Oh, dear, poor Lu. I think it might be my fault."

"Why is that?"

"She wanted to share a room. We always share a room. Besides saving money, we can look after each other—y'know, call for help if one of us takes ill. But this time my sister Evie came along, and she wanted me to share with her. What could I say? Blood's thicker than water. Right? And Evie has high blood pressure and . . . and—"

"I'm sure nothing could have been done to save her." He patted her shoulder. "Mrs. Curtis, do you think you'd be able to tell if any of her belongings were missing?"

"Her belongings?"

"Money? Jewelry?"

"Well, maybe. She kept everything over there in that suitcase she called a purse."

With a hand on her shoulder, Loweman guided her to the dresser where the imitation alligator bag was being dusted for prints by a crime scene investigator. He gestured for Jay to follow.

When the man was done, Loweman asked him to show the contents to Mrs. Curtis. With gloved fingers the investigator carefully revealed the contents of each compartment.

"Any drugs missing?" Loweman asked her when that compartment was reached.

"Oh, good heavens, I wouldn't have an inkling. LuLu took pills for everything. She has—*had* one of those pill-pushing doctors. Y'know, she'd just give him a ring, tell him what ailed her, and, presto, another new pill."

Jay and Loweman exchanged looks. Loweman jotted something on his notepad.

In the zipper section, they saw credit cards, traveler's checks, cash, and finally the corduroy pouch. The investigator opened the pouch. Loweman listed each item of jewelry.

"I s'pose it's all there," she said. "If someone were going to rob her, wouldn't he take everything that's worth anything?"

At those words Jay felt a tightening in his chest. He wanted to say something yet thought better of it.

"Yes. Usually," Loweman said. "Thank you, Mrs. Curtis. I have your number if I need anything more."

"I intend to call her daughters and give them the news," she said somewhat defiantly. "I think it should come from me and not the police."

"That's fine, Mrs. Curtis."

Jay saw Epson standing in the hall. He joined him. "Pin the room until the police give you the okay. So far it looks routine, but just in case." He started to walk away, turned back. "Oh, Mark, comp Mrs. Curtis and any guests of hers to dinner tonight, any restaurant. Flowers with condolences would be nice, too."

The Monk watched the attendants wheel the gurney out to the waiting coroner's van. Several minutes later, he watched the hotel owner, dressed in a tuxedo, exit the elevator on the casino floor with a blond man in a cheap gray suit.

Cop. It took one to know one.

Both men seemed calm, unruffled. They talked like a couple of guys who knew each other, bullshitting, catching up, the cop's attention divided between Jay King and a cocktail waitress in a skimpy skirt, breasts overflowing a low-cut top, passing with a full tray of drinks.

Nothing to sweat, the Monk told himself. Not that he really ever let things get to him. What was life if not a constant challenge? A constant conflict? When things calmed down, he'd take a run up to the eighth floor and check it out.

Five

The following morning in her mother's kitchen, having made the trek across the yard unnoticed by Snickers, Kasey poured coffee and stared at an 8x10 photograph taped to the cabinet in front of her. She turned, leaned against the counter, and scanned the kitchen, her interest piqued. Everywhere she looked she saw black-and-white photographs. Tacked to walls, stuck to the refrigerator and range with magnets, taped to the curtains, spread over the microwave and dryer.

"What's this," she asked her mother, waving a hand.

"George is finally going to put that picture book together. He wants everyone's input."

George Quackenbush, seventy, and his thirty-year-old grandson, Danny, were lodgers in her mother's rooming house. George had been a photographer most of his life, shooting the famous, the not-so-famous, the infamous—using as his background the colorful entertainment and political field of *The Biggest Little City In The World*.

When George's wife died six years ago, he turned to the only family he had left, the son of his deceased daughter. The son, born autistic and placed in an institution in his late teens, went meekly with his grandfather to settle in at the Atwood house. Danny had a passion for television and would tune in every waking minute if his grandfather would let him.

Kasey went around the room, studying each picture carefully. Included in the montage were photos of casinos, before and after new face-lifts and tower expansions; showgirls; politicians—local, national, and global; there were celebrities, from the here-today-gone-tomorrow cabaret personalities to the super megastars and legends such as Sinatra, Garland, Redford, Monroe, and Wayne.

"Don't take too long on the ones in here; the whole house is full of them." Her mother stood at the sink peeling and paring a basket of peaches. "He wants us to flag our favorites with those little tabs over there."

Kasey took a green tab and stuck it to a photo of Whoopi Goldberg in a nun habit with the Reno arch as a backdrop.

"Are you still at the *Silverbar?*" her mother asked.

"Nope. Finished there Friday. I'm on my way to *King's Club* this morning."

"King's Club? That's the place where you ran cocktails way back when, isn't it? You and that pretty little thing, Dianne, the one who married Ralph's oldest boy. Does he run the place now that Ralph's gone? What was his name? Ralph's boy?"

"Jay. And yes and yes. In fact it was Dianne who called me in on this job."

"That girl set her sights high, didn't she? So how does she like being married to a club owner?"

Kasey shrugged.

"She's unhappy?"

"Let's just say she has problems that money can't solve. Or maybe it's the money that's the root of the problem, who's to say? But Dianne has always been resourceful; she'll make out okay."

"A new job, huh?" Marianne dropped a peach pit in the trash, wiped her hands on the towel, crossed to the table to the morning newspaper. "Shall we find out what the stars have in store for you today?"

Like I have a choice, Kasey thought, stirring dry creamer into her coffee. Every morning her mother read her horoscope aloud to her. Her mother was the most superstitious person on earth, relying on fate and the stars to guide her. Most days, the predictions for Kasey were way off, like yesterday's promise of a true love nearby. Some days, however, it was uncannily right on.

She picked up the prefolded section and read, " 'A new job will require you to work behind the scenes. A loved one who is feeling down will perk up at your unexpected visit.' "

A loved one who is feeling down. Her father? She felt a pang of guilt. What had it been—two weeks? three?—since she had dropped in on him? Maybe if she had time later in the day . . .

"See there," her mother gloated. "It says you'll be on a new job and working behind the scenes."

"I always work behind the scenes, Ma."

"Just my point. How many people do?"

Kasey had no answer for that. She didn't even try to make any sense of it. Reminded of her father, she wondered if he were doing okay. It was only the middle of the month. He should be all right for a week or so. It was at the end of the month, just before his social security check came, that things got rough. It couldn't hurt to pay him a visit. She'd make time. Period.

"Read mine," Sherry Kidd said, coming into the kitchen towing Danny by the hand. Sherry was barefooted, wearing knee-high leggings and a cotton shirt with Garfield on the front. She pulled out a chair for the young man and gently pushed him into it. "What's mine say, Marianne?"

Sherry was twenty-five, with natural strawberry blonde hair, large amber eyes, and honey-toned skin. With no makeup and certain clothes, like what she had on now, she could pass for a girl of twelve. About to begin her final year as a student at the University of Nevada, majoring in political science, she put herself through school doing something only Kasey knew about—hooking.

Marianne picked the paper up again. "Gemini, right?"

Sherry nodded, leaned down to Danny. "Dannyboy, orange or cranberry juice?"

"No salesman will call," Danny said to the floor.

Sherry poured a glass of orange juice and placed it in Danny's hand, making certain his fingers had a firm hold before she let go.

"Okay, Sherry, here it is. 'Your charm has a galvanizing effect on a member of the opposite sex.' "

"That must be you, Danny." Sherry tousled his hair. "No one loves me like you do."

Danny's head bobbed. He sipped his juice.

Kasey took a peach from the bowl on the table, washed it to tame the fuzz, cut it in half, leaned over the sink, and began to eat.

"That's all you're going to have?" her mother said, handing her a napkin.

"Ummm," Kasey said, wiping juices off her chin with the back of her hand.

"No eggs, no oatmeal?"

Before Kasey could answer, her mother groaned something about another rosebush. She rushed to the door, flung it open, ran down the steps and across the yard, calling "Snickers! Snickers, bad dog. Stop it, y'hear. Bad, bad dog!"

Grinning, Kasey rinsed her hands, said a hurried goodbye and rushed out, hoping to make a clean getaway while the dog, now muddy from the garden, was intent on wrestling a rosebush to the ground.

"Jay, Detective Loweman is here to see you," Gail said over the speaker phone. "He says it concerns Mrs. Steiner."

Jay sat at the dark mahogany desk in his third-floor office of the King's Club. "Mrs. Steiner?"

"The woman who died in Room 814 over the weekend," she said quietly.

His stomach tensed. "Thanks, Gail, send him in." He worked his necktie back up, stood, walked around the desk. The double doors opened; and Gail Foster, a thin woman in her mid-sixties who had been his father's secretary when Jay and his brother were mere kids making chains with the paper clips on her desk, stood aside to allow a heavyset, red-haired woman in a pair of lime-green walking shorts and a bright tropical shirt to enter. She was followed by the detective.

Loweman introduced the woman as Ms. Gordon, Louise Steiner's daughter. Jay extended his hand. "Ms. Gordon, I'm terribly sorry about your mother's death."

"Not as sorry as I am."

He nodded, released her damp hand, and looked to the detective for an explanation.

"Ms. Gordon has come to claim her mother's body and to make arrangements to have it sent back to California for burial. But there seems to be a slight problem."

"Regarding the body?" Jay asked.

"No—not yet anyway. According to Ms. Gordon, something of Mrs. Steiner's seems to be missing. Something of substantial value."

Jay invited them to be seated. Ms. Gordon sat in a club chair. The detective chose to stand, taking his familiar stance of a hand in a trouser pocket, coins clinking together. Both declined his offer of coffee. Jay leaned on the edge of the desk and waited.

"My mother's ring, a three-carat solitaire. It's nowhere to be found."

"Perhaps she left it at home?"

"No. My sister is there now, at mother's house. She's looked everywhere. Mother always took her valuables with her in a jewelry pouch." Loweman and Jay exchanged glances. Jay remembered the pouch. The one he, Frank, and the dead woman's friend, Mrs. Curtis, had gone through. A diamond ring was not among the jewelry.

"It wasn't on my list, and I don't remember seeing a ring with a big diamond," Loweman said.

Jay pressed a button on the phone and spoke to his secretary. "Gail, check with the main desk, see if anything was put in the vault for Mrs. Steiner, Room 814, please."

"Someone stole it," the woman said. "Someone who had an opportunity to go through her personal things when no one was around. The hotel staff, the cops, the paramedics. It was probably like a circus in that room. I want you to know I hold the hotel personally responsible."

"Ms. Gordon, at no time was anyone alone with your mother after she died." Loweman explained the circumstances leading up to the discovery of the body. "Mrs. Curtis assured me she waited with the hotel manager in the hallway outside the room until the police and paramedics arrived. Mr. King, Mrs. Curtis, and I myself went through her personal belongings, at which time I listed them. A list I showed you at the station. The only ring found was a plain gold wedding band on the left hand of the deceased."

"Well, I don't trust Ruth Curtis either."

The secretary's voice came through the speaker phone. "Sorry, Jay, nothing in the vault for Mrs. Steiner."

"I wanna go through her room," the daughter said brusquely. "Maybe it fell on the floor or something."

"I'm afraid that's not possible," Loweman said. "Until we determine the cause of death, no one's allowed in there."

"You said she died of a heart attack."

"I said it *appears* she died of a heart attack. When a death is sudden, unexplained, and unattended by a physician, there's a certain procedure we gotta follow. Namely, secure the scene, perform an autopsy."

"How long's that going to take? I can't hang around here forever. I have things to do back home. My sister and her no-good clan are there now and she—" The woman abruptly clamped her mouth shut. She rose, looked from one man to another, her dark eyes hard. "If that ring don't turn up, you'll be hearing from me." She marched out, slammed the heavy door behind her.

Jay sighed, dropped his head, and shook it slowly back and forth.

"Wanna know what I think?" Loweman asked, staring after her.

"What do you think, Frank?"

"I think the ring was left at home and little sis got her hands on it first. From what Mrs. Curtis told me about them, those two were always squabbling over who was entitled to what. One would cut the other out in a New York minute if there were something of value. I wouldn't doubt if the sister hasn't already cleaned out mother's house lock, stock, and barrel. Damn shame the way people act when a loved one goes. Talk about your vultures, huh?"

"Yeah." Jay looked at Loweman, smiled. "So how's that beautiful wife of yours?"

"A trooper, as always. She does better in the summer, you know. The dry heat seems to help her arthritis."

Frank and Jay went way back. High school buddies, they participated together in basketball, football, and then, later on, the ski team at Mt. Rose. Frank had joined the Marines straight out of school, while Jay had gotten his degree in business before going into the Army. Ten years later, both men married within months of each other. The two friends, hoping to reestablish their earlier relationship, made an attempt to bring the wives together. They had one another over for dinner, backyard barbecues mostly, with the men doing the cooking—Jay on his brick-and-cast-iron rotisserie, and Frank on his Weber. After a couple of dinners, Dianne begged off without any explanation. The two friends settled for an occasional day on the slopes together or a brief lunch.

"Buy you breakfast?" Jay asked.

"Can't. Gotta look in on the medical examiner in a few."

"Lunch, then. Bring Marlene along."

"Well . . ." Loweman glanced at his watch. "Ah hell, sure. Why not? Marlene would like that. She's always asking about you. I'd be jealous if I didn't know how crazy she is about me."

Jay clapped Loweman on the back. "The way you chase women with your eyes, I'm surprised *she* doesn't get jealous."

"Aw, she's cool. There's no harm in looking. She knows only an idiot would settle for chopped liver when he's got sirloin at home."

As he walked Loweman to the door, Jay said, "You mentioned an autopsy for the Steiner woman. When?"

"Want your room back, huh? Can't blame you. Height of the tourist season. Helluva time for a good room to sit empty."

"I don't care about the room; I just want this cleared up and behind me."

"The M.E. had it scheduled for this morning; but, well, it got bumped. A couple of sheriff's deputies found a decomposed body in the hills north of town last night. Skull bashed in. This one's a homicide for sure. It'll take precedence."

Jay didn't dwell on the discovery of an unidentified, decomposed body dumped in the hills. Just as long as it wasn't at his hotel, he thought. There was enough going on right here under his own nose to cause him grave concern.

Six

Jay King descended the wide carpeted stairway from the convention area to the lobby and casino floor. At least twice a day he made rounds of the facilities. As owner of the casino, he liked to make himself visible, to oversee the operation first-hand. The morning rounds he made alone, starting in the basement with the laundry, wardrobe, maintenance, and repair departments, on to the main floor to inspect the behind-the-scene operations of the hotel and casino, then upstairs to the convention center and business offices. He toured the main casino last.

The casino in the early hours was quiet and subdued. Without the crowds, he could see from one end to the other. It was at this time, as Jay descended the grand staircase, that he took it all in with a sense of great pride. He often liked to make believe he was seeing the interior of the club for the first time, as if through another's eyes.

The effect was impressive. Neon glowing in the darkness. Tinted mirrors, primary colors, designs, shapes, sounds, lighting, and temperature appealing—seductive, even—all carefully orchestrated to entice those passing beyond its doors. Drawing them in, ensnaring them for a time.

Jay was pleased with what he saw. His family had worked long and hard to establish King's Club, and yet the work was far from done.

Jay was headed for the keno lounge when Howard Cummings, his head of operations, approached. "Morning, Jay."

"Howard. Everything running smoothly?"

"Could be better. Yanick tells me there's a purse-snatching ring working the clubs in this area. Could be as many as four of them. These guys sound pretty sharp."

"Have LeBarre run a sting. Maybe we can flush them out before they rip off any of our customers." The purse sting was common in the industry. Decoy purses were planted throughout the casino and monitored by surveillance cameras. When the purse went out the door, the carrier was then detained and the police notified. Once word got out a sting was in operation, the number of purse thefts markedly declined.

"Got extra guys on the escalators and elevators and mingling with the conventioneers," Cummings said. "One of LeBarre's men busted a pickpocket last night."

"Good. An ounce of prevention . . ." Jay saw Kasey Atwood push through the glass doors at the valet entrance. "We'll talk later." He excused himself to meet her.

Heading toward the elevator, Kasey was halfway there before she noticed him. She was wearing a blue-green straight skirt and matching jacket over a white blouse. The skirt's hem was several inches above her knees. She had very nice legs, he noticed, and found himself slowing, not wanting to cut short her approach. He might be married, but he wasn't blind. He could still appreciate the sight of a good-looking woman gliding across a room in heels.

When they met, she smiled and extended her hand.

After taking it, Jay looked around guiltily; and with a half-grin, he said, "Uh-oh, I hope I haven't blown our cover."

She laughed softly. "You've been reading too many espionage novels. I'm just part of the team now."

"Let's talk in my office." He directed her to the elevators.

As they passed a bank of slot machines, Jay stopped, bent, picked up a quarter from the floor, and handed it to a young woman perched on a stool playing the machine. After cautioning her about leaving her purse unattended on the floor, adding that having her purse stolen was not the way the club wanted her separated from her money, he and Kasey continued on.

They got no more than ten yards when an elderly man in a maroon duster, carrying a broom and dustpan, approached a waste receptacle littered with discarded cocktail glasses. Jay recognized the porter whom everyone called Captain.

"Morning, Captain. I'm surprised to see you here so early. When did you change shifts?"

Captain grinned, showing a gold-capped front tooth. "Just this week, Mr. King. Been working swing all these years, but recently the late hours been getting to me. The missus never liked them. Getting old, I s'pose. Oh, say, don't tell the boss I said that."

"Your secret's safe with me," Jay said.

Kasey looked around Jay King's tastefully decorated office, so much like his office at his house. Again the golds, reds, and greens, dark woods, Oriental carpet and Renaissance period art work transported her back to another era. It reminded her of pictures of libraries in old European manors.

Coming in from the casino floor where everything flashed, glittered, and cried out for attention, she found that the rich, warm colors had a certain calming effect. Perhaps that was why this man seemed so in control and laid back, she thought, as she allowed him to guide her to an area away from the massive desk, to a grouping of chairs designed for conversation. She sat on a blood-red mohair settee and immediately felt at ease.

He offered her coffee. She declined.

"Brad will be along in a minute." Jay sat in the center of the settee across from her. "I sent him on an errand. I wanted a moment to talk with you alone."

"About Brad?"

"No. About what you and Dianne discussed at the house

after I left the other day. She told me she showed you the newspaper clipping of the MGM fire."

"Jay, she's your wife; it's only natural she be concerned. Threats of any kind should be taken seriously."

He nodded. "I'm not faulting her. If threats in the mail were the extent of it, I'd probably dismiss it. But it involves more than just me and the hotel. What Dianne doesn't know is that two of them pertained to her."

"By name?"

"No, but it was clear she was the intended target. It would be easy enough for someone to find out who she is and what she does in the course of a day. There's *this* group and *that* charity. Well, you know."

Not firsthand she didn't. "Death threats?"

"Not exactly. More of a sexual nature. Crude. Ugly."

"Do you still have them?"

He nodded. "There, in the safe. I didn't want her to see them. I wouldn't have told her a thing; but the last one, the fire clipping, came to the house and out of curiosity, she opened it."

Kasey was glad he was the one to broach the subject. She had promised Dianne she'd look into the situation, and having Jay's cooperation was essential if she were to do the job right.

"What else? Anything specific?"

He leaned forward, let his hands dangle between his legs. "For starters, a rash of room thefts. As you know, there's always a certain amount of complaints from guests. Real and imagined. Some get drunk, gamble their bankroll away, and don't remember losing the money. Others leave valuables in their rooms and return to find them missing."

"How many complaints?"

"Four last week. The week before, three. Cash and jewelry mostly. A trinket here, a few chips there. Never enough at one time to suggest out-and-out burglary. The guests seem hesitant, embarrassed even, to report it. I can imagine what's going through their head. . . . Did I misplace it, lose it? Did that woman—or man—I picked up downstairs in the bar last night lift it while I was sleeping? One fellow claims he had a thousand dollars in cash in a briefcase and the only thing missing was some medication."

"Housekeeping?"

"Could be anyone. Anyone with access. A guest on the fourth floor swore both her diamond earrings were there when she went to bed, yet one was missing in the morning. Last week a male guest complained that someone had tried to enter his room in the middle of the night. He'd thought it was his wife—she often stayed up to gamble—but when he called out, whoever was there quickly closed the door and left. When his wife came in minutes later, she denied being there earlier. She had no reason to lie.

"We stress the importance of using the deadbolts and safety chains," he went on. "Yet people have unrealistic expectations regarding safety in a hotel. A hotel, even the best hotel in the world, is no more secure than one's own home or office. We do the best we can: security officers, safety locks, fisheyes, and surveillance cameras. Hell, I know a lot of our equipment is antiquated, but it works if people would just use their heads."

"What's Surveillance doing?"

"The past couple of days they've been monitoring the elevator banks on each floor, both regular and service."

"The guest that died here Saturday, what happened?"

"She was old, had a bad heart. No sign of illegal entry or a struggle. Nothing missing—or so it seemed at the time." Jay told Kasey about his visit that morning from the detective and the sister of the deceased.

"Maybe I'm too skittish. Hot August Nights is just around the corner. The hotel's been booked solid for months and will stay booked through the season. In October, construction on the expansion and tower gets under way. The last thing I need right now is adverse publicity." He came to his feet, began to pace. He stopped, turned, and looked down at her. "Damnit, Kasey, I have a bad feeling about all this. A real bad feeling."

"Jay, these guest complaints, are they concentrated on any particular floor?"

He hesitated. "Good question." He crossed to his desk, pressed a button. "Gail, contact security. Have them go through their logs for the past month. I want to see the full reports regarding guest complaints. Missing items in particular."

Kasey wanted to see the logs. Not everyone knew what to look for. Patterns. She always looked for patterns.

"Jay, I'd like to have a copy of those logs. All shifts."

He nodded. "Gail, have them bring up the logs for—" He looked at Kasey. "How far back?"

"One—no, two months . . . for comparison."

To Gail he said, "May through today." He straightened, removed his jacket, and draped it over a chair.

"The dead woman's room, was it sealed by the police?"

"Pinned. No one goes in there unless I say so."

"I'd like to see it. Could you let me in later this afternoon?"

"I'll be here when you're ready."

There was a tap on the door, and Brad King poked his head in. "Hello. Am I interrupting?"

Jay waved his nephew in.

Brad entered, closed the door, and crossed to them. From pale blue tux to a wheat pin-striped suit and a handpainted tie. She'd almost forgotten how young he looked—Michael J. Fox with stature. Again, she noticed the slight resemblance to Kevin.

He extended his hand to Kasey. His handshake was brief and businesslike, nothing like the pawing display of the other day. He greeted her pleasantly, stated how much he was looking forward to her guidance and training.

Good, she thought, this was more like it. Either his uncle had sat him down and set him straight or her little finger-twisting demonstration on the dance floor had done the trick.

The moment his uncle turned his back, Brad gave Kasey a wink. She groaned inwardly. This wasn't going to be easy, though probably not boring either.

"I don't know how you want to work this," Jay said. "I imagine you don't care to have it known what you'll be doing here."

"No, I'd rather not. For all intents and purposes, it should look as if I'm working for the club as a new employee. Have you told any of your key people about these threats?"

"No. No one."

"Good. Let's try to keep it that way for a while."

"What about Howard Cummings? He's my chief exec."

"Not even Cummings." She turned to the nephew. "Brad, what's your present title and position?"

"Well, I'm training for Assistant Manager—" He glanced at his uncle, grinned. "But . . . until I return to school next month, I'm Hotel Casino Service Manager. My staff and I cater to premium customers—"

"Perfect," she cut in. She knew the operation. The chief function of the service manager and his hosts was to provide special services to the repeat high roller. Customer service, to be precise. A very demanding role, often a twenty-four-hour one. The host had to know his or her way around the entire hotel and casino—housekeeping, kitchen, gift shop, and so forth. The host served as travel and booking agent, secretary, upscale valet, golf and card partner, and good friend to a particular customer and his family during his or her stay at the hotel. The host, who was above a hotel "greeter," was sometimes known as a credit executive and worked in close contact with the casino floor supervisors and the credit department.

Times, however, were changing and the VIPs, mega-celebrities, and junkets were all becoming a thing of the past. Today's casinos geared up to accommodate senior citizens, families, and everyday folks. *Grinders,* gamblers on a fixed income with a limited amount of cash to blow, were now earnestly being wooed. Even in Las Vegas, with its glitter, glamor, and elaborate theme structures, gaming had changed. Slots were hot, and middle America now gravitated to them in droves. The money stayed the same, but the players were changing. Perks, freebies, and the bizarre brought them in and kept them coming back.

She turned to Brad. "We switch roles. For the next week or two, it'll appear you're training me," she said. "You'll show me around, introduce me as a new casino host to the staff in each department. That way the two of us can go just about anywhere without suspicion. How many are on staff now?"

"Floating hosts? None full-time," Jay answered for Brad. "We had to fire our top guy for comp abuse when we learned his friends were forging the name of our premium guests. A second went on pregnancy leave, and the last was hired away by the Hilton. We have a department staff of about four who man the office and handle in-coming calls. Brad and our two managers, Yanick and Epson, and a few pit execs have been doubling as hosts. Epson has an in-house employee in mind."

"Can you hold off for a bit?"

"Sure," Jay said. "Three VIPs are due in this month. Twice that the following month. I'm sure Brad and the two managers can handle them. If not, I can step in."

"What about Dianne?" Kasey asked.

"Dianne?" Brad said, clearly amused. "Dianne King catering to someone? You gotta be kidding."

"Cool it, huh?" Jay said to Brad. He turned to Kasey. "Can you start immediately?"

"Yes. We'll get the introductions out of the way today, then we'll start on typical surveillance stuff. We'll need to do a surveillance shift in the eye. I'll let you know ahead of time so you can pull those guys off."

"You don't trust my men?"

I trust them more than I trust your nephew, especially alone in a dark room, she thought. Aloud, she said, "I don't trust anyone."

She thought she saw a glimmer of respect mixed with amusement in Jay's clear blue eyes.

"I'll get you keys, ID, and anything else you need," he said, going behind his desk and sitting. "You're on your own, you two."

Kasey turned to Brad. "Shall we begin?"

Seven

At 2:30 P.M., the Monk tossed aside the *Penthouse* Magazine and sat up. His bed was a double mattress on the floor, covered with a sleeping bag, unzipped all the way and laid flat. For a pillow he used a large stuffed panda he'd won in the arcade at Circus Circus one night trying to impress some stupid bimbo. He couldn't remember the outcome of that evening, but the fact that he had possession of the panda probably meant he'd struck out.

The Monk had found the two-room shack twenty miles north of town the first week. The place was a dump with little or no amenities. He could afford better, a lot better. But out here, backed up to the foothills, there were no neighbors, no one snooping around looking into his business. Privacy, all he wanted, was his. It would come in handy one day soon.

He stretched his arms out in front of him. Made fists. The word on his forearm expanded. *Monk*. He liked the epithet, liked it so much he'd had it tattooed on him. He was given the name while in the service. The Monk. A solitary person. A recluse. That was him. He hung with no one, relied on no one, was solely devoted to a discipline prescribed by his own exacting order. Behind his back he was called the Madmonk or the Monk of Mayhem. He liked those, too. If the shoe fit . . .

He stood, stretched again, then slapped his bare chest, hard, in rapid succession. The stinging on his nipples evoked instant alertness as no coffee or controlled substance could. He wondered what it would be like to have a nipple pierced. A gold ring through it. Maybe someday he'd find out.

Rooting around in a duffel bag, he found one of the capsules he had swiped from the purse of the old deaf woman at the club. The one he had killed with the dry cleaner bag. He swallowed the capsule with tepid coffee. The miracle pill, doing its work while he played. Killing whatever nasty germ it came in contact with before the little bastard could take hold. Not that *he* had anything—not anymore, that is. And never again. For the Monk, prevention was the name of the game. The memory of his dying grandfather was enough to make him vigilant. The Monk had been just a kid; but after all these years, he still couldn't get the sight or smell of that hospital or the old man out of his mind. At the time he had known nothing about venereal disease. Had never heard of syphilis: *Neapolitan disease, French pox, a dose.* Yet he would never forget the sight of that repulsive old man, blind and staring, his paralyzed body a wasted lump between the coarse hospital sheets. Every vital organ, including his brain, diseased.

So simple to cure. The fool had never sought treatment.

The Monk learned about VD in high school, and caught his first and only dose two years after he came out of the service. Her name was Jimmy Sue Blanco. She was tiny, reddish-blonde, brown-eyed, freckled, and incredibly shy. She was unlike any woman he'd ever met. Pure. Innocent. The Monk, in the habit of taking what he wanted, often forcibly, all of a sudden became tender and patient. He courted her for months, seeing no one else, the perfect gentleman settling for whatever she was willing to give, allowing her plenty of time in which to surrender her virginity, to become his completely. When they made love for the first time he was the happiest man alive. They talked of marriage, of children, and for weeks he was madly in love until the day he noticed a curious red bump on the underside of his penis. He confronted her on a Sunday-afternoon drive in the mountains. While she wept and begged for forgiveness, he opened the door of the speeding

car and pushed her out. He kept right on going across eight
states and never once looked back.

The rising heat in the bedroom had the Monk sweating. He
dressed quickly. He would shower at the club, as he did everyday, right after his workout in the hotel gym, then change
into the two-tone blue uniform. He liked his job. Anytime he
could wear a badge and strap on a gun, he was happy.

At four o'clock, Kasey and Brad entered the Esmeralda
Lounge, a hot spot for club workers, and took stools at the
bar. The majority of casinos welcomed, solicited even, their
own employees by offering certain promotions to keep them
around at the end of their shift. Paychecks were cashed on the
premises, accompanied by free drink tokens which could be
redeemed at any casino bar, bars that offered keno games and
video poker machines. The casino giveth; the casino taketh
away.

The lounge was a deep, dark room with tables at the back.

The day had flown by. Literally starting at the bottom, she
and Brad had covered most of the hotel basement, a maze of
concrete twists and turns, long stark hallways with low-watt
lighting—extension space given over to laundry, wardrobe,
boiler room, slot repair, food and beverage preparation, equipment storage, and employee lockers. Wherever Kasey and Brad
went, the staff was pleasant and cooperative, yet it was obvious
their presence was not well received. Kasey expected as much.
Although very little pilfering went on at this level—storage
rooms were kept locked and no one entered without a security
escort; the big losses were upstairs where cash, chips, and
coins readily changed hands—interruptions by upper-level employees, especially by the nephew of the boss, were merely
tolerated at best.

By 2:30 they had moved up one level to the main floor.
Brad showed her her office: a tiny room with a chair, desk,
and fax/telephone, cluttered with boxes of promotion pam-

phlets and flyers. His office across the hall, adjacent to the front desk, was slightly larger. And instead of boxes, he had a sofa and a Stairmaster. After meeting the Service staff, they moved on to the main casino floor where she was introduced to the casino manager, Robert Yanick. Yanick took over the introduction of his floor supervisors and the credit manager. Brad became quiet and withdrawn around the casino boss. Kasey wondered if he disliked Yanick or was merely resentful of the man's position, a position that Brad hoped to have one day.

Now that they were through for the day, Kasey allowed herself to relax. All day she'd waited for the other shoe to drop. After the wink in his uncle's office, she'd expected Brad to make some juvenile pass, but was surprised by his good behavior. He'd actually behaved like a gentleman—like a responsible junior executive. For the past seven hours he had paid close attention and seemed eager to learn. Kasey was impressed. She figured there was hope.

They sat in the middle of the nearly full bar. As they sipped their drinks, a beer for Brad and lime tonic for Kasey, she quietly explained that mid-bar, between both cash registers, was the best vantage point for spotting. The bartender, out of earshot at the far end, flirted openly with two young women.

She didn't expect to see any action today, not with the owner's nephew sitting beside her. Yet, no sooner had the thought crossed her mind, then she watched the bartender serve the two women. He took no money or drink tokens.

Her senses kicked into high gear. "Does that bartender know who you are?"

Brad shrugged. "I've never seen him before."

"Keep your eye on him, I have a feeling you're going to get your first lesson."

They chatted, pretending to be engrossed in conversation. By facing each other they were able to watch the bartender's every move.

Up and down the bar he collected for the next four drinks,

let two more slide. Within an hour, he had served freebies to at least five of his buddies. Another unpaid-for round went to the two young women. The tips were generous where the drinks were free.

"He's pouring heavy. Instead of the regulated four count, which is an ounce, he's pouring about five, and in several cases, as much as seven," she said quietly. "He's also pouring call drinks and premium liquor for well drinks."

Kasey had seen enough. "C'mon, let's go."

"But—" Brad looked toward the barkeep.

"Not now."

They left the bar.

"Are you going to report him?" Brad asked when they were out of earshot of the bar.

"That's what I'm here for."

"Hey, that's pretty cold. He seemed like an okay guy. So he gives a few drinks away. The club gives away drinks all the time. Shit, Kasey, he wasn't skimming the till."

"No, he wasn't skimming the till, but he was giving away liquor, which costs the club money." She had seen it again and again. Diminutive acts of dishonesty, like a live ember in dry grass, tended in a short time to catch hold and quickly spread out of control.

"The guy was breaking his butt in there," Brad said. "He was friendly, fast, and he sure as hell knew his stuff."

"He knew his stuff all right. And I guarantee he's gonna get faster . . . at taking what doesn't belong to him." She turned to face Brad. "Look, Brad, I don't do the firing. I only turn in a report. It's up to his supervisor to decide if he's salvageable. A warning may be enough for now. Most of the time that's all it takes."

They stood in an area near the stairs and elevator. Brad's eyes locked onto hers. One corner of his mouth lifted in a tiny grin.

"What?" she said warily.

"Man, I can dig a woman who has the balls to make heads roll. 'Off with their heads!' God, that's cool."

"I'm glad you approve."

"What now?" he asked.

"I guess that's it."

Brad looked disappointed. He brightened, pointed to a waiting elevator. "The garage. I'll show you where to park your car."

He steered her inside of one of the two parking garage elevators and pressed a button.

The doors opened on the second floor. They stepped out onto the cool, dim, concrete expanse.

"This floor's reserved for the brass. The executives park along the west wall," Brad said, pointing across the garage. "There's a private entrance into the conference rooms there. Park anywhere that's not assigned to someone. I'll get you a sticker for your windshield."

In the distance, sounds of a scuffle reached them. A woman cried out. Kasey and Brad looked at each other.

"It's coming from over there, that row of cars under the pipes." She grabbed at his sleeve, and they began to run in that direction.

From a hundred yards away, Kasey saw a man and woman struggling at the driver's open door of an old-model white Valiant. The man had a hold of the woman's upper arms, and she was trying to break free. She kicked at him, made contact. He swore. A purse lay on the ground near the rear tire, its contents scattered about.

"Hey!" Kasey shouted. "Let go of her!"

The man, dressed in a blue security uniform, turned and looked at them. He released the woman, stepped back, his hands falling to his sides. At that moment, the woman took a swing and hit the man on the side of his nose. The impact made a sharp sound.

A look of rage, of chilling malevolence, flashed across the man's face. He shoved the woman back down in the seat, then covered his nose with his hand. Blood oozed through his fingers. A moment later when he turned back to Kasey, the look was gone; she saw only pain in his eyes.

The woman bent over and vomited between her legs, splashing the black shoes of the guard.

"What's going on here?" Kasey demanded.

"Hey, what the hell are you doing to that woman?" Brad asked behind her.

The guard backed away, out of range of the splashing vomit. He pulled a white handkerchief from a back pocket and roughly swiped at the blood on his face and hand.

"This is none of your business," he said. "Both of you, move along."

"Who the hell do you think you're talking to," Brad questioned. "Do you know who I am?"

Kasey put her hand on his arm, hoping to shut him up. "Brad . . ."

"I'm Bradley King. My uncle owns this club. He happens to be your boss, mister."

The guard glared at Brad over the top of the bloodied handkerchief; then, as if by way of dismissing him, he blew his nose.

Kasey knelt down at the woman's side. She had stopped retching and had her head buried in her arms across her knees.

"What happened?" she asked.

The woman lifted her head; it wobbled. She tried to focus on the tall man in uniform. "He tried to attack me." Her speech was thick; she reeked of beer and wine.

Kasey looked up at the guard, who still held the handkerchief to his face. She searched for his ID tag, but saw none.

"She's about as drunk as they come, and I've seen plenty of drunks. I saw her get off the elevator, stumbling and staggering. No way could she drive. I was only trying to get her to come back into the casino so I could get her a cab."

"He's lyin'." Her head lolled, her eyes going from Brad to

Kasey and finally to the guard. "He was . . ." the words seemed to die in her mouth.

"Was *what?*" Kasey asked.

The woman quickly looked away. Her hands began to tremble. "Nothin'. I just wanna go home. My car keys, where're my damn car keys?"

Kasey began to gather the woman's belongings together and return them to the purse. She found a King Club ID tag. Her name was Paula Volger. She was an employee.

Kasey handed her a crumbled tissue from the purse. "Paula, the officer was only trying to help. He's right, y'know; you're in no condition to drive. You'd never make it down this spiral ramp. Let's go back in and get you a cab."

Paula wiped her mouth. "I can't leave my car here."

Kasey knew it was forbidden for any employee at any time to use the parking garage. "It'll be okay."

"I'll go with *you*, not *him*. I ain't going nowhere with him."

"That's fine." To the guard Kasey said, "I'll take care of it. As the club's new host, guess this will be my first official duty. And your name is . . . ?"

"I'll log it and make out a report," he said, ignoring her question and turning away from them.

As Brad and Kasey helped the woman across the garage to the elevator, Kasey looked back to see the guard locking up Paula Volger's car.

Eight

Once back inside the club, Kasey and Brad parted. Kasey took Paula Volger into the nearest ladies' room and, after helping her clean up, sat her in the lounge area and attempted to make some sense of what had happened in the parking garage. The only thing she learned for sure was the woman worked for the hotel in the housekeeping department. It was her day off and she had come in to cash her paycheck, play a few slots, and have a drink or two, as she did every Monday.

Paula, looking more ill with each passing minute, refused to file a report or even discuss the incident. In the end, there was nothing to do but put her in a cab at the hotel's main entrance and let it go for the time being.

At 6:30, Kasey stepped off the elevator onto the third floor. The sector housing the executive suites was quiet, without activity. The desk in Jay's outer office was unmanned, computer and printer under plastic covers.

As she tapped lightly on the closed door of Jay's office, she glanced at her watch. Jay had probably gone home for the day as well. She wondered if his secretary had remembered to leave the security logs on the desk for her.

Kasey went to the desk. Behind her, she heard the double doors to Jay's private office open.

"Kasey?"

She turned. In shirtsleeves, top button and tie loosened, Jay stood with a hand on each door. He smiled when he saw her.

"Oh, good, it's you. I was about to have you paged."

"Sorry I'm so late getting back. Brad and I ran into a little trouble in the parking garage."

Jay ducked back inside and returned with his suit jacket. "Tell me about it on the way. Security's waiting for us upstairs," he said, slipping on the jacket. "Oh, and those daily logs you wanted, they're on my desk. You can pick them up on your way out."

In the elevator, Kasey told Jay about the two employees in the garage. "Are there surveillance cameras on each floor of the garage?" she asked.

"There aren't any. Security patrol, that's about it."

Parking garages were a hotbed of crime. "How many guards?"

"One per shift. Maybe two on grave if it's a big weekend."

"Have you had any complaints about any of your security personnel?" she asked.

"Not that I know of. But then we hired on a dozen or so at the beginning of the season. There are always one or two that don't fit in. Complaints would go to LeBarre. He's head of security."

"How many guards total?"

"Eight to ten per shift with supervisors. Twenty-five, maybe thirty."

On the eighth floor they walked to the end of the hall and joined a guard, an elderly man with gray hair who had been summoned to unpin Room 814.

They exchanged greetings.

"How's that daughter of yours doing, Harry?" Jay King said. "Have we lost her to the competition?"

" 'Fraid so, Mr. King. Vegas Hilton hired her on last year. She likes the faster pace. Says we're too folksy here up north. Couple years and she'll be back. They always come back."

When the door had been unlocked, Jay said, "I don't know how long we'll be, Harry. I'll call when we're ready to lock up."

Kasey pushed the door open to the wall. The room was dark

except for a sliver of light coming through a three-inch opening in the blackout drapes.

"Did the investigators dust for prints before you pinned the room?" Kasey asked.

"No."

"Guess we don't touch anything, then." With a ballpoint pen, she pressed the light switch. A lamp in the entry and another in the room proper came on. "Do you remember if this is how the room was when it was pinned? Drapes, personal effects, and so on?"

Jay carefully took in the scene. "Looks the same. Frank took her purse."

Kasey stepped into the bathroom. The sink, tub, and toilet were spotless. No toiletries lying about. A white Samsonite cosmetic case sat on the counter.

She turned to Jay, who stood in the entry watching her. "Has housekeeping been in since the body was discovered?"

"Couldn't. The room was pinned immediately."

She left the bathroom, glanced into the closet where several articles of clothing hung on wooden hangers, and paused. In addition to the hotel hangers, there were two metal hangers. On one hanger, through the thin dry cleaner plastic bag, Kasey saw a beaded blouse. Attached to the neck of the other hanger, which was empty, was a Lina Roble Dry Cleaner receipt that read *beaded bls* and *angor swtr*. She scanned the summer cottons and light polyesters for a sweater. No sweater.

"Something?" Jay asked.

"I'm not sure. I'll come back to it later." She moved past him to the dresser and, with the pen, pulled open several drawers. Neat stacks of folded clothes, mostly underthings.

She crossed to the unmade bed. On the lower sheet, a yellowish stain was clearly visible—the woman had died in bed, her bladder voiding upon death. Kasey looked around. Except for the hearing aid and eyeglasses on the nightstand, the surfaces of the furniture were bare. No items of clothing draped over chairs or on the floor, no cigarette butts, no tourist pamphlets or coupons, no clutter of any kind. A neatnick, Kasey observed, a place for everything and everything in its place. Probably even rinsed out the sink and tub after she used it, then wiped down the chrome fixtures. Hotel maids, who on a daily basis waded through messes most foul, adored guests like Mrs. Steiner.

Kasey turned slowly in a circle. "The woman was tidy, beyond tidy. Fastidious. Not the type to casually leave a three-carat diamond ring sitting around. She straightened up the room, went to bed, and died before she could call for help. It must have happened very quickly. I don't see anything out of the ordinary."

"But you feel something?"

Yes, she definitely felt something. But it wasn't just in this room. It encompassed the entire hotel casino. She smiled. "I've been known to be wrong."

"Gut feelings should never be ignored," Jay said. "I usually go with mine."

"So do I. But in this case only a trained investigator and a forensic team can do justice to a scene this orderly."

Jay looked relieved. "Is that it then?"

She took one last look around, nodded, and crossed the room.

Jay used the two-way radio to call the security guard to return to pin the room again. As Jay held the outer door open for Kasey to pass through, she hesitated, then turned back to stare into the area to her left.

"One sec." She strode to the closet. She reached out for the metal hanger, stopping within inches. Instead she took the pen and maneuvered the hanger from side to side. On the backside of the receipt, stapled to it, was a ragged piece of thin plastic. Dry cleaner plastic. She looked down. Deep in the shadows behind a matching Samsonite suitcase, she saw a trace of pastel. When she reached down to retrieve it, she felt Jay's fingers close around hers.

She stopped, turned to look into his face.

"Should you touch it?" he asked. "Crime scene contamination and all that?"

"I don't think we have to worry about fingerprints here, but you're right, just to be safe . . ." She held up the pen. When he released her hand she bent down on one knee, balancing on the balls of her feet, and used the pen to hook a piece of something soft and furry. She lifted a pink Angora sweater a few inches.

"Well, looky here."

Jay moved in close to see. She could smell his aftershave, feel the stiff but smooth material of his pants along her thigh and knee as he crouched beside her.

"The sweater fell off the hanger. Is that . . . something?"

"It might be. This doesn't seem consistent with the rest of the room, with the dead woman's fussy habits. A woman who neatly folds used towels and wipes down water spots on chrome fixtures wouldn't allow an expensive sweater, just out of the cleaners, to slip off the hanger and lie on the floor. And what's happened to the cleaner bag? Two separate pieces, two separate bags."

"She wore the sweater that night?" Jay offered. "Threw away the plastic?"

She shook her head. "I checked the wastebaskets. No plastic."

"What makes you certain it was in the cleaner bag when she left home?"

"A sweater like this tends to shed. If it were *my* sweater, I'd keep it covered, and I'm anything but finicky."

"So what does it mean?" Jay asked, helping her to her feet.

She ran her fingers through her hair, changing the part from left to right. When she looked at Jay, he was staring at her with an expectant expression on his face, as if waiting for her to say something incredibly profound. She suppressed a smile. "Probably nothing."

They waited in the hall until Harry showed up, then they left.

The elevator stopped on the third floor. Jay reminded her that the security logs she'd asked for were in his office. Moments later, as he ushered her through the double doors of his office suite, she was surprised to find Dianne sitting behind the massive desk. And by the expression on Jay's face, he hadn't expected to see her either.

"Kasey, you're still here," Dianne said. "I saw Brad downstairs. He said you'd left some time ago." She rose, came around the desk, and lightly kissed her husband on the corner of his mouth. "Overtime?" she said to no one in particular.

Kasey waited. Dianne, she remembered, had a sharp mind that tended to jump to conclusions. She had a tongue to match. The best way to handle her was to avoid letting her addle or trap you.

"I asked Kasey to have a look in 814. A relative of the woman who died there claims an expensive ring is missing. She's suggesting it might have been taken from the room after her mother died."

"I see." She looked from Jay to Kasey. "Don't we have a police force for such things?"

"The police don't give a damn about my liabilities or the reputation of this hotel, Dianne."

Kasey said quickly, "Well, I'll just take those security logs and head out."

Jay went to his desk, lifted a fat manila envelope, and handed it to Kasey. To his wife he said, "Do we have some sort of function tonight that I've forgotten about?"

Dianne took a cigarette from a pack in her purse, started to light it, then thought better of it. She put it back into the pack and snapped her purse shut. "Function? Oh . . . no, darling, I just thought we could have a nice quiet dinner together." She turned to Kasey. "This is the only place where I can pin him down. If he's at home, the phone calls never quit and I know he wishes he were here. At least here he'll relax long enough to enjoy a decent meal. He has a suite upstairs that gets a pretty good work out. We have a perfectly lovely home that without me and the housekeeper would sit empty a good part of the time. Kasey, if you had a place like ours, would you choose to live in a hotel?"

"I guess it would depend on the circumstances."

Dianne smiled. "A diplomatic answer." She joined arms with her husband. "Well, I'm starving. Shall we, darling? Kasey, you're more than welcome to join us."

About as welcome as walking pneumonia. "Thanks, Dianne, but I have to be going. I have another job across town."

"Oh, too bad. Listen, now that we're in touch again, let's do lunch soon. We have loads of catching up to do."

So absorbed in the day's events, Kasey got as far as the lobby door when it dawned on her she hadn't played the three quarters in the slot machine nearest the exit. She turned back, found a red, white, and blue 7 machine on the end and dropped them in. The first reel stopped on a blank.

Kasey moved on without waiting for the remaining reels to stop.

On her way home, Kasey pulled into the mall entrance and drove to *Clementine's*. The restaurant, a rustic wood building looking like a lodge at summer camp, was independent of the shopping mall, nearer to the main thoroughfare. This early in the evening and this early in the week, Monday, only a handful of cars were in the lot.

She circled the building, checking the exits, then drove on. She'd come back at the end of the week, Friday or Saturday, when bar business was at its peak, and she'd bring along a companion. Aside from having a double set of eyes and ears, two people were less conspicuous. Over the years she'd used her mother, father, friends, and even the boarders at the house. All except Sherry had been more hindrance than help. Her father's taste for booze had him jolly and talkative, distracting her, and worse yet, drawing attention to them. Her mother's distaste for booze had her counting the number of drinks a customer ordered and shooting disapproving looks at those who tilted more than three. George was good, but he was reluctant to leave his grandson for too long. Once, years ago, Kasey had even taken her ex-husband, something she had vowed never to do again. The night had ended in a shouting match in the parking lot when she learned he had made a drug buy in the men's room.

Ten minutes later, she turned off the highway onto a private road and followed the row of sycamores to her mother's house. Every time she neared the property she felt an overwhelming sense of pride. She couldn't imagine the ranch belonging to anyone outside the Bane-Atwood family.

A late afternoon breeze rustled the leaves, bringing an end to the oppressing dry heat of the day. Above a jagged ridge of the Sierra, the sun burned into her eyes. As she drove to the back of the house, she watched Snickers loping toward her, wagging his great head back and forth like a prancing colt, trailing a rainbow of colors behind him.

What has he gotten into now?

She parked her car under the carport between the two houses and honked the horn. She eased the door open, feet going out first in an attempt to ward off the dirty paws. "Down, boy, down. What the hell have you—"

Then she got a clear look. Fastened to a nylon line with bright plastic clothespins were towels, washcloths, and several old lace dresser scarves, items her mother insisted upon drying in the sun for that clean, sweet smell. "Oooh boy, you, my furry friend, will be one dead dog when Ma sees this."

Kasey gathered up the nylon line and towels, engaging in a tug-a-war with the dog for the remaining ten feet. She heard the squeak of the back screen door.

"Kase? What in the world—Oh, for petesake, what has that harebrained animal done now?! Oh, lord, not your great-grandmother's handmade dresser scarves," Marianne Atwood wailed from the back porch. "Kasey, stop him!"

"I'm trying to." The cord wound around her ankles and

threatened to pull her off her feet. "Ma, grab him before he drags me across the yard along with the doilies."

Her mother jumped off the top step and grabbed the dog around the middle. For a moment the two looked like they were dancing, nose to nose.

Kasey rushed toward the house, towing the clothesline. She charged into the kitchen, reeled in the line until the last grimy length of lace and terrycloth slid across the threshold. The screen door banged shut. With a loud exhalation of breath, she pivoted, leaned against the refrigerator, and began to brush at the dirt on her skirt and jacket.

She looked up to see Danny sitting in a chair at the table. "Hi, Danny. Hot enough for you?"

"You're in good hands," he said under his breath without looking up.

"I have magazines for you from Dr. Chambers. *Sunset* and *Fishing the West.* I'll bring them over later."

No answer. Kasey didn't expect one and would have been surprised to get one. The only person Danny ever responded to aside from his grandfather was Sherry Kidd. Sherry had something special. Something that charmed him out of his own private world of bright paper and TV slogans. Love, maybe. Only Danny knew for sure, and he wasn't about to tell.

His head was bent, thick blond hair like a mushroom cap falling into his eyes, his attention focused on the piece of colored paper in his hands. His fingers painstakingly worked at the paper, folding, turning, bending, twisting. This one would be a bird of some kind, the beak and wings already distinct.

Every time Kasey looked upon one of his paper masterpieces, she felt a sense of wonder. No one had ever taught him *origami,* a technique of paper folding originating in Japan, and where he had picked it up was a mystery even to his grandfather. Yet, limited only by his imagination, he produced the most astonishing creations—flowers, animals, many-sided boxes, and birds, like the one he was constructing before her eyes. The only problem was a shortage of paper. His fingers, although slow and at times unmanageable, remained busy every waking hour. Kasey and the roomers collected all the paper, magazines, and newsprint they could get their hands on. Slick paper with colored pictures held the most appeal.

Behind him on the tea cart sat the portable Sony TV, the volume turned low. Danny absorbed everything and, like a parrot, repeated the more repetitious phrases.

Kasey opened the refrigerator door, careful not to disturb the dozen black-and-white glossies stuck there with magnets, more photos from George Quackenbush's endless collection. She stared inside, debating between a diet Pepsi and an ice tea Snapple.

"Thirsty, Danny?"

"Have you driven a Ford lately?"

She opened a blackberry Snapple and set it in front of Danny. George insisted his grandson eat and drink products that were as close to natural as possible. She took a Pepsi for herself, popped the tab and drank it down, stopping only when she ran out of air and the ice-cold carbonation began to burn in her throat. She breathed deeply, rolled the can against her wrists, and studied the photos. The one that caught her eye was of the entire cast of *Bonanza*. The set for the original series was located on the Ponderosa Ranch, a local tourist spot no more than forty minutes from Reno-Sparks. When she was a kid, her father had taken her there and she had guzzled sarsaparilla from a tin mug, a mug that featured the entire Cartwright cast on it. She wondered whatever had happened to that mug?

"That was shot right after their first episode in '59," George said, entering. "Did you know Michael Landon was doing stand-up comedy in Sparks at the time?"

Kasey shook her head. "I thought the only comedy he did was in that werewolf movie. What was the name of it?"

George chuckled. *"I Was a Teenage Werewolf."* He tousled his grandson's hair before sitting down next to him.

Kasey glanced out the window. Her mother and Sherry Kidd were trying to drag Snickers out of the vegetable garden. Sherry, wearing hiking boots and OshKosh bib shorts over a tank top, tugged, then fell backwards on her bottom. When Marianne bent over to help her up, the dog jumped both women, knocking them to the ground.

Kasey opened the back door and called out, "Want me to find that spray bottle, Ma?"

"Very funny," she called back. "Get the BB gun. No, make that the 20-gauge." Both women struggled to their feet, doubled over with laughter.

Kasey shook her head, chuckled, gathered up the clothesline of dirty linen, and put it on the washing machine. She was removing the clothespins when her mother and Sherry entered.

The women were still laughing, picking leaves and dirt from each other.

"What a sweetheart," Sherry said of the dog. "I can't wait for him to get all growed up." She brushed at the seat of her overalls, stepped to Danny, and gave him a quick kiss on the cheek. "Hi, handsome, did you miss me today?"

Without raising his head, Danny nodded. He thrust out his arm and pressed the paper bird against her stomach.

"For me? Oh, Danny-love, it's the best one yet."

"Go for the gusto," he said. "Be the best you can be."

"Wise words."

"Sherry, are you busy Friday or Saturday night?" Kasey asked. "I could use you on a new assignment."

"Friday looks okay. How long?"

"A couple hours. Ten to twelve?"

"Yeah, I'm free. As long as I'm in bed before midnight."

Kasey knew she wasn't referring to her own bed here at the house. Sherry worked on the weekends at the better hotels downtown, where the companion—usually a conventioneer or highroller—was registered. There was no safer place

than a casino hotel. High security and the hotel's preoccupa-
tion with guest privacy gave her a certain peace of mind.
Prostitution was legal in certain counties of Nevada, but not
in the downtown clubs where Sherry hung out. She resisted
the local cathouses, the famed Mustang Ranch east of Sparks,
and the Kit Kat Ranch outside Carson City. She preferred
to take her chances in the clubs, working for herself. Sherry
thought of herself not as a hooker, but a companion, a business woman. The difference, she told Kasey, was that although she accepted a fee for accompanying a certain man
for the evening, she slept with only those she liked. She
wasn't interested in developing lasting relationships with her
customers; she never accompanied the same man twice. Her
goal in life was to one day become active in politics, and
the less time spent with a companion, the less likelihood of
his remembering the encounter later on.

Sherry was Kasey's favorite work companion. The girl was
funny, friendly, and sharp. Accustomed to sizing up people and
keeping her eyes open for potential danger, Sherry had an innate creep detector and could usually hone in on trouble well
in advance.

Years ago, hoping to steer Sherry away from the clubs and
hooking, Kasey had offered her a full-time consultant job.
Sherry had refused, explaining that she liked her job. "I'm
fussy, Kasey. *I* pick the guy, not the other way around. If it
turns out bad, it's my goof. I don't goof too often."

But she *did* goof. And on those rare nights, Sherry would
tap on the door of Kasey's bungalow. Like a battered, hurting
child, the smell of sex still on her, she'd curl up in one of
Kasey's comforters on the living room floor. Kasey would
make her a hot chocolate with miniature marshmallows and,
with no words between them, rock her until she fell asleep.

Kasey finished her Pepsi, then crossed to her own bungalow.
She made up a plate of deli potato salad and pickled herring
on wheat crackers and poured a chilled soave. She sat on the
natural wicker in the bright kitchen with its potted herbs and

flowers filling the garden window and paper mobiles hanging
from the ceiling, basking in the last rosy glow of the setting
sun. When she had eaten all of the salad and half the herring,
she opened the envelope and began to go through the security
logs, sipping wine and nibbling crackers.

Two hours later, she stuffed the last sheet of paper back into
the envelope. Three months of daily logs, three shifts, told her
something was certainly out of kilter there. The past several
weeks showed a substantial rise in hotel guest complaints and
what seemed like an excess of unauthorized entries throughout
the hotel casino. She made notations of the reports she intended to pull and go over the next day.

She stretched. Where had the day gone? The first day on a
new job always flew by. Many jobs were completed in one
sitting. Others were ongoing, one day a week or month. She
usually had more than one going at a time, and no two were
quite the same.

She finished the last of the wine in her glass. It had become warm, tasting of vinegar. The sourness took her back
in time, to her youth, to the many times before the divorce
of her parents when her father had worked all-nighters at the
bar in the resort they owned along the Truckee River. On
those mornings when Kasey came in to help with the
cleanup, he reeked of vinegar, bitters, and sourmash whiskey.
The bitters he drank at first light in an attempt to ward off
the hangover. The vinegar smell, brine from the pickled eggs
kept in a two gallon jar on top of the bar, permeated his
shirt front and both arms to the elbow. Whiskey consumed
throughout the night seeped from his pores and fouled his
breath.

Kasey tried to recall her daily horoscope. Something about
a loved one being perked up by a visit. She sighed, ran fingers
through the front of her hair. She had planned to look in on
her dad. She'd completely forgotten.

Dotus Atwood was a night owl. He'd still be awake at eleven.
She dialed his number, heard it ring in his basement apartment

across town. After seven rings, she waited for the answering machine to pick up. Another ten rings and Kasey finally gave up. He was either out or passed out. As she hung up, she wondered what had happened to the answering machine she'd given him for Father's Day.

Nine

The Monk got the call on the two-way radio at half-past midnight, minutes before the swing shift ended. *Guest escort.*

When he showed up at the cashier cage, he found a very drunk and belligerent man talking in a loud voice with the floor manager. The man was shoving hundred-dollar bills into his pockets when the Monk joined them. The Monk remembered him from the main pit: loud, obnoxious, and on a hot streak on the dice table. One task of security was to keep close tabs on drunks and heavy losers. They were the most likely to cause a scene. The Monk liked to keep an eye on the big winners as well, particularly the ones who got soused.

The floor manager, a skinny guy with black, thick-framed glasses, was saying, "Mr. Nicker, we have security boxes for our guests right here at the cage. I really wish you'd reconsider and take advantage of it. I'm afraid we can't be responsible for anything lost or stolen in the hotel unless it's been secured."

"What kinda place you running here, anyway? You telling me it's not safe to carry cash around in your hotel?"

"Well, sir, you did win a lot of money tonight and there were dozens of witnesses at the table, and you have had . . ." the floorman let the sentence hang in the air.

"Yeah, yeah, yeah, so I've had a couple drinks, zat a crime?"

"As a precaution—"

"Look, I'm ready to turn in. If the rent-a-cop wants to tag along, make sure I get to my room in one piece, that's fine

with me; but my winnings go with me. You, in the uniform,"
Nicker pointed at the Monk, "do your duty."

The Monk nodded to the floorman, then followed the man.
In the elevator, the man rambled nonstop about himself, his
life, his business. He had his own vending company in Auburn
and occasionally he took these two or three day jaunts to Reno-
Sparks to have some fun and get away from the family grind.

"You ever win a lot of money? Ever win five grand at a
table? Eighteen straight passes. Eighteen. You ever roll eighteen
straight passes, buddy?"

"I don't gamble."

"You drink?'

"No."

"Drugs, huh?"

"No."

"Well, hell, Mr. Clean, what *do* you do?"

"I do my job."

"I do my job," Nicker mocked. "Okay then, do it. Get me
a broad. A blonde. One with big tits, I like 'em full-bodied,
if y'know what I mean. Have her in my room within a half-
hour."

"Not part of my job."

"Don't shit me. Isn't that what you guys do when you're
not hassling derelicts or busting heads or just wandering
around trying to look like big important men?"

The Monk stared at the lighted floor numbers.

"Not very talkative, are you?" The man bobbed drunkenly,
tilted his head, looked at him askew with one eye. "You're
kinda young to be a security guard, aren't you? I mean, most
of the ones I've seen around here are old geezers. Military
and retired cops. You're too young to be retired. What are you?
Thirty-five, forty?" When he didn't get an answer, Nicker went
on. "Betcha wanted to be a cop, huh? Wanted to be, but
couldn't cut it for one reason or another. You like the uniform,
the gun. Yeah, I betcha like to play cop."

The elevator stopped on the sixth floor; the doors opened,

and the stocky man lurched forward. The Monk grabbed his arm and the back of his neck. The hand at his neck squeezed hard, forcing the man to one knee.

"Ooww!" Nicker quickly came up, pulled away from his escort, rubbed at his neck. "Hey, you stupid sonofabitch, what're you trying to do? Shit, that hurt."

"Yes," the Monk said flatly.

"Get lost." Nicker pushed at him. "I don't need you."

"Which room?"

"I said . . ." As he looked into the Monk's icy eyes, his jaw suddenly went slack. "I . . . uh, I can manage from here." The mocking tone gone.

"Which one?" the Monk repeated quietly.

Nicker glanced nervously down the abandoned hallway. He swallowed, his Adam's apple seeming to go into a spasm. "It's clear down at the end. Really, I can—"

The Monk took him by the arm and began to walk down the hall. The man stumbled along, turning to look behind him several times before they reached Room 634. "Hey, thanks, buddy, I . . ."

"Open it."

"Listen, if I said anything back there that didn't sit right—"

"Open it."

The Monk thought he heard the man moan as he reached into his shirt pocket and brought out a keycard. With trembling fingers, he attempted to insert it in the slot. The Monk took the card and unlocked the door, holding it open. Once inside, the man quickly turned and tried to close the door. The Monk's shoulder blocked it open. In the dark entry, the Monk could see the light from the corridor reflected in the whites of the man's eyes. Light, overshadowed by raw fear.

The man dug into his pants pocket, brought out a bill, and shoved it at the Monk. It floated to the floor. The Monk held the door open, bent, retrieved the hundred-dollar bill. He slowly turned it over in his broad hand. He rose, again staring hard at the man.

At that moment a door across the hall opened. From the corner of his eye, the Monk saw a young couple come out, saw them glance their way. The Monk kept his back to the couple, watched Nicker's face, which seemed to go into a paroxysm of darting eyes and twitching muscles.

The Monk carefully pressed the bill down into Nicker's shirt pocket. "Auburn's not a very big town, is it, Mr. Nicker? If I get down that way, I'll look you up, check out your operation. Maybe meet the wife and kids. I like kids . . . most kids."

It took the drunken man only a second to assimilate the threat, and the comical look on his face was almost enough to placate the Monk. Almost, but not quite.

Ten

The following morning the Monk made his way through the underground maze, the vast back-of-the-house operations of the King hotel casino.

It was 10:00 A.M., well into the day shift, the time in which most services operated at full capacity. The Monk was dressed in dark-brown pants and a tan shirt. Downstairs in the basement, pager on his belt and a phony ID card clipped to his breast pocket, he could pass for maintenance. Upstairs in the hotel corridors, without the ID and pager, collar open and sleeves rolled up, he could pass for a guest. He had made these unauthorized rounds many times in the past without incident.

The Monk had just stepped off the freight elevator when he heard footsteps on the metal stairs. He ducked into the shadows. A man, a short Hispanic in kitchen whites, passed quickly without seeing him. The Monk knew the employee had no business in that area without a security escort, no legitimate business, that is. Whatever the punk was into, the Monk thought, it was either illegal or against club rules. He knew all the rules. He had personally violated most of them.

The Monk waited several minutes before following.

He jiggled a doorknob here and there along his way. Locked. This far northeast section of the building housed hotel and restaurant supplies such as food and liquor, and to leave storage rooms unlocked was to invite thievery on a high scale. The Monk knew the entire layout by heart. In his three weeks on the job he'd explored every inch of the building's 49,000 square feet and had come across some interesting things.

His investigation went well beyond the hotel casino to its proprietor, Mr. Jay Garner King. He knew where he lived, the names and ages of his family members, the cars each drove, right down to the people he associated with on a daily basis, both business and pleasure.

The Monk knew King from another time and place. Twenty years ago, they had butted heads; and if everything went according to plan, they would again. Just thinking of the arrogant sonofabitch with his sexy wife and growing empire made the Monk want to smash something with his bare hands. He absently rubbed the clenched knuckles on his right hand as he made his way down the deserted corridor.

As he neared the end of the building and a large open area at the southern corner, a construction area designated as a second food-storage warehouse, he slipped into the shadows. This was the only place the sneaky little spic could be. The cold concrete space was dark, closed off by cartons, wood braces, and draped sheets of clear plastic.

Hushed voices ahead told him the man was no longer alone.

The rubber soles of the Monk's shoes made no sound. He closed the distance, slow, deliberate, like a predator stalking prey, his presence concealed by a wall of stacked boxes. He paused within ten feet of the man and woman locked in each other's arms. Lovers.

The Monk wasn't surprised. Aside from sticky fingers and drugs, illicit sex often went hand in hand with the twenty-four hour business, mainly during swing and graveyard. In large casinos with the work force ranging upwards of 25,000, any dark, secluded corner became a possible site for a lover's tryst. One of the duties of a security officer was to patrol those areas, all of which were quite familiar to the Monk, and roust the culprits. Today, two day-shift workers had found themselves a cozy niche.

Watching them now, his eyes fully adjusted to the dim light, the Monk recognized the dishwasher from the main kitchen. A few times in the past weeks when their shifts had overlapped, the Monk had escorted him to the basement supply room. The woman was a stranger to him. From the color of her uniform, the Monk knew she was a maid. She was pretty, a thin body with large breasts, also Hispanic.

They leaned against a large tin duct padded with strips of soft, pink insulation. They were fully clothed—she in the tan housekeeper's uniform, he in kitchen whites. Their union was one of newness, of discovery, and consisted of kissing and groping. The woman kept the man in check. Either she was playing hard to get or she sensed they were not alone.

A banging door in another part of the basement quickly parted them. A few rapidly spoken words in Spanish and they were scurrying off in different directions.

The Monk knew they'd be back.

Her horoscope for the day warned of a back-stabbing acquaintance. . . . Romance was again on the horizon. . . . Money was all around her. Kasey accepted the part about the money, ignored the romance prophecy, and gave little more than a passing thought to the back-stabbing acquaintance.

At 10:00, the start of the day for most casino executives, who on average worked a twelve- to fourteen-hour shift, she met Brad and Jay King in a conference room on the third floor for a staff meeting. Present were Howard Cummings, the chief executive, Epson and Yanick, the top managers in the casino and hotel, and the heads of the various other departments.

Except for Howard Cummings, the CEO, she'd met the others the day before.

Jay introduced her as their new casino host.

The hotel manager, Mark Epson, turned to Jay. "Wait a minute. What about Syd Land? I thought we were going to consider him?"

"We are considering him," Jay said.

"Then I can bring him in now?"

"Not just yet."

"When?"

"I'll let you know."

"I had someone in mind, too, Jay. My gal is experienced. Has a helluva resume." Yanick, the CM, turned to Kasey, "Ms. Atwood, what qualifications do you have? Where did you work before?"

"She knows the job, Bob," Jay said.

"Well, that's dandy, but I think the rest of us should be aware of her qualifications."

"Bob," Jay said patiently, "I've already hired her. Are you challenging my decision? My authority?"

"I'm only—no, sir."

"I brought her in. She answers to me."

Kasey wasn't surprised by the reaction of those around the table—uncomfortable seat shuffling, eyes lowered; the more brazen of them pursed lips or nodded knowingly.

"Make no mistake, however," Jay went on, "she's perfectly qualified. With Hot August Nights fast approaching, I suggest we all work together to make this promotion the best yet. Do I have everyone's cooperation?" He let his gaze touch each person at the table. "Good."

Kasey thought his approach brilliant. She had wondered what she would say to those who asked where she had worked prior to King's Club. As a rule, hosts came up the ranks in-house or were stolen away from rival establishments. Occasionally, a host without prior experience might be hired and trained if he or she were sharp and personable, with a good memory for names and faces. But now, hired by the boss himself, though she could expect little or no respect, she knew that probing questions would be kept to a minimum, as well as any close alliances with other employees. The less she was taken seriously, the better the opportunity for her to move around undetected and with little suspicion. Like Brad King, she'd be just another family friend or relative giving orders and pulling in an undeserved paycheck.

"Anything else?" Jay asked, closing that particular discussion.

Howard Cummings cleared his throat, then said, "Yesterday's surprise sweep by the immigration authorities hit us pretty hard. We lost about three percent of our work force, mostly in the hotel and kitchen areas. We're scrambling to fill the holes. Usually when this happens, the other hotel casinos are in the same fix; but it seems this time we were singled out. With all these fake green cards, we don't know anymore who the hell is legit."

"Have personnel increase job advertisement," Jay said. "Next."

Yanick began to chuckle. "Guess whom I spotted walking the block last night?" he said. *Walking the block* meant the common practice of a rival casino or *store* sending out a spy to check out the competition. "None other than Tony Bartona from The Harbor Club. You know, that dive on the lake's north shore that Mr. Vegas himself, Ansel Doyle, just bought into."

Jay suddenly came to attention. "Was he concentrating on anything in particular?"

"Not that I could tell. I'd say he was just checking out the operation. He had dinner in the Steak House, saw a show, and took a room for the night."

"Is he still here?"

"I don't know. I can check."

"Do that. Get back to me."

"Tony's nothing," Brad said. "I saw him last night, too. Bought him a drink, in fact. Teased him about spying."

"I'm not so sure you should be encouraging him, or the likes of him, Brad," Cummings said. "Bartona is trouble in my book. He or any of his goons just setting foot in the place leaves a stink."

Brad shot Cummings a hard look, then said brusquely, "You're too paranoid. You think every guy with a vowel at the end of his name has mob connections. He was shopping, nothing more." Brad smiled. "You know what they say about imitation being the most sincere form of flattery."

Kasey had watched the exchange between the two men with interest. She remembered Brad's coolness yesterday toward the casino manager. Now with the CEO. It seemed he had a personality problem with his uncle's key men.

"Hmmm, well, Brad's probably right. But if he shows up again, I want to know right away," Jay said. "Okay, what's next?"

The meeting dragged on with several department heads coming under fire for one infraction or another. Blame was passed with no one taking responsibility. It was obvious the managers resented one another and, like children, accused and denied. Kasey had begun to tune them out, her mind drifting, when something Barney LeBarre, the head of security, said brought her back abruptly.

". . . . The guest in question wasn't the one who complained. The complaint—more an observation, I take it—came from guests in the room across the hall. They thought the man in . . ." He consulted a clipboard. ". . . 643 was attempting to signal them. They—the wife, actually—thought maybe he was being threatened by one of our security guards."

At the mention of a security guard, Kasey and Jay exchanged glances.

"Which one?" Howard Cummings asked.

"I can't say at the moment. Last night's swing log had nothing about the sixth floor, or an officer being up there."

"She was certain the man was security?" Jay questioned.

"Yes. The husband confirmed it, though he didn't notice anything out of the ordinary. Said he was eager to get back to the tables."

"Has anyone talked to the guest in 634?" Epson again.

"Yeah," LeBarre said. "Name's Nicker. Said there was no problem. Said he was pretty racked last night and doesn't remember much. Seems this Nicker guy hit the dice table a good lick before his brain checked out for the night. Six, seven grand worth."

"So what's the problem?" Cummings piped up. "Don't we have enough problems without inventing more? How long is he staying? I hope to hell someone comped him for another night so he doesn't walk with our money."

"I don't know about that," LeBarre said, "but if ever a guy were hiding something, it was this one. He broke out in a major four-star sweat when I brought it up . . . about security, I mean."

"Well, there's nothing we can do If he doesn't want to talk about it. We have to respect his privacy." Jay turned to Kasey. "If he's still registered, comp him to meals and another night in the hotel."

She wrote down the name and room number, then made a mental note to ask Cummings or Yanick to show her the premium-customer ledger. The ledger detailed each customers gambling record, credit limit, and net worth. It also listed personal information such as favorite foods, beverages, sports or activities, even the clothes size of each member of the family. The job of a host had great possibilities for those who liked working with the public, rubbing elbows with the rich and famous. Kasey preferred working behind the scenes. She found hotel guests, particularly guests accustomed to being catered to, a hard cross to bear.

Jay was called away, and the meeting continued without him for another tedious, combative hour. They adjourned for lunch. She and Brad returned to the main floor and were crossing the casino to the Steak House to meet the head maitre d' when Kasey heard her name paged over the intercom. She excused herself and stepped to a white courtesy phone on the wall near the cabaret bar.

Left to his own devices, Brad greeted a cocktail waitress standing at the bar. The waitress, an attractive woman about Kasey's age—so Brad *did* go for older woman—waited as the bartender filled her floor-drink order. In the short time it took for Kasey's call to be put through, she watched Brad stroke the waitress's arm, her cheek, and the back of her hand as they spoke.

"Kasey, it's Jay," he said, coming on the line. "Can you come up to my office for a few minutes?"

"Right now?"

"Yes."

"And Brad?"

"Just you."

"I'm on my way." She hung up.

Brad, glancing her way, saw she was off the phone. He gave the waitress a smile and a tender pat on the rear and walked away. When he reached Kasey, she stared somberly at him.

"What?" he said, looking around. "What'd I do now?"

"Is that your wife? Sister? Fiancée?"

"No, she's just some waitress I know. What's the problem."

"The problem is harassment. What you just did could be construed as sexual harassment—big time."

"Oh, come on."

"Didn't your uncle go over that with you?"

"Well, yeah, but it doesn't apply here. That's Trish; she likes it. She knows I'm only kidding."

"Are you sure? Are you one hundred percent sure? Does Trish like it here? Does she need this job? Does she have a kid or two she's working her fanny off to support?"

"I don't know. What's the big deal anyway?"

"Ask your uncle about sexual harassment and the courts. It might give you a whole new perspective on fanny patting."

"Okay, okay," Brad said. "I get it. I get it. Not in the workplace."

She shook her head. "And definitely not when you're in a supervisory position. You're cute, Brad, a real charmer, and I bet the girls are just crazy about you. But that won't prevent one of them, or more than one, from slapping you and this establishment with a sexual-harassment suit. Something like that could really hurt your uncle, screw up his plans for expansion."

She left Brad on the casino floor to mull that over. Five minutes later she was in Jay's office meeting Detective Loweman of the Sparks Police Department.

Eleven

"Homicide."

Det. Loweman looked from Jay to Kasey. He ran his fingers up and down his blue flowered necktie. When he couldn't mess with his pocket change, he fiddled with his tie.

The three were seated in the conversation area of Jay's office. Jay had introduced Kasey as a private consultant for the hotel casino.

"Great," Jay said. "That's all I need."

"I've got men upstairs now going over the scene."

Jay stood. "Then you might as well know Kasey and I had a look around in there yesterday."

"Shit," Loweman said, obviously perturbed. "Damnit, Jay, you know better. The scene of a murder—"

"What murder?" Jay calmly cut in. "No one said anything about a murder, or that Room 814 was officially a crime scene."

"Officially, no, but—ah, hell, what's done's done," Loweman said impatiently. "I'll need to get comparison prints from you two."

"It was *treated* as a crime scene, Detective Loweman," Kasey said. "Nothing was touched or disturbed."

"Well, thank God for small favors."

"So the medical examiner found something?" Jay asked.

"Yeah. There's conclusive evidence she was physically assaulted the night she died," Loweman said. "It's not certain if she died from suffocation at the hand of the killer or from a coronary brought on by the attack. But that's for the legal system to decide once we get our man.

"The M.E. didn't get around to the postmortem until this morning. And what the coroner suspected when he initially examined the body turned out to be correct. Some bruising on the upper torso just prior to death revealed two cracked ribs. Also a finger was broken. Now that particular break happened to be postmortem."

"The missing ring?" Jay asked.

"Most likely. Once the victim is dead, there's swelling . . ." Loweman demonstrated on his own finger, made the sound of a snapping twig. "The M.E. found fibers in the woman's mouth and air passage."

"Fibers?" Kasey said. "Like fur? Were they pink?"

"Pink? Yeah, how'd you know that?"

Kasey rose. "Let's go up. I'll explain there."

Jay, Loweman, and Kasey went directly to Room 814. Two crime scene investigators, already inside, moved around the room snapping pictures, dusting for prints, sketching, taking measurements, and carefully collecting trace evidence. Reporters from two local newspapers were in the corridor interviewing anyone who would talk to them. A uniformed officer stood at the door to keep the rubbernecks and any unauthorized persons out of the way of the officials.

The investigators hadn't gotten to the closet yet. Kasey pointed to the suitcase on the floor. "Behind that is an angora sweater. It belongs on that hanger with the cleaner receipt."

Loweman called to one of the investigators and had him retrieve the pink sweater. As the man slipped it into a large evidence bag, Loweman studied the hanger. "Get this, too," he said to the man. He turned to Kasey and Jay. "You sure you didn't touch anything?"

"Positive."

"The cleaner bag, huh? He tears it off, uses it to suffocate her—no visible marks on her neck or throat—then disposes of it somewhere else. He knows by the heart medication that she's got a bum ticker, so after he kills her he plants the pill bottle in her hand. Looks about as close to a natural as you can get. Slick. And it might've worked if he hadn't broken a couple bones in the process."

Knowing how it was done didn't seem to make the detective any happier. It was murder now. Kasey knew he was upset because the case was no longer fresh. The woman had died sometime late Friday night. The body went undiscovered until late Saturday afternoon. Today was Tuesday. In a homicide case, four days was an eternity, leaving the trail nearly cold. It was doubtful they'd find many guests still registered in the hotel who had been there that night. And of those, how many would have remembered seeing anything?

"He wasn't greedy and he didn't panic," Loweman said almost to himself. "He takes the time to get the plastic bag, kill her and forcibly take the ring."

"That's all he took?"

"Maybe not. We found an empty prescription bottle. Antibiotics. The friend of the deceased said Mrs. Steiner had had an abscessed tooth and had just gotten the medication the day before. Which might explain why she skipped the sightseeing tour. Anyway, there was no way she could have taken all of them in just one day."

"He thought it was dope?" Jay said.

"If he did, he's not very drug-wise. I don't take the man for an idiot. She had Valium, Demerol, Percodan. He didn't bother with them. Who knows, maybe he has a dose and he doesn't like doctors."

"He left everything neat and tidy," one of the investigators said, passing by. "I doubt if we'll get much of anything."

Loweman looked grim. "Those are the killers I dread, the calm, collected ones. You can bet your boots they've done it before. And they'll do it again. Give me the character who out of fear, hate or passion, does the deed, panics, and runs. The crime scenes are a helluva lot messier, but that kind of killer usually gets caught. Leaves stuff all over for us. Trips himself up somehow. Brags to someone or confesses as soon as the pressure is on."

Mark Epson arrived with Harry, the security guard. The guard carried a laptop computer.

They all stood in the hallway and watched Harry take out a special tool and go to work on the metal plate below the lock. Once the plate was off, Harry plugged the computer cable into an outlet in the lock.

"How does that work?" Loweman asked Harry.

Without looking up, Harry said, "Well, can't tell you much about computers, but this is a pretty simple operation. The lock has a memory. Lock Interrogation. All the keys are coded and every time one is used to open a door, information is logged into the lock's own mini-computer. From the key's code, the person assigned to it, along with date and time, is automatically entered. It can go back months. If someone used an unauthorized card to open the door, it'll show up. It'll also tell us who signed out that card."

A long list of dates and numbers scrolled by on the monitor. Harry stopped it on the last dozen entries. The readout showed that on the day the victim had last been seen alive the door had been opened with the occupant's key at four P.M. and again at ten—the time her friends said she'd turned in for the night. The next entry read eleven-forty-two. The code matched a key issued to the occupant. The following two entries were after her body was discovered and therefore accounted for.

"Hell, somehow he managed to get a key to her room," Jay said. He turned to his hotel manager. "Mark, check downstairs and see if there's a record of the guest requesting a second key. Maybe the first one was lost or stolen."

Epson jotted in a notebook.

Det. Loweman stepped forward. "Mr. Epson, when you and Mrs. Curtis found the body, was either the deadbolt or the security chain engaged?"

"No. I got in with a master. If the deadbolt had been engaged, I would have had to use a special tool."

"Who has access to keys in the hotel?"

"Lots of people. We have what we call one-shot keys. Those are signed out by bell captains and room service. Then there're the mini-masters or floor keys; they can be used on a certain floor only—by maids, engineers, phone repair, and so on. All keys are signed in and out. Stolen keys or an extra key made up at the front desk will code to the guest. If the computer says the door was opened at two P.M. by the guest, but he denies it, then an illegal key is suspected."

"Well," Loweman said, hitching himself up, "it's about time I earned my pay." He flipped a page on his notepad.

"Before you start knocking on doors, Frank," Jay said to the detective, "let me find out who was here and who wasn't. If they weren't here then, they don't know anything."

"Jay, this is a homicide investigation. I can't be tiptoeing around to suit you or your guests."

"I know. I don't intend to get in your way."

"Good." Loweman paused a beat, then relented. "Okay, look, get me a complete list of the people that were registered on this floor that night. And everyone on the bus the deceased came up on. If they are no longer at the hotel, I want names, addresses, whatever you have. And I want it like yesterday."

Jay looked to Epson.

"Got it," Epson said.

As Epson headed toward the elevator, Kasey met Jay's troubled gaze. The only thing more disconcerting than having it publicly known that a murder had taken place in his hotel was the probability that the killer might still be here, employed at the hotel. Out of nearly 19,000 employees, at least a fourth of them had access to room keys.

Minutes later, back in the executive office, Kasey leaned on the credenza and watched Jay pace. He had removed his jacket.

She stared at his back when it was turned to her. Jay, she noticed, had the broad shoulders of a swimmer, which he was. She had learned from Brad that Jay swam an impressive number of daily laps in either the pool at his home or the indoor one on the fourth floor of the hotel. His body looked hard, solid. At forty-two, his abdomen was flat, his waist narrow, his rear—

She quickly looked away, focused on a Renaissance painting of a parasoled couple in a small boat on a beautiful lake and said, "I'm afraid you're not going to like what I have to say."

He turned. "Say it."

"I went over the security logs last night. There's definitely a pattern. Someone is getting into rooms and helping themselves to whatever they want. Det. Loweman was right. Whoever it is, they're not being greedy—not yet, anyway. But they will. As I said, a pattern is developing and it's slowly accelerating. Only now there's been a murder, and a rather cold-blooded one at that. The killer broke the woman's finger to get at her ring when less than five feet away—relatively untouched—was a purse with cash, credit cards, and jewelry. He knows there'll be other opportunities, and he's in no hurry."

Jay had stopped pacing and was somberly staring at her. "You think he works in the hotel, don't you?"

She met his gaze. "Yes."

He nodded, then resumed pacing.

The unasked question, the one she knew was heavy on his mind, was whether there was a link to the previous thefts—and to the threats against himself and Dianne.

On the sixth floor, two floors below where the police were busy processing the crime scene, the Monk casually walked down the empty hotel corridor. He passed an unattended housekeeping cart which blocked an open doorway. Although he couldn't see anyone inside, the sound of a vacuum told him the maid was making up the room. He stopped at the next room, inserted the keycard in the lock, opened the door, and slipped inside.

Twelve

Paula Volger closed the door of Room 601 and wheeled the housekeeping cart to the adjacent door. Her head was pounding; her stomach churned; her tongue felt like a wool sock stuffed with sawdust. She had a hangover—a four-star, grand-slam, twenty-one-gun-salute hangover. And to top it all off, her arms hurt where that security asshole in the parking garage yesterday had squeezed them until they were black and blue. Nazi prick.

She glanced at her watch: 3:00. One more long, torturous hour to go before she could change into her street clothes, claim her stool in the Esmeralda Lounge, and partake of the hair-of-the-dog, which—if not a sure cure—would at least give her a reason to live. Inez Ramos, a fellow maid and Paula's best friend, had promised to meet her.

Paula took a moment from her own self-absorption to think about her friend. Inez, usually so serious, so grounded, had been acting weird the past couple of days. *Spacey* was the only word for it. She was a straight shooter, didn't gamble or do drugs, so it had to be a man. Paula hoped she was wrong.

Men were bad news. Wanted just one thing. Like Mr. Rent-a-Cop yesterday afternoon. Using muscle, trying to take advantage of a lady who'd had one too many, then lying through his fucking teeth. Better her than Inez. Inez woulda caved in, given him what he was after. She was too damned meek and shy, afraid to raise her voice or call attention to herself. Paula was gonna have to drag her to one of those women's self-defense classes they always had on tap at the Y.

Paula rapped on the door of 603, rolled her stiff shoulders, and called out, "Housekeeping!"

The unlatched door moved inward an inch.

Paula hesitated, her hand in the air. Open doors of occupied rooms made her wary. "Hello. Maid. *Hel-lo?*"

With her foot she pushed the door open far enough to see inside. Clothes in the closet, an open bag on the bed, an overflowing ashtray on the round table by the window.

She took several steps forward, pausing just beyond the threshold. Inside the dark bathroom, scattered over the sink top were cosmetics, toiletries, a travel case.

Definitely an occupied room. An *unsecured* occupied room. Something Paula didn't come across often. Thank God. Because if anything were missing, you could bet your sweet ass she, Paula Volger, minimum-wage housekeeping engineer, would be the first to be fingered.

The pounding in her head intensified. Forget this room, she told herself. Turn around, go out, close the door, report it and hope to Christ there's nothing missing.

From the corner of her eye she saw movement through the crack of the open bathroom door, then a swatch of blue fabric. She froze.

Paula struggled to remain calm. *Rape.* Maids ambushed in hotel rooms. It was high on her list of things to avoid. It had happened to a good friend of hers four years ago—a pillowcase forced over her head from behind and she never caught so much as a glimpse of the rotten sonofabitch.

The blue fabric shifted.

Paula grabbed the doorknob to Room 603, backed out into the hallway, quickly pulled the door shut, and—positioning the linen cart across the doorway—turned and ran. She heard a noise behind her. She rushed down the corridor, her heart pounding in sync with her head, the sound of heavy footsteps keeping close pace at her back. When she reached the bank of elevators, she turned to scream, to fight if she had to.

No one was there.

Kasey was with the hotel manager in his office going over the guest ledger when they heard a commotion beyond the closed door. She followed Mark Epson out to the receptionist's desk where a woman in a maid uniform stood arguing with the receptionist. Kasey instantly recognized the inebriated woman from the parking garage, the one who had struggled with the security guard the day before.

"What's going on?" Epson asked.

"Mr. Epson," the receptionist said, "she insists—"

"Someone's in Room 603," the blonde maid said, words coming out in a rush. "The door was unlocked—y'know, ajar like, when I went to make up the room. I stepped in to see if it was occupied and . . . and someone was hiding in the bathroom, behind the bathroom door."

"And?" Epson said.

"And I got the hell outta there. The hotel don't pay me enough to double as security."

"Start again. You went in, saw someone in the bathroom—"

"Not just in the bathroom, *hiding* in the bathroom." She told them what had happened. "Look, if there's anything missing from the room, it wasn't me that took it."

Kasey knew the housekeeper was first to be suspect, and with good reason. Maids had access and opportunity. In gaming operations, however, where employees were state bonded and required to carry an ID police card, and with polygraph tests, lock interrogation, and sophisticated surveillance, in-house pilfering had been reduced significantly.

Epson called the front desk and learned the guest registered in 603 was a female doctor in town for a medical convention in the hotel. He dialed the room. When he got no answer, he had her paged.

Several minutes later, the call came through. The doctor had been in a seminar on the second floor. After identifying himself, Epson explained the situation and asked her to meet him and a female associate at the door to her room. He asked that she not enter her room until they had arrived.

Within minutes, five of them—Kasey, Epson, Paula Volger, the doctor, and a security guard, one Kasey had never seen before—gathered around the housekeeping cart in front of 603.

The officer opened the door and went in first. He searched the room and found no one inside.

Epson then asked the doctor to go through her possessions and look for anything missing or disturbed. While she looked, the security officer ran a computer readout on the memory lock. The computer indicated the last keycard used had been assigned to the guest, but was used at a time when she was downstairs in a conference session. The maid had told the truth.

"As far as I can tell, there's nothing missing," Dr. Cooke said. "Everything looks the same as when I left."

"You're a medical doctor?" Kasey asked.

"Yes," she said. "I know what you're thinking, but as a rule I don't take drugs with me to conventions. If that's what they were looking for, they found aspirin, antacids, and birth control pills, nothing more." The doctor tossed a suitcase on the bed, opened it and began to pack.

"You're not leaving?" Epson asked.

"Yes, I am. The last session of the conference was the one you interrupted. I intended to stay another night, but I don't think I can after this. I'll be looking over my shoulder and jumping at the slightest noise."

Kasey stepped up to her. "Dr. Cooke, I understand how you feel. Please allow us to move you to another room on another floor. Naturally, for the inconvenience, the hotel will be happy to comp your stay in that room."

"Well . . ."

"Along with front-row seats in the main showroom? We want your stay at King's Club to be a memorable one."

The doctor considered a moment, then nodded.

"Good, you won't be sorry."

Epson went to the phone on the credenza, spoke to the front desk, and made arrangements to have a bellman take the doctor and her luggage to a new room.

Kasey and Epson joined the others in the hallway.

When the hotel manager began to chastise the maid for over-reacting, Kasey put her hand on his arm. "Mark, she was only doing her job."

Kasey met Paula Volger's keen blue eyes. Behind the defiance there, she saw something else. Gratitude? Respect? Kasey was sure Paula remembered her from the day before. Twice in two days, Kasey had come to her defense; and although the woman probably felt a certain amount of gratitude, it was obvious she didn't trust Kasey.

Epson turned on Kasey. His eyes, behind round metal frames, narrowed. "If I were you, Miss Atwood, I'd be less inclined to worry about someone else's job and I'd worry about my own duties. What the hell did you think you were doing in there? Giving the damn hotel away? You don't make decisions like that on your own, at least not the first day on the job."

"I was only—"

"Check with me first. You hear?"

"Yes."

This time when Kasey met Paula's gaze, her eyes expressed, if not trust, at least a measure of camaraderie.

On the way down in the elevator, Kasey's mind raced. It seemed Paula Volger had inadvertently come upon the person who had been breaking into the rooms the past couple of weeks. Paula had taken the appropriate measure. She had gotten the hell out of there to report an intruder. Kasey made a mental note to have Epson circulate a memo to each hotel department asking all personnel to be on the alert, to report anything out of the ordinary. The typical hotel burglar was anything but aggressive, preferring to use stealth and cunning. But surprised in the act, he could be unpredictable, even violent. If there were a connection between the dead woman in Room 814 and the rash of room thefts, and Kasey hoped there wasn't, this intruder was cunning and indeed violent.

When she returned to her office behind the concierge desk, she learned Brad, in a chauffeur-driven limo, had gone to the airport to greet a high roller and that he would be tied up with the man and his entourage for the rest of the evening. She typed up a memo for Epson and returned several calls. Two messages, taken by the office staff from tour operators, regarded prospective conventions, and those she passed along to the sales department. At 5:00, an hour into the swing shift for standard workers but still hours away from quitting time for most top-level management, she looked around the neat office and realized that, without Brad, there was little for her to do in her pseudo-position as host.

She rose, picked up her purse, and started out. She planned to drop by Jay's office, fill him in on the open door incident in 603 before driving across town to meet with another client.

On the far side of the hotel lobby, Kasey saw Dianne coming through the main glass doors. Dianne was dressed casually—leather boots, split skirt, and vest—as casual as one can get in a designer outfit of denim, leather, and silver studs.

Kasey raised her hand to wave, but Dianne, eyes straight ahead, strode across the lobby to the bank of elevators. They were both going to the same place, to Jay's office. If Kasey hurried, they could ride up together.

Suddenly, going to Jay's office didn't seem like such a good idea after all. For the second day in a row, Dianne had come to the club to be with him. Let her have her private moments with her husband, Kasey told herself. According to Dianne, they were few and far between. The staff meeting in the morning would be soon enough to discuss business. If her instincts were right, she and Jay would be spending a lot of time together the next several weeks. It was a good possibility she would see more of Jay than his own wife. At the thought, her pulse seemed to quicken.

She bit down hard on her lower lip. The last thing she wanted to do was revive that go-nowhere crush of years ago.

She wondered if physical attractions, crushes which were never to be consummated, ever went away by themselves? Or did they only smolder like dying embers, to blaze again and again by a breeze of emotion?

Kasey turned and dropped three coins in the end slot machine. A moment later, empty-handed, she pushed through the doors into the bright afternoon sun.

Thirteen

The kids, four of them ranging in age from three to nine, screamed and shrieked. Water splashed on Kasey's skirt as she sat poolside in the padded lounge chair. She had come straight over from the club. Allen Czeczko reclined on a chaise lounge. Directly beneath his wrap-around Ray Bans, a white strip of Scootie sunscreen made his large nose appear broader, more porous. Between pale toothpick legs and a hairy Buddha belly, a canary yellow bikini was stretched to the endurance point.

Kasey, not comfortable looking at anyone that big with so much exposed skin, kept her eyes on the kids and their mother splashing in the shallow end of the pool. Where Mr. Czeczko was openly uninhibited regarding his body, his wife was not. The heavyset woman wore a matronly swimsuit with a built-in bra and a flared skirt that only accentuated what she had hoped to conceal.

"It's that sneaky little chink Lee, isn't it?" Czeczko said. "Karla warned me about him. She wanted to boot his kiester out of there, but I told her to hold off."

The week before, under the guise of a new employee, Kasey had been hired to discover which one of the six sales clerks at Koko's Gift Shop was moving valuable items out the back door. Sales were down while shoplifting theft was up. Czeczko also had a shop in Vegas and another in Palm Springs that Kasey had been commissioned to check out, but it was the receipts in the Reno store that initiated immediate concern.

Koko's was no nickel-and-dime operation. No stock of logo

T-shirts, souvenir plates, or cheap trinkets. Czeczko catered to the elite. The gifts he carried were the sort wives selected when their spouses hit it big gambling; the sort beautiful young things received from their wealthy, married lovers as a matter of course. Specialty items, custom jewelry, designer clothes, figurines, music boxes, paintings, and numbered prints by notable artists. With the price of merchandise inflated as high as three hundred percent, shops like Czeczko's had little trouble meeting the exorbitant lease rates in the lower level of the 2,000-room, 100,000-square-foot Reno Hilton.

Czeczko and family lived in a custom home in a neighborhood where the smallest house with an inferior view was valued at close to a million. Czeczko's house was large, with a view that wouldn't quit.

Kasey had wound up her assignment for Allen Czeczko the week before. He had been in Vegas, at his main store, until this morning, and this was her first opportunity to fill him in on her findings.

"No, Mr. Czeczko, it's not Kim Lee. He's probably your most honest and dedicated employee."

"Who, then? Lynch? Hess?"

"It's all in here." She held out a manila folder.

He sat up, leaned forward, the yellow strip of cloth completely disappearing beneath his huge belly. He took the folder, opened it, and began to read. A moment later he rose.

"Let's go in," he said.

She followed him inside the tri-level house to his ground-floor office. Wearing nothing but the yellow bikini and a pair of lime-green thongs, looking ridiculously out of place among the gray ledgers, Bragg lithographs, and hi-tech computer and office equipment, he continued to read as he paced. Sounds of children laughing filtered in through the French doors.

"As you can see by the report," Kasey said, "there's absolutely no doubt where those items are going or who's taking them. I'd say by her actions, by her sheer audaciousness, she's been at it for some time and has, in my opinion, little fear of castigation."

"You're accusing my manager."

"Yes."

"Karla's been running that shop for two years."

"Yes. And probably stealing for just as long, though not as aggressively as now. I couldn't get to the receipts, but I'll bet there's some very creative bookkeeping going on there."

Czeczko crossed to his desk, sat in the massive chair, and opened a check binder. After a moment's hesitation, he laid down the pen and closed the binder. He bent over, opened a drawer in the desk, his bare skin on the leather making a rude noise, and counted out a number of bills. He rose and, with a somber expression, handed her the money.

"That's the amount we agreed on for this job. Take it because it's all you're going to get. You can just forget about doing those other jobs we spoke of."

She took the money, waited.

"You're fired." He tore the manila folder in half, then in half again. "This, Miss Atwood, is what I think of your lying report. Your work was shoddy. This . . . this—" he said, shaking the torn papers, "—is nothing but made-up garbage. You weren't there long enough to learn a damn thing, so you had to pick the most obvious employee to accuse . . . my manager. I wouldn't be surprised if you didn't pocket a thing a two yourself while you were there."

Kasey wasn't surprised by his reaction. She'd been here before. She had two strict rules that had to be followed without question before she agreed to take a job. One, the person hiring her must stay away. Two, no one else was to know who she was or what she was doing there. Either Czeczko trusted Karla Hite so much that he thought her above consideration in any wrongdoing or he was a very stupid man, thinking with a part of his anatomy that was now swaddled in bright yellow spandex. Kasey wondered how long the affair had been going on.

"She's not working alone, Mr. Czeczko. There's a man. Twice in three days he posed as a customer and she waited on him personally. He purchased some very expensive jewelry items. I think he got a deal, a very *good* deal. Later, at closing, he parked behind the shop. I saw her open the back door for him and hand something out. It's all there in the report."

"As far as anyone is concerned, I never hired you. You never stepped foot in my place of business. I want every copy of this report, you understand?"

"Photos, too?"

His face turned sanguine, then purple. "You can find your own way out," he said. He brushed past her and marched through the door, the green thongs slapping against his soles and rolls of fat jiggling at his waist.

From the Czeczko house Kasey drove back downtown. Ugly confrontations made her think of her father—not that *she* ever argued with him, for years her mother had had an exclusive on that. What she did was worry about him. She had tried to reach him again that morning with no success, the line ringing on and on, the answering machine obviously disconnected—

Or hocked.

Good ol' dad was a gambler. A horseplayer. Ponies were his life. His home-away-from-home was a race-and-sports book on Commercial Row near the railroad tracks. Most days, from ten A.M. to eight P.M., he could be found there pouring over racing forms for the more than half-a-dozen open tracks across the country. The second love of his life was sourmash whiskey, which came free with the price of a wager. Kasey's mother had divorced him not long after they were forced to sell their riverfront resort to cover his outrageous gambling debts.

Whenever Kasey thought about the resort, she felt a rush of bittersweet nostalgia. Most of her childhood had been spent there—formative years, good years. Located six miles out of town on the Truckee River, the resort had consisted of casino, tavern, restaurant, and twelve bungalows adjacent to a natural hot springs and bathhouse. Lined up along the wall in the tavern like neon soldiers, the three-reel, single-coin, one-armed bandits had blinked and clanged, their bells ringing day and night. In the evening her mother had operated the wheel of fortune while her father dealt blackjack. On weekend nights he had dealt until he became too drunk to count the cards and handle the bets, at which time he closed the game and moved on to the bar. Behind the bar, he'd fished for pickled eggs and tossed back shots with the customers until he'd passed out.

When not in school, Kasey had been everywhere, doing everything at the resort. Early morning had found her making up rooms in the motel, helping in the kitchen and dining room until around midday when her father, pale and lethargic, finally rolled out of bed. That was when Kasey had found things to do as far as possible from her parents and the constant one-sided bickering. Her mother, who worked harder than all of them put together and was more than justified in her feelings, nagged and carried on until Kasey had begun to feel sorry for her father, who shamefaced, could only nod and swear before God and all his disciples to get it together.

Years passed where Kasey worked, played, and, on a daily basis, witnessed the hired help pilfering the Atwood goods. In the beginning it was difficult for her to believe that these people whom she loved, who teased, joked, and watched over her, could possibly steal from her family. She soon changed her mind.

Uncovering the thefts became a game with her. Who was taking what, when, and where. She never bothered with the *why,* that was far too perplexing to deal with. Once, she did ask a maid why she stole towels and linen. "Why, honey, it's expected. Everybody does it. Your folks got insurance. It don't cost them nothin'." In her own backyard, Kasey became well educated in the art of in-house sleight of hand, and she would put it to good use later in life.

Shortly after the resort sold and her parents divorced, Grandma Bane had become ill and Kasey and her mother had moved to the ranch to care for her and to take over the chores. While they tended bees, fruit trees, and a vegetable garden and took in boarders, her father turned to a life of full-time drinking and gambling.

Although her mother criticized her for enabling the "old souse," Kasey could never forget the good times spent with her dad, usually in the hours between lunch and dinner when the bitters he took for the hangover finally kicked in, the color returned to his face, and he could almost tolerate the daylight. At those times, father and daughter had gravitated to the river, gathering driftwood, tubing the rapids, or sitting on the deck of the restaurant fishing for trout—a menu item—while Kasey read, softly so her mother wouldn't hear, the following day's entries from the racing form to her father.

Remembering those days made Kasey smile. To a young, impressionable girl, her father was the coolest person she knew.

Kasey parked in front of the olive-green complex, left the car, and made her way down to the tiny basement apartment where her father had lived for a dozen years. She knocked, waited, knocked again.

"He ain't home."

Kasey stepped back and looked up. Above her on the second-story balcony stood an elderly woman with iodine-red hair caught in a frizzy knot on top her head. Ashes from a smoldering cigarette drifted down on Kasey.

"Do you know when he'll be back?"

"Not for a while. Says he's got something going in the ninth at Belmont. You a friend of his?"

"I'm his daughter."

The woman pushed the cigarette out of her mouth with her

tongue. She grinned wide. "No shit? I been wanting to meet you. You're Kasey, right? I'm Sasha."

"Hi."

The grin melted away. "He never talked about me? Sasha? Sasha Micorn?"

Her expression, disconcerted, told Kasey that whoever she was she thought she was important to Dotus Atwood. "Well, he might've mentioned you . . ."

"Aw, don't bullshit me, honey. He didn't say diddly-poop about me. Hell, that's okay, though. We both know most men got priorities, an' women ain't one of 'em." She began to cough, a thick, phlegmy smoker's cough.

Kasey glanced at her watch: 5:42. The race was an hour away. It would take another ten minutes for him to walk home—her father had been on foot for over ten years, his driver's license pulled after his third DUI citation.

"You wanna wait inside? I got a key." Looking smug, she pulled one from the pocket of her shorts.

"No, that's all right. Maybe I'll look him up." Kasey left Sasha coughing and fumbling for another smoke. She returned to her car and drove to the race book.

"And they're off!"

Kasey stood in the open doorway of the Winner's Circle and scanned the vast room with its poster collage of champion racehorses on one side and famous sports players on the other. At her back, the air was hot and arid. In front, it was cool, refrigerated, smelling of popcorn, tobacco smoke, and stale beer. The green naugahyde seats on the race-book side were nearly all occupied with hunched backs and lowered heads. Tables, joined together in rows like schoolroom desks, each with a green plastic lamp, were cluttered with overflowing ashtrays, drinks, newspaper, and discarded betting tickets.

When her eyes had adjusted to the dimness, she stepped

inside and let the door shut behind her. She looked for the distinctive silver hair that was a bit longish for a man his age. She spotted him seated in the middle of the room. He sat hunched over a racing form, a drink in one hand and a magnifying glass in the other.

She crossed the room, came up behind him as he turned to chat with the two men on his left.

One man wadded a ticket into a ball and threw it toward a board displaying the track and racing lineup. ". . . didya see that? Didya see her die in the stretch. She got all rubber-legged and then just friggin' died. *Chriiiist!*"

"Hey, John, the ol' girl ran her heart out," Dot said.

"Heart, fart. She folded. Well, that's it for me. I couldn't catch a cold today." The man stood and tossed his racing form in the wastebasket. It tipped over at Kasey's feet. He looked contrite as he picked it up again. "Lemme give you a solid tip, little lady. Best tip of the day. Don't bet the ponies. Stick to slots or bingo. Mechanical gambling. It won't break your heart like these damn fillies and mares. Just like a woman— sucks ya in, takes ya for what you got, then smacks ya down, laughing all the way."

"I'll remember that," she said.

Kasey's father leaped up from his chair. "Hey, sweetheart, how you doing?"

She nodded. Smiled.

"Hey, guys, this is my daughter. Kasey, say hello to a couple bums I hafta put up with every day. Lou and Dinty, my little girl Kasey."

Lou grinned. "Your daughter, huh, Dot? Guess I don't have to tell her to lay off the ponies. You're testimonial enough."

The other man, a tiny fellow in a plaid cap, stood, took her hand, and held it. "Your father told us he had a pretty daughter. Of course no one believed him. Of late, he has the eyesight of a slug, and his perception and judgment are no better. But in your case, he was grossly deficient in his praise."

Kasey thanked him.

"That's enough, you two. Go back to what you were doing. I'll have a word alone with my girl," Dotus Atwood said, wadding up at least a dozen paper bets and tossing them into the basket. He steered Kasey to the small bar in the corner. Under his breath he said, "One's as smooth as the other is crude."

After clearing a table of empty beer bottles, ashtrays, and food remnants, Dotus asked her what she was drinking. She offered to buy but he refused.

"Your money's no good here. It's on the house."

He detoured to a betting window and spoke to the writer. When the man shook his head, Dotus pointed to Kasey sitting in the bar. The writer sighed, again shaking his head, but handed over a couple of drink tokes. Minutes later, Dotus was back with two beers.

"This isn't tonic, Dad."

"Carbonated water's a waste of a good drink toke, not to mention the barkeep's time. I'll finish what you don't drink." He sat and drank down half of the first beer.

Kasey knew it was pointless to argue with him. Her father was a drunk, had been a drunk for as long as she'd known him, and he wasn't likely to change in the near future. It was early enough in the day to catch him relatively sober— well, not exactly sober, he was never that. *Lucid.* There was a certain window in the day where he was at his best. Too early found him hung over, slow-thinking, whiny. Too late and he became incomprehensible, on his way to being catatonic. One thing he never was and that was mean. If he had been a mean drunk, she might have given up on him long ago.

He wore clean cotton chinos and a polo shirt. His wardrobe was supplied by Kasey—gifts at Christmas, his birthday, and Father's Day. He had shaved that morning, and she caught a whiff of Mennen aftershave.

She touched the silver strands that curled over his collar. Kasey had begun trimming his hair years ago. She suspected he'd let it grow halfway down his back if she didn't cut it. Money for haircuts was not in his budget. She gathered the hair at the back of his neck. "How 'bout a trim, Dad? Another inch and you could wear it in a ponytail."

"Yeah?" He said, sitting up straight. He grinned. "You think it'd make me look cool, like those guys in Hollywood?"

"Which guys? The pimps? Drug lords? Which?"

"Not cool?"

"Depends on what image you're after."

He slumped back down into his seat. "I gave up trying to impress folks a long ways back."

"I've got some time this afternoon," she said. "How about it?"

"Ah, honey, appreciate the offer, but I can't leave. There's this old race-book crony who owes me money. He hit it big last night. Said he'd be in today to square up. Gotta get it, y'know, when they got it. It comes and goes so quick. Maybe tomorrow, yeah?"

"Yeah. Sure."

"How's your mother?"

He always asked about Marianne. Kasey knew he still loved her. She suspected her mother loved him still; but after years of pain and disappointment, the bitterness went far too deep. Marianne had made a decision, and she would never reconsider. Dotus Atwood was like a poison to her.

"Mom's good. She's putting up peaches and honey. Ready for more honey?"

"God, no. My cupboards are full of the crap. Only thing honey is good on is cornbread. You can only eat so much cornbread." He drank his beer. "What'cha doing now? You on a job?"

She told him about spotting at the club. She made it sound routine, boring almost.

"Isn't that the hotel that old lady was killed in?"

She had found his lucid window for the day. He was sharp, up on events, giving her a rather fatherly, concerned look.

"How'd you know about that?"

"Lou freelances for the Trib. He mentioned it not more than half-an-hour ago. You in on that?"

"Well, not exactly. I'm not a private detective or a cop. But I'm keeping my eyes open."

He seemed thoughtful for a moment. "You be careful. Okay?"

She nodded. "Dad, I tried calling you a couple times earlier in the week."

"I'm not easy to catch."

"I know. That's why I gave you the answering machine. What happened to it?"

"I'm not one for those modern contraptions, Kasey. I don't know enough people to even make it worthwhile to use the thing."

"Where is it?"

He shushed her, pointing at the TV screen anchored above them. "My race. Watch the number-six horse. This one'll pay over thirty bucks to win. Got it tied to the nine horse in the seventh."

She watched his face as the horses raced around the track. His eyes danced. His muscles seemed wired, twitching like slight electrical charges under his skin. Out of his seat, he pounded the table, chanted: "C'mon, Jamie Boy, c'mon, c'mon, c'mon." The horses were only halfway down the final stretch when he let his arms drop to his sides. With dejection written all over his face, he sank into the chair. "Can't win 'em all."

"The answering machine. Where is it, Dad?"

He avoided her eyes. "I got the ticket on it. I can redeem it anytime."

"You hocked it?"

"It seemed like such a damn waste hooked up to a phone that didn't ring. If you want it back, I'll get it out on the first when my check comes."

She pushed the beer away. She reached into her purse, pulled out two twenties and pressed them into his shirt pocket.

"What's that for?" he asked. "The answering machine?"

"Forget the answering machine." She stood, kissed his cheek. "In case your pal doesn't pay you back. Buy a few groceries, will you?"

Fourteen

" 'Romance builds in the workplace—' "

"Ma, enough with the romance, okay?" Kasey said, sipping coffee. "I don't have time for romance. I don't know where I'd squeeze it in."

"That's not what it says here. Besides, there's always room for romance. It's like JELL-O."

"Interesting analogy."

Marianne Atwood folded the newspaper and looked at her daughter with genuine concern. "Kasey, you work too hard and you're much too young to be . . . well, uninvolved. What's wrong with killing two birds with one stone? Didn't you say you were working with a young, single man on this job?"

"He's ten years younger than me, Ma. A baby, for cryin'-outloud."

"Times have changed, Kase."

"I consider a twenty-three-year-old male still a boy." She grinned. "Maybe in ten, twenty years I'll think differently."

Kasey opened the refrigerator door. One of George's photos fell to the floor. She picked it up. It was a color print of the Reno balloon races. "How long is George planning to leave these pictures lying around?"

"Until he decides, with our help, which ones he wants for the book. The more we help, the faster it'll go."

By now many of them had green tabs stuck along the borders. Kasey studied half a dozen. She tagged two more. One of the old Reno arch and the other a current photo of an A&W

Drive-in, its parking lot filled with classic cars of the fifties in town for the Hot August Nights festivities.

Kasey went to the sink, rinsed out her mug, and set it in the drainer. She looked out the window and saw Snickers lying in the shade of an apple tree. "That dog must be sick. It's only eight o'clock and he's lying down."

Her mother snorted good-naturedly. "He's resting up."

The moans, soft, muffled, told him they were there again this morning.

In the corner of the basement, from his hiding place behind the cartons, the Monk watched the two lovers.

They stood in the same place as before with the supply duct at the woman's back, their hands buried inside clothing, kissing wantonly, urgently—illicit lovers fearing discovery at any moment, rushing to beat an intrusive clock.

He watched them, feeling the heat rise in his own body as the woman fumbled to open the man's fly and the man lifted her skirt and none-too-gently lowered her panties. The two came together abruptly amid moans and heavy breathing. He watched them copulate, the moans soon turning to grunts and soft cries, their bodies thumping against the padded tin shaft. Within minutes it was over. Like rabbits, he thought.

As he watched them quickly straighten their clothes, he grinned. The *puta,* whore—that's what he thought of any woman who lifted her skirt so readily the way this one had—she would have one itchy ass later from the pink fiberglass insulation.

The Monk waited to see who would leave first. He hoped it would be the man. He liked the looks of this woman. She was busty with a small waist and glowing skin . . . like his stepmother. Would she taste like her? Smell like her? Would her skin feel as hot or have the same creamy smoothness?

The man in white lit a cigarette, settled against the supply duct, smiled a self-satisfied smile, turning away just enough to confirm his dismissal of her.

The woman stood there uncertainly for several moments, then without a parting word, she whirled around and strode off.

"Inez, later, at quitting time, hey?" he called after her.

The Monk waited until he heard the metal door to the main floor close, then he left his hiding place and silently headed for the service elevator. He had wasted enough time. He had business on the sixth floor.

Jay King sorted through the morning mail. His secretary had already gone through it, tending to whatever did not require his individual attention. One unopened envelope with the red embossed King's Club logo, addressed to Mr. Jay Garner King, was marked *Personal*.

Jay felt an involuntary tightness in his gut. The other anonymous letters had arrived at his office on hotel stationery.

He held the envelope to the light, then ran his fingers over it, feeling for a bulge, a wire, anything that might indicate the thing could be lethal. A poison-pen letter was one thing, but a letter bomb was quite another.

He felt nothing. With a letter opener, he carefully slit the top and pulled out a folded *Gazette* newspaper photograph. Jay unfolded it. This one, from the society section, showed two women, one elderly, the other young and pretty and quite familiar—*Dianne*—presenting an oversized check to a representative of the Nevada Theater Arts Coalition. Dianne's head was circled in red ink. Below the photo the message read: *Nice. Not my type, but I'm willing to make an exception in this case.*

With a clenched fist, Jay pounded the desk top and cursed. He snatched up the phone. "Gail, get Kasey Atwood on the beeper. Ask her to come up when she's free."

* * *

The Monk stood on the landing of the sixth-floor emergency stairway and peered through the small, wire-mesh window. Not more than four feet away he saw a housekeeping cart parked in front of 634, the last room on the floor, the room to which Mr. Nicker, the vending machine man from Auburn was registered.

Last night, the Monk had spotted the drunken little prick flashing a fistful of hundred-dollar chips and running off at the mouth. Apparently he'd had another lucky streak at the dice table. At midnight, just as the Monk's shift ended, Nicker had gone up to his room, again taking his winnings with him. The Monk had changed from uniform to street clothes, punched out for the night, then, allowing plenty of time for Nicker to pass out, he had gone up to the sixth floor and with a keycard for Room 634 tried to gain access. He had been thwarted by the deadbolt.

No problem with the deadbolt now. Someone had to be in the room to engage it, and at that very moment Nicker was downstairs in the coffee shop ordering breakfast. The only hitch was the maid, whom the Monk hadn't counted on.

He poked the nozzle of nasal spray into each nostril and shot the antihistamine home. He sniffed, clearing his stuffy head, and settled back to wait.

A short time later he saw the maid backing out of Room 634. He watched her close the door, test the lock, then turn to her cart and dump the soiled towels. He quickly pulled back, pressing his body flat against the wall. He had only caught a glimpse of the maid, yet he recognized her as the one he'd watched earlier in the basement with the spic dishwasher. Inez. Pretty, dark-haired Inez. So this was her floor. He would remember that, maybe pay her a visit one day soon. Only they'd use a nice big bed, not an insulated duct. He wondered if her ass had started to itch yet?

Moments later he chanced a peek. The door to the utility closet was open, the maid nowhere in sight.

Impatient to get in and out before Nicker returned, which

could be any moment, the Monk pulled on thin leather gloves, left the stairway, unlocked the door to Room 634, entered, and closed the door behind him. He quickly went to work, deftly patting down the clothes hanging in the closet area. He knelt, lifted a pair of cowboy boots and shook them. Something shifted inside. He grinned. *Too easy.* A favorite place to conceal valuables. He tipped the boot, caught the bulky sock. He rolled it down to expose casino chips and a wad of hundreds. He was about to stuff the money into his pocket when the door behind him suddenly opened. The maid strode in, towels draped over her arm.

She looked at him, surprised. "The, uh, extra towels you . . ." Her gaze dropped to the money-filled sock in his gloved hand. Awareness, along with fear, sprang into in her large brown eyes.

She moved backwards, her hand reaching behind her. She grabbed the doorknob and whirled around, pulling the door open.

"Inez!"

Her name made her hesitate for a split-second. It was enough time for him to throw himself at her. He grabbed her around the waist, clamped a hand over her mouth, and slammed the door shut.

With his body he pressed her into the corner behind the door. She struggled, trying to scream through the hand that covered her nose and mouth.

"Be nice, Inez," he whispered in her ear. "Be nice to me like you were nice to that little potscrubber downstairs in the basement this morning." He saw her blush, felt the heat of it through her thin uniform. "Thought you were all alone, didn't you? Thought that was your secret place." He chuckled. "Yours and every other horn dog in this shitty place."

He pressed against her. His other hand glided over her buttocks. "That was fiberglass you were rubbing against down there. Does it itch, huh, Inez?"

The Monk heard a faint sound on the other side of the door.

The door handle moved. The Monk pushed against the door, twisted the deadbolt. He tightened his grip on the maid and warned her with his eyes and the pressure of his body to stay quiet. She moaned softly.

The handle jiggled.

A voice on the other side muttered, cursed. The handle jiggled again.

For what seemed an eternity, the Monk held tight to the maid, staring hard into her eyes until she finally closed them. Beads of sweat broke out across her nose and forehead. She trembled.

The handle had ceased its jiggling.

"I'm going to open the door," the Monk whispered to her. "You do anything to tick me off and I'll gouge out your eyes and feed them to you, do you understand?" He brought his thumb up to her eye and pressed. *"Understand?"*

She nodded.

"Okay. Good. Now look out there and see if he's gone." Holding her, he turned the deadbolt, eased the door open, and pushed her forward.

She nodded.

The Monk looked. Except for the housekeeping cart, the hallway was empty.

"Do exactly what I say. Don't make me hurt you." He pocketed the sock of money, tossed the towels on the bathroom counter, pulled her out of the room, then made her push the cart into the utility closet.

Moments later they were in the stairwell going down the steps.

Fifteen

Kasey and Brad King had to hurry to keep up with the hotel guest. This was her second trip down this corridor to Room 634. Yesterday afternoon, after the staff meeting, she had carried out the casino manager's instructions to contact Mr. Nicker with an offer of dinner and another night's lodging, compliments of the hotel. Yanick, concerned that the casino's money might leave the premises and not find its way back into the pit where it belonged, now had more to sweat about. In addition to the five grand, their comped guest had scored another thirty-two hundred the night before.

"I'm telling you," the man was saying, "I couldn't get the door open."

Brad, acting as assistant hotel manager until Epson reported in at ten, said, "Are you sure you had the right floor, Mr. Nicker. Except for the color scheme, the floors look pretty much alike."

"I had the right floor. I had the right room. What I didn't have was the right key."

"You say you used that key last night when you turned in?"

"Yeah, sure. So that means someone changed the code on me."

They reached 634.

"That's not possible, Mr. Nicker—"

"Just watch." Nicker inserted his keycard into the slot, waited for the green light, then pulled it out and turned the knob. The door opened.

"Well, what the hell?" He turned to Brad. "I tell you it wouldn't work before."

Brad and Kasey exchanged glances. Wrong floor? Wrong room? Or he had turned right instead of left when stepping off the elevator? All common mistakes.

"Hey, hold it," Nicker said when Brad and Kasey turned to go. He stepped into the closet area, dropped to his knees, lifted a pair of cowboy boots and shook them. "Sonofabitch! I've been robbed. Goddamn sonofabitch, it's gone, all of it. Eight thousand bucks. Gone!"

Both Kasey and Brad knew about Nicker's luck at gambling the past two nights. They also knew he had refused to put his winnings in a hotel safety deposit box. Legally, the hotel was not responsible for lost or stolen goods which were not properly secured.

"I'm calling the cops," Nicker said, his face turning crimson. "I've been robbed, and you people are gonna make it good. It was one of your hotel maids. The cart was right there . . ." He pointed at the utility closet ". . . . She must've been in my room when I tried to go in. She deadbolted the damn door, then swiped my money. What kinda people have you got working here? Psycho security guards, thieving maids—"

"Mr. Nicker," Brad said, "calm down. We can straighten this out. All of our employees are bonded. They're issued police cards, which means they're fingerprinted, photographed, and are thoroughly checked out through the FBI."

"Ah, great. That's a big comfort. She's probably on a plane to Guatemala right now with my ten grand—"

"You said eight a minute ago," Kasey said.

"It was ten. I said ten. What difference does it make? With that kind of money she and her whole family can live it up pretty good across the border."

"I doubt—"

"Find her then," Nicker said. "And if you do, make her take a goddamn polygraph."

"That's exactly what I intend to do," Brad said, relieved to have a direction. "May I use your phone?"

"Make it quick. I'm calling the cops."

Kasey wandered down the hall to the utility closet. She found a housekeeping cart inside. Brad joined her as she was looking it over.

"He's on the phone to the police," Brad said of Nicker. "He's gonna make a big stink over this."

"There's nothing we can do about that."

"What do you think?" he said. "The maid?"

Kasey shrugged. "If Nicker's eight grand is gone—and I'm sure it's eight, not ten—it's more than possible. There's used linen in this cart, and some of these towels are still wet. I'd say this is the cart Mr. Nicker saw in the hall awhile ago. It's too early for the housekeeper to take a midmorning break and it's certain she hasn't finished rounds on this floor, so what is this cart doing here? Give LeBarre and Epson a call. As chief of security and hotel manager, they both need to be in on this."

"What about my uncle?"

"Him, too." She started out the door. "I'm going to find out who was assigned to that cart."

From her office Kasey called the housekeeping department and had them pull the month's work schedule, which confirmed that Paula Volger, the maid who the day before had reported a possible intruder in 603, was assigned duty on the same floor all week. Two other maids worked in different wings of the floor, Inez Ramos and Betty Olcutt.

Several minutes later, Kasey got a second message that Jay King wanted to see her. Believing he had heard about the theft in 634, she gathered as much information as she could regarding the three employees in question before going up to the executive office. She knew nothing about Miss Olcutt or Miss Ramos except that both were considered reliable, hardworking, and had been with the hotel several years and that neither had prior citations. Miss Volger, on the other hand, had come to her attention twice in as many days.

When she passed Brad's office, she heard her name called. She went back, stood in the doorway.

Brad, jacket and tie removed, sleeves rolled up, was on the *Stairmaster,* stepping vigorously. "Where you going?" he asked.

"To your uncle's office. He wants to see me. Are you coming?"

"He didn't ask to see me."

"Hmmm," she said. "You have time to workout?"

"It's my way of coping with a crisis. I've done all I can do for now."

"Well, I'll check with you later." Kasey turned to go.

"Wait. Come in a minute." When she was inside, he asked, "What are you doing after you finish here today?"

He was looking at her in a way that made her uneasy. "Why?"

"Well, maybe we can do something together."

She looked away. Aside from one or two long glances or a lingering hand on her lower back when they entered and exited the elevator, Brad had pretty much behaved himself since they'd started working together. "That's not a good idea, Brad."

"Why not? And don't say it's because I'm too young."

"You're too young. For me, anyway."

"That's bullshit and you know it."

"Brad, we're co-workers. I don't fraternize with co-workers."

"What about when your job here is finished?"

"Nothing will have changed; you'll still be too young for me."

"Okay. I can see this is going to take a little time. I'm all for a challenge. I can be very persuasive, Kasey."

When Kasey entered Jay's office, he was on the phone. He motioned her in.

She crossed to the window and stood looking out.

"Has she turned up?" Jay said into the receiver. "Damn. Look, does anyone know her? Does she have friends working here? Okay, okay, put LeBarre on this. Have him find out anything he can. Send someone to her house. How far could she have gone in just an hour or so?"

Kasey could feel Jay's eyes on her as he talked on the phone. She continued to stare out the window, pretending not to notice.

Several moments later, he ended the call. He hung up, stood.

She looked over at him. They both began to talk at once.

Jay smiled, nodded for her to go first.

"Which maid?" Kasey asked.

"Ramos. Inez Ramos. Excellent work record. Nothing on her sheet. She turns all overlooked items into the lost and found, even booze and loose change."

"Maybe she was having financial problems? Eight thousand dollars isn't loose change. It's a lot of money."

"I guess."

"The police have been called in?" she asked.

He loosened his necktie and came around the desk. "Yes. I know, I should just leave it in their capable hands. But damnit, Kasey, what happens in this hotel is my responsibility."

"I know that."

Jay took Kasey's hand and pulled gently. "C'mere, I want to show you something." His hand was cool, his grip firm. He guided her to a paneled wall opposite his desk where he pressed a spot midway between ceiling and floor. A door, camouflaged within the dark woodgrain, opened inward. With a hand at the small of her back, he led her into a second office. The door closed with a whisper behind them.

There were no windows in this room. The overhead lighting was turned low, controlled by a wall dimmer. Along one wall stood a bank of monitors, five in all, screens blank. Laid out on a large-mahogany conference table in the middle of the room was a detailed architect's model of the forthcoming hotel-casino expansion with its upscale parking garage, twin towers, and the completely remodeled exterior of the existing structure—wrought-iron railings, shingled roof, and lofty cupolas—in keeping with the town's Victorian theme.

He pointed. "The future King's Club."

She moved slowly around the table, taking it in.

"Right there, next to the amphitheater, I want an outdoor skating rink," Jay said. "Roller skating in summer and ice skating in winter. Can you see it, Kasey? It's the holiday season; carolers fill the amphitheater; the town Christmas tree is brightly lit; people are ice skating, and right there, an impressive backdrop towering above the scene . . . King's Club."

Kasey rounded the corner. "It will be the biggest thing in this town," she said.

"And the best . . . I hope."

"The best, without a doubt." Their eyes met and held for a brief moment. Kasey felt a slight rush. She looked away, reached out and touched one of the towers. "I thought only one tower?"

"For now, yes. I'm being optimistic." His expression took on a look of rapture. "It was a dream of my father's. And now mine. He opened the club in the early sixties with very little gaming experience. Carny roots, penny pitching, pinball, that was what he knew. He and a handful of men like him, carny and bingo men, pioneers in the business. The road stories they'd tell when they got together! Pappy Smith knew how to run a show, and a casino. Dad learned a lot about the business and how to treat people from the Smiths. To them, Harold's Club meant everything, and people were important. Employees as well as customers."

"What about family? Where does family come in?"

Jay looked up at Kasey. In his blue eyes she saw a measure of guilt and contrition.

"Yes, of course, family. When my father started the business, we were all involved. My father, mother, brother, and me. Business, family—it was all the same. We all worked it, took pride in it. That family's gone now. There's just Dianne and Brad. Brad is definitely part of the business, and his interest will grow as time goes by. Dianne, by her own choosing, is not. I regret that, Kasey; I really do."

He leaned over, righted a miniature tree on the model. His fingers were long, well formed—the hands of an artist or surgeon. "When I married Dianne, I was young and in love and I thought my father would live forever, with me planted firmly in his shadow. Well, he didn't live forever. I've had to step out of the shadows into the harsh light of responsibility. Now that it's been forced upon me, I realize I want the same things for King's Club that he wanted. And it's up to me to make it happen. If that means not spending as much time with those I love until I can pull it off, then so be it. Securing financing for this project, working with bankers, contractors, licensing bureaus, and God-only-knows-who-else has taken up every moment of my spare time. I'm afraid Dianne will just have to be patient for a while longer."

Kasey looked away. Knowing Dianne as well as she did, she realized that was a tall order, one she wasn't sure Dianne could handle. *But it's none of my business,* Kasey told herself.

"Speaking of Dianne . . ." Jay said as he pulled an envelope from his breast pocket. "This came in the morning mail."

Kasey pulled out the grainy photograph. It took her only a moment to digest the contents.

She checked the postmark. Reno. With the hotel logo it could have been mailed right here, deposited in the mail drop at the front desk.

"Has she seen this?"

"No, and she won't."

"I'm not sure I agree with that, Jay. I know you're trying to protect her, but unless she knows she could be in danger, she'll go tripping along without a care or a clue."

"She will anyway, Kasey."

"Maybe . . . but all the same."

"Okay, I'll tell her in a couple days. In the meantime, I'll have one of the security guys keep an eye on her."

"Why wait?"

"I'm going to find out who's doing this." He flicked the envelope.

"How? Have you changed your mind about bringing in the police?" she asked.

"Uh-uh. You, Kasey, are going to find him . . . with my help, of course."

Kasey laughed softly. "You give me too much credit, boss. I catch bartenders with their hands in the till. I catch dealers and their partners rigging games. This is big. Too big for me or you, Jay."

"Right now, he's just some nut making half-baked threats. If we keep on top of it, maybe we can catch it before it goes any further." With a hand on her upper arm, he led her to the door and pushed it open. "Together we can do it," he said.

"Do what, darling?" Dianne said from the built-in bar. She poured scotch over ice, turned to them.

Kasey started guiltily. She quickly composed herself. She had nothing to feel guilty about.

Jay went to her, kissed her lightly on the temple, and said, "Catch a thief."

"Like that old TV show," Dianne said.

"I wouldn't know; you know I'm not into TV." He sat on the edge of his desk. "Dianne, if you've come to have lunch, I'm afraid I can't take the time today. We've had some trouble this morning and I'll be tied up all day."

"Then I'll just take Kasey. Start without her; she can catch up later."

Kasey turned to Jay.

"Go ahead," he said resignedly. "I'll put Brad on it. He's been complaining about not having enough responsibility. He wants to get more involved in the inner workings. He knows the situation. He'll fill you in when you're through with lunch."

Once in the lobby, Dianne refused to even consider eating

at the hotel. "I hate hotel food. Come on, the Jag's parked right outside."

"Where to?"

"Someplace utterly snobbish."

Sixteen

In the Clubhouse—so named because someone had scrawled the word on the back of the door—a tiny dark room just off the now obsolete catwalk, a room the Monk had discovered the first day on the job, he took a moment or two to compose himself. The adrenaline still raced through his veins. The sense of potency, of domination, of total power throbbed throughout his entire being. With his arms outstretched, a palm braced flat against the wall on each side of him, chest heaving, he closed his eyes and savored it.

Only when the image began to break up and the thundering vibration in his body had dulled to a mere quivering of muscle and flesh, did he open his eyes and take stock of his quiet surroundings.

Grinning, he tucked his arms in tight to his body, took a boxer's stance, and made mock jabs in the air with gloved fists. After a series of grunts and deep breathing, sparring with the hot air in the close space, he stripped off the leather gloves and flexed his fingers. He felt a slight soreness, a soreness he had been oblivious to at the time he used them to subdue the pretty little mex maid. The tenderness gave him a renewed sense of gratification.

With a penlight he examined his shirt and pants. Blood spattered the shirt, but not the pants. He touched the drying flecks and smiled. A job wasn't worth doing if you couldn't see the results, if you didn't get a little dirty. With that old lady in 814, there had been no blood, no visible evidence of his handiwork. The only gratification had come from hearing the sharp snap of bone when he had forced her ring from her finger. He had hoped to make that death look natural, and he'd almost pulled it off. Almost. Taking the ring had probably been a mistake. But, shit, he wasn't worried. There was nothing to link him to the old woman. And when he finished here, there would be nothing to link him to the maid.

He stripped the blue shirt from his sweat-drenched torso. Using the shirt he bent down and rubbed hard at the reddish black flecks on the tops of his shoes. He rolled the shirt into a ball, reached up and shoved it and the gloves deep into the corner between the ceiling and the overhead tin duct. Before leaving the room, he slipped on a dark-blue nylon windbreaker and zipped it all the way up.

Five minutes later, downstairs in the employee locker area, the Monk paused at a metal locker. After looking around to make certain he was not being observed, he forced two items through the slotted vents. The third item, the maid's crucifix, he would plant later that evening when he was on duty. It was too risky now.

Paula Volger stood at the access door on the second floor, the same door she had seen the security guard, the one who had tried to attack her in the parking garage, come through only minutes ago. He had glanced around suspiciously, as she was doing now, before he'd casually sauntered to the door of the service stairwell and disappeared.

She wondered what he was up to now. Was he stealing from the club and hiding his contraband somewhere beyond this door? Or had he found a dark, secret place to shoot up or maybe meet a lover? She thought of Inez, wondered if this man could be the one her friend was seeing on the sly, then just as quickly rejected the notion.

There was only one way to find out. She lifted her keychain and began to try in the lock. The fourth one, a multipurpose key that opened the linen and storage rooms, worked. Paula quickly opened the door and went through. Five steps down, she entered a dim, narrow passageway with overhead pipes, beams, and metal ducts. The now seldom-used casino catwalk.

She followed the walk to the end, so intent on the view of the casino below through the two-way mirrors that she almost missed the narrow plywood door at the junction. She paused, put her ear to the door and listened. There was no door latch. She pushed. It opened inward. Paula searched for a light switch and found none. From her uniform pocket she took a book of hotel matches and lit one. She stepped inside.

Someone had been in the room a short time before. The strong odor of sweat hung in the air. Another match revealed a metal toolbox on the floor. Two matches later she uncovered the bloody clothes.

Frightened now, she quickly exited.

The Monk had one more stop before he was through. He retraced his steps to the second floor. He had decided to hide the third piece of evidence in the room where he had stashed the bloody clothes until he could plant it later that evening. No sense taking a chance getting caught with it on him.

He entered the convention floor and rounded the corner. Ahead, from the door that led to the catwalk, he saw a woman in a hotel housekeeper's uniform come through. She quickly made her way to a service elevator, hit the button, and paced impatiently until the doors opened. She had stepped inside and turned to press a button when their eyes met.

He recognized her—the drunk from the parking garage. And by the expression on her face he could tell that she recognized him as well.

He started to walk toward her. She pounded on the button panel with the edge of her palm. Even from a distance he could read the fear in her eyes. *What the hell was she up to?* he wondered.

He stepped up his pace, but the elevator doors closed before he could reach them.

Several minutes later in the tiny room off the catwalk, as the Monk was hiding the crucifix, he spotted the four burnt matches on the floor. He knelt, picked one up and examined it curiously. His hand balled into a tight fist. In his mind's eye he saw the frightened face of the maid in the elevator.

"You're dead, bitch."

Seventeen

The Windsor blue surface of Lake Tahoe was mirror smooth, rippled now and then by a speedboat or ski jet. Kasey and Dianne sat in the open patio of Hobie's on the north shore. Overhead in the towering pines, bluejays hopped from limb to limb, screeching. Yellow jackets buzzed, occasionally landing to sample the food. Water lapped softly at the pilings at the edge of the deck.

Kasey picked at several pine needles that had fallen into her bowl of clam chowder—soup, with ground pepper, accompanied by freshly baked bread and real butter, were a weakness of hers—and listened patiently to Dianne lament her boring, boring existence.

"What good is being married if your husband has no time for you?" Dianne said. "Eddie, at least, was always there."

"As I recall, that was one of the reasons you divorced him."

"I divorced him because I was in love with Jay. Jay was everything I wanted. Gorgeous, rich, incredible in bed. Only it didn't turn out the way I imagined. He's one of the most influential men in town; the social invitations arrive daily, but we don't go anywhere. He speaks Russian, German, and Spanish, but we've yet to leave the country."

"He has a hotel to run, Dianne."

"I knew you'd side with him, being a workaholic yourself. Where's it gotten you?"

That rankled Kasey. "Right where I want to be. Status isn't important to every—"

Dianne cut her off. "What's the good of being rich when you don't take advantage of it?"

"Those aren't Wal-Mart clothes you're wearing; this isn't Burger King, and that car out there—"

"Oh, Kasey—" Dianne shook her head sadly. "—somewhere over the years our desires and ambitions took entirely different roads."

No argument there, Kasey thought. Different roads was an understatement. Different worlds was more like it. On a daily basis, Kasey dealt with ordinary people—the working class. Although she was her own boss, she relied on others for her livelihood; and without cheats and undesirables, she'd have no business. She wondered how she had ever been all that close to Dianne.

Kasey shrugged and absently waved her hand at a hovering yellow jacket.

"Don't slap at them; it only pisses them off," Dianne said of the wasp. She took a bite of poached salmon and sipped her wine. "Jay showed you the hotel expansion plans. Do you have any idea how much all that is going to cost? We'll be in hock up to our eyeballs."

"It's for the future, Dianne. You should know that."

"The future?" She laughed sarcastically, brushing a strand of pale-blonde hair from her eyes. "What future? Gaming is opening up across the board. Nevada no longer controls it. Anything can happen. Gaming here could dry up. We could be living in a ghost town in a few years. Vegas, with its multimillion dollar theme palaces will probably be okay. Tahoe has the lake; Laughlin, the Colorado River, but what about us? What do we have? Instead of adopting a wait-and-see attitude, Jay is taking us deeper into debt. He's gambling with our future, Kasey, and this is one time the odds are not in favor of the house."

"Maybe he feels he has no choice."

"Oh, he has choices all right. He could sell the club. Get

out while the getting's good. Ansel Doyle made him an offer. A very generous offer, I might add. He won't sell."

"What would he do with himself if he didn't have the club?"

"We could travel for a while. We should enjoy life while we're young. He could find something else, another business, another hotel maybe."

"Dianne, get involved in this hotel. *Your* hotel. I guarantee it will make Jay very happy."

"Jay *is* happy. It's me who isn't." With her fork, Dianne shooed a yellow jacket away.

They finished their meal in silence.

When the plates were cleared away, Dianne excused herself to go to the ladies' room. With wry amusement, Kasey watched as the eyes of half the male diners followed her progress across the patio and into the restaurant. Dianne, wearing a lightweight miniskirt and blouse in pale aqua, seemed to exude a combination of style and sex.

Kasey focused on the lake. Like something from the pages of *Tom Sawyer* and *Huckleberry Finn,* the U.S. *Dixie* cruised majestically over the bright-blue water with banners waving, the faint sounds of a calliope drifting in the breeze. As Kasey stared absently at the paddle wheeler, her thoughts shifted to Ansel Doyle.

Twice in two days his name had come up. Doyle, a big-time gaming mogul with a vast interest in casinos throughout Nevada, Vegas in particular, had a reputation for getting what he wanted. He also had a reputation for purchasing family-owned operations, turning them into something cold and impersonal, often neglecting the business once it began to go downhill, which was usually the case with his northern Nevada properties. Generous offer or not, if Kasey knew anything at all about Jay King, Ansel Doyle would be the last person he would sell out to.

Dianne returned. "I ordered Irish coffee for both of us."

"Shouldn't we be getting back?"

"Relax. Look, it was my idea to hire you. Jay can do without his super sleuth for a couple of hours." She lit a cigarette, inhaled deeply. "By the way, have there been any more threatening letters?"

"Jay's the one you should ask."

"Jay is too closemouthed about his affairs. What little information I get I pick up from snatches of conversation at dinner meetings with the top brass and business associates. I would have never known about the offer to buy the club if Doyle hadn't brought it up at dinner awhile back."

"Maybe Jay doesn't think you're interested."

"Actually, I'm not, but I'm beginning to realize that showing an interest is the only way we can converse." Dianne's voice quieted, she looked down into her coffee, "We haven't been alone much lately . . . for conversation or anything else."

Kasey sipped her coffee. It tasted bitter.

Dianne looked directly into Kasey's eyes. "Do you know how long it's been since my husband has approached me with genuine desire in his eyes? Do you? Months. Oh, we fuck—he'll oblige me whenever I make the first move. But I'm talking *desire*. Pure, sexual desire. The kind that brought us together. Not to sound conceited, but I could have just about any man I want. Any of these men." She twirled her finger to indicate the surrounding tables. "I see desire in their eyes when they look at me. They want me." She leaned forward. "So what's with my handsome, virile husband?"

"Dianne . . . I . . ."

Dianne laughed softly. "I've embarrassed you. Oh boy, times *have* changed. We used to be able to talk about anything. Sex in particular. Remember?"

How could Kasey forget? Before Dianne and Jay were married, Dianne, not one to be shy or modest, had told Kasey and the other cocktail waitresses everything about her affair with Jay. In vivid detail she described their lovemaking until the women were fanning flushed faces with their drink trays and, little by little, falling in love with Jay King.

"I'm afraid I don't have much to share with you in that

department," Kasey said with a slight grin. "My social life is somewhat stalled."

"I know one or two men who could change that."

Kasey raised her hands, palms toward Dianne as though warding off a curse, "Please, no—"

"Okay. But you don't know what you're missing."

"Is this a personal recommendation?"

Dianne merely smiled.

"Dianne, you've cheated on Jay?"

"Cheated is such an ugly word. I like to think of it as marriage enhancement. I'm careful. I'm discreet. And I'm sure Jay is, too."

"You two have—what?—an open marriage?"

Dianne smiled again. "Let's just say we're both open-minded."

She was lying, Kasey told herself. Jay had more scruples than that. Uncomfortable with the subject, Kasey changed it.

At 5:00, Dianne dropped Kasey at the hotel. Minutes later, in the executive office, Jay's secretary told her to go right in.

Jay was reclining in his chair, feet crossed on his desk top, reading from a file. He wore rimless reading glasses, which Kasey thought gave him a studious yet provocative look. He didn't hear her enter.

"Sorry it took so long," she said.

He quickly dropped his feet to the floor and began to rise. "No, don't get up."

He settled back down, glanced at his watch. "You're back early, considering." He smiled, removed the glasses. "Lunch with Dianne is usually an all-day affair. Sit."

She sat in a ball-and-claw, pub-back chair of oxblood leather that faced the desk. "Anything?"

He shook his head. "No sign of our Miss Ramos anywhere in the hotel. CSI dusted the scene and naturally found no prints since housekeeping employees are required to wear gloves. Police are waiting for her at her house."

"Does she have a family?"

"Single. Lives with her sister's family."

"Where's Brad?"

"I sent him home. I knew you'd be back. There wasn't enough for the three of us to do. The police are handling the room burglary. If it was the maid who was going through the rooms all along, then at least we know it's over. Like most thieves, she got greedy and went for it when she came across a bankroll large enough to make a hit and run worthwhile."

"I hope you're right. About her being the one."

"But you don't think I am?"

"No. It's too pat. There's something going on here, Jay, and it's anything but pat. We can't overlook the threats. Has anything happened lately to warrant threats?"

He swiveled around, gazed out the window. Moments later, he turned back. "A couple months ago, Yanick spotted Dan Carne in the club. He had him tossed out."

"Dan Carne. A reputed mobster, convicted mostly for sports-fixing, but has a hand in just about everything from loan-sharking to slot-cheating."

"You know him?"

"I had the pleasure once." Several years ago, while on a job, Kasey had witnessed the arrest of a Black Book member who by merely entering the casino and playing the slots violated the state law. Nevada's infamous Black Book presently consisted of approximately two-dozen people lawfully excluded from casinos due to unsavory gaming backgrounds and or alleged mob connections. Dan Carne had been with him at the time. "I hear the Gaming Control Board is considering Carne for a spot in the state's Black Book."

"Can't be too soon for me. He raised hell when we gave him the boot. Said we couldn't keep him out." Jay rubbed his chin. "You may have hit on something, Kasey. It's certainly worth looking into."

"Dianne told me Ansel Doyle made an offer on the club. She said you turned it down."

"That's right."

"Could there be anything there?"

"Ansel has made offers on dozens of casinos over the years. I'm sure he's been turned down a time or two."

"Was it an earnest offer?"

"Yeah, it was. Which made no difference since I don't plan to sell the club at any price."

Kasey wondered if the recent incidents in the hotel might have something to do with the gaming mogul's interest in the property. Doyle had a reputation for less-than-ethical business tactics. Nothing illegal, nothing to jeopardize his gaming license. However, if he could slow down or interrupt business, or in some way tarnish the good name of the club, the loss of revenue to the King family could be devastating.

On the desk top Jay lifted a large ivory paperweight shaped like a stacked pair of dice, took the envelope beneath it, and handed it to Kasey.

Inside, a single sheet of hotel notepaper read: *Working for King's Club could be hazardous to your health*. She turned over the envelope. It was addressed to Howard Cummings, Jay's right-hand man.

Kasey looked up at Jay quizzically.

"Howard thinks whoever mailed this to him also tried to run him off the road last night at the look-out point on Windy Hill. He banged up his rear fender and blew a tire, yet managed to stop before he careened over the edge. He was pretty shook up afterward and damn mad. Figured it was a drunk or some kids driving recklessly . . . that is, until this afternoon when he received that." Jay pointed at the note. "Now, of course he's having second thoughts."

"Did he get a good look at the car?"

"Nope."

"Did you fill him in on what's going on?"

"No. I thought I'd run it by you first."

"Were there witnesses to last night's incident?"

"No. Which is why he didn't bother to report it to the police."

Cummings could have made up the story and even sent himself the warning. "Tell him he should be careful, but don't go into a lot of detail just yet. Just say you've been getting threats, too."

"My thoughts exactly." He inhaled deeply, rubbed the back of his neck. "Kasey, you might as well go on home. I have a few things to finish up here, then I think I'll head out. I haven't been home at a decent hour in weeks."

"Dianne will be glad to see you."

"Surprised is more like it." He looked down, shuffled some papers on his desk. "Is there someone waiting for you? A special guy?" He looked up. "I wouldn't want to be responsible for keeping you away from . . . well, whomever."

"There's no one."

She was almost to the door when he stopped her.

He wrote something on a pad, tore it off, and handed it to her. "It's the number for my private line here in the office. You should have it in case . . . well, you know, in case something should come up. You already have my home number and the car phone, yes?"

"Yes."

In the elevator Kasey hit the button for the lower level. She had an idea, wanted to check it out. Inez Ramos and Paula Volger worked the same floor. It was possible they were friends.

In the Esmeralda Lounge she found Paula sitting on the end stool, her back to the door. When Kasey took the stool next to her, Paula swiveled around quickly.

"Christ, Inez, where the hell have you b—Her words were cut off abruptly at the sight of Kasey. "Oh, I thought you was . . . well, was someone else."

"Inez Ramos? Is she meeting you here?"

Paula turned back to her beer. "Maybe."

"She's late, isn't she?"

Paula faced her again. "Look, I know what's been going around. I hear things. I just want you to know, you and anybody else who's interested, that Inez Ramos is just about the most upright person in this whole stinkin' place. If something's missing, Inez had nothin' to do with it."

"Where is she then?"

Paula slid off the stool, grabbed her purse.

Kasey held her arm. "Paula, talk to me. I want to help. I'm not the cops."

"Just what are you?"

"My name is Kasey Atwood. Right now I'm with the hotel. That's all I can say."

"Same thing. Look, Inez is my best friend. She—hey, I don't want to talk about her until I know exactly what's goin' on."

Kasey nodded. "Can I buy you a drink?"

Paula tapped a pile of complimentary drink tickets in front of her. "You want somethin', I'll buy." Paula gestured to the barkeep.

"I'll have what she's drinking," Kasey said to the bartender who, Kasey recalled, liked to give freebies to his friends.

He placed two Coors in front of them and a glass for Kasey, took two drink tokes, and moved away.

"A considerable amount of money is missing from one of the rooms Inez was assigned to. Her housekeeping cart was found in the supply room hours before her shift was over. She's nowhere in the hotel. If what you say about her is true, then it's possible she may be in danger. When was the last time you talked with her?"

"This morning."

"Did she say anything? Anything that might explain what's happened or where she is?"

Paula looked away; her fingers scratched on the bottle's label. "Well, she has been acting weird lately. I figured it was a guy. Inez is shy, trustin'. She's not too smart where men are concerned. We met in here last night. She was all dreamy and . . . well, distracted, like people get when they're falling hard for someone. She seemed okay in wardrobe this morning; but when I saw her on the floor a little later, she was bummed out about somethin'."

"You don't know who it is she's seeing?"

"I don't even know for sure if she is seeing anyone."

"Is she having financial problems?"

"Inez? Naw. She lives with her sister's family. They love having her there. She minds the kids for 'em. Five of them. Inez leads a real low-maintenance existence. She's pretty content with what she's got, not at all materialistic. No way. That's why she'd never risk her job by stealing. There's nothing she'd want that bad. 'Cept maybe a good, lovin' man."

"What if someone else put her up to it?"

"You mean . . ."

"She wouldn't be the first gullible woman to be influenced by a lover."

"Yeah, well—listen, I think we've talked enough about Inez."

"Can I ask you something else? This doesn't concern Inez."

"Guess I can't stop you from askin'."

"Paula, will you tell me what happened to you in the parking garage on Monday?"

"You ain't gonna let up, are you?"

"I don't like to see women abused."

"Me, neither." She paused, then said, "Hell, there's no denying I was plastered. Only it wasn't like that wormy bastard said. Look, there's something creepy about that guy. If anyone's got something to hide, it's that one. This afternoon I saw him coming—" Paula abruptly stopped talking. She stared straight ahead, her mouth open.

Kasey followed her gaze. At the opposite end of the room, a uniformed guard stood in the other doorway, backlit by the lights in the corridor. He seemed to be looking their way. It was too dim for Kasey to see the man's face clearly, but his size and shape were familiar.

"Is that him?" Kasey asked.

Paula slid off the stool.

"Paula? Paula, don't go."

Paula rushed from the bar. Kasey turned back, looking for the guard. He was gone.

Back in her office, Kasey found a message to call Peggy Randall. Peggy was Kasey's rock, and vice versa. Kasey, Peggy, and Dianne had worked together ten years ago. For Peggy, the beautiful daughter of an Irish mother and a black father, the job at the club had been short-lived under the Walker and Smart reign of sexual harassment. At the time, Peggy had little or no will to fight yet another form of inane prejudice; today, given the same situation, she would not have caved in so easily. Between Dianne and Peggy, Kasey had been the friend in the middle—a neutral point of a triangle. Over the years as Dianne and Kasey drifted apart, Peggy and Kasey had become best friends.

Peggy was engaged to Artie Brown. Artie, an intermittent boarder at the Atwood house, spent the majority of his time with Peggy at her condo in Reno. But because their relationship was anything but tranquil, Artie maintained a room in the boardinghouse. When Peggy threw him out, which was once or twice a month, he had a place to crash until they made up and she let him back.

Kasey could guess what Peggy wanted. Both Peggy and Artie held night classes at the Y. Artie taught Tae-Kwon-Do to children and Peggy taught self-defense for women, a class that Kasey helped with when needed.

She made the call.

"Kasey, I'm so glad you got back to me in time," Peggy said. "Sweetie, say you'll give me a hand tonight with the class."

"I'll give you hand. And a foot and the other foot and—"

150   *Carol Davis Luce*

"Thanks, you're a lifesaver. 7:30? We'll get a bite afterwards?"

"Sounds good."

They said goodbye. It was 6:30. Enough time for her to go home, change clothes, and return to town.

In the lobby, across from the reception area, Kasey saw Jay talking with a security guard. At the same time, at the side entrance, she saw a police car pull up, then another. Jay looked around, spotted her, gestured for her to join him; then he intercepted the two policemen entering the hotel. As she approached, she heard one of them say, "Basement. Homicide."

Eighteen

"Who found the body?" Det. Loweman asked the guard.

In a far corner of the basement, behind the yellow crime-scene tape, Frank Loweman stood with Jay and Kasey. The detective had arrived as the area was being secured.

"A maintenance man," the security guard said. "Says he saw one of the dishwashers hightailing it outta here like Satan himself was on his backside; and since it's an unauthorized area, he was curious, came back here to see what the guy was running away from. That's what he found." The guard nodded toward the dead woman in the tan housekeeping uniform lying spread-eagled on the concrete floor. Her head was twisted at an odd angle against a blood-splattered tin duct.

"Where is he?"

"The maintenance man or the dishwasher?"

"Whoever we got. Preferably both."

The guard called to a man in brown work clothes. The man hurried over.

"You found the body?" Loweman asked the maintenance man.

"Yes, sir. Name's Bill Hogan."

"And you saw a guy running from here, Mr. Hogan?"

"Yes, sir. His name is Ruiz. He works in the main kitchen. I believe your men have him upstairs in the holding room."

"Well, that's a break."

A C.S.I. man wearing two pairs of rubber gloves, a surgical

mask, goggles, and paper booties over his shoes was in the process of collecting blood samples, which he placed in separate bags labeled CAUTION: BIOHAZARD—May Be Contaminated. Another officer drew a chalk line around the body.

"Biohazard?" Jay asked Loweman.

"A precaution. All articles or evidence dealing with body fluids, especially blood, have to be flagged that way. HIV. Can't be too careful these days."

Kasey asked, "Detective, is that Inez Ramos?"

"We don't have a positive yet, but it's a good guess. The ID card found nearby says Ramos. Course, right now she doesn't look anything like the woman in the picture. The victim is a maid and Hispanic, and we got a missing Hispanic maid. We also got a Hispanic dishwasher observed leaving the scene. It don't come easier."

Kasey looked back at the body, then at the people bustling around it to collect evidence, so cold and impersonal. Whoever she was she deserved better than this. Kasey wished she could go to the body and tenderly arrange it, cover the bare legs, give the woman a measure of dignity. Her final moments had been cruel and harsh. And it seemed it was not over for her yet.

"How was she killed?" Kasey asked.

"Can't say for sure. The M.E. will have to make that determination. She died hard, I'll say that. Face was pretty well pounded, bruises on her throat. Neck looks broken. The position of the body and the fact she has no underpants indicate sexual assault."

Kasey thought of her visit in the bar with Paula Volger less than an hour ago. Paula and Inez had been best friends. Paula, tough, street-wise Paula, who only the day before had had the common sense to back away from a potentially dangerous situation in Room 603, would soon learn about the brutal death of her friend. Paula had said Inez Ramos was shy and gullible, looking for nothing more than a stable relationship with a decent man. Kasey looked away from the bloody corpse. *That would never happen now.*

It was cold in the basement. Kasey shivered, hugged herself, and rubbed at the rippled flesh on her arms. A moment later, she felt the weight of Jay's suit jacket as he draped it over her shoulders. It was warm from the heat of his body and smelled lightly of his aftershave. She thanked him with a smile.

"Jay, my friend," Loweman said ruefully, "you musta did something to piss off the hotel god, 'cause you're sure having some bad luck here. Two homicides in two weeks. I barely got started with the other investigation and now—Aw, shit, here comes the chief. Stick around." Loweman went to meet a tall, thin Oriental man.

Kasey and Jay stood side by side, silently gazing at the murder scene. A uniformed policeman with a camcorder carefully moved around the scene, narrating as he filmed. Kasey focused on both the uniform and the camera.

"Jay, I want a list of all security officers. Names and shifts. Get me a schematic of the building. I want to know the location of every camera, two-way mirror, egress, and anything else that involves surveillance. Oh, and there's this particular security guard—"

"Not here," he said, putting his hand on her lower back and urging her forward. "Upstairs. We'll go to the office and have something sent up. Are you hungry?"

Hungry? "Oh, God," she glanced at her watch. 7:19. It was a ten-minute drive across Sparks to the Reno Y. She would scarcely have time to make it there before the class started. "No—I can't. I'm sorry, I have to be somewhere."

She broke away, was halfway to the service elevator when she realized she still had Jay's suit jacket over her shoulders. She turned. Jay was standing where she'd left him, watching her. She went back, handed him the jacket, and thanked him.

He folded it over his arm. "Where are you parked?"

"In the garage."

"I'll walk you."

"No, that's okay. I've got to run. I'm late already." She was already hurrying away.

"Be careful. Hear?" he called after her.

Running as late as she was, she'd had no time to play her obligatory slot machine before leaving the club. It was times like this, rushing through town, squeaking through one yellow light after another, that Kasey wished she had a car phone. If there were one thing she hated, it was being late, making people wait on her. Kasey arrived at 7:31, in time to catch a pair of sweats Peggy tossed at her as they passed in the hallway.

"Meet you on the floor," Peggy said.

She changed from her skirt and blouse into the freshly laundered sweats. In bare feet she joined her friend and a group of about fifteen women of various ages who sat yoga-fashion on floor mats in the large room with basketball hoops and bleachers, the latter now folded against the walls.

After introducing Kasey to the class, Peggy continued to reiterate points from the previous class—the awareness session. Tonight was the second of two parts—the physical training and assertiveness session. Although Peggy, a fifth-degree black belt, was skilled in martial arts, she opted to instruct what she called the "crash course." How many women in today's hectic world had the time or the inclination to take an ongoing martial arts class? The main purpose of Peggy's class was to give a woman, regardless of age, stature, and physical condition, the knowledge and self-assertiveness to avoid becoming a victim. Her women's self-defense program was now the Y's most popular class.

Thirty minutes later, in a room filled with screams and grunts, Peggy and Kasey, taking turns on each other, demonstrated various self-defense tactics. They used knees, elbows, hands and feet or whatever weapons were at hand—keys, pepper spray, the heel or toe of the shoe. Screams served a number of purposes: to scare off the attacker, to alert passersby, and to get the fight or flight adrenaline rushing through the would-be victim's veins.

Well into the session Kasey was glad she had come. This was just what she needed. An outlet for the tension that had been building for the past couple of days. She found herself screaming a little louder, putting a little more thrust into her defense moves. She felt alive, exhilarated. It was over all too soon.

The room emptied quickly. Peggy and Kasey folded the mats and stacked them against the wall.

"Hungry?" Peggy asked.

"I could eat."

"Clementine's?"

"Not Clementine's. I have a job to do there at the end of the week. If I go there tonight, I'll wind up working. How 'bout Keppy's?"

"Perfect. Tonight's potato leek."

"It's not like you to be late. What happened?" Peggy asked Kasey after they were seated at a wicker table in the garden room of Keppy's, where plants and trees flourished everywhere in artificial humidity.

"A maid was murdered at the club today. Her body was found in the basement just before seven tonight." Kasey pushed a palm frond away.

"Murdered?" Peggy leaned forward. "Did they catch the killer?"

"Maybe. A hotel dishwasher was seen running away."

"So tell me."

Kasey and Peggy shared everything. What was said never went beyond the two of them. Despite Peggy's mixed heritage and a somewhat traumatic past, this petite woman with the soft brown eyes and caramel complexion was the most normal, most grounded, most compassionate friend Kasey had. Whenever Kasey needed a reality check, she called Peggy.

She told Peggy what had happened. They discussed it for several minutes, then the conversation turned to less gruesome news.

All through their identical meal of potato leek soup, spinach salad with hot bacon dressing, wine, and freshly baked sheepherder bread—even their tastes ran alike—Kasey's mind kept wandering. Peggy talked of Artie and their relationship, but Kasey listened with only half an ear, commenting when appropriate. Her mind was back at the club, on the latest chain of events. Two murdered women—one a guest and the other a maid—Paula Volger and the security guard, the threats, the burglaries, far too much to be merely coincidental. Someone was out to make Jay King suffer, to punish him for some infraction—someone who knew Jay well enough to know just how important the club was to him. She wished she had the schematic and surveillance information she'd asked for. Was he still at the club, she wondered, or had he gone home—to Dianne?

The table was cleared, coffee and dessert ordered. Kasey glanced at her watch: 10:13.

"Am I keeping you from something," Peggy asked sweetly.

"What? Oh, I'm sorry, Peg, no. I'm just a little distracted, I guess."

"A *little?* A cardboard cutout in your likeness would've been more sociable."

Kasey grinned sheepishly. "Sorry. Next time I'll be better company. Promise."

While Peggy moaned ecstatically through a caramel custard flan, Kasey excused herself to use the rest room. A bank of telephones outside the ladies' room caught her eye. She slowed. *No,* she told herself, *I will not call him.* It can wait until morning. He's home with his wife, where he belongs.

Her body seemed to move independently from her brain. She stopped, took a quarter from her purse, dropped it in the slot, and dialed his private line at the club. As the phone rang, her heart pounded. What would she say if he answered?

The phone rang on and on. She hung up slowly, relieved that he wasn't there to answer, wasn't there to hear her lame excuse for calling, wasn't there to indulge her.

As she approached the table where Peggy sat waiting for her, she coaxed her mouth into a pleasant smile.

Nineteen

At 8:00 A.M., her arms filled with magazines for Danny, Kasey opened the door of her bungalow to find Snickers sitting on the porch, front legs covered with fresh mud up to his chest, a young rosebush at his feet. He placed a paw on the bush as if it were a trophy kill and whined happily.

Kasey felt like a zombie. Everyone in the Atwood household had waited up to ask her about the recent murder at King's Club. All the local stations on both the early and late night news programs had covered it. When finally she had climbed into bed, sleep had refused to come. She'd lain awake thinking about the recent events at the club, attempting ineffectually to piece it all together. At 5:30, she finally left her bed to tackle some overdue paperwork.

Tangling with a muddy dog the size of a small bear in her new off-white linen outfit was the last thing she wanted to do this morning. She closed the door and strode to the phone.

Across the yard she heard the ringing. "Ma," she said when Marianne answered, "we gotta do something about that dog."

While Marianne lured Snickers to the side of the house with a bowl of honey-laced ice cream, the dog's favorite, Kasey managed to make it to the main house undetected.

On this already hot, and guaranteed to get hotter, Thursday morning, the Atwood kitchen bustled with activity. The noise level was acute. George sat at the table reading aloud the news-paper account of yesterday's murder while Danny folded an-other section of it into the likeness of a cat. Sherry stood at the sink transferring honey from a half-gallon canister to the little bear-shaped honey dispenser; the blender at her elbow whirred furiously with a peach-colored concoction. The TV at Danny's back was tuned to cartoons; the dishwasher chugged and hissed, and Artie pounded nails in the laundry area.

"Artie, hi, long time no see."

"Hey, Kasey, how you doing?"

"So-so."

"Nice duds. If you're lookin' to impress someone, you're gonna do it?"

She felt heat rise to her face. The day before yesterday, after leaving her father at the racebook, Kasey had gone to the mall. She'd bought a few pieces she could interchange, telling herself she had nothing to wear. Each day on the job she found herself taking a little more care with her appearance, aware of what she was doing, yet unable to stop.

"Is this a visit or are you staying awhile?" she asked.

"That depends on Peggy, I guess."

"Another fight?" Kasey poured coffee.

He grinned and went back to his hammering.

Sherry said over the noise, "He's helping your mom put up shelves for all these honey containers. He and Peggy are getting along great. Right, Artie? What's it been, a record three weeks now?"

Marianne entered, blocking the dog with a leg until she got the door closed. On the back of her blouse, a series of mud prints in the shape of giant paws stood out like a cartoon pattern.

"New magazines. Your favorite, *National Geographic*," Kasey said to Danny. "I'll put them away till you're ready for them."

"Have you driven a Ford lately?" Danny muttered.

Kasey pushed through the swinging door into the dining room. The room was dim and cool and blessedly quiet compared to the kitchen. She deposited the magazines in the knee-high stack in the corner between the hutch and the credenza.

Not ready to return to bedlam, she took a moment to sip coffee and browse through more of George's tacked-up photos. This batch seemed to concentrate on women: show girls in all their jeweled and feathered regalia, bathing beauties in swim wear, debutantes in evening dresses, pretty women of all sorts—the cheesecake segment, no doubt. Kasey flagged the show girls and three more.

As she was about to leave the room, her gaze fell on a framed photograph on the credenza. A photograph that had been there for years, yet had gone unnoticed for so long. She lifted her wedding picture and carefully studied it as though for the first time.

Her dark hair had been long, flowing over her shoulders, turned slightly under at the ends. She had worn more makeup then, which made her hazel eyes seem larger, brighter, more defined. Her face was fuller, too—thirteen years had melted away the baby fat. The bride and groom had had a traditional wedding among the roses in Idlewild Park: Kevin in a white tux and she in a full-length white dress, veil, bridal bouquet, complete with something borrowed, something blue.

When she finally allowed herself to look at Kevin, a sad tugging worked at her stomach. Kevin looked so very young. Had he really looked that young on their wedding day? Now, to her, he would stay young forever. His features had faded with each passing year until even his likeness in the photograph became little more than that of a gentle, attractive stranger linked to her by entwined fingers wearing matching wedding bands.

Kevin Mason had been her childhood sweetheart. His mother had cleaned rooms at the Atwood's river resort while he had bussed tables. From the eighth grade on, Kasey and Kevin had been practically inseparable. When Kevin entered high school, his mother began to come and go with the frequency of a merchant marine, staying away for weeks at a time, leaving her son to fend for himself. Marianne Atwood, humanitarian that she was, took him under her wing, made certain he was fed, clothed, sheltered, and even given the emotional support his mother had failed to provide. In return for that kindness, he continued to work at the resort after school and during summer vacations for little or no wages. Nothing in the world could have made Marianne happier than to see her daughter marry Kevin. His death was as much a blow to Marianne as it was to Kasey.

Oblivious to the racket in the other room, Kasey lightly touched the face of her dead husband. "I love you," she whispered. "Take care, huh?"

Kasey had scarcely stepped back into the kitchen when her mother waved the newspaper and began to read the daily horoscope.

"Ma, skip it for today. I can't hear a thing you're saying with all this noise."

Marianne raced around the room silencing first the blender, TV, and dishwasher. "Artie! Cool it for a minute. Take a break, will ya? I wanna read Kasey's horoscope."

The room quieted. All eyes turned to Kasey, waiting.

"For godsake, Ma . . ."

"Hush." Marianne cleared her throat. "It says here, 'A trusted friend can provide you with a second set of eyes today.' "

"Oh, that reminds me," Kasey said, turning to Sherry. "Can you do Clemetine's tonight? I have a feeling I'm going to be pretty wrapped up at the club for the next couple of weeks."

"Sure," Sherry said. "Tonight's good."

"There! How much more proof do you need?" Marianne flapped the newspaper in the air.

Kasey shrugged, winked at Sherry.

"There's more. It says, 'Someone is watching you. Stay alert!' " She looked at her daughter. "There's an exclamation point after 'alert.' "

"What, no romance today?" George asked.

"I bet that 'someone' who's watching her is a secret admirer," Sherry said.

George tapped the newspaper. "The murder's front page, Kasey. Must be real exciting being right in the thick of it."

"I'm not sure 'exciting' is the right word."

Marianne folded the newspaper. "Kase, we have a room to rent out. Would you mind checking around to see if anyone you know might be interested?"

"Grandma's room?"

"No, I don't think I'm ready to let strangers in there yet. If ever."

"Then who's leaving?" Kasey looked at each boarder.

"Me," Artie said from the laundry room. "Peggy and I are getting married. Finally."

"What?! I just had dinner with her last night," Kasey said incredulously. "She didn't say a word."

"Yeah, she did. She tried, anyway. She said you were comatose."

Kasey vaguely remembered Peggy talking about Artie and some special event. "Artie, that's great! Congratulations. When?"

"Maybe next month or the month after. If we don't tear into each other before then."

"Work out your aggressions on the mat, both of you."

"She'd beat the tar outta me," Artie said, grinning. "That's one mean woman when she's riled."

"When are you moving out?" Kasey asked.

"I guess I'm sorta out now. Most of my stuff is already at the condo."

"We're gonna miss you."

"Maybe not. Your ma said I could crash on the living room couch whenever Peggy—well, y'know, needs time to herself."

"Where's the wedding?"

"Better talk to her about that. She just has to name the place and I'll be there. Nothing fancy, though. You know Peggy."

Peggy hated frills and fuss.

"Ma, I'll see what I can do about getting us a new roomer."

"Make sure it's someone who'll fit in," her mother said.

Kasey nodded, drained her coffee, blew her mother a kiss, turned to Sherry, and said, "Clementine's. Nine."

Kasey was surprised to find Jay waiting for her at the main entrance to the club, his expression grim. When he saw her approaching, the tension in his face seemed to ease and a certain look came into his eyes, a look every woman recognizes. A look of appreciation, which told her she looked nice. Suddenly, she no longer felt like a zombie.

They walked the casino, talking.

"Have you seen the papers?" he asked.

"Yes. And the news reports this morning."

"Then you know the police have a suspect in custody. The guy's a dishwasher here at the hotel."

Kasey nodded. She walked alongside Jay in silence and thought how much easier it would be for Jay, Dianne, and the club, if this murder could be solved so easily. Internal rift. One employee kills another out of passion, greed, hatred, whatever. Only one other thing could make it ideal: If the police could tie the suspect to the other incidents—to the death of the elderly guest, the room burglaries, the mail threats to Jay. Wrap it all up in one nice, neat package for the courts to deal with.

When she didn't respond, Jay said, "Talk to me, Kasey. Tell me what's on your mind."

"I was thinking how great it would be if this dishwasher was behind everything that's been happening here. Wishful thinking, I'm afraid."

"Why?"

"Again, too pat." She stopped, turned to Jay. "Do you know who he is? Have you seen him in the club?"

"His name is Juan Ruiz. He's been with the hotel a couple of months. He's young. Twenty-nine, thirty. That's all I know. I saw him before Loweman's men took him away last night. He didn't look familiar."

Jay's pager beeped. He excused himself, walked several yards to the Blue Keno Lounge, and picked up a white courtesy phone.

While Kasey waited for Jay, she watched the activity in the casino. Business was always slow at this time of the morning. Several young unattended children ran up and down the wide, red-carpeted stairway that led to the convention floor. With broom and dustpan, a porter cleaned up empty coin wrappers between the slot machines and on the floor. Cocktail waitresses in sequined vests and black shorts carried loaded trays of coffee, juice, and Bloody Marys to gaming patrons.

Kasey watched a tiny, gray-haired woman wearing a pair of new white tennis shoes, brown housedress, and a long, pea-green sweater. A large, canvas handbag hung from a drooped shoulder as she meandered through a bank of quarter slot machines. She appeared to be looking for a machine to play, but it took Kasey only a second to mark her for a silver-miner. She stopped at a machine, placed a cupped hand in the change tray, and hit the *cash out* button. Overlooked credits—quarters accumulated in play from the previous player—dropped into her palm. She shoved them into her bag and moved on.

Not many people knew it was illegal to silver-mine. It was one thing to simply play off forgotten money, but to pocket it was something else. The silver-miner made it a practice to cruise casino slot machines looking for credits and coins left behind. If caught by the establishment, repeated offenders could be arrested. Most casinos merely issued a warning. Some did not. At King's Club, a second-time offender was usually ushered out by security. If asked to leave more than once, a silver-miner had a polaroid picture taken and put in a special book. Security was trained to watch for and tag repeat offenders.

Kasey had never agreed with the casino's reasoning that money left in the machine belonged to the establishment. *Finders keepers* was her motto. She looked on it as a windfall. Times were tough.

She dismissed the old woman and turned back to watch the three young children playing on the staircase. Unattended kids in a casino were another matter. Parents, intending to play for only a few minutes, often lost track of time. She had observed young ones on their own for hours on end—tired, hungry and thirsty, cold or hot if left outside. A busy establishment, particularly a gambling establishment, was not a safe environment for unchaperoned children.

Jay, no longer on the phone, was now talking to the casino manager, Robert Yanick. If she hurried, she could round up the children, find out who they were, and have their parents paged before Jay and the casino boss were finished.

Halfway to the children, she saw a security guard approaching them from the opposite direction. At that moment, Jay gestured to her.

Kasey hesitated uncertainly. Security would handle it. But the sight of the hotel blue-on-blue uniform suddenly generated a piercing apprehension. Not all men in blue were good guys. In fact, on two separate occasions in the past, she had been hired by casinos to observe not only employees and players, but the uniformed officers as well.

The man turned toward her and Kasey was relieved to see it was the elderly guard Harry. He gathered the children, sat them on the staircase, and spoke into his radio.

When she returned to Jay, he informed her that Det. Loweman was in the hotel. They were to meet him in the main kitchen.

The good smells in the huge kitchen reminded Kasey she had forgotten to eat that morning. As they passed a steaming mound of blueberry muffins on the countertop, she eyed them but refrained from taking one. She and Jay joined Det. Loweman and another detective at the back of the crowded room, near the dishwashing machines.

"This is Det. Williams. He's one of the investigators on the case. He found this on the floor last night," Loweman said, holding up a clear, plastic ziplock bag. Inside, coiled like a sleeping snake, was a gold cross on a chain. He pointed to the base of one machine. "Right there. Couldn't have been there long, the floors are cleaned each shift. Looks like it might have been dropped accidentally. The victim's sister told us she wore a gold cross or crucifix around her neck, which was nowhere at the crime scene. There were marks, abrasions actually, on her throat where it appears a chain had been ripped away. This chain's broken."

"Has Ruiz confessed?" Jay asked.

"Hasn't said a word. We're working on him, though. We have a search warrant for his locker and his vehicle."

"The locker would be in wardrobe. If he has a car, it would be in the employee lot across the street."

"Let's go to wardrobe first," Loweman said, smoothing flat his necktie and buttoning his jacket.

They took the service elevator to the lower level. Wardrobe occupied a large portion of the northeast wing. Jay, Kasey, and the two detectives stood facing locker number 322. With bolt cutters, Williams broke through the arm of the combination lock.

Wearing gloves, Williams carefully removed a copy of *Penthouse* to reveal Ruiz's street clothes. The pants and a plaid button-down shirt were crudely folded. While Loweman held open the evidence bag, Williams carefully lifted out the shirt. Two things fell from the folds. One hit the floor and rolled several yards; the flat, round, white object twirled like a top before slowly toppling over on its side. Even from a distance it was clear it was a King's Club one-hundred-dollar gaming chip.

Loweman sauntered over to it. He squatted. "Well, lookit here. Now I wonder where he got this? Minimum-wage kitchen workers don't, as a rule, get tokes." He lifted the chip by the edge and dropped it into another evidence bag.

"Over here," Williams said. "Looks like our fella was in

a hurry and overlooked a couple important items." He was bent down, prodding at a gold object with the end of his pen. It caught the light, sparkled. A two-carat solitaire diamond ring.

Twenty

They peered through the tinted glass of the two-way mirror into an interrogation room of the Sparks Police Department. Alone in the room, facing them, was the dishwasher, Juan Ruiz. The short, muscular man slouched in a molded plastic chair behind the table. The bright orange of the county jumpsuit he wore gave his olive complexion a sickly cast. He looked bored.

Because he so obviously avoided looking into the mirror, Kasey suspected he was aware that eyes watched from beyond it. And she suspected this wasn't the first time he'd been in an interrogation room. He picked at a faded tattoo on the fleshy part of his hand between thumb and forefinger.

"He's got a sheet," Loweman said to Jay and Kasey. "Misdemeanors mostly. DUI, assault and battery, petty theft, a couple minor drug offenses. No lockup time. Probation, some community service. Small-time punk."

"Could he have killed that woman?" Jay asked.

"Oh, hell yes, in a New York minute. In fact, he's our boy. I guarantee it."

"How can you be so sure?" Kasey asked.

"For starters, he was with her yesterday. He had the opportunity and the motive. And now we have reason to believe he was involved in the death of the woman in Room 814."

"The ring?" Jay asked.

"Yep. There's no doubt that the ring belonged to the deceased. It was inscribed, and both daughters have confirmed."

The three turned to stare at the man behind the two-way mirror.

Loweman squeezed Jay's shoulder. "Stick around. You and Ms. Atwood might find this interesting."

A moment later, through the tinted glass, they watched Loweman and Williams enter the room. Ruiz remained slumped in the chair. He clasped his fingers together on the tabletop, looked at both men defiantly before lowering his eyes.

Williams took the initiative. After determining if the suspect could read and write English and again advising him of his rights, Williams asked, "So, Juan, you have anything to say?"

" 'Bout what?"

"About Ms. Ramos."

"Who's that?"

"Inez Ramos. The *late* Inez Ramos."

"I had nothing to do with that. Nothing."

"Then you won't mind helping us clear up a few things."

"Like what?"

"Like how long have you known her? How close were the two of you?"

"I don't know her. Not good, anyway. Like we talked a couple times in the lounge. I talk to a lot of chicks."

"You didn't meet her in the basement yesterday? You didn't maybe fool around a little?"

Ruiz shook his head.

"She was a nice-looking woman."

"Yeah? So?"

"You saying you didn't try to hit on her?"

"Maybe."

"So what is it? Maybe you hit on her or maybe you didn't try?"

"I hit on her. Yeah, sure, I hit on her. Is that a crime?"

"Let's cut the crap," Loweman interjected coldly. "You met her in the basement. You had sexual relations with her. Are you going to deny that?"

"I—"

"We got semen, Ruiz. The woman had semen in her vagina cavity. Someone put it there. Was that you?"

Ruiz sat up, turned around in the chair until he was facing away from his two interrogators.

"Before you answer, Ruiz, let me mention DNA. You've heard of DNA typing, right? That alone could be enough to hang you. But in addition to traces of semen, we found traces of fiberglass on your jock shorts. Fiberglass that was also on the victim and her clothes. Fiberglass from insulation covering the duct in the area where the body was found. Mister, there's no fiberglass insulation in the hotel kitchen. So how the heck would it get on your jocks, Ruiz, unless you were down there in the basement with you pants down around your ankles?"

"Shiiit, man, look—hey, I'm gonna tell you . . . this is the honest-to-God truth, man, I met her down there in the morning, before work. We like did it, man. She was willing. *Willing.* Afterward, I watched her walk away."

"Okay, that fits. She was seen on the sixth floor, performing her housekeeping duties till about midmorning. Then she disappeared."

Ruiz shrugged his shoulders, shook his head. "I don't know nothing about her disappearing."

"The body was discovered at 6:20 that afternoon. Medical examiner estimates the time of death somewhere between noon and four. She'd been dead at least two, three hours when the coroner examined the body at the scene."

"That means I didn't fucking do it."

"It doesn't mean anything of the kind. It was you the maintenance man saw running from the scene. Want to explain what you were doing down there then?"

"Okay." He slapped his palms on the table. "Okay, she called me."

"What time?"

"Eleven. Eleven-thirty. I ain't supposed to take calls on shift, but she told my supervisor it was, y'know, like urgent. She wanted me to meet her in the basement after work."

"What did you tell her?"

"I said sure. Like you said, Mr. Cop, she was a nice-looking woman. Kinda shy, though."

"How did she sound on the phone?"

"Wha' d'ya mean?"

"Did she seem nervous or upset?"

"She sounded a little nervous, yeah; her voice was, y'know, shaky like. Like I said, she was kinda shy. Not the sorta chick who feels comfortable comin' on to a guy."

"But with you she made an exception, huh, Ruiz?"

He shrugged again, looked smug.

"What happened when you got down there?"

"I found her. It's dark down in that back part. I almost fell over her. Right away, I knew she was dead." He clapped a hand over his eyes. "I . . . shit, man, I got scared and . . . and I ran. I didn't do her. I didn't! Like why would I kill her when she was willing?"

"How do we know you're telling it straight? About her being so willing and all?" Williams asked. "Maybe she changed her mind and that pissed you off. Her calling you, getting you down there, and then teasing and all." Williams opened a file folder and carefully laid out five color photographs on the table in front of Ruiz.

Ruiz glanced at them, quickly looked away.

"Take a good look, Ruiz. She isn't so pretty there, is she? Just about every bone in her face was fractured. Couple teeth knocked out in front. Her cricoid was crushed and her neck broken. Now this one . . ." Williams tapped a photograph. "See those bruises on the inside of the thigh? I'd say a knee was used to force her legs apart."

Ruiz glared at Williams. "I never had to force no chick."

Williams grabbed Ruiz's hands and slapped them down flat on the table. He took a moment to examine them. Even through the dark glass Kasey could see cuts, burns, and scratches in various stages of healing. The hands of a blue-collar worker. The hands of a killer?

Williams touched a relatively fresh abrasion. "Sarge, did the M.E. find anything under the victim's fingernails?"

"Don't know; the report's not done yet."

"Whad'ya hit her with, lover boy? Whad'ya use to crush her face in? These hands? With maybe something wrapped around the knuckles to keep from injuring them?"

"Go to hell. I don't want to talk to you guys no more."

Loweman walked around behind Ruiz, leaned against the wall, and folded his arms across his chest. "Y'know something, Juan?"

Ruiz had to turn completely around to see him.

"I believe you," Loweman went on. "Yeah, I believe you when you say you didn't force yourself on that woman. You're a lot of things, Juan, but a rapist isn't one of them. You know what I think happened? I think the two of you were working the hotel together. I think she cased the rooms when she cleaned them. Later she'd get you inside to rip off these folks. Up 'til yesterday, the pickings had been pretty much penny-ante. Then you hit Room 634, and eureka! Suddenly you score big, really big. So you decide to cut her out of the deal. Or maybe you were afraid she'd crack, turn you in. You meet in the basement, argue; you get hot, spooked, whatever. Maybe you didn't mean to hurt her, maybe you just wanted to shut her up, like you had to shut up the old lady in Room 814; but, well, things got out of hand. Is that how it went, Juan?"

"What the fuck you talkin' about? What pickings? What old lady?" He looked from one man to another.

Both detectives were silent.

"You bastards are trying to set me up. I fess up to a quickie with this chick, and next thing I know you got me raping and stealing an' . . . and killing. You know what you can do? You can take your goddamned DNA and your shitty fiberglass evidence and shove it up your asses. I had sex with her this morning; I ain't denying that. You got nothin' else on me. Nothing."

Loweman and Williams looked at each other and offered nothing.

"Shiiit, if I was supposed to have killed her around noon, why would I go back down there after work?" Near hysteria made his voice high-pitched, shrill. "Huh, why would I do that? To like pay my final respects?"

Loweman pushed away from the wall, slipped his hands in his pants pockets, and jingled the change there. "Maybe you went back to look for something. Something that could incriminate you. Something, Juan, that we've got."

"Why don't you save us all a lot of time and tell us what happened?" Williams said. "Where'd you stash the rest of the money from Room 643?"

Ruiz leaped to his feet. "Fuckers! I wanna lawyer! Get me a fuckin' lawyer, now!"

In the dark shadows of the grape arbor, the Monk listened to the soft sounds of water from the manmade waterfall cascading over moss-covered rocks into the pond below. He shifted the small flat box from one gloved hand to another and, through the sheet of vines, watched Dianne King as she lay on her stomach on an inflated raft that lazily drifted in the deep end of the swimming pool. He'd lied when he wrote on the newspaper photo he had sent to her husband that she wasn't his type. She was his type. There were two kinds of women. The kind you married and the kind you didn't. He wasn't looking to get married.

The woman, a fine oily patina covering her bikini-clad body, lifted her head and tossed the shiny blonde hair from her eyes. In a maneuver that appeared almost liquid, she rolled off the lounge and disappeared beneath the sparkling water. She dove deep and began to swim the length of the pool underwater.

The Monk chose that moment to cross to the patio. He slid back the glass slider, stepped inside, and immediately looked for the security system. He found the panel box to the left of the door. The green light glowed. Deactivated, just as he'd figured. In all his years as a cop and more recently as a security guard, he'd learned that many private alarm systems were used at night or when the property was unattended. Mrs. King had no reason to expect an intruder. And with the housekeeper inside, why bother?

The Monk knew about the housekeeper. The stout, Teutonic, middle-aged woman came at 9:00 and left at 7:00. He knew her habits as well as the habits of each member of the household. Dianne King, when at home, took a daily swim before lunch and sometimes again before dinner. Cocktail hour was at 6:00, and she drank alone if no one were there to join her. After the housekeeper left for the day, she was usually alone in the house for several hours before her husband and nephew arrived. When his majesty got tied up, which was often, the nephew kept her company in the marble-and-glass mausoleum.

The Monk turned back to the door and nearly had it closed when Dianne King shot up out of the water, her eyes closed, her mouth open as she sucked air into her lungs. He stepped out of view. The vertical blinds rattled.

"Mrs. King?"

A female voice from the kitchen. The housekeeper.

He backed behind a linen screen painted with an elaborate Grecian design.

"Mrs. King?"

From between the joints of the screen, the Monk watched the woman march across the room to the slider. He saw the puzzlement on her face as she looked at the partially open door, the swaying blinds, and then beyond to her employer who was still in the pool. She opened the door wider. A gust of wind rattled the blinds.

Seemingly satisfied that the wind had rattled the blinds, she closed the door and returned to the kitchen.

The Monk made his way to the rear of the house.

Several minutes later, after allowing himself a brief tour of the east wing, he entered the master bedroom. The room, in his opinion, was decorated like a fancy cathouse boudoir and was big enough to swallow entirely the rundown shanty he rented north of town.

He circled the room, closely examining anything that piqued his interest. He studied the photographs. A wedding picture of the bride and groom; a studio portrait of Dianne King; photos of the handsome couple on a cruise liner; a vast assortment of headliner celebrities, each posing with J. G. King at the velvet-curtained entrance of the hotel's main showroom.

"Nice. Helluva nice life you got here, Your Highness," he said with contempt. "Y'know what? I think I want some of this for myself. Yeah, I definitely want some of this." With gloved fingers, he stroked the jaw and throat of Dianne King's portrait. "How 'bout it, Sweetheart? Getting lonely enough for me yet?"

With the box still under his arm, he roamed aimlessly from the sitting room to the deep walk-in closets to the vanity with its two adjoining bathrooms of gray marble, black porcelain, and gold fixtures. He examined everything at his leisure. Inside the medicine cabinet, he found two prescription vials—one a painkiller and the other an antibiotic. He opened the second vial, poured the antibiotics into his pants pocket, capped the vial, and replaced it on the shelf.

At the high-boy dresser, he opened a drawer filled with female underthings. He lifted a pair of flesh-colored thong panties, released them to remove the thin leather glove on his right hand. These he had to feel firsthand, to experience the sleek fabric against his rough hands. As he caressed the silky smooth material, an image of the sexy woman on the inflated raft, her body shiny with oil, came into his mind's eye.

He pocketed the panties, slipped the glove back on, closed the drawer, crossed the room to the enormous bed and laid the box on top of the black-satin bedspread, placing it just so. He took one last look around and left the room.

From the hall doorway he could see across the living room and beyond to the patio and pool. Outside, the housekeeper was arranging a place setting on the patio table. Dianne King was just emerging from the pool, water beaded like shimmering jewels on her golden skin.

As she stood drying off, he thought again what a great body she had and what a lucky man J. G. was. King had everything. A beautiful wife, money, status. So maybe the Monk couldn't have it all like J. G., but he sure as hell could have some of it, even if it were only a taste.

With the housekeeper outside, he detoured to the kitchen. A prepared luncheon plate of skinless chicken, kiwi fruit, a wedge of gouda on a bed of lettuce sat on the counter alongside an open bottle of *fumé blanc*. The Monk tore a piece of the chicken away and popped it into his mouth, chewed twice, then took a swig from the bottle of wine to wash it down. He heard the sound of the slider opening as he eased out the side door.

In the rich, gracious atmosphere of an old English Tudor dining room, the hotel Steak House kept a large booth reserved in the back for Jay, Brad, the senior executives, and their guests. Today Cummings, Yanick, Epson, and Brad occupied the booth. Knowing there would be a barrage of questions and not ready to bring the others in just yet, Jay had steered Kasey to a smaller booth across the room with only a cursory nod to the four men.

Kasey felt the curious stares from the booth, and from other booths around the room. Tongues would be wagging this afternoon. *Have you heard? The boss and that attractive new host that he hired out of the blue, they left the club together earlier in the day, returned to dine in private at a small, intimate table, openly snubbing the good ol' boys. Stay tuned for updates.*

"Don't concern yourself with them," Jay said. "Sometimes they can be as bad as a bunch of old women, gossiping and whining."

"Or a bunch of old men?"

A touch of a smile. "Yes, old men. Isn't that what I said?" She smiled.

"I understand my father made that mistake a few years back. Only it was no simple slip of the tongue."

"Oh? What was that?"

"Dianne told me you worked for us years ago. She said you and another cocktail waitress were being sexually harassed and my father sided with your accusers. But instead of quitting, you hung in there, eventually getting enough on them to convince my old man to toss them out. Is that the way it went?"

"Close enough. He then offered me the manager's job."

"But you didn't take it?"

"No."

He waited, not pushing, but obviously curious.

"I didn't turn it down because of a sense of moral injustice, Jay. I had nothing against your father or the club. Eleven years ago the expression 'sexual harassment' hadn't even been coined yet. It was just time to move on. The men were fired. That much was accomplished. And if it made your father listen to the next person who came to him, then my speaking up and fighting back served its purpose."

The waiter brought their lunch, a steak sandwich for Jay and seafood bisque for her. The waiter twisted the tall pepper mill, sprinkling ground pepper over the top of her pale-pink soup. Kasey cut the end from a round of freshly baked Dutch-crunch bread and buttered it.

"Is that how you got interested in the . . . the spying business?" Jay asked. "By nailing those two?"

"I was interested long before that. We—my folks, that is—owned and operated a resort and I learned very quickly that the employees were making out better than the owners."

He nodded; it wasn't necessary for her to explain. "Which resort?"

"The River Lodge."

"The River Lodge! You're kidding? Jesus, I loved that place. That was yours? Your folks ran that place?"

She nodded.

"When I was in high school, I hung out there all the time— for the natural spa. There was this bartender who served me beer, whiskey, whatever. Never carded me. He also sold me chances on a punchboard and always gave me a freebie for good measure. I must have blown a couple of hundred bucks trying to win that pump-model Remington shotgun."

Kasey couldn't help herself; she grinned behind her napkin.

"What?"

"That was Stu. He ran a scam on that punchboard. That was another thing I learned real quick."

"You're saying he continued to sell chances after the shotgun had been won?"

"That's right. Mostly to underage kids like you who couldn't complain even if they caught on."

He seemed to reflect for a moment. "Was your father aware of this scam?"

Kasey looked down, busied herself buttering another chunk of bread. "If it weren't 86% proof, my father wasn't aware of it."

She felt Jay's eyes on her. A moment later he was cutting into his steak sandwich.

"You must have been around seven or eight when I started going out there," Jay said, shifting the subject. "I probably saw you."

She met his gaze, nodded.

"Your folks sold the place about ten years later. I remember, because the new owners closed it for renovation. I had to go out to Steamboat Springs until it reopened."

"You must like hot mineral baths."

"Best way to relieve tension. Well, second best way." He grinned. "Last year I had the two Jacuzzis put in the hotel pool. When I stay here, I try to get in a few laps before turning in. I save the Jacuzzi for last. Helps me sleep."

Brad appeared at the table. Kasey saw the other men moving toward the foyer. "Jay, I tried to reach you this morning. Gail said you were away from the casino."

"Kasey and I were at the police station. Det. Loweman thought I might know something about the suspect."

"I see." He stood uncertainly.

"The Hamiltons are due in today. Have they registered yet?" Jay asked.

"I was just about to check." Brad hesitated. "I thought Kasey and I could meet them togeth—"

"Kasey has more important things to do right now."

"But—"

"We'll talk about it later, Brad. For now just go about your regular duties. Take good care of the Hamiltons. The Peppermill and Harrah's have been courting them, so give them the best. Red carpet all the way."

Brad looked from his uncle to Kasey and back to his uncle. He nodded stiffly and strode off.

Both were silent. It was obvious to Kasey, and probably to Jay, that Brad was not happy to be excluded from the *more important things*. Jay was the boss. He would handle it. Brad was not her problem.

Jay opened his mouth to speak, closed it. He looked over his shoulder as though making sure no one else was about to intrude. "What's this about security? Last night you asked me to get a list of all security personnel. Does it have anything to do with the incident on the sixth floor? That business about one of our guards hassling a guest?"

"That's part of it. It's only a gut feeling, Jay. Probably doesn't mean a thing, but . . ."

"Let's hear it."

"Juan Ruiz may have killed that maid, but I don't believe he's behind the other things going on here. There's a security guard, a specific one—I don't know who he is, not yet, anyway—but I have this strong feeling he's involved. He keeps popping up like the zonker in a game show."

"The one in the parking garage?"

"That's him." She told him about her conversation with Paula Volger. "And remember the complaint—or whatever it was—from the woman on the sixth floor who thought she saw a security guard harassing another guest? That guest was none other than Mr. Nicker in Room 634. From the very beginning I suspected someone who works here. Someone with more access to the hotel and casino than a dishwasher or maid."

"That makes sense. Then you think Ruiz is being set up?"

"Possibly. Unfortunately, once the police have a solid suspect, they're not too inclined to look further."

"Then I guess it'll have to be up to us to bring them back around. Gail has all the stuff you asked for. Security personnel, surveillance, everything. I can make the eye available to you."

"No, surveillance needs it for the casino. If it's all right with you, the monitors in the room in your office should work."

"The place is yours. Tell me what you need and I'll have it sent up. Do you have a name for this security officer?"

"No, he wasn't wearing a name tag."

"That's a violation."

"One of many, I bet."

"It shouldn't be too difficult to track him down. Which shift?"

"I'm not sure. It was after five; the two shifts overlap. He could be day or swing."

"So we're talking about sixteen to twenty. We'll find him."

The waiter approached with a telephone. "Call for you, Mr. King. Your secretary put it through."

"Thanks, Vince." He excused himself to take the call. "King here. Dianne?" He listened for several moments, then glanced at Kasey. His brow furrowed. "Where was it? When did you find it? Did Helga put it there? You opened it, looked through it? Dianne, I don't know anything about it. Someone put it there and it wasn't me. Now listen to me, and listen carefully. Make sure the house is locked and the alarm is activated. Bet-

ter yet, lock yourself in the master bath. Take Helga and the
cellular phone with you. Call 911 if you hear anythi—I'm
sorry if I'm scaring you. Just do what I say, hear me? This is
no joke, Dianne. I'll be right there."

Jay hit the disconnect lever, dialed. He asked for Det. Loweman. While he waited, he said to Kasey, "Dianne found a box
on our bed. She thought it was from me. Some sort of slinky
nightgown. There's a note—Hello, yes. Jay King. If you can
reach him, tell him to meet me at my house as soon as possible.
It's urgent."

Kasey was on her feet and ready to go before he finished
giving the police dispatcher his address and phone number.

Twenty-one

Kasey followed Jay into the foyer of his house. He glanced at the security panel just inside the door and stopped cold.

"I don't believe this," he said quietly.

The alarm had not been set.

"Helga?" he called out.

The housekeeper rushed toward them, a dishtowel and crystal wineglass in hand. "Mr. King, it's you. Is something the matter?"

"Where's my wife?"

"Your bedroom, I believe."

Jay took Kasey's arm. She had to practically run to keep up with him as he propelled her down a long, wide hallway bright with natural light from an overhead skylight. They passed through a circular atrium, the air heavy with humidity, to a pair of double doors which Jay barged through without slowing down.

"Dianne, what the hell—?"

Dianne stood at a window facing the pool, her hands deep in the pockets of a floor-length terrycloth robe. She turned.

"Dianne, I told you to lock yourself in the bathroom. He could be out there watching you right now. Christ, he could still be in the house."

"*Who?* For godsakes, Jay, what's going on?"

He crossed to her, took both her hands in his and gently pulled her away from the window. "Are you all right?"

"Yes, yes," she said impatiently. "But if you don't tell me what this is all about, I'm going to scream."

"The alarm is off. Why is the alarm off? How many times have I told you to keep it on at all times? He just walked right in."

"Who, Jay? Who are you talking about?"

"The man who put that there." He nodded toward the box. "Dianne, someone has been in our house, can't you understand that? And he got in because the alarm was off. Opened a door and walked in. Why do you insist on making things difficult for everyone? Two women have been murdered at the club. This is for real."

"Jay, you're overreacting. You're bringing problems from the club home with you. You said the police have the killer. Besides, what does a murder at the club have to do with me?"

Kasey, standing in the doorway, felt awkward and imposing. She knew why Jay was concerned for his wife's safety. He had every reason to be worried. Kasey thought of the newspaper photograph of Dianne that Jay had received only yesterday in the mail. It hadn't been the first one, and it probably wouldn't be the last. She understood Jay's fear—a threat had been made and acted upon. Yet Kasey couldn't blame Dianne for her blasé approach to it all. Dianne didn't have a clue. Jay should have warned her.

As if he read her mind, he glanced at Kasey guiltily before saying, "I'm sorry, Dianne; it's my fault. I should have let you in on it. It involves more than the club. I've . . . well, I didn't tell you, but the same joker who sent the clipping of the MGM fire also made several other threats, these were directed at you. I kept it from you because I didn't want you to worry."

Dianne backed away from her husband. In a cool tone she asked, "Threats? What sort of threats, Jay?"

He looked at Kasey.

"Rape? Mutilation? Death? What?" she demanded, her voice strained.

"I don't know. Nothing specific. Kasey thought I should tell you, but I . . . I wanted to wait."

Dianne turned away from him, crossed to the bed. "Wait for what, darling? Wait for me to be attacked in my own home?" She flipped the top off the box and, by the slender straps, lifted out a sheer, black teddy. She held it up against her chest, looked down at it with an expression of deep reflection. Suddenly pivoting, she balled the teddy and threw it at Jay. "I should have known it wasn't from you!"

Jay went to her, attempted to hold her. At first she stiffened, shrugged off his hands, pushed at him. Insistent, he held on. "Dianne, forgive me, please. I was wrong. I was only trying to keep from upsetting you, but I realize now that I put you in more danger. Dianne . . ."

Dianne visibly relaxed. She closed her eyes, moaned, turned in his embrace, and laid her head against his shoulder. Jay held her, stroking her back.

Kasey felt a strange tightness in her stomach and quietly retreated.

Det. Loweman was being ushered into the foyer by the housekeeper when Kasey reached the living room. Without preamble he said, "What is it? Where is everyone?"

She told him. For the second time that afternoon, she walked down the long hallway to the master bedroom, this time accompanied by the detective and housekeeper.

When they were close enough to see into the room, Loweman bellowed, "Don't touch that! Don't touch anything!"

Jay, who was just about to reach into the box, hesitated. He straightened, stepped back, and placed a protective arm around Dianne.

"Hello, Frank," Dianne said when he entered the room.

"Dianne."

"How's Marla these days?"

"*Marlene* is fine. I'll tell her you asked."

"We'll have to get together for another barbecue soon."

"Yeah. Real soon."

Kasey sensed a definite coolness between the two.

Loweman bent over, used his pen to lift the teddy by one strap, and placed it on the bed. Next, he separated the black tissue paper to reveal the note. Kasey and Jay read over his shoulder.

Black becomes you. RIP

"RIP. Rest in peace," Loweman said. He turned to the housekeeper. "Did you see or hear anyone around the house?"

"Well, when Mrs. King was taking her afternoon dip, I thought I heard the patio door slide open. I looked. No one was there. I thought it was only the wind."

"What time?"

"Noon. Just before I served lunch."

Loweman turned to Dianne. "Dianne?"

"I don't recall anything. I swam, had lunch on the patio, then sunbathed for another thirty minutes or so. When I came in to shower and change, I found the box lying on the bed. I thought it was from Jay. I called him at the club to let him know I'd found it."

"You have an alarm, right?"

"It wasn't on," Dianne said defensively. "I don't see any reason to set it when I'm right outside and Helga is inside."

Loweman cleared his throat. "I'll get a team over here. I'll need comparison prints from the three of you."

"Helga, thank you," Jay said. "You can go back to whatever you were doing. Frank, can we talk a minute?"

"Am I being excused, too?" Dianne said. "Are we going to continue to play the game of sheltering faint-hearted Dianne from all the bad things in the world?"

Jay looked thoroughly admonished. "Di—no, you're right, of course. I'm sorry. This concerns you and you have every right to be in on it." He turned back to Loweman. "Frank, the murders at the club, they're tied in with this."

"How do you figure? We got our man, Jay."

"Has he confessed?"

"It's only a matter of time."

"You've got the wrong man. Whoever brought that box into this house and wrote that note has targeted me and my family. He's after me, and I don't think he'll stop at one or two murders."

"A coincidence, Jay, nothing more. The diamond ring we found in Ruiz's locker, the one that belonged to the victim in Room 814, is worth somewhere in the neighborhood of three grand. We also found close to a thousand dollars in cash and chips inside a man's sock in Inez Ramos's locker. The sock matched a pair that Nicker had. Gray argyle with a pink diamond pattern. Not your everyday jock sock. Looks like a solid connection to me."

"That only proves that Inez Ramos's killer robbed the woman in 814 and probably the man in 634," Kasey said. "It doesn't prove it was Ruiz, or that Ruiz and Ramos were partners in crime. The killer could have seen the man and woman together and devised a plan. It's easy enough to plant evidence in a locker. Where's the other six grand that Nicker claims was in the sock?"

"Ruiz hid it, of course. Or he gave it to Inez Ramos."

"Why would he leave some in his locker? No one's that stupid."

"You don't know the average criminal mind. If they had any brains, they wouldn't have to resort to crime."

"Ruiz is being set up," Kasey said. "There's a housekeeper by the name of Paula Volger. She was a friend of the dead woman. Talk to her; I think she knows something."

Loweman wrote down the name. "Why hasn't she come forward?"

"My guess is she's afraid."

"Okay, okay, I'll keep looking. Naturally, we're going to

take these threats to you and Dianne seriously," Loweman said to Jay. "From now on, I advise you to keep the alarm on twenty-four hours a day. Does your system have a panic button?"

"Yes," Jay said. "Behind the headboard."

"Is there a gun in the house?"

Jay strode to the nightstand, opened the drawer, "Right here on my si—" He stopped abruptly, looked up. "It's not here."

"I have it," Dianne said softly. She reached into the pocket of her terry robe and carefully brought out a chrome-plated .38 automatic. She looked at her husband. "I wasn't as blasé about this as I made out to be."

Kasey saw the tremor of Dianne's hand as she passed the gun to her husband. From her other pocket she brought out a cigarette and lighter.

Jay took the lighter and lit her cigarette. "You're getting a bodyguard," he said.

"The first step is to safeguard the property," Loweman said.

"That's impossible. On this ridge with its natural rock formations there's no way to put up a security fence."

Loweman pinched the bridge of his nose. "Dianne, is there somewhere you can go for a while?"

"Her mother's," Jay said. "In Utah."

"No!" Dianne said sharply. "You know I can't stay with her, not in that tiny house. She smothers me. The house smothers me. The town smothers me. No, not there."

"A friend?" Loweman asked.

Dianne took a moment to contemplate, chewed at her lip. Finally, she shook her head. "No. No one I'd want to stay with. I was never the type to bond closely with other women. Except for Kasey here, I have no—what one would call—intimate friends."

Despite the fact that Kasey believed their friendship had deteriorated over the years, she couldn't help but feel touched by Dianne's admission and, before she knew what she was saying, it was already out. "There's a vacant room at my mother's boardinghouse. It came available just this morning. It's small, but clean and homey. You're welcome to it, Dianne."

Dianne seemed to blanch at the idea of living, even temporarily, in a boardinghouse. "Oh, you're sweet to offer, and it would be such fun to have you so near—now don't take this the wrong way, Kasey—but, I need to be a little closer to the action. It's so damn remote out there. I'd go stir-crazy. You're not upset with me, are you?"

Kasey shook her head. Secretly, she was relieved. Being that close to Dianne day in and day out could drive a final wedge into their already questionable relationship. But aside from how the friendship would hold up, Kasey's greatest concern was for the safety of the others at her mother's house. If a killer were out to get Jay and the members of his family and he were as clever as Kasey thought he was, he'd have little trouble finding Dianne at the ranch.

"The hotel," Dianne said, crushing her cigarette out in a tiny crystal ashtray. "We'll move into the hotel. What better place? It's like a fortress, security all around."

"I don't know about that," Jay said. "I'm not sure security is any better there. The room burglaries—"

"Hire more security," Dianne cut in. "Besides, no one can get into the rooms if the deadbolts are in place. It's settled. We'll sleep in the suite tonight." She turned to Kasey. "Will you help me pack, Kasey?"

Kasey looked at Jay. When he nodded, she said, "Sure."

For the first quarter-hour Kasey had moved from one side of the room to the other, trying to stay out of the way of a crime scene investigator as he dusted for prints and Dianne, who moved from closet to high-boy to bathroom gathering clothes and personal items and packing them into a half-dozen Gucci bags.

"What can I do?" Kasey asked for the third time.

Dianne looked up, puzzled. "Do? Oh. Of course. Jay needs

some things. His bathroom's on the left. Would you get his toiletries?"

"Is it okay?" Kasey asked the investigator as he left the bathroom.

He nodded.

"And that's his closet behind you. Four changes should be enough."

"Dianne, I don't know what he wan—"

"Nonsense. Four suits, one of each color, and a tie to match."

In the bathroom Kasey found an empty nylon travel bag. She felt strange, intrusive, about to go through Jay's private medicine cabinet and drawers; but at the rate Dianne was going, they would be here all day. Into the bag she put a green toothbrush with yellow and white bristles, toothpaste, mouthwash, and roll-on deodorant.

On a shelf above the sink, she found an old, worn leather case, rolled up and tied. Inside, lined up like battle-scarred soldiers, were six straight razors. Fascinated, Kasey examined them. Each one bore a different handle: bone, mother-of-pearl, brass-lined steel, ivory. What appeared to be the most used razor was also the least adorned. The handle, a dull-luster finish, had the initials RGK crudely carved at the bottom. Ralph G. King. Jay's father.

On the sink sat a mug with a shaving brush and soap. She touched the brush. Damp. It was hard to believe that a man in the '90s would shave the old-fashioned way. Kasey's own grandfather had given up the brush and straight razor for an electric Remington when her father was a boy. Either Jay was spoiled from barbershop shaves or he was sentimental. She suspected the latter.

When she opened the medicine cabinet, a plastic bottle fell into the sink. She shook the bottle. Empty. Odd. Why would Jay keep an empty medicine container? She put it back.

Bottles of after-shave and cologne filled an entire shelf. All were full except one. Navarro. She put it to her nose and

breathed in. Yes, this was the clean, fresh fragrance that Jay
wore. Several times she had caught a subtle whiff of it on him.
In the elevator the first day, on his jacket yesterday in the
basement when he had put it over her shoulders, and again in
his car that very morning. Kasey closed her eyes and breathed
it in again, the fragrance evoked sharp images of Jay.

Kasey's eyes snapped open. The bottle fell to the floor. She
quickly snatched it up, capped it, grabbed a wad of tissue, and
wiped up what had spilled. She shoved the after-shave bottle
deep into the bag with the other toiletries, struggled several
seconds with the zipper until it finally caught and closed. On
her way out, she found the razor strop hanging on the back
of the door. She crammed it into the bag.

"Kasey, never mind Jay's clothes; Helga is going to take
care of it." Dianne closed the last suitcase. "Ready?"

She couldn't explain it, but knowing she wouldn't have to
enter Jay's closet and go through his personal wardrobe gave
Kasey a feeling of relief. "Ready," she said, almost too eagerly.

Twenty-two

After helping Dianne get settled into the suite that Jay kept available on the top floor, Kasey found Jay in the screening room that adjoined his office. He sat at the table of monitors, his shirtsleeves rolled up, a pile of papers and envelopes spread out in front of him.

"Dianne finally released you," he said, standing and pulling off the frameless glasses he wore when reading.

She walked past him, switched on a monitor. "You should have told her, Jay."

"I know that, Kasey. Didn't I admit as much to her? Christ, I never thought he'd be so brazen as to go to my house."

"He's playing games," she said. "He could have hurt her. He was inside the house, in her bedroom. All he had to do was wait for her to come to him."

Jay was silent. She could guess what kind of pictures were going through his mind. Why was she being so hard on him? Was it payback for the deceptive images that had come to her in his bathroom earlier that afternoon? Did she want to fight with him so that she wouldn't fall in love with him instead?

"I don't want anything bad to happen to Dianne," he said quietly. "She's had to put up with a lot of crap lately. I know what she wants from our marriage. I know what she wants from life; but until my needs are fulfilled, I can't fulfill hers. Does that sound terrible, Kasey?"

Kasey looked away, ran fingers through her hair, then shook her head. "I don't know."

She felt his eyes on her again. She knew that if she looked at him, he would hold her gaze a moment longer than necessary; and ridiculous as it sounded, each of those moments drew her in closer, bound him tighter to her.

She switched on another monitor. "Shall we get to work?"

He handed her a key. "It opens the door to this room from the hallway. Come and go whenever you like. If I'm not here, feel free to anything in my office . . . bar, phone, whatever. You remember how to open the connecting door?"

"I think so."

He pushed out the chair beside him. When she sat, he leaned over her, pulled the stack of papers to her. She caught a whiff of his cologne before he leaned back.

"The stuff you asked to see. Security personnel. Names, positions, shifts. Structural blueprints. Schematics indicating every egress, emergency or otherwise, every surveillance camera, catwalk, two-way mirror, and . . . well, you get the picture."

"Let's start with security."

"I did a little homework before you showed up. It might save some time. Omitting graveyard and concentrating on the other two shifts, we have a total of twenty officers, not counting the shift supervisor or the chief of security. Nine of the twenty came on this spring. Seasonal temps. Of the nine, two are women and one is black. That leaves six."

"Photos?"

"Black-and-white photocopies of the police shots. Pretty much worthless. Sparks PD have the originals."

"Okay, then, this is what we're looking for. He's about six foot even. Approximately forty-years-old. Brown hair, very thin in front. Average build—no, above average; he filled out his uniform better than most. Don't know his eye color. I only saw him once in the parking garage, and most of that time he had a handkerchief to his face." She told Jay about Paula Volger hitting him in the nose and making it bleed. A chilling image of the man's eyes flashed across her mind—eyes filled with rage and malevolence. "However, I think I would recognize his eyes. His complexion was tan, though he seems to be of Nordic or Scandinavian ancestry. Likes the sun. Sportsman, probably."

"Doesn't sound like anyone I know. Temp, I'd say. If we don't spot him tonight, you can have a look through the police files." He tapped a paper in front of her. "Anyway, here are the names of the six."

Kasey turned to look at Jay. She grinned. "Very good. I'll make a spotter out of you yet."

"Yeah. I may have to find another line of work in the near future. Whoever's trying to bring down the club is doing a pretty good job of it. Three maids quit today. Head of housekeeping told me they were scared out of their wits. I guess having a fellow worker found dead in the basement goes beyond an occupational hazard. We've had room cancellations—enough to know the two murders being played up by the media is definitely responsible. The Gaming Board is starting to snoop around, and the bank is asking leading questions. And now this thing at the house today."

"I'm sorry, Jay."

He shrugged. "Let's just find the bastard, and quick."

"Naturally, the simplest way to go about this is to interview each security officer. But I'd rather not have him know we suspect him, not yet anyway. It may take a little longer doing it this way, but when we do find him—this man who seems to always be in the wrong place at the wrong time—we can observe him without his being aware of it. It's a game of time and circumstances, Jay, and it could take awhile. Are you prepared to play?"

"What choice do I have? Discovering who he is and firing him isn't going to make him stop. Something is driving this man, and until I find out what it is, I'm completely at his mercy."

"It's possible the guard may not be involved at all. As I said, it's more a gut feeling."

"I trust your gut feelings."

Kasey checked the time: 4:04. For the next two hours, the security day and swing shifts would alternate completely.

Jay switched on the rest of the monitors, then dimmed the overhead lights.

Two monitors were keyed into the pan-n-tilt camera at the Time Office—a check-in point for hotel casino workers. The remaining monitors were keyed to fixed-focus cameras which were set at every entrance. The picture quality varied from one monitor to another.

Jay fiddled with several controls. "After the renovation, the first thing to go will be this outdated surveillance system. Nothing but state-of-the-art equipment, color cameras, the works for the new club. It's expensive, but in no time it sure as hell pays for itself."

"Anything is an improvement from the days of two-way mirrors, catwalks, and peepholes," Kasey said.

"When my brother and I were kids, we used to sneak into the old eye and play war on the catwalk, looking down on the casino action through the mirrors, pretending we were on a reconnaissance mission. That all ended the night Travis accidently dropped his rifle and it broke through the mirror, landing right in the middle of a crowded dice table. He felt the old man's razor strop for that one."

"What about you? Were you punished?"

"Uh-uh. I hid out in this tiny room that no one knew about but Travis and me. It was sort of our clubhouse."

On the monitor, Kasey saw a handful of employees enter the Time Office. She tapped the screen. She and Jay sat back, their full attention now on the monitors.

KA-BOOM! The report echoed through the canyon. It sounded like a small cannon, followed by rolling thunder.

"Gotcha," the Monk said under his breath.

He put the end of the gun's muzzle to his mouth and blew

the fine ribbon of smoke away. He breathed in the cordite, a pungent odor that he liked, an odor as intoxicating, as stimulating as a woman primed for sex.

"Gotcha good, ya littl' bastard."

The Monk sat in a patch of shade on the gritty desert soil, his legs drawn up, knees bent, his back against a large, smooth boulder, the holster snug over his shoulder. The sun was behind him. He examined the gun, a powerful Smith & Wesson .44 Magnum, Dirty Harry's monster choice. The pistol was heavy, solid, ominous-looking. Though not as accurate as some of the longer-barrel handguns, he liked the size, the feel, the way it fit his hand, the way it recoiled, ejaculating close to 1,000 foot-pounds of energy.

At seven o'clock, the hottest part of the day long gone, when desert animals crawled out of burrows and from under rocks and brush to eat, drink, or catch the sun's last warming rays, the Monk chose this time to get in a little target practice. He relished the heat. The hotter the better. He craved the outdoors, which was why he picked the swing shift to work. His favorite rambling times were in the heat of the afternoon and the hours after midnight. He worked and slept the rest of the time.

When working as a cop, he always put in for swing or graveyard. The hours when crime and criminals flourished. When junkies, drunks and whores came alive, claiming the streets, dives, and back alleys for themselves. The hours when the Monk of Mayhem prowled, targeting the predator as well as the prey. He wasn't all that picky. If they were on *his* streets, they answered to *him*.

He rubbed the long barrel caressingly along the side of his jaw. He hadn't had the Magnum when he was on the force. Law enforcement agencies in big cities frowned on such massive, unwieldy firepower. This particular piece he'd taken off a dead pimp in LA. It was virtually untraceable, the serial number and manufacture marks obliterated long ago. Macho metal was cool, but only as an extension of his own capabilities.

The Monk reached under his arm and pulled a pint of tequila from the holster there. Leaning his head back on the boulder, he took a long swig, used his tongue to cut off the flow of burning liquor, swallowed hard, and in this same manner drank until the bottle was empty. Then, like a sharpshooter in a cheap western, he tossed the bottle high into the air, whipped the pistol upward, and fired. The bottle shattered, raining booze and thick shards of glass over him. He shook his head, laughed. He reached into the pocket of his pants, drew out the silky flesh-colored panties, and used them to wipe the droplets of tequila from his face and hair.

With one finger he twirled the panties round and round and thought about the woman. Not the one who owned the panties, but the other one. The brunette. The one who wasn't what she pretended to be.

She was beginning to catch on. He'd come face to face with her twice now—if he counted the brief encounter in the downstairs bar yesterday. She was no dummy. He counted on that. Fed on it, actually. He had no use for stupid women. This one, the brunette, Ms. Kasey Atwood, new host for the club—he chuckled at that—was already catching on.

"Let the games begin," he muttered.

It was getting late. Time for him to check out the action. Time to plan his next move. Earlier that afternoon, parked in his car on the ridge above the King house, he had watched the two women load the Jag with suitcases. He could guess where they were going; but just to be sure, he followed them anyway, straight to King's Club.

A ground squirrel popped its head up over the top of the rock pile, then quickly retreated. The Monk rested his wrist on the top of his knee, sighted the .44 at the point where the squirrel had first appeared. He waited.

When the squirrel popped up again, the Monk carefully

squeezed off a round. Chunks of splintered rock exploded. The squirrel ducked out of sight.

"Next time, amigo."

He holstered his gun, pushed himself away from the boulder, and came to his feet. He stretched. Took one last look around.

For as far as the eye could see, small rock piles dotted the landscape. Scattered about the first dozen or so mounds, those within range of the mighty .44, lay pieces of fur, tissue, and bone, bloody remnants of the creatures, curious by nature, who inhabited the area. A shooting arena with countless prey. No one could say he didn't give them a sporting chance. He could have used the Winchester .243 with its high-power scope or even the .12-gauge shotgun. But he was a sporting man. Yes, sir, popping squirrels with a handgun was indeed a practiced art.

"How well do you know yourself?" Jay asked. He leaned back in the chair, the row of monitors glowing, and studied Kasey.

It was after eight o'clock. Up until now, conversation between them had been merely small talk. Shop talk.

"How do you mean?"

"Well, you seem so good at judging others, I just wondered how well you know yourself."

She shrugged, tucked hair behind one ear. "It's not something I've put a lot of thought into."

"Who is Kasey Atwood?"

"You're serious."

"Very. Kasey Atwood, do you know her?"

She glanced at him, her smile timid. "Not as well as I should. I guess, like a lot of people, I'm afraid to really look inside."

"Why?"

"Afraid of what I'll find."

"Such as?"

This time she laughed softly. Looked away.

"You mentioned your father was an alcoholic. Do you worry that you might follow in his footsteps?"

"My mother does my worrying for me in that department. Every time I have a drink, she develops another worry wrinkle." She scratched at an imaginary speck on the monitor. "Do I worry? No. I've come to the conclusion that most families are dysfunctional. Either you follow in your parents' footsteps or you don't. What about you? Did you have a so-called *normal* family life?"

He seemed to ponder her question. It was his turn to laugh softly. "I never thought of my family as being dysfunctional, but I suppose it was. My father was a workaholic and my mother . . . my mother was a hypochondriac. It started with headaches, then heart palpitations and dizziness. From there it held no bounds. She could come up with the most incredible diseases. All in her head, of course. She only had to read about something and she had full-blown symptoms the next day."

"Was she always that way? A hypochondriac?"

Jay reflected. "No. It wasn't until after my father became really involved in the club that she started to—Jesus," Jay said, laughing again. "Jesus, why wasn't I able to see this before? She became—she used her illnesses to get his attention, and he worked longer hours to get away from her and her constant ailments. That's it. That had to be it. I always thought I was the reason he stayed away."

"Why would you think that?"

"I don't know. Don't kids always blame themselves for their parents' shortcomings?"

Kasey thought of her relationship with her father. Maybe she didn't blame herself for his weaknesses, but she certainly felt responsible for his well-being.

A silence fell over them. She pretended to be engrossed in the monitors before her. She felt his eyes on her, and the air surrounding them grew heavy, charged. She found it difficult to breathe.

"What now?" Jay asked quietly.

Kasey stood and stretched, breaking whatever confidential web they had spun. "It's time for me to call it a night. Either it's his day off or we missed him," she said. "I go on to another job and you go upstairs to your wife. Tomorrow is another day."

He sighed, shook his head ruefully. "My wife. I'm not a very good husband to her, am I? She has every right to be fed up with me. Tonight of all nights I should have spent with her. I meant to leave hours ago. I—"

"Jay, don't be so hard on yourself. What you're doing is for her, too. She should understand."

"I hope you're right."

"Besides, the night's still young."

On her way out of the club she played three quarters in the triple 7 machine at the back door that she had come to regard as "her machine." It paid her even money. She pocketed the quarters and left to meet Sherry across town.

Twenty-three

Kasey and Sherry arrived at *Clemetine's* at the same time.

Waiting for Sherry at the entrance of the restaurant, Kasey watched her jockey her '74 GMC pickup into a tight space alongside a new, bright-red Porsche. The Porsche's driver, in an attempt to avoid a door ding, had taken up two parking spaces. There were other parking places in the lot, but Sherry had ignored them and squeezed in.

The old battered truck, with the two right wheels on a planter curb, sat askew like a drunken, armored warrior begging for a kiss from the shiny lady in red. It evoked quite a picture, one the Porsche's owner was not likely to appreciate, which was exactly the point.

Sherry waved at Kasey through the rear window, hopped across the seat, and exited on the passenger side. She ran across the parking lot, her enormous suede handbag slung over her shoulder and bouncing against her back, fully stocked with at least one change of clothes, condoms, corkscrew, Mace and siren alarm, umbrella, cosmetics, reading material, bottled water, and an assortment of snacks. If trapped or abandoned anywhere, Sherry could live out of that bag for days.

Tonight she looked older, more mature. At home, with her hair in a ponytail and no makeup, she could easily pass for a teenager. Her reddish-blonde hair had been twisted into a loose chignon at the back of her neck. Under a shapeless beige tunic she wore a black miniskirt. Her long, thin legs were stockingless, ending with a pair of unadorned leather sandals on pale, tiny feet. Sherry's choice of dress seemed in contrast to the girl herself. Classy, yet slightly tacky. Sexy, yet chaste. Looking at her now, no one would guess that she made a living hustling in the better hotels in town. Or that she used the money to put herself through school.

They entered the still-crowded restaurant and made a bee-line for the lounge. The bar was full. Two-deep in several places. They slid into an empty booth at the back of the room.

"Keep your eye open for a couple places at the bar," Kasey said over the loud jukebox music. "We're out of the loop back here."

"Does the owner know you're coming tonight?" Sherry asked.

"No. He doesn't even know who I am. We've only spoken on the phone."

Kasey took in the action. There were two bartenders and two cocktail waitresses. People ate at the bar, on cocktail tables, and in the booths—overflow from the restaurant. "Business is certainly good. The man should be making money."

"A manager?"

"Nope. This guy owns and operates. He's here nearly every night. Either he's a lousy businessman or he has some pretty brazen employees. Can you see the registers?" When Sherry nodded, Kasey said, "I'll take the right. You get the left."

Sherry had worked with Kasey enough to know the routine by heart. Bartenders were always scrutinized first. Managers and relatives tied for second.

A cocktail waitress wearing jeans and a tank top with *Clementine's* printed on it placed napkins on the table. Before she could take their order, a large man with curly black hair, glasses in thick black frames, and a grin that looked plastered on, approached them. "I'll take care of these ladies, Abby. Tell Hank to throw a steak on the grill for me. I'll eat it at the bar."

He placed both palms flat on the table and leaned forward, exposing a chest as hairy as a shag mat. "First timers, am I right?"

They nodded.

"Welcome. I own the joint. Name's Leroy Tate. We have a policy here. For pretty ladies, the first drink is on the house."

"What if the lady is not pretty?" Kasey asked.

"You don't have to worry about that," he said, winking. "Anything you want. What'll it be?"

"Champagne?" Sherry asked.

He squinted at Sherry. "Say, are you old enough to drink?"

She unflinchingly stared him down. "Yeah. I'm old enough."

"Yeah. Okay." He straightened. "Well, sorry to disappoint you, honey, but we only sell champagne by the bottle. House wine's real good, though."

"You said anything I want. I want champagne. The bottle. On the house, naturally."

Kasey was about to nudge Sherry under the table. A low-profile was essential in this line of business. Sherry nudged her instead. Kasey sat back, waited.

The owner laughed. "You got me there. Pretty clever. Okay, little lady, you'll get your champagne. Only because I like you. And what's your friend going to have? A kegger?"

"Thanks, I'll just share her champagne."

"Now I'm only doing this for you two this one time, so don't go blabbing it around. At this rate I'd be broke in no time."

When he was gone, Kasey turned to her companion. "What was that all about?"

"I know his type. Relax, you'll see."

The waitress brought an ice bucket, champagne, and three glasses. A moment later, Tate popped the cork and filled the glasses, taking one for himself. He nudged his way in beside Sherry, told a couple raunchy jokes to break the ice, gulped down the champagne, then excused himself, telling them to save his place, he'd be back soon.

They watched him return to the bar, to a heaping plate of food and a bottle of red wine.

In the course of two hours, he comped every woman in the lounge with drinks and appetizers, some more than once. He took change from the till to feed the jukebox and four slot machines, put away two sixteen-ounce steaks, and drank non-stop until he could no longer sit a stool at the bar. Mr. Leroy Tate was having a good time.

"This jackass doesn't need crooked help. He's his own worst enemy," Kasey said, loading a chip with guacamole. "How'd you know?"

"I knew the minute I laid eyes on him he was an 'impress the ladies' sort of guy and a really good sport. That's always expensive. He's a boozer. That gets expensive, too.

"And the help are right there, filling their pockets, going along for the ride. I bet plenty of those nice juicy steaks, like the ones he had for dinner, are going out the back door every night."

"Sssh, here he comes," Sherry said, lighting a cigarette. She only smoked when she drank, and she neither drank nor smoked at home—Atwood house rules.

Tate flopped down in the booth, practically sitting on Kasey. "How're my two little bubble gals doing?" he asked thickly. "Got everything you need? Want you to come back. . . . Have a good time."

He squeezed Kasey's thigh, tried to kiss her. When she pulled away, he whined, "Hey, don't start getting righteous. You two been suckin' up freebies all night. Y'know, I can still charge you for the champagne and those finger foods."

"I don't think so. Mr. Tate, my name is Kasey Atwood. You called me on Monday. Hired me to check out *Clemetine's*."

His brow furrowed. When it finally sank in, his frown deepened. "Well, hell, why didn't you say so before?"

"Could we talk in private?"

"Yeah, sure. My office."

They left Sherry in the booth. His office was a cluttered room filled with cases of liquor, pamphlets, extra furniture, and odds and ends. He leaned back on the desk, both hands bracing him, head bobbing drunkenly.

"First question," Kasey said. "How are the day receipts?"

"They seem okay."

"You have a manager?"

"Yeah."

"Mr. Tate, this is my first time in the place. Because it's my first time, what I have to say may not be a fair evaluation. But since I don't intend to return, I'll just have to go by what I saw here tonight."

"How could you see anything sitting in a back booth?"

"I saw plenty. I could have sat anywhere in the bar. If your employees are stealing from you—and I'm sure they are—it's because they can get away with it. This is a business, Mr. Tate, not your own personal playground."

"What's that mean?"

"If tonight is an example of every other night, it means that much of your profits are going into your own gullet. My advice to you is to stay out of the place until you can get yourself dried up. Hire a good night manager."

"Who the hell do you think you are, telling me my business?"

"You hired me to find out where the profits are going. I told you what I thought." She opened the door. "I'll send you the report and my bill."

"Dock the price of the champagne," he said sourly.

"Sorry, that falls under the heading of expenses."

Kasey went back to the booth to find Sherry gone. Her cigarettes and lighter were on the table. The waitress informed Kasey that her friend was in the ladies' room.

The champagne was gone, the bottle upended in the bucket of melting ice. She dropped several bills on the table for the waitress, picked up Sherry's cigarettes and lighter, and went to the bar to wait.

She ordered a plain tonic and lime and laid several singles and change on the bar. The bartender served her. He took the exact change. The money never made it into the register, but went directly into his pocket. She watched him work the bar. In a short time, his pocket had fattened considerably. He wasn't even trying to be discreet. Open stealing. A proprietor, even one not on the premises every night, would have figured out what was going on in no time. Any *sober* proprietor, that is.

She sipped her tonic, scanned the faces along the crowded bar. On the end stool, facing her, a man with a dark baseball cap stared at her. He looked familiar. Where had she seen him before? It was difficult to make him out in the dim, smoky room, and with that cap—

It was *him*.

Kasey quickly lowered her eyes. *What was he doing here? Was it just a coincidence or had he followed her from the club?*

By the way he was watching her, his gaze intense, she could tell it was no coincidence.

She and Jay hadn't spotted him coming or going through the club's employee station because he wasn't on duty today. Would he be there tomorrow? Who was he? How long had he been sitting there watching her?

She picked up her change along with Sherry's things and hurried to the rest room. She found Sherry at the vanity freshening her makeup.

Sherry had removed the loose tunic to reveal a black sheath dress underneath. Black high heels replaced the sandals. She looked at Kasey in the mirror. "How'd he take it?"

"Who?"

"Tate, of course."

Kasey had forgotten all about Tate after seeing the man at the bar. "Oh. Not bad, considering. Not bad for a guy who's bombed and has just been told he's raping his own business. I only hope . . ." Kasey's thoughts returned to the man at the bar.

"Kase, what is it?"

While Sherry finished fixing her face, Kasey told her about the security guard at the club. "He's sitting out there now."

Sherry had risen. She tossed her bag over her shoulder and pulled on the door handle. "You want me to nuzzle up to him? Find out who he is?"

Kasey abruptly closed the door. "No, it's too dangerous. He might know we're together. Maybe not, though. He wasn't at the bar when I left the booth to talk with Tate, that much I know."

Kasey left the rest room first and, much to her relief, the man with the baseball cap was no longer at the bar.

Kasey and Sherry left the restaurant together and separated in the parking lot. Kasey, who was parked closer to the restaurant, waited inside her locked car until Sherry was safely inside her truck, which now leaned forlornly toward a wide, empty parking space. They drove out together, turning in opposite directions on Highway 395. Kasey headed for home. It had been a long day, and she wanted only to fall into bed and sleep. Sherry might also fall into bed, but not to sleep; her work day was just beginning.

Traffic on the highway just before midnight was light. As the miles slipped by, she periodically checked her mirrors, side and rearview. Would the man try to follow her? When she turned off the highway, two cars behind her made the turn. Kasey slowed. Within several minutes one of the cars pulled out and passed her. A pink Thunderbird. The other car dropped back.

Kasey's mind raced. There was little doubt in her mind that the car behind her was being driven by the man with the baseball cap, the security guard at the club. Her mother's ranch was less than a mile away. The last thing she wanted to do was lead this nut to her doorstep.

Without slowing further, Kasey whipped the wheel to the right in a turnout and, with tires squealing, gravel crunching and flying every which way, she executed a sharp U-turn. The

other car, a black Camaro with tinted windows, passed, then
did the same.

Stomping her foot down on the accelerator, Kasey sped back
the way she had come, the bright lights of the Camaro oblit-
erating her rearview mirror, blinding her.

She raced back to the highway, the stop sign looming ahead.
Without slowing, she laid on her horn and barreled across two
lanes of the four-lane highway. The Camaro stayed on her tail,
narrowly missing a van in the opposite lane. Amid squealing
tires and blaring horns, her Pathfinder fishtailed for a hundred
or so feet before straightening. Kasey floored it, intermittently
hitting the horn. For once in her life, she hoped a cop would
spot her and take pursuit. She headed for Sparks.

Once on the freeway, the Camaro quickly caught up. It
stayed on her rear bumper. It was doubtful she could lose it.
There was only one place to go.

Minutes later, when she changed lanes to exit the freeway,
the Camaro zoomed along the right side of her car, refusing
to yield, forcing her to stay in the middle lane. When she sped
up or slowed, the Camaro kept pace. Ahead of her, Kasey saw
the twelve-story King's Club. She missed the Nugget Avenue
exit. Again she sped up, racing for the next off-ramp, hoping
for a chance to get into the far lane. Traffic thinned; and as
the miles passed, she realized they were the only cars on the
freeway on that particular stretch of road. If she didn't get off
within the next exit or two, she could find herself alone with
this madman on the secluded outskirts of town where anything
could happen.

As she neared the McCarran exit, Kasey slammed on her
brakes. The Camaro slowed, but not enough, and Kasey
whipped in behind it, stomped her foot on the gas, and quickly
passed on the right, the passenger wheels bumping along the
dirt shoulder. The Camaro was alongside in an instant, veering
in front of her Pathfinder in an attempt to run her off the road.

She took a chance. Turned the wheel sharply to the left. The
two cars made contact. By the muted thumping sound, she

guessed her front bumper had hit his rear wheel and, like two bumper cars, they glanced off each other. Kasey cranked the wheel, narrowly missing the veed divider barrier, and raced down the ramp. From the corner of her eye, she saw the Camaro brake, then go into a spin. When she pulled back onto the freeway, now heading west, she caught a glimpse of the Camaro's taillights descending the off-ramp.

Minutes later, her knees shaking so badly she had difficulty braking, Kasey pulled into the valet entrance of King's Club. Under the brightly lit portico where cars, limos, and tour buses moved steadily along its three lanes, she instantly felt a measure of security. There were fewer places safer than the valet parking of a large casino. She could exit her car at the main entrance, amid groups of people, waiting attendants, and surveillance cameras, knowing that trained security personnel were nearby.

A valet attendant opened her door. Kasey scanned the cars around her, looking for the Camaro. She spotted it idling at the curb on the street parallel to the hotel. Dark tinted windows concealed its driver.

She hurried inside, stopped at the valet desk, and identified herself as hotel management. "Get security on the phone. Quick."

The girl dialed, handed Kasey the receiver. Officer Dobbs came on the line. After identifying herself again, she told Dobbs about being followed and nearly run off the road by the black Camaro. She told him it was idling at the entrance to the club. He said he would send a unit to check on it and get back to her. The moment she hung up, the Camaro pulled away.

Dobbs called back five minutes later. No sign of a black Camaro, he told her. She asked if he knew of any security officers who drove a black Chevy Camaro with tinted windows. The answer was no. "Would you like to make a report to the police, miss?" Dobbs asked.

She considered a moment, then decided against it. She had

no proof, no witnesses. It was her word against his—against a black Camaro, actually. After all, she hadn't seen the person behind the wheel, hadn't caught so much as a glimpse through the tinted windows. Having him picked up would only show her hand, and she wasn't ready for that yet. She would talk to Jay first.

"No. No police. But tell security keep their eyes open for the car. If they see it, have them report to Mr. King immediately."

Kasey hung up. Uncertain what to do now, she leaned on the desk and looked around. Before her wild ride through town and country, she'd been tired, exhausted; all she had wanted to do was crawl into bed and sleep. She was still exhausted, but now she was keyed up, as revved as her engine on the highway. She needed time to think, to plan her next move. She couldn't go home now. Not until she knew she wouldn't be followed. She could wait awhile and take a chance the man had given up and gone away, or she could spend the night at the hotel.

While she made up her mind, she decided to go upstairs, let herself into the monitor room adjoining Jay's office, and, in the peaceful solitude, think.

The Monk used a lobby elevator. In civilian clothes, he could go about the hotel like any other guest. No one was likely to stop or interfere with him. The cap offered a measure of anonymity. The elevator stopped at the top floor. Before exiting, he glanced up at the surveillance camera in the elevator lobby, saw it was directed at the two elevators across the way, slowly panning toward him. He moved quickly to the corridor, out of the camera's limited range.

He had come up to check security on this floor. He needed to know firsthand what he was up against. The executive suite took up an entire end of the southwest wing. The Monk stared down the long corridor to Room 1214-15 where King and his wife were holed up—both of them no doubt feeling safer, more secure, barricaded behind those thick double doors.

Aside from the elevator camera, there were none in the corridor. And no guards posted at the door to the suite.

He grinned. Good. Good. A guard would only complicate things. Although there wasn't a door in the entire place he couldn't open and there wasn't an employee he couldn't bribe or coerce, he preferred to not have to reach too deep into his bag of tricks just yet.

King's Club, for all its rooms, departments, and closed-circuited surveillance, was as good as his.

But there was no rush. He was enjoying this little game. It was actually going better than he had ever thought it would. He was in no hurry to kill them. Once done, he'd have to leave, change his identity and disappear. He was being paid well for this. Had carte blanche. No reason in hell not to have a good time. He would milk it for all it was worth.

The episode tonight with Kasey Atwood should leave no doubt in her mind that he, a security guard at her client's hotel, was up to no good.

The Monk smiled. The little lambs, skillfully herded by him, their shepherd, were flocked together under one roof. And if they had any sense, they would be more than a little anxious. The Atwood woman in particular. Because she was going to be the first to go.

The Monk returned to the elevator lobby. He pushed the *down* button, keeping his back to the rotating camera. While he waited, he shot a quick blast of nasal spray into each nostril. He sniffed. The doors opened. He stepped inside and pressed LOBBY.

"Hold the elevator!"

The Monk instinctively gripped the rubber-edged door as a man in a warmup suit rushed in.

"Thanks," the man said.

The Monk realized too late that the man was Jay King. He lowered his head, the bill of the baseball cap masking the upper part of his face, and moved to the back of the car. He wasn't ready to be recognized yet. He wanted King to wonder a bit longer just who was after him. Because once he discovered the *who*, the *why* would become crystal clear.

King held a cellular phone. Nice touch. He and the wife were only seven digits away from each other.

King pressed four—the floor with the swimming pool.

The Monk spotted a rolled-up towel tucked under King's arm. A nightly ritual. A couple of times in the past months while on his security rounds, he had come across the hotel owner in the pool late at night. Of course he had promptly retreated without being seen. It was rumored King swam at least fifty laps whenever he stayed over. Sometimes, on a sleepless night, he would get in more than one set of laps. The pool opened at 9:00 in the morning and closed at 10:00 each night. King then had it all to himself. No lifeguards. No attendants. Nobody.

From now until the Monk decided to put an end to the game, J. G. King would have many sleepless nights.

Kasey let herself into the monitor room from the main corridor. She had no sooner closed the door behind her when she heard someone in the adjacent office. Jay's office.

Assuming it was Jay and eager to tell him about her wild drive through the city with the black Camaro on her tail, she opened the inner door and strode in without knocking.

The room was dim; the only lights glowing were behind the bar. And at the built-in bar, riffling through the open safe, stood Brad King.

When he saw her, he quickly dropped the papers in his hand.

"Kasey . . ."

"Brad?" She looked around the otherwise-vacant office. "What are you doing in here?"

"I might ask you the same question." His tone was harsh,

accusing. "Do you always just barge into private offices without knocking?"

"Well, no . . . I . . ." He had her on the defensive. She didn't like being on the defensive. She wasn't the one rummaging through Jay's safe late at night in the dark.

"Yes?" he said.

"I was in the monitor room and I heard something. I thought you were Jay."

He shut the safe, pulled the panel closed, then walked up to her. He smiled his charming, boyish smile. "I was just putting some papers away."

To Kasey it didn't look like he was putting anything away. It looked more like he was trying to find something.

Brad moved in close, forcing her against the back of the bar with his body. He reached up and took a bottle from the shelf. She stepped to the side. Brad uncapped the cognac bottle and poured two glasses. He handed her one.

She shook her head. "It's late."

"What are you doing here, Kasey?"

Under normal circumstances she would have told him about seeing the security guard at the bar and what had followed. But finding him in Jay's office this way made her reluctant to share. He was lying. If he were lying about what he was doing here, what else would he lie about?

"I had an appointment in town and it ended early. Thought I'd watch the monitors for a while and then head home."

"You didn't get enough earlier tonight?"

"It's addictive. Like a video game."

"Want some company?" He moved in closer, so close she could smell his light cologne and the lemony scent of his freshly laundered shirt.

She shook her head again. "I'd kind of like to be alone for a while. You know, to think, to sort things out."

"Think about what? Sort out what?"

When she didn't answer, he shrugged.

"Okay. I'll leave you to your own private demons." For once, he seemed relieved by her rejection.

He downed the cognac, squeezed her upper arm, moved around her, and left the room without a backward glance.

Twenty-four

Twenty-four

Jay pulled himself through the water effortlessly. He was on the final laps, face down, stroking by rote, no longer conscious of the water which smelled strongly of chlorine or the burning pain in the muscles of his abdomen and shoulders. At this point he allowed his mind to wander, to free-associate, to bring this nightly ritual to a gratifying and grateful end.

He thought of Dianne in the suite upstairs. Behind a locked, bolted, and chained door she waited up for him. In the event she fell asleep, he had brought along the cellular phone. He would call when he was about to return to their room.

Suddenly he felt a tightness in his gut that had nothing to do with swimming. Lately, time in Dianne's company was becoming less pleasant and more combative. They seemed to have nothing in common anymore.

Had they ever? he wondered.

Dinner that evening had been ordered in and somber. They had sat at the elegant dining table amid flickering candlelight, looking through a wall of glass at a breathtaking view of city lights and mountain vistas. Dianne seemed testy, snapping at the room service captain, picking at her food, and complaining about everything. Afterward she had sat in the wading pool-sized jacuzzi, offering little by way of conversation. Jay was familiar with the pouting Dianne. He'd been exposed to it enough over the years and more so lately. He supposed she was upset because he had chosen to work with

Kasey in the monitor room instead of staying with her in the suite.

He felt a tinge of guilt again. If Kasey hadn't had an appointment elsewhere, he might very well have missed dinner entirely, so caught up was he in this thing with the hotel.

His thoughts turned to Kasey Atwood: Kasey, whom he'd spent more time with in the past week then his own wife. When Dianne had suggested he hire her, Jay had been dubious, only going along to humor her. He had not intended to take his wife's friend or her consultation service seriously. Yet, day by day, he was learning to trust, respect, and rely on Kasey's expertise. Jay was impressed by her astute reasoning and her quickness. And to complicate it all, not only was she bright, she was also very attractive. A dangerous combination.

He found himself comparing the two women. Both were lovely—one like a crystal prism, the other like a neon sign—each reflecting light and color, and that's where the comparison ended. Like night and day, they were. Dianne was as intelligent as Kasey, but she no longer had the drive to improve her mind, to advance her skills or knowledge. She had no special interests other than snow skiing and tennis. No hobbies. It seemed all she cared to do lately was shop, travel, and play. Things he had no desire to do until his aspirations—aspirations once meaningful to his father and brother—had been realized. The death of his brother had intensified his goal. He and Brad were the last. He wanted Brad to carry on the family name with a first-class establishment that would be everything his father had envisioned. By this time next year, the tower and a good part of the renovation would be completed. Then, and only then, could he begin to think about travel and good times.

Jay finished with a backstroke across the length of the pool and climbed out. In the eerie aquamarine glow from the pool, ripples of light dancing along the wall and ceiling, he toweled off and, skin still damp, pulled on his sweatsuit.

The clock on the wall said 1:20.

He glanced longingly at the two jacuzzis. He usually finished with at least fifteen minutes in the hot tub, but tonight he would have to settle for the small one in the suite. Dianne was waiting.

Dianne, the night owl. She stayed awake watching movie after movie, sometimes into the wee hours of the morning. The only nights she succumbed early to sleep were after they had made love.

When was the last time they had made love? *Love?* Was what they did an act of love or was it merely sex? Sex for Dianne had to be intense, fierce, with a passion bordering on savage. Sometimes Jay thought of it as hand-to-hand combat. A battle of groping, thrusting, stabbing, of being impaled and even consumed, where in the end the victor cries out triumphantly before shoving the vanquished away. Afterward, when they lay exhausted, their bodies still slick with sweat, their breathing still labored, Dianne quickly sank into a catatonic slumber while he was left with battle wounds and empty, yearning arms.

In the elevator, he punched 3 instead of 12. He wanted to pick up some files from his office to read later in the suite.

Instead of going through the executive offices, he let himself into the monitor room from the corridor. Three glowing screens provided enough light for Jay to see someone curled up on one end of the short leather sofa, her head propped on the armrest.

He closed the door softly. He stepped in close and gazed upon a sleeping Kasey Atwood.

She's beautiful, he thought. Her facial features in repose seemed even more gentle and fragile, her slightly parted lips soft and full. A strand of silky hair crossed her cheek. He wanted to lift it, tuck it behind her ear as he'd watched her do dozens of times. He wanted to lean down and kiss those soft, full lips, wake her with a kiss like in the fairy tale.

Instead, he stood above her, content for now just to watch her sleep.

Even before Kasey opened her eyes she knew she was not at home in her own bed. Her neck felt stiff, one arm was asleep. She awoke to pale luminous light, no sound, and the feeling that she was not alone, that she was being watched.

Jay King, standing above her, his wet hair combed straight back, gazed at her with a slightly puzzled expression.

"Hi," he said.

"Hi." She sat up, rubbed her neck. "What time is it?"

"After one. Are you on overtime?" he asked softly, in keeping with the quiet surroundings. "Or are you just overly dedicated to the job?"

"More like hiding out."

He stepped toward her. "Hiding out? What do you mean?"

She lifted her arm by the elbow, pins and needles now stabbing into the numbness. "Our security friend, I ran into him in a bar tonight. He followed me home. Well, almost home. I turned back and came here. But he stayed right on my tail. Tried to run me off the road, in fact."

"Jesus," he knelt, took her hand. "Are you all right?"

"Yes. I managed to ditch him at the McCarran exit. I came here, called security. They're looking for the car."

"You're sure it was him?"

"As—" She cleared her throat. "Could I have some water, please?" she asked, rubbing her eyes.

Jay squeezed her hand. He went into his office, returned with a glass of water, and handed it to her. When she spilled some trying to shift around on the sofa, Jay dabbed at it with his towel.

She drank half of it before speaking. "Thanks. I'm sorry, what did you ask me?"

"The security guard, you're sure it was him?"

"As sure as I can be. The lighting in the bar was dim, but

it looked like him. He was wearing one of those billed caps, but I recognized his eyes. He has very distinctive eyes. Slanted. Somewhat Mongolian."

"Why would he try to run you off the road? You think he knows you're suspicious of him?"

"He may be putting it together. I was with Brad when he went after Paula Volger in the parking garage." At the mention of Brad's name, Kasey recalled her encounter with him in Jay's office a short time ago. Should she tell Jay? No, she decided quickly, not just yet.

"And you saw him since?" Jay asked.

"Yesterday. He saw me talking to Paula in the downstairs bar. He may have seen Dianne and me together or maybe he was watching your house this afternoon when you and I and Det. Loweman showed up. He's not waiting for us to find him. He's meeting us halfway." She nodded. "Yes, damnit, *he knows.*"

"When you saw him in the bar yesterday, was he in uniform?"

"The man I saw was. Yes."

"What time was that?"

"Between five and six. I know what you're thinking, but it still doesn't narrow it down. The shifts overlap two hours."

Jay sighed heavily. He looked past her, frowned. "You say he was wearing a cap tonight. What color?"

"Black or deep blue. It was dark in the bar. His shirt was dark, too."

Jay whirled around and threw the rolled-up towel against the wall. "Shit! The sonofabitch was in the elevator with me. He was on my floor. I didn't get a good look at his face; he kept his head down. But I remember the black cap. I thought there was something weird about the way he was acting. Evasive. He was going down to the lobby, so I didn't dwell on it."

"When was this?"

"Less than an hour ago—*Dianne.*" Jay reached into the

pocket of his sweatsuit, pulled out a cellular phone, and began to punch buttons. He paced as he waited. "Pick up. . . . *Pick up, damnit.* Dianne, thank God! Are you all right? . . . Has anyone called or come to the door? . . . Okay, listen, I'm on my way up. Don't open the door to anyone, under any circumstances, do you understand? Especially if it's a security officer. . . . No, no, it's probably nothing. I'll be there in three, four minutes. Use the peephole, and don't open until you're certain it's me." He hung up and turned to Kasey. "The bastard. He's having a real good time."

Kasey pushed hair out of her eyes, shook her head. She rose from the sofa, crossed to the dimmer, and turned it. Light filled the room.

Jay strode to the door, paused. "What about you? What are your plans for tonight?"

"I haven't decided."

"I don't want you leaving the hotel. He may be waiting for you."

"Then I'll get a room. For now, I thought I might check the monitors, see if I can spot him."

Jay took her arm. "Forget that. It's late. You're coming with me," he said. "Our suite has two bedrooms. If this character is on to you, I can't have you wandering around the empty halls alone. After tonight, there'll be a room available for you at all times."

"Jay, I can take care of myself."

"I'm sure you can. Humor me."

On the way up to the top floor, Jay used the cellular to call security and surveillance. Several minutes later, Dianne cautiously opened the door to the suite. If she were surprised to see Kasey with her husband, she didn't show it.

"What's happened?" she questioned, stepping aside to let them in. "Is he here in the hotel?"

A thick layer of cigarette smoke floated in the air. The phone on the bar rang. Jay went to answer it. While he talked on the phone, Kasey filled Dianne in. She told her about spotting him in the bar, her race across town to the hotel, and finally about Jay being in the elevator with him.

"Who is he? Why does he want to hurt us? What have we done to him? Can't the police protect us?" Dianne asked with an irritated edge to her voice.

Jay put down the receiver and joined them. "That was the security shift supervisor. He's got men looking for him, watching the exits. They're also checking the lots for a black Camaro."

"Did you mention he might be a fellow officer?" Kasey asked.

He shook his head. "No. No telling who he's in contact with around here. We have to speed this up a bit, though. First thing in the morning, we'll go to the station and have a look through the police cards. We have at least six possibles. We need a name and address to go with a face."

"What if he's only posing as a security employee?" Kasey suggested.

"We'll find that out tomorrow."

There was a knock at the door.

"That's security." Jay kissed Dianne lightly on the temple and headed for the foyer. "Get Kasey settled for the night in the other bedroom. I'll be back soon."

"Where are you going?" Dianne asked.

"To the eye. The camera should have gotten him on tape in the elevator lobby."

"Jay, no."

"One man will patrol the floor and watch the elevator and stairway. The other will go with me. I doubt if this crackpot would be dumb enough to attack me in a public place with armed guards around. And if he does . . . then he does. I can't—*won't,* allow some punk to keep me holed up in one of my own suites."

"Wait," Kasey said before he reached the door. She went ahead of him into the foyer and peered through the fish-eye in the door. Two bare-headed, uniformed guards stared blankly into the lens. Neither man was the one they were looking for. She stepped back. "Okay."

"Lock up," Jay said, joining the guards in the corridor.

Twenty-five

In the dream, Kasey treaded water in the middle of the hotel swimming pool. It was dark. Icy-blue rays rolled in waves over the walls and ceiling. She smelled chlorine and mildew and a trace of familiar after-shave. All very mystical, as dreams go.

As her legs and feet scissored back and forth to keep her afloat, she felt yards of a soft substance, like fronds from underwater plants, gently stroking her bare skin. She looked down and was surprised to see herself fully clothed. Surprised because she had expected to be nude; had always wanted to swim in the nude; and, after all, this was her dream.

Wrapped around her, like intricate petals on a rose, was a long, white gossamer gown; her flesh was clearly visible under its many sheer layers. With each scissor motion, the panels twisted and clung, beginning to impede her movement.

Unafraid, she slipped beneath the surface.

Deep beneath the warm silky water, with a profound sense of awe, she observed her chest rising and falling, aware that she breathed as naturally as any sea creature. Lithe as a ballet dancer, she pirouetted again and again, her hair caressing her face, the layers of cloth caressing her body. She had never felt more alive, more free, more attuned to her surroundings.

As she twirled underwater, the gown enfolded her like the wings of a newly emerging butterfly. Too late she realized she was caught in a cocoon of her own making. With her arms pinned to her sides, her legs bound tightly in yards of fabric, she slowly sank to the bottom of the pool. She struggled. No longer could she breathe. Within seconds, she felt a crushing weight on her chest, her heart and lungs in agony, about to burst. She was losing consciousness; the pool lights dimmed further. She willed herself to wake up, to put an end to the suffocation; but instead of waking, she felt strong arms take hold of her. Slowly, gently she was lifted to the surface.

She filled oxygen-starved lungs with cool air.

Safe now, nestled in masculine arms, she instinctively clung to him. Her eyes remained closed. She felt cool tiles beneath her, felt the binding cloth being peeled away layer by layer. Intuitively she knew her rescuer. Knew because it was her dream and she had willed him into it.

She opened her eyes and saw Jay, his hair dark and shiny with water—the way it had been when she had awakened to find him watching her sleep earlier that evening. Once again, she stared into those cool blue eyes—eyes filled with longing, desire.

Cradled along the length of him, she felt his heated nakedness against hers. His hand cupped her breast. He leaned forward and brushed his lips across hers, light and feathery. She arched her back and pressed her mouth firmly to his.

The warm mouth that covered hers seemed to breathe life back into her, more than life—passion and fire—an awakening. Every kiss, every caress, every touch of pleasure, she committed to memory. When she felt herself waking, she resisted with all her might. *No, please. This is all I'm going to get. What's the harm?*

Yet even as her eyes fluttered opened, the last of the dream fading, she knew the harm. She knew quite well the harm that a mere dream could have. Particularly a dream of this nature. She was attracted to Jay. And if that were all, she could probably handle it. But she sensed the attraction was not one-sided and Jay was married to a friend of hers. There was no way on earth to make it right. No way.

For the second time that night, she awoke in a strange room

filled with a certain man's presence. Only this time she was alone. Or was she? Like his after-shave, the essence of Jay King filled the air, penetrating her to the core.

Kasey rose at five. The suite was dark, quiet. For two hours she had lain awake acutely aware that the main character in her erotic dream slept only feet away, on the other side of a thin hotel wall. Coming face to face with Jay this morning would be more than she could stand.

Anxious to be gone before he awoke, she dressed quickly and quietly slipped out.

On the drive home she thought about Jay, the job, and what she was going to do about both of them.

This can't go on, she told herself. She was spending far too much time in his company. She counted the days they had worked together. Five. *Five?* Impossible. How could she feel this wretched in such a short time? Maybe it wasn't so short, she told herself. Hadn't she felt something the day of the wedding—the moment she'd walked into his study and had seen him standing there in his tuxedo, greeting her with a warm smile. But if she wanted to be truly honest with herself, she had to go back even farther than that, back to when she worked at the club, when Jay and Dianne were involved in their steamy, illicit affair. *Back when the shock and pain of Kevin's recent death drowned out all else—or so she had thought.*

What did it matter how long she had been attracted to him? That was then and this was now. She had a job to do. If she intended to do the job well, she couldn't continue to work with him, not alone like before. She would suggest they split up, each take a separate role in the investigation. Perhaps Brad should be brought in to act as a buffer.

Give up the job, a voice in the back of her head whispered. *No,* another voice countered, *it can be worked out.*

She shut out both voices and turned her attention to the road. Traffic at that time of the morning was light, especially heading south. In an hour, weekday commuters from the smaller towns of Minden, Gardnerville, Carson City, and the valleys in-between would have the northbound highway clogged.

She repeatedly checked in the rearview mirror. This time when she turned north off the highway onto Forrest Lane, no car turned behind her.

As she neared the ranch house, its green roof and dormer windows visible through the row of sycamores, it occurred to her for the first time that her mother might be worried about her. Out of respect and common courtesy—because parents of grown children worry, too—Kasey usually called her mother if she planned to be away all night. With everything else on her mind, she had forgotten.

As she pulled under the carport, she saw her mother standing at the kitchen window. The stern, anxious expression on her face suddenly grew slack with relief. When Kasey waved, Marianne turned away from the window without responding.

Kasey would patch things up with her later.

She went into her bungalow, checked her answering machine, showered, dressed, then crossed the yard to the main house.

Her mother was sitting at the table with Danny. Both were busy with paper. Danny's fingers worked bright sheets of construction paper into geometric shapes. Marianne was cutting out a stack of *proof of purchase* seals. Her mother was one of those consumers who actually mailed away for rebates, free samples, and coupon merchandise from the various manufacturers. Nothing was thrown away until Marianne had inspected it. If a member of the household threw so much as a candy wrapper in the trash with the seal intact, there was hell to pay. Every day the postman delivered something from one nationally advertised retailer or another and the mailbox was crammed with catalogs and leaflets—more paper for Danny.

"Morning, Ma. Morning, Danny." She patted Danny's shoulder and bent to greet her mother with a kiss on the cheek. "Where's Snickers?"

"They didn't have phones where you were last night?"

Straight from the hip. No pussyfootin' around.

Kasey straightened slowly, but before she could respond, Marianne took her hand, shook it, and said, "Oh, honey, don't pay any attention to me. It just popped out. You don't have to check in with me, for heaven's sake. You're a grown woman. It's just that, well, sometimes your job can be dangerous and . . . and—"

"It was late, Ma, I didn't want to wake you."

Marianne looked away, nodded, and smiled.

"No, Ma, you're right, I should have called. I'm sorry. I know you listen for my car. Even when you're asleep you still listen for it." She squeezed the rough, callused hand. "I worked late at the hotel. I fell asleep."

"But Sherry said . . ."

"What did I say?" Sherry asked, strolling into the kitchen. She looked spry, full of spunk for someone who kept late hours and loved champagne. It was doubtful she had been to bed yet. "Kasey, where'd you go last night? I thought you were heading home when we split? I was worried when your car wasn't here this morning."

"I changed my mind. There was something—"

"Ahhh, there's our little wanderer. Home safe and sound," George said, entering with a box of photographs. "I told your mother you could take care of yourself. She was worried sick about you. When Sherry said you were headed home around midnight—"

"Was everybody up waiting for me last night?" Kasey asked with mock sarcasm. "Where's Artie? Out scouring back alleys, checking hospitals? Danny? Were you up? Would you like to know where I was all night?"

"It keeps going and going," Danny said under his breath.

"And so does this conversation. How 'bout next time I get written permission?" Kasey said, picking fried potatoes out of a pan on the stove and popping them into her mouth. "I must lead a helluva dull life if everyone gets excited about my staying out once in a millennium."

"Kasey worked late at the hotel and she fell asleep. It could happen to anyone. Now, is everyone satisfied? Go about your business, leave the poor girl alone," Marianne said gruffly and lightly slapped Kasey's hand when she reached for more potatoes.

Each boarder went about his or her business, saying nothing more.

George began collecting all the photographs in the kitchen and laundry room, putting the green tabbed ones in a separate stack. "Has everyone had a chance to pick a favorite from this batch?"

"This batch? There's more?" Marianne asked.

"Oh, sure."

"How many more?"

"Hundreds and hundreds."

On the TV monitor in the boardroom, they stared at the black-and-white video. The camera panned from one set of closed elevator doors to another, four in all. As it returned to the first elevator, they saw the doors were wide open, yet the interior was empty. The doors slowly closed, and the camera continued to pan.

"He timed that one just right," Jay said to the four other people in the room: Brad, Kasey, Dianne, and Barney LeBarre, the head of security. Jay fast-forwarded the tape. The elevator doors, one after another, flashed by in fast succession, looking like a revolving scene in an old Hitchcock movie.

A dark figure entered the picture. Jay stopped, reversed the tape until the figure was again seen entering the frame.

"There he is," Jay said. "We're not going to get much more than that. It's obvious he knows about surveillance and cameras. We see what he wants us to. A man in dark clothes wear-

ing a baseball cap. It could be anyone. No way to tell how
tall he is or whether his hair is dark or light. With this grainy
quality, he could be any nationality. Can't tell for sure."

"Fingerprints?" LeBarre asked. "He wasn't wearing
gloves."

"Look at how he presses the button. With a knuckle. No
prints."

The camera moved on. When it returned to the number two
elevator, the area was empty and the doors were inches from
closing.

"Kasey, I know there's not a whole lot to go by, but can
you tell if that's the same guy who followed you last night?"
Jay asked, rewinding again.

"Sure looks like him. The cap and shirt look right, and—
hold it! Go back." Kasey leaned forward. "What was he doing
just before the camera moved away from him?"

Jay played it back. They watched the man press the *down*
button, then reach into his pocket, pull something out, and put
it to his face. His head jerked back twice in rapid succession.

"There! What was that?" she asked.

"He popped something into his mouth," Brad said.

"No, not his mouth. His nose," Kasey said. "Nose spray."

"So we look for someone with a cold?" LeBarre said.

"Or allergies." This from Dianne.

"That could be half the people in Nevada. Everyone I know
is allergic to something around here, including me," Kasey
said. "Not many people use antihistamine in nose spray form,
though. Too addictive."

Jay rewound the tape until the capped figure was in view
again. He hit *pause,* freezing the frame.

For several moments no one spoke.

Finally, LeBarre cleared his throat and said, "What do you
want me to do, Jay? If this guy is the one causing you problems
and he's on security payroll, I'll find him. And when I do, he
won't work for anybody else in the state. Hell, he won't work,
period. I'll personally see to that."

Jay felt immense relief. Barney LeBarre seemed to be taking the news of a possible conspiracy, harassment, extortion, or whatever it was to heart. That morning when Jay had confided in him, LeBarre had appeared genuinely surprised and then outraged, expressing responsibility for the perpetrator and his actions. His eyes had flashed with anger. He stated that to have someone under his supervision jeopardize the welfare of the club was unforgivable and would not be tolerated.

The decision to confide in LeBarre had been a difficult one for Jay. He had no idea whom he could trust. Particularly since it was apparent that the bad guy, whoever he was, was well-connected in some way, moving about more freely than an average security officer. As head of security, LeBarre had access to every lock in the hotel and casino. But Jay had to trust someone and the man had a sterling record. Twenty years with the club, twelve of them in a supervisory position.

"Barney, when we find out who he is, I don't want you to do anything. I don't want him to know that we're on to him. Is that clear?"

"Geeze, Mr. King, I don't know. That could be bad, real bad . . . for the club, I mean. No telling what this flake can do if we don't cut him off at the knees."

"First we have to ID him. Then we need to catch him in the act. Someone killed a guest and a maid. Someone is making threats toward me and my family. It may be the guy in the video, and again it may not be." Jay pointed at the figure on the screen. "If he's an employee here, Sparks PD will have a police card and photo on file. Kasey should be able to spot him."

The meeting went on for a few more minutes and ended with Jay reminding everyone to keep what they knew to themselves. "There's a dangerous man running around the club, so watch yourselves. Dianne, Brad, Kasey, don't go anywhere alone, and be on the lookout for anything out of the ordinary."

Everyone stood.

"Uncle Jay, can I have a word with you? In private?" Brad asked.

After everyone filed out, Jay turned to his nephew. "What is it, Brad?"

"I'd like to know what's going on here. Why am I being left out of everything? You hired Kasey to work with me; now it's just the two of you. She gets the important stuff while I get the crap."

"Brad, I hired Kasey to look into some threats I'd gotten. If that wasn't made clear to you, then I'm sorry. Working with you was only a front."

"That may be, but it's no reason to shut me out. I have a vested interest in what happens here, don't I? The club could be mine someday. You told me so yourself. Is that true or were you just jerking me around?"

"No, Brad, I wasn't jerking you around. You and your sister inherited a sizable percentage from your father; and when you've been on board awhile and after you've been made a partner, that will entitle you to even more."

"But right now you have controlling interest. And if you die, Dianne gets it."

"I doubt your aunt will want to be saddled with the club. We both know how she feels about it. But if it comes to that she's not going to just hand it over to you. You'll have to buy her out."

"I intend to."

"Good. Nothing would please me more than to know the club will stay in the immediate family." Jay knew Brad needed an occasional dose of assurance. At present, the boy was not as responsible or conscientious as Jay would like him to be. But Brad was no different than Jay had been at his age. So how could he expect more from his nephew than he, himself, had been willing to give?

Maybe things were about to change. Wasn't Brad asking for more responsibility? More involvement in the club?

Or did the focus of his complaint concern not the club or his duties, but Kasey Atwood and the fact that Jay and not Brad was spending time with her? Jay suspected, by the way his nephew looked at Kasey, by the way he jockeyed to be near her, that the boy regarded her as more than a co-worker. Brad's next words served to confirm Jay's suspicion.

"You and Kasey have gotten pretty tight. Joined at the hip, practically. People are starting to talk."

"Who's talking?"

"Start with the top brass and go down."

Jay, about to hotly deny that anything was going on between them, abruptly changed his mind. He realized it didn't matter who was talking, if indeed anyone were. Brad was jealous. If Brad were jealous, then Dianne had to be wondering what was going on. Hadn't she, too, complained about being excluded? It was only a matter of time before she would begin to question her husband's relationship with her friend.

Jay felt a twinge of guilt. He was certain Kasey had no physical interest in him. But, God help him, he couldn't in all honesty say the same about his feelings toward her. He thought back to the night before, standing in the dim monitor room watching her sleep, thinking how delicate and vulnerable she looked when her guard was down. He had wanted to touch her, kiss her, but he had resisted. How much longer, though? he asked himself.

This morning when he had arisen, Kasey had already gone. And at the meeting she had been unusually quiet, refusing to meet his eyes. Was she aware of his feelings?

Jay buttoned his jacket. "Okay, Brad, you want in on it, you're in. Meet with Kasey this afternoon at four in the monitor room. She can fill you in on everything."

"Who's going with her to the police station?"

"She can go alone."

"You're backing off on this?"

"The two of you can handle it," he responded a bit brusquely. "I have a business to run and a wife to look after."

* * *

At police headquarters, Kasey sat in a large central room filled with file cabinets, microfiche machines, and computer equipment, looking through the photographs attached to a stack of police card applications. Within a short time, Kasey had three probables.

From a phone on the desk, she called Jay's private line at the club and wondered if he were in. After the meeting that morning, he had left word with his secretary that he would be out most of the day and that Kasey was to go to the station without him.

Was Jay avoiding her?

When he came on the line, she said, "Jay, it's Kasey."

"Yes, Kasey," he said evenly.

"I'm at the station. I have three possibles. The men in the photographs look enough alike to warrant confirmation. Should I call LeBarre?"

"Yes. I'm all tied up here. As soon as you know for sure which shift this character works, then that's the shift you'll take. No sense in the club monopolizing all your time. I'm sure you have other jobs, other engagements . . ."

"I'll be in at four. I'm fairly certain he's on swing." She waited through a long, uncomfortable pause. "Well, until then . . ."

"Kasey . . ."

"Yes?" she responded, almost too eager.

"There's a keycard waiting for you at the front desk. Stay at the hotel until we get this mess cleared up. You're too vulnerable coming and going late at night."

"We'll see." She was ill at ease in hotels, especially for more than a couple nights. Unless she felt imminent danger, she would continue to commute. "How's Dianne?"

"Antsy. She doesn't like being confined. This isn't going to be easy. Find this guy, Kasey. The quicker the better."

Kasey nodded absently and replaced the receiver without saying goodbye.

Sweat poured down his face, into his eyes, stinging. Pressure, from gnashing his teeth, built along his jawbone and shot daggers of pain upward into his temples. He struck out, his gloved fists pummeling, crushing. With hard, solid blows he punched, jabbed, punched again.

Oblivious to the others around him in the men's gym and equipment room on the fourth floor of the hotel, the Monk was in a world of his own. A familiar world of power, pain and, more often than not, payback. Today, instead of the long, heavy bag that dangled before him, his fists pounded into muscle and flesh, breaking the ribs and bruising the kidneys of his old nemesis Jay King. He launched his entire body into the assault, the impact from each blow more damaging than the preceding one, calculated blows meant to disable, to maim—to kill.

There was a time years ago when he was nowhere near as disciplined as now. A time when a combination of pain, the sight of his own blood, and the prospect of being bested were enough to shatter any and all rational thought. Twenty years ago when he was stationed at an Army base in Germany, a young soldier on the boxing team, undefeated and cocky, he had come close to killing an opponent, a big Swede with an iron jaw and a relentless left jab. At the close of the tenth round, bleeding from a broken nose and a cut across his brow, sensing he might lose his first bout, he went berserk. He had never been beat. Would *not* be beat. The mere thought of defeat infuriated him. Blinded with rage, his battered body had suddenly exploded with a burst of superhuman strength. It had taken five men to pull him from the bleeding, unconscious Swede tangled in the ropes.

It was possible Jay King, also on the boxing team, had sat in on that final match. But it would be another beating that would bring the two men together and seal the fate for the Monk's military and boxing career. Jay King had butted in where he shouldn't have and he would have to pay.

Now, twenty years later, it was payback time. He knew King hadn't forgotten him. Four years ago their paths had crossed again and, though the Monk's appearance had changed considerably in the past two decades, he was certain King had known who he was. It was a simple matter of putting it together now, of making the connection. How many enemies could a spoiled, rich kid have? A kid whose father had handed him an empire worth tens of millions on a silver platter?

The Monk thought of his own father, a motorcycle patrol cop with the Los Angeles Police Department. An image of red flashed before his eyes. He could never think of his old man without thinking about red boxing gloves—and pain. Pain was no stranger to him. He had lived with it every day of his childhood. Pain that had been inflicted not out of rage or anger, not indiscriminately or haphazardly, but with utter precision, under controlled circumstances until, in his late teens, he had managed to clear out for good.

The Monk punched the heavy bag and muttered, "It's for your own good." . . . *for your own good . . . make a man outta you . . . No son of mine is ever gonna back down from a fight . . .* The Monk envisioned the pair of red boxing gloves being flung into his face. . . . *Put 'em on. . . . Hurry up. . . . You're lucky, kid. My ol' man never gave me the comfort of gloves. . . . It was bare knuckles and sometimes the heel of his boot. . . . Hurry up. I ain't got all day. . . . It's for your own good. . . . Quit your crying, you little pussy. . . . C'mon, c'mon, take a swing. . . . Hurt me. . . . You know you wanna, so c'mon, try an' hurt me. . . .* Night after night before dinner, his father would toss him those fucking red boxing gloves and they'd go several rounds in the backyard, or the garage when the weather turned. He dreaded most the times when his father stayed out late drinking with his buddies on the force. On those nights, he was dragged from his bed half-asleep and knocked around senseless until ultimately he began to cry. The *weenie whining,* as his father called it, always got him extended time, while his mother—his weak, worthless mother—stood by, silently wringing her hands. Then later, in his teens, it was his stepmother who stood by in her tight jeans and low-cut tops watching—gleefully, no hand-wringing there—father and son duke it out. By then he was giving nearly as good as he got. Nearly as good, but not quite.

Because he was never allowed to lose or even be second best at anything for fear of his father's retaliation, he learned at an early age to lie, cheat, and bully his way through life.

The Monk punched the heavy bag, slick now from the sweat that flew from his face, and grunted with the effort. This was the way he wanted to take out the King, with his bare hands. But before he confronted his majesty, there were a few others who had to be taken care of first. There was no hurry. One thing he had learned over the years was patience. He savored the payback. Sometimes he waited years. Like with his stepmother.

His father's untimely death from an armed robber's bullet to the head had cheated the son of that particular payback. But getting even with Lillie, prick-teaser Lillie with her tight clothes, foul mouth, and subtle come-ons, had more than made up for it. It was a payback that lived on and on, kept on giving. As a matter of fact, he told himself, it was time for a visit with his dear stepmother. He had some time on Sunday. He'd jump a plane, be in LA in an hour and at the sanitorium before noon. They'd have the whole afternoon together. How he enjoyed those visits.

A flurry of punches sent the bag swaying, spinning. He grabbed the bag, hugged it to him for a moment as if it were a lover, then with an angry oath, flung it away from him. The swinging bag hit a portly man passing by.

"Hey, watch it, fella," the man said.

In two strides the Monk was upon him, his hand at his throat. He slammed him into the wall. Their eyes locked.

Frightened now, the man pressed his back to the wall, then raised his hands, palms out, in a sign of submission.

The Monk let go, moved back.

The man stood frozen, unable or unwilling to move.

"Hey, man, look, I'm sorry." The Monk leaned forward, straightened the towel around the man's neck. "Let me buy you a drink. My name's Tom. Tom Andrews. I work here in the club. Security. I was letting off a little stream just now and . . . well, I got carried away. Look, I'm really sorry."

The man backed up. "No problem. Everything's cool." He quickly disappeared through the door of the sauna.

The Monk grinned and headed for the showers.

Twenty-six

At four o'clock, Kasey stood in the third-floor hallway, used the key Jay had given her, and let herself into the monitor room. The room was dim, all six screens glowing. Instead of Jay, Brad turned to greet her. He sat before the screens, the light giving his dark hair pale-blue highlights.

"Hello, there," he said.

"Hi." She glanced at the closed door to Jay's office, exposing her thoughts.

"It's just you and me. Unk asked me to sit in for him."

"Will he be in at all tonight?" She tried to sound nonchalant.

"I doubt it. Why? You need to talk to him?"

"No," she said too quickly. "No. It's okay. I asked LeBarre to send up a couple of files. Have you seen them?"

"Yeah, they're right here." He pushed the folders toward her. "Andrews, Werner, and Cage. One's on grave, so he's out. The others work swing. We're down to two."

Kasey separated the two files. Lucas Cage. Thomas Andrews. Both had been hired on at the beginning of the season.

"Does Jay want to be notified when we spot him?"

"Yep. And I'm to see that he gets a nightly progress report."

"Is everything okay? I mean, I thought he wanted . . . well, to be . . ." she let her words die away.

"To be in on everything? Yeah, he does, only not so directly. We do the legwork and get back to him. I think he realized he doesn't have time to play detective. He said, and I quote, 'I have a business to run and a wife to look after.' "

It was obvious Jay was avoiding her. He had made it quite clear she was again working with Brad and that Brad, not she, would report directly to him.

Wasn't this what she wanted? Now she could concentrate on doing what she'd been hired to do. She should feel relief, a burdensome weight lifted. So why the sudden lack of enthusiasm for the job? Why did she feel empty, adrift?

She knew why, but damned if she'd allow herself to dwell on it.

"Let's get started then." She tossed her purse onto the sofa and sat at the table. "Remember the security guard in the garage who we thought was attacking the woman?"

"Was he? Attacking her? You talked to her afterwards, what did she say?"

"She clammed up about the whole thing. I think she would've talked before her friend was murdered, but not now. Now she seems terrified. She knows something. My guess is the man we're looking for got to her first. Possibly threatened her."

"So we're looking for the badass in the garage?"

She nodded. "He seems to be everywhere there's trouble. Can you remember what he looked like?"

"Sure. I'm good with faces."

"Okay." She pushed the files back to him. "Give me a little background on these two while I watch for them."

Brad began to read. "Cage, Lucas T., age 40. Single. Lives at number 6 Pioneer Trail," Brad said. "Caucasian. Six foot, hundred and ninety pounds. Last resided in Tahoe. He worked security at Caesar's and Harvey's."

"Citations?" She watched monitor number two, the one with its camera set up in the employee check-in desk. A stream of employees were coming and going, some already dressed for work and others in street clothes. She heard Brad shuffling papers.

"Nothing."

"What else?"

"That's it for Cage. The other one, Andrews, Thomas Andrews, is 41. Unmarried. He lives in an apartment on Greenbrae, right here in Sparks. Caucasian. Five-eleven, hundred and ninety. Previous employment . . ." Brad whistled. "The guy's got police-force background. Moved around a lot. Watts, Miami, Vegas. Big crime hot spots." Papers rustled. "Citations? Wow, this joker's got citations. Sexual harassment, insubordination, excessive force in removing D and D's from the property."

D and D stood for drunk and disorderly.

"Let me see that." Kasey took her eyes from the monitor to read the report on Andrews. Only two months on the job and he'd been cited four times. The harassment charges had been filed by a fellow employee. No doubt Paula Volger. Insubordination from a superior, and two customer complaints. She knew from past experience that complaints from drunk and disorderly customers held little or no credibility.

"There he is!" Brad said, pointing at the screen.

On monitor number four Kasey watched a man in street clothes check in at the desk. He looked about the right height and weight, and his thinning hair, nearly bald in front, was the right length. He certainly looked like the man she'd seen on the past three occasions; yet because of the high angle of the camera and the poor quality picture, she couldn't make a positive ID. Except for that time in the garage, the other meetings had been brief and in bad lighting.

"Are you sure, Brad? Remember, Cage and Andrews look enough alike to pass for the same man, at least on camera."

"I never forget a face. That's the asshole in the parking garage."

Kasey turned a knob. The lens zoomed in on the man's ID tag. Thomas Andrews.

"Well, the file fits the man. Abusive, lack of regard for authority, sexual harassment."

Brad dialed Jay. He put him on the speaker phone so Kasey could hear.

"Jay, I think we found our man."

"Good work. Is Kasey with you?"

"Yeah, she's right here." Brad glanced at her, then went on, "His name is Thomas Andrews. Swing security officer. He even has citations. What do you want us to do now?"

"Monitor him if you can. I'll have LeBarre put someone on him right away."

"Why don't we just bust him? 86 him?"

"I explained it at the meeting this morning. So far we can't prove that he's done anything wrong. At least nothing the police could bust him for. Besides, even if we were successful in keeping him off the premises, it doesn't mean he can't and won't cause trouble. It's best to keep him under surveillance and hope to catch him in the act."

"In the act of doing what?"

"Assault, robbery . . . . maybe attempted murder. We've had it all in the past week. Have Kasey brief you. I'll be in the suite the rest of the night if you need to reach me. I want you two to stay put. Don't do anything except monitor him. I don't want either of you to place yourself in jeopardy. Understand?"

"Sure," Brad said.

"Kasey, are you there?"

"Yes."

"Do I have your word?"

"I'm no hero, Jay. I'm a consultant, not a cop."

"Good. Don't hesitate to call if anything comes up. Anything at all. I'll relieve you when I know LeBarre has him under complete surveillance."

Kasey and Brad went back to the number two monitor. While they continued to watch the check-in desk hoping to spot the other officer—the one named Cage—Kasey filled Brad in.

After Brad's call, Jay dialed the eye and talked to LeBarre. The chief of security had no trouble locating Andrews on one of the monitors.

"Can you put someone on him, someone who can work around the clock if necessary? Someone who doesn't work here at the club?"

"Sure, no problem. I know a couple a unemployed officers. They dig free-lance and could use the bread. I have just the guy. Ex-boxer. If your man spots the tail and gets tough, Corky can take care of himself. I'll get right on it."

"Good. And Barney, if this Andrews gets anywhere near a member of my family, I want to know immediately."

"Right."

"Who's on the twelfth floor?"

"Hollise. He's staked out in the storage room by the ice machine. From the eye, I can see everyone who comes and goes on your floor. All I gotta do is get Hollise on the radio when someone gets off the elevator. To anyone walking toward your suite, he looks like the guy restocking the vending machines. There's no way this bastard's gonna get anywhere near your door."

Jay thanked him and hung up. The bastard might not get near his door, Jay told himself, but he bet he sure as hell would try.

Two hours later, when no one resembling Lucas Cage logged in at the employee desk, Kasey and Brad turned to the other four monitors. They kept two monitors fixed on the elevator lobbies—one on the main floor and the other on Jay and Dianne's floor. Brad took charge of these while Kasey, who was used to camera surveillance, switched from camera to camera throughout the hotel and casino.

Ensconced before the monitors, drinking cup after cup of coffee, picking at a meal ordered from room service, Kasey found herself inadvertently doing what came naturally—spotting.

On the number five camera located in slot section two, she noticed that a bald man playing slots near the exit was acting suspiciously. Instead of concentrating on the reels of his own machine, he seemed distracted, uptight, surreptitiously looking around the packed casino.

Kasey had Brad call down to the eye and have surveillance focus on the man and his immediate surroundings. The camera zoomed in. A large woman perched on a stool played the machine next to him, her brimming tub of dollar tokens sitting between his machine and hers. Less than a minute later, the bald man made his move. He grabbed the tub of tokens and ran for the nearest exit. Security, in contact by radio, managed to bar the door before he could slip through. An hour later, a team of professional purse snatchers again had her calling security. Theirs was a familiar subterfuge, used often in crowded casinos. While one thief distracted the player, his partner lifted her purse from the floor or between the machines and quickly made off with it. Although this pair had split up, both were apprehended before they could leave the premises.

In another slot machine area on the opposite end of the casino, Kasey spotted an old, stooped woman in a limp house-dress, a woman who looked like hundreds of elderly women who passed through the doors of the casino every day. It was the large canvas totebag and new tennis shoes that marked her as the silver-miner from the day before. The woman seemed more stooped than before, her movements slower. Must be past her bedtime, Kasey thought. But Kasey knew as well as the silver-miner that the later into the night it got the better the pickings. Gamblers got tired—some tipsy from one-too-many free drinks, others eager to move on to something else—their concentration and attention lowering considerably with each passing hour.

Kasey watched her for a while, marveling at the woman's adeptness and stamina, before moving on to the other monitors.

In the course of the evening, Kasey spotted Thomas Andrews several times conducting his various duties—chip runs to the pit, escorting bar and restaurant employees to storerooms, carding minors, or just patrolling the floor looking for drunks, rowdies, street beggars, and suspicious characters such as pickpockets and thieves. At one point, she witnessed Andrews escorting a drunken Indian off the premises. Kasey nudged Brad, and together they watched to see if he might use excessive force. But the stocky Paiute went out the door without further hassle and Andrews returned inside and was promptly swallowed up by the crowd.

Kasey chewed her lower lip, raked fingers through her hair. Something wasn't quite right about the whole thing. About Andrews. She had a distinct feeling they were watching the wrong man.

At the end of the swing shift, Kasey and Brad turned their attention back to the number two monitor. It was twelve-twenty when Thomas Andrews checked out.

While they waited for Jay to contact them, they turned away from the monitors, stretched stiff muscles, and rubbed burning, tired eyes.

Brad went into Jay's office and returned with two snifters of cognac. He handed one to Kasey, sat on the sofa, and pulled up a chair to prop his feet.

He twirled the glass, inhaled the liquor's bouquet, twirled the glass some more. He peered at Kasey, then lowered his gaze. "Are you good friends with my Auntie Di?"

"Used to be. We lost touch over the years," Kasey said. "Do I detect a note of disrespect for your aunt?"

"There's not much love lost between us, if that's what you mean. And it's not for lack of trying on my part. My mother died when I was a kid. Uncle Jay married Dianne when I was twelve. She was the only adult female in our family. I thought she'd, y'know, be kinda like a mom. I really missed having a mom. She straightened me out real quick. She's jealous of me and my sister. Has been all along."

Kasey sipped the cognac.

"Where'd you two meet?" he asked.

"Right here at the club, running cocktails."

"When?"

"About the time you were begging your father, in a voice that was still changing, to let you cruise around with your new driver's permit."

"You don't miss an opportunity to remind me that you're a lot older than I am, do you?"

"I would have phrased that somewhat differently," she replied with a slight smile.

"Does old age scare you?"

"No. But youth seems to bother you. Brad, there's nothing dishonorable about being in your early twenties. The years go by fast enough as it is. Enjoy each one."

"What were you like in your twenties?"

"Oh, I don't know. Serious, I guess. I was married, widowed, married again, and divorced in a very short span."

"How'd your husband die?"

"Train hit his car."

"Bummer. That must have been tough on you."

"Devastating. He was barely twenty-two. He was my best friend. I knew everything about him."

"And you were crazy in love."

"I loved him very much, yes."

"So why'd you get married again so soon?"

"I guess I thought it would help me forget. Help make the pain go away. It didn't."

"What happened to that marriage?"

"It didn't work." She grinned and added, "He was younger than me."

"No shit? How much younger?"

"It doesn't matter." She turned away, pretended to study one of the monitors.

"Did the second husband remind you of the first?"

"They couldn't have been more unalike. Kevin was kind, considerate, and loving. Marty—Martin Zane the Third—was, and still is, bad news. Always in trouble with the law, drugs, creditors. After the divorce I didn't want my name linked with his, so I took back my maiden name. Went from A to Z and back to A again."

Brad sipped the cognac. He seemed to reflect upon her words. Then, he said, "We don't have to date or go steady or anything. We could just sleep together."

Kasey couldn't help but laugh. Brad's approach was unlike anything she had encountered before. Coming from anyone else, the proposition would have seemed crude, tasteless. From this young man with his dimples and easy grin, it was amusing and, she had to admit, somewhat flattering.

"Shades of Mrs. Robinson?"

"Who? Who's Mrs. Robinson?"

"My point exactly." She faced him again. "Brad, don't you have a special girl? A good-looking guy like you with such a bright, promising future should have the women crawling all over him."

"I do. But none interest me."

"Why?"

"Too immature. They haven't done anything, haven't experienced life. Now you, you've been around. You have your own business. You know as much about surveillance and the backside of the gaming world as most general managers and CEOs."

"And that makes me exciting? The fact that I spend eight to twelve hours a day in dark rooms like this spying on people makes me seem special to you?"

"Well, yeah, sure. Women my age are either married, still in school, or working for minimum wage—ZZZZZZ. My last date was with a girl who flipped all-beef patties at McDonald's. That burger aroma was all over her, like perfume. Couldn't have been a better endorsement for the product. I was hungry all night for a Big Mac and fries."

The phone rang.

Brad snatched it up. "Brad King here. Sure, Jay. Hold it a sec." He switched to the speaker phone.

Jay's voice, soft, yet resonant, filled the small room. "Le-Barre's man followed Andrews home and he'll keep tabs on him throughout the night. I'd like you both to stay at the hotel tonight. No sense taking any chances. He may decide to come back."

"I have a date," Brad said.

"Here at the hotel?"

"No. Uptown."

"Cancel."

"But—"

"Kasey, can you stay?" Jay asked, cutting Brad off. When she hesitated, he added. "Keys are on my desk. Room 1246. I don't know what your preference is, or if you have a preference, but you'll also find a master key to the pool and gym. Everybody seems to be into the workout scene nowadays. You should find everything you'll need for the night in the room. If not, call room service, the front desk, or me. I'll be in the suite all night."

"I guess it's settled then," she said.

"Good."

"Will you need me tomorrow night?" she asked.

"Tomorrow night . . . and for as long as it takes. Consider, if you will, the hotel your temporary home. Sign for everything. Brad," Jay said, again addressing his nephew, "see that Kasey gets safely to her room."

"I'll do that."

" 'Night, you two. Be careful." The line went silent.

Brad hung up. "Buy you another?" he asked, pointing at her glass. "The night's young and my big plans have been shot all to hell."

"No thanks, Brad. I think I'll turn in." Kasey went into Jay's office and picked up the keycards. As she passed the bar with its concealed safe, she thought of Brad. She'd had several opportunities to tell Jay about Brad and the safe, but had decided to keep what she'd seen to herself, and she wondered if she were doing the right thing. Over the years Kasey had encoun-

tered all kinds. There were the innocent and the not-so-inno-
cent. Brad King, by his words and actions when caught in the
act, definitely fell into the second category.

Brad walked her to her room. He tried to kiss her at the
door and got a cheek when she saw it coming.

"I'm a patient man, Kasey. I don't give up easily."

"Young men have little patience."

"There you go again."

"Brad, it would never—"

"Never say never. Remember, it doesn't have to be a commitment. I'll settle for raw, unadulterated sex."

"You're easy to please."

"In more ways than you can imagine." Brad unlocked her
door. "I better have a look under the bed," he said, stepping
forward.

Kasey grabbed a handful of jacket and tugged, pulling him
back. "That's okay. I can check under my own bed."

"You make it hard for a guy to be a hero. How am I going
to prove myself to you if you don't give me the chance?"

"Prove yourself by showing me you're as patient as you
claim to be."

He sighed, looked into her eyes, one corner of his mouth
quirked up. He pressed the card into her palm, his hand holding onto hers. "I'm right down the hall if you need me. Room
1230. Sweet dreams."

He waited at the door until she was inside. Kasey heard him
whistle softly as he walked away.

After locking the deadbolt and engaging the safety chain,
she turned the TV on low and called her mother. Marianne
answered halfway through the first ring. Although her mother
insisted it wasn't necessary to check in, she seemed pleased
that she had.

Just as Jay had promised, the bathroom was stocked with
the basic sundries. On the bed she found a white terry bath-
robe, white nightshirt, a cotton two-piece workout suit, and a
pair of slip-on sandals—all items carried in the hotel giftshop,

the tags still attached. The hospitality bar and refrigerator were fully stocked as well. She was set for the night.

She undressed, got into the nightshirt, which reached mid-thigh, and lay down on the bed. The remote lay limp in her hand.

Staring at the TV screen reminded her of the row of monitors her eyes had been glued to all evening. A grainy, black-and-white image of Tom Andrews in his security uniform came to mind. Damnit, instinct told her something just wasn't right.

Twenty-seven

The next morning Kasey went home. After changing into a pair of shorts and a sleeveless top, she found her mother and George in the orchard, each on a ladder at respective trees, picking peaches. Danny sat on a blanket in the shade of the grape arbor, a box of cut-up magazine pages at his knee, his fingers carefully creasing and twisting the bright, slick paper into new creations.

She greeted them, grabbed a gunnysack from the pile on the ground and secured it under her belt. At the tree where her mother worked, Kasey climbed to the first elbow, straddled it, and began to pick the fruit within reach.

"It's gonna reach about a hundred today," her mother said. "It feels like it's there already. George and I have been out here since seven."

"What will you do with this batch?" Kasey asked her. Inside, the refrigerator and fruit bowls were filled with peaches. All the neighbors had been visited at least twice; and George, Sherry, Artie, and Kasey had made the rounds of friends and acquaintances.

"Jam. I've exhausted every other avenue. Yesterday when I took another lug to Janet Mendosa, she refused to answer the bell. She was inside; I saw her peeking out behind the blinds."

"Ma, why do you keep the orchard if you have no outlet for the product? It was different when you sold to the markets, but now . . ."

"Kasey, I will not cut down one, single, precious tree. Your grandmother and her mother before her tended this orchard and they found plenty of folks thrilled to get the fruit. Why, there's no fruit sweeter than ours. Lord knows those hard, wood-tasting things in the stores today can't hold a candle to the real thing. Picked ages ago. Never allowed to tree-ripen like these."

It was useless to argue. Her mother was like a whirlwind, always on the go, spinning this way and that. More important than finding an outlet for the hundreds of pounds of peaches, apples, grape jelly, sunflower seeds, and pinion nuts that ended up in the crowded cellar every year, it was her mother who needed an outlet for her excess energy.

"I was thinking that maybe next year we'd get a booth at that open-air marketplace in Sparks. It's too late this year." She paused before solemnly adding, "I hope it won't be too late next year."

Kasey knew she meant their financial problems and the possibility of losing the house.

"We won't lose the house, Ma, I promise you." If Kasey had to take a second job, she would.

They picked peaches in silence, each into her own thoughts.

"Oh, Kasey, someone's coming out to look at Artie's room today," Marianne said. "He called early this morning."

"Yeah? Male or female?"

"Male. Retired. Young, helpful fellas like Artie don't come along every day, so I take what I can get. I just hope this one's not looking for a nursemaid like that poor wretch, Mr. Houseman. Not only was I a caregiver to him for two years, I had to bury him when his time came."

"No other calls?"

"Calls, but no takers. Too far out of town for most. Mr. Flynn—Irish name, isn't it? Do you think he drinks? I mean heavy drinking?"

Kasey shrugged. "You'll have to ask him."

"They don't always tell the truth. They'll say whatever they think you want to hear. Oh, well, what's important is that we all get along." Marianne chuckled. "Remember that heavyset woman—now what was her name?—the one who walked in her sleep?"

"You mean the one who raided the kitchen every night?"

"She had a sleep disorder."

"What she had was an eating disorder and a good flashlight," Kasey said. "Ma, you're too gullible."

"I know. Look, if you can, hang around until this man comes, okay? You're such a good judge of character. It's so much easier to take them in than it is to get them out."

A good judge of character. True. Except where the men in her personal life were concerned.

She told her mother she would be staying at the club for a while, then packed a bag to take back with her. The rest of the day was spent helping around the house, orchard, garden, and bees. She worked hard, hoping to keep her mind off Jay and the club.

At three, an elderly man in a pale-green '49 Hudson pulled into the yard. Kasey and Marianne showed Mr. Flynn through the house, which he took an instant liking to. Before the tour was completed, Kasey had to leave. She blew her mother a kiss and promised to call her as soon as she arrived at the club.

Later that afternoon, the Monk made his call. He listened to the ringing; and on the seventh ring, someone finally picked up. The woman sounded breathless.

"Mrs. Atwood, please?"

"I'm Marianne Atwood," she said.

He introduced himself as Thomas Andrews. "I work at King's Club. I was told you had a room for let in your home. Is that correct?"

"Well, not exactly, Mr. Andrews. Just this afternoon someone was out to look at it. He seemed very interested."

"I see. Kasey . . . well, she made it sound so appealing. Just what I was looking for."

"My daughter told you about the room? You know Kasey?"

"Yes, ma'am. She indicated you were very careful, most selective, if you will, about whom you rented to. But if the room has already been taken . . ."

"May I ask how old you are, Mr. Andrews?"

"Forty-one. I'm healthy, have a strong back, and I'm good with my hands." He lifted his hand, made a fist, and jabbed at the air. "And I don't drink or smoke."

The Monk knew the silence on the line boded well for him.

Then, "If Kasey told—Mr. Andrews, if you'd like to see the room, I think it can be arranged. I can't promise anything, but . . ."

The Monk stood in the kitchen of the ranch house waiting impatiently for the Atwood woman to finish bullshitting with the old fart in the living room who had wanted her opinion on some out-of-date black-and-white pictures.

Thirty minutes earlier, the landlady, all smiles, had greeted him at the front door. Of course he had put on the charm—but not too much charm; he didn't want her to think he was too smooth or too slick—although, after only a couple minutes, he sensed this woman was about as gullible as they came.

She had taken him through the two-story house, rattling off all the house rules and regulations: No loud TV or music, no musical instruments, no booze, no smokes, no drugs, no handguns, no cooties, no nothing. Cons had more rights, he thought.

She had sent him into the kitchen with instructions to help himself to a cool one in the fridge while she helped the old guy. He was certain the "cool one" didn't mean a brew. As he poured ice water into a tumbler he looked out the window above the sink into the rear yard. That's when he spotted the young woman with the strawberry-blonde hair.

Something deep inside him stirred.

In the shade of an elm tree, she trimmed the hair of a young male in his late twenties. He sat on a piano stool. She swiveled him this way and that, snipping, singing, and blowing away sheared hair from the back of his neck. The boy-man seemed to like the attention; he smiled, rubbed his knees with the palms of his hands. But he acted strange—retarded.

The Monk instantly dismissed him and focused on her. Jimmy Sue. She looked just like Jimmy Sue, the only woman he had ever loved or wanted to marry. Sweet, innocent Jimmy Sue, who had given him his first dose. Seeing the pretty little thing in bare feet, her face scrubbed of makeup, her hair pulled up into a ponytail, brought back bittersweet memories of Jimmy Sue.

"A water man. Well, good for you," the landlady said, entering the room. "People just don't drink enough water these days. It's cola this and soda that. And the stuff they call purified water, don't you believe it. That water you're drinking comes from an artesian well we have right here on the property. Doesn't come purer."

"That's reason enough for any health-conscious person like myself to want to let a room in this fine house, Mrs. Atwood," he said with an admiring eye on the young woman in the yard.

Twenty-eight

The Monk, clutching his carry-on luggage, a gray nylon satchel, hailed a waiting cab at the curb of LAX. Once clear of the airport, the Sunday traffic was light. On the twenty-minute drive to the Rosemount Sanatorium, after silencing the cabby with a stony glare, he sat back to anticipate his long-overdue reunion with his stepmother, Lillie.

Repeatedly breaking into his thoughts was an image of the young woman with the strawberry-blonde hair he had seen at the Atwood house the day before. At first glance, he had felt something he hadn't felt in years and had been convinced he would never feel again. Feelings like that disturbed him. To feel was to lose control. It disrupted his life, made him lose sight of what was important. He wasn't looking for a relationship. Hell, no. But . . .

With the right woman . . . with the right woman . . .

He always said there were two kinds of women, the kind you married and the kind you didn't. That little woman, with her scrubbed face and her bib-overalls, singing as she worked, was the kind you married.

"We're here," the cabby said. "Hey, buddy, Rosemount."

The Monk shook his head hard to clear it. He exited the cab, paid the driver; then, standing on the cracked sidewalk on the quiet, tree-lined street, he took a moment to take in his surroundings. The Los Angeles sky was just as he remembered it, a multitude of muted colors, none of which were blue. The hospital looked the same, only older, more rundown. The spiky fronds of yucca and palms now overtook the walkway. His last visit had been three years ago.

The Monk checked in at the desk on the main floor. A moment later, a nurse he remembered from other visits appeared. Her greeting was somber.

"I didn't think you would make it," she said. "You said early afternoon."

"I live out of state now. It's not easy—commuting. I had some business in Nevada that took a little longer than I expected. I missed the first flight and had to catch a later one."

"I see." She cleared her throat. "I tried to reach you."

"Oh?"

"About your stepmother—"

"Is Lillie all right? When I spoke to you yesterday, you said she was doing fine."

"Well, she was. But when I informed her of your visit, she became quite agitated."

"Agitated?"

"Excited."

"Which is it?"

"Well, I can't be sure, since she isn't able to communicate. Either way, I'm not sure she's up to—"

"I came five hundred miles to see her. And I know she wants to see me. After all, I am family, the only family she has. Now, would you deprive the poor woman what little pleasure might come her way these days?"

The nurse shifted uncomfortably. Finally, she nodded curtly and said, "All right. But I don't want you to overdo it. Keep the visit short, and please don't say anything that might upset her. Remember, she's very frail."

"Of course."

"She's in her room. The blue wing." She turned to leave.

"Oh, nurse, it's such a nice day, may I take her outdoors?"

A smile touched her lips. "I think that would be all right. For a few minutes, anyway. Make sure the sun isn't too much for her. Call for an orderly. He'll settle her into a chair."

He nodded.

He needed no help. He would tend to dear, sweet Lillie himself.

The Monk followed the blue strip on the floor to the west wing. He took his time reaching his stepmother's room. He had made certain she knew he was coming. She had had all night to reflect upon it, and he wanted to prolong her anticipation—or should he say *apprehension?*

But then it was impossible to know what Lillie was thinking these days. She no longer shared anything with anyone. Not since that terrible night when she went from a heartless, teasing sexpot to a pathetic, mute quadriplegic.

Twenty-two years ago, less than a week after his father was shot and killed by a street punk, an intruder forcibly broke into their house and brutally beat her with a bat as she slept in her bed. There were no suspects, no arrests. Naturally he was questioned, then released after supplying a solid alibi for his whereabouts at the time of the crime.

If the Monk lived to be a hundred, he would never forget the feeling of power, of sheer ecstasy, wielding the bat that night had given him.

He reached her room and stood outside. Unable to stall any longer, he pushed open the door to his stepmother's room and entered. Three of the four beds in the room were unoccupied. The bed by the window held a small, twisted lump.

He moved across the room slowly, each step sounding on the brittle linoleum. She watched him advance, her eyes open wide, staring; her lips moved, yet no sound issued from them.

"Hello, Lillie. It's been awhile. You look lovely, as always. A little thinner, maybe. You're not dieting, are you? I know how much your figure means to you, how hard you always worked to keep it in shape. Tell me you're not dieting."

Her eyes darted back and forth.

"Good. You're just perfect, so let it be." He let the satchel drop from his shoulder. "I have a surprise for you. I know you're going to like it." He pulled the zipper an inch, then stopped when he heard a toilet flush behind the closed door of the bathroom.

A moment later, an elderly woman came out. She was wearing a large pair of men's pjs. The cuffs dragged on the floor, and her hands had disappeared into the end of the sleeves. She stared hard at him, but said nothing as she climbed into the bed across the room.

He turned back to Lillie. "On second thought, I'll save the surprise for later, when we're outside."

Lillie's lips moved faster.

He fetched a wheelchair from the corner. He pulled the bedding away from Lillie's emaciated body, then placed her in the wheelchair, using a pillow to prop her. He took a blanket from the bed and tucked it around her.

"Here we go," he said, pushing her from the room.

Moments later, they were on the hospital grounds, strolling down a path that gradually became swallowed by overgrown shrubs and bushes, into a copse of mature eucalyptus. The Monk found a secluded spot on a knoll beyond the trees, far from the hospital and prying eyes.

He parked the wheelchair facing west. The mid-afternoon sun, though filtered through layers of smog, was still bright enough to be uncomfortable, especially to the sensitive eyes of someone not accustomed to being outdoors.

Lillie blinked, lowered her lids, tried in vain to avert her face.

"Hope the sun isn't too bright for you?" he said, unzipping the satchel. "I need the light. This won't take long. We're gonna have fun."

She looked down at the satchel.

"Remember how you loved to make yourself up? The way you'd get all gussied up on the weekend." He took one item after another out of the satchel. He saw Lillie straining to see, a muscle in her jaw twitching spastically. "You've missed that, haven't you, Lillie? Missed the pretty colors, the nice smells, the tight clothes. Missed all that flesh hanging out there for everyone to see. Above all, you missed the attention."

He worked quickly. Time was running out. He didn't want to be interrupted before he had finished what he had come to do. Although he had never done anything like this before, he had no trouble with it. Perfection was not a criteria. A little eyeshadow, rouge, lipstick. Lillie jerked her head when he was applying the lipstick. It smeared across her chin. He left it there.

"You had a great body. And you liked to flaunt it. Yeah. Liked to give the kid a little thrill, didn't you? A quick flash here and there. Look, but don't touch."

He yanked her plain cotton gown off her shoulders and pulled it down low to expose a pale, bony chest with a hint of cleavage. He hiked the hem of the gown up above her knees. Her legs were flesh-padded bones, twisted to one side, the muscles shriveled and wooden-like.

"Almost done," he said, and pulled a brassy blond wig from the bag. He slipped it on her head, adjusting it with a tug here and there.

Standing back, he examined his handiwork. "Perfect. Lillie, you look like your old self. Who says you can't get it back?"

He reached into the bag again and brought out a Polaroid camera. "I was going to bring a mirror, but then I thought, hell no, a picture." He began to snap. "Pictures are forever."

Click. The camera whirred. "Remember the time you posed for Dad and he took all those Polaroids? They're all faded and brittle now. Time for a new set."

Click.

He shifted her around, posed her.

Click.

When he was finished, he removed the wig, washed her face with a packaged towelette, and adjusted her clothes. He took out his wallet and removed a picture from a plastic envelope. He turned her wheelchair until her back was to the sun. Once her eyes had become accustomed to the dimmer light, he showed her a picture of herself before the attack—a twenty-five-year-old in a string bikini.

She looked at it, looked away, her expression pained.

"Remember that one? The ol' man used to carry it around in his wallet, flashing it to all the guys at the precinct, bragging about the fox he'd married." He looked at the new Polaroids, then held them up for her to see. "What'd'ya suppose they'd think now?"

She squeezed her eyes shut. He pried them open. "Now, Lillie, I want you to look at these. I went to a lot of trouble, so you look."

After she had looked at the each photo, he dropped them in the bag, zipped it up, tossed it over his shoulder, covered her with the blanket, and began to push the wheelchair back the way they had come.

"Oh, by the way, I'm thinking of moving back to LA. That way I could visit more often. Would you like that?" he asked, squeezing her shoulder. "Only one problem. I'm running out of surprises for you. Shit, I'll have to think really hard to top this one."

Twenty-nine

Over the weekend, Kasey and Brad worked undercover. They alternated sitting at the monitors and making rounds through the club in the capacity of host. Whenever they were together, true to his word, Brad laid on the charm, refusing to give up.

Kasey, Brad, and half the plainclothes surveillance team monitored Thomas Andrews. There wasn't a second that someone didn't have him in sight, even in the men's room. The subject went about his duties without as much as a slight infraction—just as someone who suspected he was being watched would do, Kasey told herself.

Yet, in those few days a number of disturbing things happened, beginning gradually and escalating rapidly.

On Saturday, a dozen guests claiming confirmed reservations arrived to find no such reservations and a full hotel. There was no question the reservations had initially been made, some as long ago as three months. But according to the hotel computer, all had previously cancelled. Premium customers wore accommodated, while others had to be put up in other hotels or turned away.

On Sunday morning, the hotel computer went down, followed by the switchboard telephone lines. Two of the four elevators began acting up, repeatedly trapping guests between floors, once for as long as an hour. Guests reported receiving crank calls in the middle of the night. When a small fire broke out in a storage room on the second-floor Convention Center, hundreds of conventioneers had to be evacuated until the fire department gave the all-clear. The reaction of inconvenienced guests ranged from peevishness to outright anger. Many checked out amid curses, complaints, and even a threat or two of litigation.

Late morning, a hotel PBX operator received a call from an anonymous source that a bomb had been planted in the hotel casino. Jay was notified immediately. He in turn notified the local police. After police, fire officials, and hotel personnel combed the entire building and found nothing, the directive to evacuate was called off.

With one crisis after another, Jay had no choice but to bring the top executives into the picture. Because most of the problems concerned the hotel end of the business, Mark Epson was less surprised than Robert Yanick and Howard Cummings by the news of a saboteur. Epson and Yanick were gravely concerned and disturbed. Cummings received the news with little or no emotion, as though he had expected it.

All the while, Andrews remained under strict surveillance, both at the hotel and away. The man did nothing suspicious. If he were in some way responsible, he was either very shrewd or he had an accomplice.

Kasey learned that Paula Volger, the hotel maid and friend to Inez Ramos, had drawn her wages and terminated her job at the club the day after the killing. Det. Loweman had been unable to reach her by phone or at her apartment.

Throughout the weekend, Kasey caught glimpses on the monitor of Jay and Dianne in various places in the club—coming or going into one of the four restaurants, at poolside, entering the showroom, the lounge. There was no keeping Dianne sequestered. On Saturday evening, escorted by two surveillance men, Dianne dropped in on Brad and Kasey on the third floor. She sipped scotch, watched the monitors until she became bored, then left.

Kasey's only contact with Jay was by phone. Each night, he called the monitor room and asked for a report which she or Brad promptly supplied. There had been one chance encounter between them late Monday afternoon. At the twelfth-floor elevator, Jay, Dianne, and the surveillance men were exiting as Kasey was rushing to enter. Jay's hand overlapped hers when both grabbed the door to hold it open. The physical contact zapped Kasey with the force of an electrical shock. And for hours afterward, like an exposed nerve, she felt a throbbing, burning ache.

Thirty

Monday night, swing shift over, Kasey turned Brad away at her door as she had done each night since Friday. It had become a nightly routine for them—a nightcap in Jay's office, after which Brad escorted her to her room and tried to worm his way inside.

She tossed her keycard on the dresser, flipped on the TV, and attempted to mentally prepare herself for another night of insipid TV in an effort to obliterate any thoughts of Jay King. The past three nights she had lain awake for hours, listening to the soft footfalls in the hall, wondering if his were among those she heard. Did he pass her room without slowing, without a thought to her being inside? Or was he as acutely aware of her behind the closed door as she was aware of him behind the double doors at the end of the corridor? Had he felt the same charged energy through his hand that she'd felt when they touched at the elevator only hours ago?

The room was hot, stuffy. She turned the air conditioner to *high* before going into the bathroom to shower.

When she returned, the room was a little cooler, though still warm. She sat cross-legged on the bed and dialed her mother. Marianne answered before the second ring.

"Still up, huh, Ma?"

"Hi, honey. Just capping the last of the jam. You know how it is, once started there's no stopping till it's finished."

"Ma . . . my horoscope . . . What was it for today?"

"Why, Kasey Atwood, have you become a believer?"

"I wouldn't go that far. I'm not committed like you, but . . . well, what harm can it do to dabble, huh?"

"No harm. No harm at all. Have it right here." Newspaper rustled. "It says, 'Pay attention to your gut feelings; they are right on target.' "

"That's it?"

"The rest is romance stuff. I won't bother you with it."

"Read it."

The pause was long enough for Kasey to picture a look of motherly concern on her face. " 'You may feel as if you're treading water in your love life.' "

Gut feelings. Treading water. Kasey rubbed her eyes. She was suddenly very tired. "Good night, Ma. See you tomorrow."

The Monk, wearing a security uniform, exited the emergency stairway on the third floor and made a beeline to the executive offices. He used a master key to enter the monitor room from the outer hall.

After switching on the five monitors, he set to work selecting the areas he wanted to observe: swimming pool, the third floor where he now was, and the twelfth floor. If King or any of his cohorts left their rooms or if anyone got off the elevator on this floor, he wanted to be prepared.

Over the weekend he had gotten word—from a reliable source—that he and another guard were being monitored.

He smiled. Everything was progressing like clockwork.

Kasey awoke with a shiver. The hotel air conditioner made a loud whirring sound, louder than she was used to. And the room was now cold. Freezing cold.

After talking to her mother, Kasey had tried to fall asleep, had dozed lightly until the bone-chilling air had brought her wide awake.

She hurried across the room to the air conditioner, rubbing the raised flesh on her arms, and turned it down. Shivering, she rushed back to bed and bundled up in the thin covers in an effort to get warm.

The glowing digital clock read 1:40. She was wide awake and cold to the bone. At home, if she couldn't sleep, she'd try a long soak in the tub with a book and a glass of wine or brandy.

Wrapping the blanket around her, she was headed for the bathroom when she spotted the key to the hotel pool on the dresser top. The indoor pool had a jacuzzi. The warmth, plus the massaging action of the jets would relax her as no routine bath could. And she'd have it all to herself at this hour. The pool closed to the public at ten. Jay was the only one who used it after hours; but according to Dianne, he hadn't left the suite at night since she'd moved in.

She put on a black two-piece swimsuit under a black warmup suit, slipped on sandals, took a towel from the bathroom, grabbed the keys, and left.

As she approached the elevator, she was fully aware that this floor, above all others, was being videotaped by a surveillance team. Everyone coming and going was tracked. She avoided looking at the tinted ceiling dome with its rotating camera as she stepped into the elevator.

Their bodies were slick with sweat, their breathing raspy, harsh. She moaned loudly, uttered oaths and unintelligible words. She rode him hard, thrusting, twisting, her buttocks pounding down against his pelvis as she straddled him. Jay felt himself deep inside her, to the hilt, the soft tissue surely being battered in a way he could neither initiate nor carry out if he were in control. But he wasn't in control; Dianne was. Dianne, who didn't feel fulfilled unless there was a measure of pain, unless she could draw blood.

Stinging, burning, he felt the half-dozen places on his shoulders and back where her fingernails had ravaged the skin. Her long nails were buried into his hands as she clutched them, grinding them against her breasts, her moans turning to sharp, piercing cries.

He held back, waiting for her to reach orgasm first. At times it seemed as if she could stretch it out endlessly. Usually, in order to last, he had to think of other things: the new tower, the balance sheets, and so on; but tonight he was having trouble just keeping his libido charged. His mind wandered; and in that one unguarded moment, *she* was in his head.

Sweet, sensual images of Kasey Atwood. Kasey wrapped around him, under him, her long fingers caressing his back, her full, alluring lips tenderly kissing him, her moans soft. Everything about the act was slow, seductive, tender. He could see Kasey clearly now, could almost smell, taste, and feel her.

His climax was abrupt, explosive. Hers followed a split second later. He cried out, pulled her to him and clung tightly, sought her lips. She rebuked his kiss to bury her teeth into his shoulder. It was then, feeling the sharp pain, that he realized it was Dianne in his arms and not Kasey. Not Kasey.

Long moments later, when their beating hearts and breathing had become less labored, Dianne whispered in his ear, "Man, oh, man, now that was more like it, Mr. King. For a moment I thought you were going to fizzle out on me, but wow, you really got with it there at the end. That, dear lover, is the kind of enthusiasm I've missed lately."

Jay didn't comment. He was afraid that if he did he might tell her what had been on his mind for the longest time. That he was too old for this. That somewhere over the past several years he had grown tired of rough, raunchy sex, sex without tenderness. He didn't need gymnastics to be sexually satisfied, had never really needed it, but Dianne had been adamant. The times he tried to go slow, to make love and not engage in a battle of lust that teetered on the brink of violence, she appeared bored, had then taken over to the inevitable conclusion.

He had to admit that in the beginning he had been excited

by her sexual prowess, her insatiable appetite, her erotic imagination. Yet, he had assumed that with time they would settle into something a little more conventional. Tender, even.

Sometimes he wondered if it mattered *who* her sexual partner was as long as she was satisfied. Jay was certain she cheated on him. The signs were less than subtle. The wrong numbers when he answered the phone. Bruises on her breasts and inner thighs that he had not put there. A certain contentment at times, like a wild cat being stroked, purring, yet capable of attacking at the slightest provocation. In a way he blamed himself if she found their relationship wanting. Work for him came first. It had to if he expected to realize his dreams.

Dianne sighed with contentment and rolled off him, away from him. A moment later, she was fast asleep.

He envied her ability to just pass out afterward. This act, this sexual combat, did little to relax him. It always left him agitated, hyper.

Jay quietly slipped out of bed and dressed. From the living room phone he called Corky Saget, the man LeBarre had hired to follow Andrews. Saget reported that the subject's car was still in the carport and he had a very clear view of his apartment. In fact, Andrews had just come out on the deck with a woman.

"They're acting real cozy-like," Saget said. "He ain't going nowhere soon. I'll call if he does, Mr. King."

Their prime suspect, at least three miles away entertaining a lady on his deck, was accounted for. After several more calls to hotel security and surveillance, Jay felt confident enough to leave the suite. He would be gone an hour, maybe less, and the place was more than secure.

With great interest the Monk watched Jay King approach the elevator in his nightly pool attire, complete with towel and cellular phone. Not more than thirty minutes earlier, he had watched Kasey Atwood make the same trek.

King looked into the camera as he stepped into the number four elevator.

"Evening, Mr. King, sir," he said to the image on the monitor. "Hope you have a nice swim."

Time for the Monk to get on with the business at hand.

Thirty-one

The Monk had found his employee file in King's office. After shredding the contents and burying the folder at the back of the file cabinet, he left the monitor room; mission accomplished. Actually, he had gotten more than he bargained for. He had learned that both King and Atwood had left their quarters, which made what he had to do that much easier. The two would soon meet up in the pool. How very cozy.

Completely relaxed and nearly dozing, Kasey was submerged to her chin in the smaller of the two round jacuzzis, steam rising around her, when Jay entered at the far end of the pool area.

There was no doubt in her mind it was Jay King. Even in the darkness she recognized him—his profile in silhouette, the confident way he moved. He strode to the deep end of the pool, undressed down to skin, dove in, and began swimming.

Damn, she cursed to herself, he had decided to come after all. And to make matters worse, he swam in the nude. She had considered doing the same, but had chickened out, not knowing who had a master key and if they would choose this particular night to use it.

By his direct approach to the pool without as much as a glance her way, it was obvious he thought he was alone. The time to make her own presence known had passed. If she got out now, Jay would see her for sure. If she waited, there was a good chance he would finish his laps and leave without ever knowing she was there.

She pushed across to the other side of the jacuzzi. If her back were to the swimming pool, Jay was less likely to see her. For an indeterminable amount of time she listened to the steady, fluid sound of his body moving through the water.

While she waited, the jacuzzi jets, set on an automatic timer, shut down. The water around her began to settle. Without the cover of the foaming bubbles, she felt exposed. Her mind raced. How many laps? How long would it take? Would he decide to jacuzzi afterward? She knew on any other night he would, but things were different now. Dianne was probably waiting up for him. He'd do his laps and go. *Please, Jay . . . do your laps and get the hell outta here.*

The sounds of swimming ceased. Kasey drew her legs up until her chin rested on her knees, trying to make herself small, imperceptible. She closed her eyes and waited.

The jacuzzi suddenly erupted in bubbles again. Her eyes flew open.

"Kasey?" Jay said, stepping into the water. "Is that you, Kasey?"

She nodded and looked away, embarrassed. "I guess I should have coughed or something."

"Mind if I sit?"

She waved him down. "Sit, *please.*"

He eased down into the bubbles several yards away. "I can leave if my being here . . . ah, makes you uncomfortable. I thought I was alone."

"It's your pool. Your hotel." She rose to her feet. "If anyone leaves, it'll be me."

"It's big enough for the both of us. Stay. please," he said quietly. "I could use the company."

She slowly lowered herself back down.

He sighed deeply. "Oh, how I've missed this." He winced when his upper back touched the hot water. On his shoulder she saw a long scratch, then another, and what appeared to be a human bite.

Her stomach twisted. She felt her cheeks and chest grow warm from within. Jay had just left the arms of his wife. By the marks on him, it was apparent they'd had some very intense, physical sex. Which should have been no surprise to Kasey since Dianne had never been one to keep her sexual exploits with Jay to herself, describing every detail, boasting how their lovemaking went on for hours with no holds barred.

Jay rested his arms along the concrete lip, laid his head back, and closed his eyes. A jagged scar parted one wet eyebrow. "Couldn't sleep?" he asked.

"No."

"Me neither."

"Dianne doesn't like to jacuzzi?"

His eyes opened slightly. "She's fast asleep."

"Is someone with her?"

"Oh, don't worry; she's safe. I doubled-checked security. There are men all over the place. Saget has Andrews staked out at his apartment. No one's going to get near the suite without raising an alarm."

"Speaking of Andrews . . . you saw him on the monitor, does he look familiar?"

"There's something, yes. It could be as simple as seeing him around the club. I'll need a closer look. I get this feeling I knew him in the past, or someone who looked like him. Some background on the guy would help. School, college, service, something we might've had in common. I've got people working on it. So far nothing."

"Jay, what if it's not Andrews?"

Over one partially opened eye, an eyebrow went up.

"Well . . . I was—oh, forget it," she said. "I see phantoms where there are none."

"You think we're watching the wrong man?"

"I don't know how to explain it, but it just doesn't feel right. Andrews doesn't feel right."

"You've only been monitoring him for a couple of nights."

"I know. I wish I'd've gotten a better look at him the two times I came in contact with him. Brad is certain it's him. But Brad . . ." She let the words die. She couldn't say that she didn't trust Brad either, not since finding him in Jay's office safe the week before.

Jay lifted his head. "Brad, what?"

"Nothing. It's nothing. I was about to say that the only thing I know for sure is that the man who I think is the culprit drives a black Camaro and that he isn't a nice guy. The bit about his not being a nice guy is, however, strictly instinct."

"Trust your gut feelings," Jay said.

Pay attention to your gut feelings. Her horoscope.

Jay closed his eyes again. Kasey studied his face. In the dim interior, he looked drawn out, tired. So much had happened in the past few weeks. And until they learned who was responsible, there was no guarantee that things would improve anytime soon. Plans for the new tower, for the future of the club, hinged on stopping a saboteur, perhaps a killer, with a grudge against Jay.

Kasey changed the subject. "How many laps do you do?"

"It depends. At least fifty."

"You're very disciplined."

He lifted his head, looked at her. "Not as much as I should be. Most nights I want to skip the pool and just come straight in here."

"But you don't."

"No. Putting myself through the paces only makes this, my reward, that much sweeter. Discipline was something my father practiced faithfully, and he drilled it into my brother and me. He took nothing for granted. Hell, there is no gamble greater then the gaming business. Right? In the start-up years we never knew from day to day how it would go, if we could keep the doors open." Jay rubbed the scar above his eye. "The pressure never seemed to ease, not even after our club ranked right up there with the best. A run of bad luck in the pit, a couple big payoffs back to back and we could be right where we started, flat broke. Competition forces us to forever expand, renovate, take one risk after another. Hell, look around at the number of clubs that crumbled in the seventies and eighties."

She nodded, remembering George's photos of the bankrupt Mapes and Riverside, landmark hotels on prime riverfront property, each destined to fall under the wrecker's ball, or if lucky, to go out in a blaze of glory and fireworks in the tradition of the Dunes extravaganza of '93.

"Hey, I didn't mean to go off on a tangent." Jay sat up. "Do you swim? Work out?" he asked.

She shrugged. "Nothing as disciplined as you. Once or twice a week I assist a friend who teaches self-defense for women. And there's plenty to do at home. My mother has a small ranch south of town. Orchard, bees, garden. She also runs a boardinghouse. She's always getting in over her head in something. I help out when I can. Summers are invariably hectic."

"Your parents, they're divorced?"

"Yes, years ago. My father is semi-retired. He draws a little social security which he seems able to get by on. Unless, of course, the ponies turn on him."

"He's a horseplayer?"

She nodded.

"What does he do when he works?"

"Whatever he can find."

"If he needs a job, send him around. I can see that he gets work whenever he wants it."

Kasey nodded, looked away. She appreciated Jay's offer, but she would never impose on his generosity, particularly where her father was concerned. Dotus would surely take advantage. Not because he was bad or without conscience, but because he was weak.

Jay reached out and took Kasey's hand. He turned it over, exposing a wrinkled, water-logged palm.

"You've been in too long," he said.

She drew her hand away, feeling the same vibrations as before in the elevator. "Yes, I know."

Using the rail, she pulled herself to her feet, realizing just how much her over-long stay in the hot water had sapped her strength. She was conscious of his eyes moving over her body.

She turned, took one step up; but before she could take another, Jay's arms circled her waist, pulling her back down into the jacuzzi. Startled, she uttered a soft cry of surprise. His fingers lightly covered her mouth. "Don't make a sound," he whispered in her ear.

A shadow passed over them. Backlit from the lighted corridor, a man-shaped shadow stretched from the main glass door across the tiles to the center of the jacuzzi.

Together, they slid down until the tops of their heads were out of sight.

"Security?" she whispered back.

"I don't know. Either way, we don't want to be sitting ducks."

They were sitting ducks no matter who it was, Kasey thought. Anyone seeing them together, like this, was going to get the wrong impression. She, for one, would not want to explain this to Dianne.

"Jay . . ."

"Sssh."

The double glass doors rattled gently several times, as if someone tested them. The shadow was of a man; and from the bulge at the hip where the revolver was, Kasey surmised he was a security officer. Somehow that didn't make her feel any less nervous. She thought again of her horoscope: *Pay attention to your gut feelings. . . .*

The shadow drew back, disappeared.

"He's gone." Kasey was about to move away from Jay when the shadow returned. Jay's arm tightened around her.

Was the man at the door playing games with them? Did he know they were in the jacuzzi? Her pulse raced.

A faint sound of jangling keys. More shadows. The door

opening, the man-shadow growing shorter, though more dense, as it moved inside closer to the jacuzzi.

The jacuzzi shut down; the bubbles stopped, and the water began to clear. Kasey could make out their submerged bodies. Instinctively they pulled in tighter to each other, becoming as one. She held her breath, aware now that Jay's heart was beating as fast as hers.

Then, as suddenly as it had come, the shadow retreated. The door closed, and the shadow disappeared.

It seemed an eternity before either dared to stir. Jay made the first move. He leaned across Kasey to the pump, hit the button to reactivate the jacuzzi, and as he leaned back their eyes met and held. Something magnetic passed between them. Although for the past several minutes he had held her in his arms with nothing more than a film of water separating them, it was the contact of their eyes that seemed to irrevocably draw them together. In the shimmering light she saw within his blue eyes a blend of emotions—passion; anguish; and something more, something that made her shiver deep inside. And she knew, without a doubt, her own eyes mirrored his.

She focused on the scar across his eyebrow. He touched her lips, his fingertips lightly tracing the contours of her mouth. Her lips parted. His hand moved to her hair, his fingers weaving into the damp strands. She felt herself being gently pulled toward him, toward his parted lips. And she felt powerless to stop it.

He pulled back abruptly, released her, and turned away.

Like a hypnotic subject in a B-movie, Kasey snapped out of it with a start. Propelled by a vast array of emotions, she sprang from the jacuzzi, snatched up her clothes, wrapped the towel around her, and headed for the exit.

She heard a muted splash as Jay dove into the main pool behind her. The sounds of vigorous swimming followed her out the door.

* * *

The Monk took the stairs, climbing the nine floors with little effort, slipping through the door on the twelfth floor. His luck held. No one had thought to post a guard at the stairs. With cameras in the elevator lobbies only, his presence in the corridor went undetected. He paused at the door to Kasey Atwood's room. With his master key he could enter and wait inside for her to return. There was nothing he wanted more than to settle up with the hotel snoop. The fact that she worked for King, that King was probably screwing her behind his wife's back, suggested that King cared for her. And what King cared for, the Monk felt the urge to destroy.

Last week when he'd followed her from the bar, she'd thought she was pretty damn clever doubling back to town and outmaneuvering him on the freeway. There would be no getting away from him the next time. She was as good as dead.

There was no hurry. He knew where to find each and every one of them. And unless something unforeseen happened, time was on his side. In fact, after he finished down the hall, he might just pay her that visit.

He took a moment at the ice-and-vending machine to check it out. The door to a storage room was slightly ajar. He passed without incident.

He continued down the corridor to the door of the King suite and, feeling vulnerable standing out in the open, quickly inserted the keycard. If King's wife had deadbolted the door behind her husband, he was out of luck.

The green light glowed. He removed the card and turned the handle. The door eased open.

The Monk checked the empty corridor, then ducked inside and closed the door. He turned the bolt.

Thirty-two

Jay had completed five more vigorous laps, yet the strenuous exercise did little to stop his mind from racing. Instead of erasing thoughts of Kasey, the physical exertion only served to bring her to life—bigger than life. The sight of the dark stripes along the pool's bottom reminded him of the black bikini she wore, and the warm water was so much like the silky feel of her skin.

Exhausted, he left the pool area. Instead of returning to the suite, he went downstairs to his office. The thought of returning to bed with Dianne while Kasey was still on his mind seemed sacrilegious somehow. He needed time away from both women who, like twin scales braced across his shoulders, weighed heavily upon him.

Jay turned on the desk lamp, crossed to the safe, and opened it. He took out the envelope on the hotel stationery and slid out the newspaper clipping. This one was dated August 27, 1980, and showed a photograph of a large building engulfed in a cloud of smoke. The caption read, "Harvey's: Explosion cripples Lake Tahoe resort-hotel." Printed across the bottom was: *I'll bring you down—brick by brick if that's what it takes.*

Jay had received the clipping that morning and had not shown it to anyone, not even Kasey. Resort fires and bombs, the hotel-owner's greatest nightmare. He returned the envelope to the safe. He would have to tell Loweman, and soon.

At the built-in bar he splashed Wild Turkey into a rock glass, then entered the monitor room. The screens were blank. Jay switched on all five and absently stared at them as he sipped his whiskey.

With the exception of the employee check-in area, where a uniformed guard sat at a counter, the other four screens were devoid of people: three elevator lobbies and the swimming pool.

Jay frowned. He stepped back, studied the other screens. The main lobby and the twelfth-floor lobby and, lastly, the lobby on the third floor, the floor where he was now.

Odd. Why would Brad and Kasey monitor the third floor or the pool, especially after hours?

He called Brad's room and when his nephew answered, he asked, "Brad, were you and Kasey monitoring the pool or the third floor?"

"The pool? Not us. No reason to. Why?"

"Did you both leave together?"

"Sure, I walked her to her door like I do every night. Like you asked me to. What's going on?"

"I'll get back to you." Jay hung up and quickly dialed Saget's cellular phone. When the man answered, Jay said, "King here. Has he left his apartment?"

"No, Mr. King. He and his female friend are kickin' back on the deck. I can see them real good."

"They've been out there the entire time?"

"No, sir. Ducked inside for a while. Ten minutes, tops. Now they're back out, enjoying a smoke and a cool one."

"You're sure it's Andrews? You're sure he never left the apartment?"

"His Pontiac never left the carport."

"Pontiac? Andrews drives a Pontiac?"

"Yeah. An old blue one. Most of the paint's oxidized and faded—"

"Shit." Jay disconnected. He quickly dialed again.

* * *

Dianne King lay on her back, one arm above her head, the other across her stomach. The sheet covered her to the waist. Her blonde hair, still slightly damp at forehead and nape, stuck to her skin in wispy spikes. The bed smelled of sex.

The Monk stood at the side of the bed and watched the woman sleep. He shifted the knife to his left hand, the shiny steel glinting in the pale moonlight. King's wife was a sexy lady, one he could look at all night if he had the time. Which he didn't.

He leaned down and lightly stroked her left breast with the backs of his fingers. She smiled in her sleep, moaned.

His hand covered her breast, squeezed.

"Yes," she murmured, still asleep.

The bedside telephone rang.

She struggled awake; but before she could open her eyes, the Monk grabbed her arm and roughly rolled her over on her stomach. His knee bore down hard on her lower back as he pressed her face into the pillow. She fought, bucked, and thrashed, but was no match for his size and strength.

The phone rang twice more.

"Jay!" She cried out into the pillow.

He grabbed her by the hair and turned her head until it was facing away from him. He didn't want her to suffocate. Didn't want to end it too soon. He needed this beautiful wife of his number one enemy. She was an important player in the game.

"Jay?"

He bent down and whispered in her ear, "No, Mrs. King, not Jay. Jay's gone to his other woman, your friend. I watched them in the jacuzzi. Very cozy. It's all on tape if you'd like to see it."

The phone continued to ring. She lay very still, her eyes wide open.

The Monk gathered the sheet in his fist and savagely whipped it from her body, flinging it away from the bed. He shifted, easing his knee from her lower back, holding her down with an arm across her shoulders. He laid the flat of the knife's blade against the side of her face. Seeing the blade, she moaned and squeezed her eyes shut.

Using the tip of the knife, he lightly ran it across her neck, then over the smooth flesh of her back and buttocks. She shuddered.

"Do you know where your husband is?" Without waiting for an answer, he went on, "He's not in the suite. He left you alone. He shouldn't have done that. Your dear, devoted husband will have to take full responsibility for whatever happens to you tonight. He shouldn't have relied on others to protect such a fine piece of property." He felt her stiffen. "You resent that? Resent my referring to you as his property? You, Mrs. King, belong to him. And I can have anything that belongs to him, make no mistake. There is nothing he, you, or anyone can do about it. Do you understand?"

When she failed to respond, he pressed the cool blade against her skin.

"Understand?"

She nodded.

The phone stopped ringing. The silence seemed deafening. A moment later, it began again.

"How much time do you think we have?" He traced her spine with the blade's point. "Enough? The door is bolted. It will take a while to get it open. Shall we race against time or shall we wait until a time when we won't be interrupted? You decide, Mrs. King. Now or later?"

She whispered something.

"What? Did you say something?" He leaned down, placed his ear to her lips.

"Later."

"Later. Don't care to be rushed. Good. Good. I agree." He twisted around and snatched up the receiver in mid-ring. "Yes," he said evenly.

"Who is this? Where's my wife?"

"Good evening, Mr. King. Your wife is right here with me. You left her all alone. Shame on you. I hope you'll be able to live with yourself after such flagrant and gross negligence. Was the swim worth it? Was the hot tub worth it? Was your companion worth it? Wasn't your wife enough for one night? Because of you, Mr. Kingpin, she'll be forced to live with a reminder of this night for the rest of her days."

"Don't you touch her!"

The Monk carefully placed the receiver close to Dianne King's mouth. The Monk pressed the tip of the blade into her flesh where the lower back curved at her right buttock. The blade broke the skin. She gasped, made a mewling sound deep in her throat. He took his time making his mark.

When he had finished, he said, "I'll be back."

After letting himself out of the suite, he hurried down the hall to Kasey Atwood's room. He used the master to unlock the door. But the door refused to open. He cursed. She had to be inside already with the deadbolt engaged.

Down the corridor, a phone in the storage room adjacent to the ice machine began to ring. The Monk rushed to the stairway and entered. As the metal door closed with a hiss, he caught a glimpse of Jay King and a man in a tan uniform running full speed toward the suite.

Thirty-three

Kasey stepped out of the steamy bathroom. As she pulled the sash tight on her robe she heard footsteps in the corridor thundering past her room, men calling out. She quickly unlocked the door and looked out. At the end of the corridor, Jay and a man in a tan uniform were charging through the double door of his suite. Two security guards raced by, joining the others.

Kasey grabbed her room key and, in bare feet and robe, followed.

Inside the suite she followed the voices to the master bedroom where she found a chaotic, anger-filled scene. Dianne, stark naked, stood on the bed, erratically pacing back and forth while Jay tried to cover her with the sheet. Dianne screamed and cursed and swung at him, clawing the sheet away.

Jay turned to the three men standing uncertainly just beyond the door. "Wait in the other room." When he saw Kasey, he said, "Kasey, help me."

"Help *you!* What about me?" Dianne screamed. "Who was here to help me when I needed it?"

"Dianne—" Jay grabbed a wrist.

"He was here! Right here in this room. On the bed. His . . . his hands all over me." She cupped a breast with one hand and pounded her thigh with the other.

"Dianne, come down off the bed. We want to help. Let us help you." Jay reached for her again. "Are you hurt? Did he hurt you?"

She reached behind her. Her palm came away smeared with

blood. She dropped to her knees, and Kasey saw more blood on the back of her right thigh.

"Jesus," Jay groaned. He pulled her to him, wrapped his arms around her, and gently lifted her from the bed.

Kasey found a silk kimono at the foot of the bed and handed it to Jay. He released Dianne long enough to force her arms into the sleeves. Then he turned her around to have a look at the wound.

"I'm calling Dr. Hammond," Jay said.

"I want a drink," Dianne said harshly. "Goddamnit, somebody get me a drink!"

Kasey hurried from the bedroom to the wet bar in the living room. With shaky fingers she poured a hefty shot of scotch into a tumbler. The three security men stood in a clump by the white sectional and watched her. A cellular phone lying on the couch began to ring.

"Someone get that," Kasey said on her way back to the bedroom.

Dianne snatched the glass from her hand and downed the scotch in two gulps. She then marched to the bar, kimono flying out behind her, poured another shot, and drank it down.

The men shifted uneasily, looked down at their feet.

Jay joined Kasey in the doorway.

The guard who had answered the cellular phone said, "Mr. King, someone by the name of Saget is on the line. He says you and he got disconnected. Wants to know if there are any new instructions."

"Tell him to drop the stakeout. He's tailing the wrong man." Jay ran fingers through his thick hair. "Then call the police. Ask them to contact Det. Loweman."

Dianne whirled around, as though to protest; then perhaps thinking better of it, she marched back into the bedroom, pushing Kasey and Jay aside, spilling scotch.

"Andrews isn't our man?" Kasey asked.

Jay shook his head. "He never left his apartment tonight.

He drives an old faded Pontiac, not a black Camaro. Guess your gut feelings were right on."

"Cars! Gut feelings! Who cares? When is someone going to care about me?" Dianne said angrily. She strode to the mirrored closet, turned, lifted the hem of the kimono, and examined the bloody area at the top of her buttock.

From across the room, Kasey saw a cut in the shape of a crescent. Given the sparse amount of blood which was already clotting, the wound looked superficial.

"That bastard," Dianne said. "That fucking bastard. He branded me. It's bound to scar. I'm going to be scarred from this." She strode to the bed, tossed down the liquor, then threw the heavy glass at the large plate mirror, shattering it.

Jay went to her. He again tried to put his arms around her, but Dianne jerked away. "What happened, Dianne? How did he get in?"

"You tell me. You tell me why you went waltzing out of here in the middle of the night, leaving me all alone . . . alone and *unprotected*. Where the hell were you?"

"I couldn't sleep. I went for a swim. But before I left I double-checked security. I made certain—"

"Made certain of what? That I was in good hands?"

"I thought so, yes."

She turned on Kasey with fire in her eyes, "And where were you, my good friend? Enjoying a little dip, too?"

Kasey's eyes met Jay's. *How had Dianne known?*

As if reading her mind, Jay said to Kasey, "He was in the monitor room tonight. He was watching the pool."

"So it's true," Dianne said. "He said the two of you were together. Said it was all on tape."

"Nothing happened, Dianne, and the tape will prove it." But even as Kasey said the words she realized that the tape could be incriminating. Jay nude. The two of them huddled together at one point in the jacuzzi. And if that weren't enough, there was the intimate moment that had passed between them; Kasey was sure it spoke volumes. Although Jay had come to his senses and pulled away, Kasey had not. Even in the dimly lighted room, on a black-and-white tape, any fool would be able to see the magnetic attraction between them. And Dianne was no fool.

"Can we put that aside for now?" Jay requested curtly. "There'll be plenty of time for accusations and recriminations later. Right now, tell me what happened. Who was he? What did he say and do?"

Dianne didn't seem eager to drop the subject. "I want to know—"

One of the guards rapped lightly on the bedroom door frame, interrupting her. "Sir, Det. Loweman." He held out the cellular phone.

Jay took the phone. "Frank, sorry to bother you at home. Can you come right over? We've had some trouble." He glanced at the two women, then turned his back to them and said quietly, "The bastard who was at the house the other day—he got into the suite tonight. He assaulted Dianne. No, no, but Christ, he *cut* her."

As Jay spoke to the detective, Kasey felt Dianne's eyes on her. She turned, faced her, and in a hushed tone said, "Dianne, nothing happened. I swear. It's not what you think." Even as she spoke the words, Kasey felt a sense of guilt and betrayal. *It's worse than you think,* she said to herself. *I'm in love with your husband. Nothing happened because Jay didn't let it happen. Tonight, if he had wanted to make love to me, I wouldn't have tried to stop him. I would have welcomed it with every fiber of my being.*

"What I think, what I *know,* is that the two people I thought I could count on were nowhere around when I needed them."

It suddenly occurred to Kasey that Dianne's anger had little to do with Kasey's possible involvement with Jay. She was upset that she had been left alone.

"Dianne, I think you're being unfair to Jay. His being here may not have made a difference. We're not dealing with your typical criminal. This man is determined. He has a purpose.

He's playing with Jay. Playing with all of us. And he's not going to stop until he gets what he wants."

"He wants *me*."

"Is that what he said?"

"He said he'd be back. I believe him."

"Would you feel safer somewhere else?"

"What's safe? He's been in my house and now here. Where would I be safe? Kasey, that man is bad." Dianne grabbed Kasey's hand in both of hers and squeezed. Her eyes were filled with fear. "He's real bad. He got a kick out of cutting me, scaring me. God only knows what he would have done if Jay hadn't interrupted him. He's coming back. I know it."

"He won't get to you, Dianne. You have my word." She brushed back a strand of hair that had fallen across Dianne's eye. "Go splash some cool water on your face. It'll make you feel better."

Dianne went into the bathroom and closed the door.

"What's going on?" Brad asked from the doorway.

While the family doctor tended to Dianne, Jay called the chief of security with instructions to mount a security camera at the suite's entrance without delay. He ordered around-the-clock plainclothes surveillance officers to occupy the rooms adjoining the suite. They were to act as personal bodyguards to Dianne. Jay considered blocking off the entire floor for himself and his party, but that meant putting registered guests out on the street and into a town where all the hotels were booked to capacity.

Thirty minutes later, Frank Loweman arrived. After interviewing the surveillance man who had been staked out in the room adjacent to the ice machine, Loweman excused everyone but Kasey and the family.

"Nobody saw him," Loweman said. "Neither coming nor going."

Jay turned to Loweman. "You have the wrong man behind

bars for murder, Frank. The man who assaulted Dianne tonight is the one you want. The one who killed those women."

"Now we've been over this before, Jay. Even if I agree with you, the chief is convinced it's Ruiz. The punk has a damn impressive sheet. Drugs, theft, assault and battery, possession of stolen property. The D.A.'s office seems to think they have a pretty solid case," Loweman said. "But, look, I promised you I'd keep an open mind. Right? If we find any substantiating evidence to go along with what you're saying, I'll take it to the brass. Meanwhile, Ruiz is it."

"You're wasting time."

"Jay, if this guy tonight was a cold-blooded murderer, why didn't he just kill Dianne? Why stop at a little cut?"

"He has a game plan. It started with threats and harassment and it's escalating. He tried to run my chief of operations off the road and he followed Kasey late one night, chasing her across town and back. Two people got in the way and he killed them. They were dispensable. He feeds off the terror, the uncertainty. Like with Dianne tonight. When he's tired of playing, I have no doubt he'll make his final move."

Kasey shuddered inwardly. She was dispensable. Was she next? And what about Brad? Yes—what about Brad?

She looked over at Brad who, for a change, had hardly opened his mouth since coming into the room. With a bottle of mineral water in hand, he had taken a position at the far end of the room. What if the killer's target were not Jay, but Dianne? she wondered. Dianne and Howard Cummings? Both had claimed to be victims of violence, both had been threatened. And both had a vested interest in the club. It was rumored that Jay was about to offer Cummings a piece of the action. Which could explain Brad's animosity toward the club's CEO. And Dianne, of course, as Jay's wife, shared his percentage. With Dianne and Cummings out of the picture, Brad stood to one day inherit the controlling interest.

"Another threat came in the mail today. A bomb threat this time," Jay told Loweman.

"I want it and any others."

The doctor finished treating Dianne and left. Dianne, pale and drawn, reluctantly joined the others in the living room. She insisted on a drink before she would say a word. After tossing down another scotch, she told them what had happened.

Loweman asked, "Was he wearing gloves?"

"Yes."

"You didn't see him at all?"

"How many times do I have to say it? I was sound asleep when he grabbed me. It was dark. He had me on my stomach with my face turned away from him. I only saw his hand when he stuck the phone in my face."

"You have no idea who this man is?"

"No. Why should I? I don't hang out with thugs, and no one I know would accost me in my bedroom in the middle of the night to . . . to *carve* on me."

"Dianne, that's not what Frank meant," Jay said patiently.

"I know what he meant." Dianne thrust her empty glass at Kasey and said, "Get me another."

Before Kasey had a chance to refuse, Jay took the glass from Dianne and gently set it on the table.

"Did security run a check on the memory lock?" Loweman asked Jay.

"No, it'd be a waste of time. It's either a maid, guest, or master key which, in any case, would be unauthorized. We know he has access.

"He's shrewder than I thought," Jay added. "Shrewder than we are, anyway. He used the stairwell, which automatically locks from the inside. If he can get by the surveillance cameras and security, if he can get around this hotel undetected, he's either invisible or he's one helluva escape artist. We know he's clever, tonight he was also lucky. I left Dianne alone with the deadbolt disengaged. This wouldn't have happened if I'd stayed in."

"Here. Here," Dianne muttered as she struggled to her feet.

She snatched up her glass and advanced to the bar, her steps stiff, wobbly.

"Dianne . . ." Jay said.

She turned her back to him. As she poured the scotch, the bottle slipped from her trembling fingers and tipped over on the bar, spilling scotch over the black-lacquered surface. She watched it gurgle out and flow down onto the plush eggshell carpet. Suddenly, the tough exterior shattered. Dianne broke down and cried. Covering her face with her hands, she sank to the floor in a tight crouch and wept.

Jay went to her. He gently lifted her and carried her into the bedroom.

Kasey rose from the couch and, without a word to anyone, left the suite.

The Monk settled himself into the corner of the tiny, dark room. After fleeing the King suite, he had furtively made his way to the second floor, to the room off the now-unused cat-walk where he had hidden the bloody clothes after he'd killed the hotel maid. The clubhouse.

Security would be watching all the exits. He had a better chance of getting out of the hotel undetected if he laid low until morning.

His head hurt. Damn sinuses.

He reached into his shirt pocket for his nose spray. The pocket was empty. He patted the other side, then shifted around to reach into his pants pockets. The sprayer was gone. He had lost it somewhere.

His heart thumped rapidly. He crawled around the tiny room searching. Think. Think, he told himself. Where could it have fallen out? He had used it in the stairwell just before entering the floor of the King suite. It had to be somewhere between this room and the suite.

He crouched, his head in his hands, his fingers squeezing, trying to ease the building pressure behind his eyes. It was too risky to go out and look for it now. Forget it. Even if someone found it, he doubted if it could be tied to him. Any fingerprints would have been smudged or worn away by his leather gloves. It was over-the-counter shit, a popular brand used by scores of people. Forget it.

Thirty-four

Kasey had stripped the bed in Sherry's room, and she and her mother were making it up with bright floral sheets which smelled of sunshine and fresh air. It was Tuesday, the day Marianne Atwood cleaned the boardinghouse and changed the bedding in all the rooms.

Of all the boarders, Sherry was by far the least fastidious. Clothes hung from lamp shades, doorknobs, curtain and shower rods. Books, magazines, and notepads covered every flat surface of the room. The bathroom was cluttered with female paraphernalia. Female roomers, Marianne often theorized, were never as neat as male roomers, and Sherry and Kasey were living proof. But since both women contributed extensively to the household in a variety of ways, their messy habits were tolerated good-naturedly by Marianne.

"I rented the room, you know?" Marianne said, pulling on a clean pillowcase as she looked out the window in Sherry's room. "He's moving in today. It was difficult to decide between the two. Both seemed like reli—Oh, damn that stupid dog! Kasey, look what he's done now."

She joined her mother at the window. In the yard below, Snickers had tipped over his water pan, chased a rivulet of water down the dirt slope and, where it puddled at the bottom, he gleefully rolled in it, covering his thick fur with mud.

"He's going to get mud all over the clean sheets."

Kasey gathered up a large mound of bedding. "I'll get these into the machine and tie him up."

"Make sure it's far from the clothesline. I don't need to do a double wash today."

She watched her mother crouch on the balls of her feet, lift the mattress at one corner and tuck in the bedding with brisk, no-nonsense motions. A strand of gray hair fell across her eye and she blew it away. Everything she did, she did with determination, putting her all into it. It occurred to Kasey that she couldn't remember the last time she had seen her mother relaxed, with absolutely nothing to do.

Clutching the bedding to her chest, Kasey said, "Ma, when was the last time you were out to dinner?"

"You mean in a restaurant?"

"Um-hum."

"Phooey, who has time?"

"You would if you wanted it. You create your own frantic little world here. You're always starting something and you won't quit till it's finished."

Marianne looked at her daughter as though she had begun talking in a foreign tongue.

"Now don't give me that look. Everybody needs time out."

"Look who's talking."

"My point exactly. What are you doing tonight?"

"Ironing. It's Tuesday."

Not tonight you aren't. Tonight, I'm treating you to a movie and dinner."

Marianne stared a moment longer, then shook her head as if to clear it and said, "Don't be silly, Kasey, I have—"

"No arguments. I'll pick the movie; you pick the restaurant afterward. Ma, it'll be fun."

"Oh, honey, I don't know. Don't you have to work?"

"They can do without me for one evening. I've been at the club every day for eight days. I sleep there, eat there; I'll be back there again tonight. I could use a break, too."

"Well . . . in that case . . ." Marianne smiled at her daughter. "Okay."

"Good."

"What would I wear?" Marianne ran a callused hand through her short gray hair and looked down at herself.

"It's the 90's, Ma. Anything goes." Kasey smiled and started out the door.

"Kasey?"

"Yes?"

"By any chance did you read your horoscope this morning." Kasey shook her head.

"While you're down there have a peek at it. Paper's on the table."

"Why don't you just save me the trouble and tell me what it said?"

"Read it," Marianne said, turning away to smooth out the bedspread.

In the kitchen, with her arms still filled with sheets, Kasey leaned down to read the paper, which had been neatly folded to the horoscope section.

Spend time doing something fun with a loved one this evening. Kasey grinned. It wasn't as if she invited her mother—or her father, for that matter—out on a regular basis. She couldn't remember the last time she had spent an evening with either of them doing something fun. Okay, so it was about time. She read on. *Someone with love in his heart thinks of you tonight.* She straightened slowly. This was ridiculous, she told herself. If she weren't careful, she might begin to take this seriously, advancing from basic astrology into tarot cards and palm reading, unable to make a move without consulting one or other divine medium.

After loading the washing machine, she filled a heavy clay bowl with water and set it out by the shed. Snickers, seeing Kasey, bounded to his feet and raced to greet her. She managed to get the tether on him without getting too muddy, then she made a dash for the house. She made it back inside just as he careened against the door with a shuddering, house-jarring thump.

Danny, seated at the table, looked up from his paper-folding. "Fly the friendly skies," he said.

George stood at the sink peeling a fresh peach. "What's scary is that that mutt is still just a pup. The way he's growing, he's gonna eat your mama right to the poorhouse."

"Too bad he can't survive on fruit and honey."

"Nut 'n'honey," Danny said.

Kasey leaned down to inspect one of George's tacked-up photographs—a classic one of the Truckee River during spring thaw, overflowing the banks and flooding downtown Reno. "How's the book coming along? Making any progress?"

"It's getting there, slow but sure." He leaned over and snatched a picture from the refrigerator. "Now, how did that one get there? One of the last people I'd want in my picture book would be a crook like Doyle. Damn riffraff."

"Ansel Doyle?"

"Yeah. Must've picked it out because of the governor. See . . ." He showed the photo to Kasey. "There he is alongside the governor and the attorney general. Just having a man with Doyle's shady reputation standing that close to government officials tends to make them all look bad."

Kasey remembered seeing the picture somewhere before and recognized all three men from previous press coverage. Several other men, dressed in suits and looking like bodyguards, stood off to the side, blending into the background.

"Here, Danny Boy," George said, handing the 8x10 glossy to his grandson. "Something shiny for you to fold."

Danny had already creased and folded the photograph in several places when Kasey, watching him work, suddenly blurted out, "Wait!" She gently took the photo from his fingers.

"What is it, Kasey?" George asked.

She straightened the folds, laid it flat on the table, and took a closer look. She pointed at one of the suited men in the background. "George, do you know who that man is?"

"Don't know his name, but I know he was one of Doyle's henchmen. The man has a hoard of 'em."

"You mean a bodyguard?"

"Call 'em what you will. I call 'em henchmen. Thugs."

Thugs. Henchmen. The man standing off to the side of Ansel Doyle was the security guard Kasey had been looking for.

"When was this taken?"

"Early this year. I took those shots when they had the grand opening for the downtown project. See the dome and towers in the background? The bowling stadium's off to the left there. I peddled that particular photo to the *Gazette-Journal*. At the time, Doyle was making a lot of flap about doing a river project even bigger than what had already been done north of the tracks."

"This picture was in the local paper?"

"Yeah. On the financial page in a Sunday edition. It went along with an article on a slew of proposed projects that were guaranteed to boost the slumping economy."

She vaguely recalled seeing it in the newspaper. Of course at the time it had meant nothing to her. Just two state bigwigs and a casino tycoon. She would never have noticed the other men in the picture's background.

She took the photograph and drove into town.

The maid reached down between the bed and nightstand and lifted the plastic object wedged there. It was an ordinary nasal spray bottle, the kind found in any drugstore. She placed it on the nightstand, then continued making up the bed in the master bedroom of the King suite.

The Monk kept the speed of the Camaro at a conservative 40 miles an hour. He was in no hurry. Just out for a little drive in the country on a hot July afternoon. Air from the open window rushed inside, cooling him. It felt cooler at his damp armpits. The car was equipped with air-conditioning, but he preferred the real thing. Artificial heat and air were for pussies, for suits. His father had always said that the true test of a *man* was how much he could tolerate. If a man couldn't get back to nature, couldn't make his own comfort or live in extremes without whining, he might as well shove a gun barrel in his mouth and pull the trigger.

Last night, he had spent seven punishing hours in the clubhouse, that airless three-by-five room on the second floor. Without his nasal spray, his head had felt as if it were caught in a giant vice, the jaws crushing his frontal lobe to the bursting point. He had been forced to breathe through his mouth like a beached carp.

At seven that morning, he had worked his way down to the casino floor to the east exit where he merged with hotel guests about to board the many tour buses lined up there. By cutting between two buses, he had stolen away into the early morning traffic.

Now, many hours later, he drove down the long lane to the white frame, two-story house with the green shutters.

He entered the yard, pulled under the massive weeping willow, and parked. He sat there a moment listening to the pings and clicks of the engine cooling and looked around, again impressed by what he saw. It must be a great place to live, he thought. An even better place to grow up. Acres and acres of land with the Sierra for a backdrop.

But all that took a backseat to the young woman with the strawberry-blonde hair. Since he had laid eyes on her Saturday, she'd been heavy on his mind. He wondered if she were at home today. He had made up his mind he would go slow with this one. If something were worth having, it was worth waiting for. Patience. When it came to important things, no one had more patience and fortitude than the Monk.

He opened the car door and eased out, stretching. He was about to close the door when he saw movement on the east side of the house. A large Saint Bernard backed out dragging a small bush in its jaws, soil-clumped roots still intact, worrying the bush like a big bone. The dog spotted him, immediately dropped the bush, made a woofing sound, then bounded forward.

The Monk opened the door wider and waited until the animal had reached him before he reacted. With lightning speed, he grabbed the dog's collar and viciously twisted, his fist becoming a makeshift garrote wedged firmly against the animal's throat, strangling him. The dog was immobilized instantly. The Monk held on a little longer until he felt it slump against his legs. He eased the dog to the ground.

"You need to learn some manners, pal," he said to the nearly unconscious animal. "That was lesson number one."

He gently closed the car door, stepped over the dog, and, with long, yet unhurried strides, made his way to the house. On the front porch he glanced back at the dog. It was sitting up now, retching slightly, seemingly dazed. There were two things he could not tolerate: unruly kids and stupid animals. Both should be seen and not heard. The less seen the better.

A short time after he rapped on the stained-glass pane of the front door, it was opened by the gray-haired landlady. She wore loose-fitting jeans, a plaid shirt with rolled-up sleeves, sneakers, and a billed cap turned backward on her head.

"Hello, Tom," Marianne Atwood said with a smile. "I thought you might show up today."

Thirty-five

Kasey glanced up at the surveillance camera on its make-shift mount above the door of the King suite. The security guard seated to the side of the door had already checked her out and radioed his boss that she was there.

Jay opened the door. He looked tired and solemn; but when he saw her, his eyes seemed to brighten. His smile was slight, but welcoming.

"Kasey."

Just that. *Kasey.* It was her given name; she heard it a dozen times a day. Yet now, spoken through his lips, it sounded very special . . . sensual, almost.

Oh God, she had it bad. How was she to get past this state of suspended emotions? she wondered. Staying away, being together, it made no difference. She was going to have these feelings for him no matter what. She could only hope it was an infatuation and that it would soon crest, then die out so she could get on with her life and begin to think clearly again. *Not bloody likely,* she told herself.

She stepped in. Jay closed the door, turned to her. They stood in the foyer, face to face, saying nothing. His blue eyes burned into hers, seared a path to a needy place deep inside her, both warming and chilling.

"Who's there?" Dianne's voice rang out from another room.

They broke eye contact. Jay's hands disappeared into the pockets of his pants; he turned slightly.

"How is she?" Kasey asked quietly.

"Come in. Sit down. I'll be right back." He turned left toward the guest bedroom and disappeared inside.

Kasey crossed to the dining room table. She remained standing. A short time later Jay came out, softly closed the door behind him, and joined her.

"She's still pretty shook up," he said. "Late last night she had housekeeping change the bedding and even replace the mattress. Then, after all that, she wouldn't spend the night in that room. She refused to sleep where he had been. She can't close her eyes without reliving the whole thing."

"I'm sorry, Jay."

"When I get my hands on that bastard, I'll tear him to pieces. He'll regret the day he chose my family to come after. This damn playing around is over. I don't give a shit if he knows I'm on to him. I want him. It's obvious he wants me. So why the hell doesn't he just come out and face me? One on one."

"Because he's doesn't like playing fair. He's killed two defenseless women. That should tell you something about his character."

At the mention of the two dead women, some of Jay's anger seemed to slip away. "At least he didn't kill her."

"No, he didn't kill her."

"But she *was* violated, and it's going to take awhile for her to work this out. The doctor thinks she should go into some sort of crisis therapy."

"I agree."

"If only she did."

"Would it help if I talked tb her?"

"Maybe. Later." He pulled out a chair for her. On the window ledge outside, two pigeons pranced and cooed. With a flurry of flapping wings, a third one joined them.

Jay watched the birds absently. "Security blocked all the exits as soon as I radioed in last night. They monitored them all through the night. Nothing. The guy's a phantom." He looked at Kasey. "Can I get you anything?"

"No thanks. Jay, I found this." From her purse she took out the 8x10 and handed it to him. "It might help."

He sank into the chair as he studied the photograph. "Where did you get this?"

She told him. "Jay, aside from the governor, the attorney general, and the formidable Mr. Ansel Doyle, does anyone else look familiar?"

He studied the picture carefully. Then he lightly tapped the picture over Doyle's bodyguard. "This one. Yes, this one. If it's the same guy I think it is, I knew him in the service. Army. We were both stationed in Germany. That was . . . hell, twenty years ago at least." His dry chuckle held no humor. "Of course. Of course."

"What? You two were army buddies?"

"Hardly. The closest we came to embracing each other was as boxing opponents in the ring."

"Let me guess. You beat him and he swore to get even?"

Jay shook his head. "He beat me. TKO'd in the sixth round. The guy was brutal. Ruthless. He could take a pounding and not go down. Talk about someone out for blood. I don't think the word *defeat* was in his vocabulary."

Jay rose, again offered her a drink, took a bottle of Foster's from the refrigerator, opened it, then leaned on the bar. "No, it was later, at the tail end of overseas duty, when we had a serious run-in. I was to be a witness for the prosecution in his general court-martial trial. Only it never got that far. The charges were dropped. Lack of evidence."

"What charges?"

"Aggravated assault and mayhem. He damned near killed a fellow serviceman one night in the alley behind a bar. He was an M.P. He claimed the soldier was drunk and disorderly and had resisted arrest. That's not the way I saw it."

"What happened?"

Jay took a moment to reflect on it. "He came into the bar all puffed up, looking for trouble, looking *like* trouble. By the way he stood at the door taking in the scene it was obvious he was searching for someone in particular, and he found him. It happened so fast. One minute this young kid is kicking back with his buddies, on leave, minding his own business; and the next, he's being hauled out back getting the holy crap beat out of him. He never had a chance to resist. He never had a chance period. We—three of his pals and I—jumped in and broke it up. A couple more minutes and there wouldn't have been anything left to salvage."

Jay sipped the lager. "Because the soldier's injuries were so extensive, CID stepped in."

"CID?"

"A department of the military that investigates crimes committed by American soldiers. As it turned out, I was the only eyewitness willing to take the stand against him. The others suddenly developed mass amnesia. The M.P. had gotten to them first, scared them off. My testimony alone wasn't enough to make the charges stick. My word against his. He walked. The allegations, however, did serve to get him reassigned to a desk position. To a man who thrives on pushing people around, that was the same as prison time. He swore that one day he'd come after me. Payback." Jay looked at Kasey. "I guess that day has arrived."

"You're sure this man in the picture and the M.P. are the same man?"

"About as sure as I can be." He scrutinized the photo again. "Yes, it's him. He's heavier, has less hair, and his face is more rugged; but it's him. You see, I'm not really surprised. In fact, I think I expected it. About three or four years ago, Dianne, Brad, and I were guests at one of Doyle's clubs in Vegas. I thought I saw him there. It came back to me then. Germany, the beating, the hearings, his threats. For a couple of weeks after returning to Reno, I looked over my shoulder. But when nothing came of it, I figured he wasn't who I thought he was. I got involved in the club again and, well, he just faded from my mind."

"Was that when Ansel Doyle made you an offer for the club?"

"No, that took place in the spring of this year. Doyle came here. Spent a week in the Executive Suite."

"Did you see this M.P. then?"

"No."

"Can you recall his name?"

Jay stared off into the distance. "Not offhand. I've tried already without any luck. His fighting moniker was something religious. *Pope, friar,* something like that."

"Does the name Lucas Cage sound familiar?"

"Lucas Cage? Lucas . . . God, that's it. Lucas . . . *monk.* Lucas the Mad Monk!" Jay paced to the window, back to the table, and dropped into a chair. "And, oh man, the name fit. Mad. You could see it in his eyes. The guy was psychotic. Before the incident in the bar, he almost killed another man in a championship bout, which pretty much ended his boxing career in the service. Who in their right mind would want to climb into the ring with a potential time bomb? They also called him the Monk of Mayhem. Jesus, I can't believe I didn't put it together."

"Why should you? It was years ago when you saw him and that was in another city clear across the state. At the time you weren't even sure it was him."

"Well, he was in no hurry to get back at me. My old army buddy, Lucas the Mad Monk, can sure as hell hold a grudge, I'll say that for him."

"What now?"

Jay snatched up the phone, dialed. "Knowing what I know about this man, there should be enough criminal activity in his past to get the D.A. involved." A moment later he was telling Lowemen they had ID'd the suspect. He hung up. "He's on his way over. Kasey, how'd you get his name?"

"He was the other possible. The other security guard. All along we had his name and file; we just followed the wrong lead. I think he was smart enough to stay off security duty.

We had Andrews and no one to compare him with." She thought of Brad, who had positively sworn Andrews was their man.

"Yes. And he managed to stay away from me, stay out of my sight. I would have recognized him otherwise," Jay said. "The game is in high gear. He's closing in now, and the stakes have become very high. Judging from his actions last night, it's not just me he's after. It's my entire family." He lowered his voice. "His assault on Dianne was meant not so much to inflict pain, but to terrify her. He didn't just cut her, Kasey, the bastard carved his initial on her. 'C' for Cage. Remember last night when she said he'd branded her? If she only knew how right she was. He intends to hurt me through the ones I care most about. C'mon," he said, taking her arm, "we need that file on him."

Dianne called out for Jay.

Kasey stood. "Look, I'll get it. You stay with Dianne."

Jay caught her wrist as she turned to leave. "Kasey . . . please . . . be careful. He came after you once, that night he chased you on the highway. If he's as shrewd as I think he is, he'll try it again, and more aggressively this time."

It wasn't necessary to ask what he meant by that. She knew. *He intends to hurt me through the ones I care most about.* Lucas Cage knew they had been together the night before in the jacuzzi.

She nodded and backed away until they were at arm's length. He released her hand. She hurried out as Dianne called out a second time.

Both files were missing. Cage and Andrews.

Kasey went from the monitor room into Jay's office, hoping they would be there. When they weren't, she picked up the phone on the desk, called down to personnel, and asked to have the files with the original documents pulled. After several moments of waiting, the woman came back on the line, "Miss

Atwood, the file on Andrews is here, but I can't find one for Lucas Cage. In fact I don't see anything for a Lucas Cage. Are you sure he's an employee here?"

Kasey wasn't surprised. Lucas Cage could alter, switch, and even remove files; but he couldn't wipe away all evidence of his existence at the hotel casino. And he was too smart to think he could. This was just another ploy on his part to spice up the game. To let them know what he was capable of doing.

She called the security department to find out when Lucas Cage had last reported to work and when he was scheduled again. Ted Lunt, the supervisor, told her Cage had reported to work on Wednesday, then called in sick. He hadn't been seen in five days.

At least someone had information on Cage. He wasn't a phantom and he couldn't destroy all the records or silence everyone through intimidation.

"Ted, what can you tell me about him? About Lucas Cage?"

"He hired on for the summer, does his job, and keeps to himself pretty much."

"Anything else?"

"Well, personally I didn't like the man. He's got a *chip,* if y'know what I mean. Doesn't take orders too well. If we weren't shorthanded, I'd've let him go after the first week."

"Can you be more specific?"

"He's got a mean streak. He's been on report two, three times. Insubordination, strong-armin' folks, making his own rules, stuff like that. He's at the limit. One more and, shorthanded or not, I'm gonna have to bounce him outta here."

"If he shows up for work tonight or if you see him anywhere on the premises, call me or Mr. King right away."

From the third-floor window of Jay's office, Kasey looked down at the street below. She saw a black Camaro turn the corner and pull into the parking garage directly beneath her. *Cage?*

"Ted, do you know what he drives?"

When he said he didn't, she hung up and rushed into the

other room. She switched on two of the monitors, tuning into the cameras focused on the garage elevators. She watched the main lobby and the lower level for several minutes. A steady stream of people exited both elevators, none of whom were Lucas Cage.

Was he on the premises? How many black Camaros with tinted windows could there be in this town? Employees were prohibited from parking in the hotel garage, but since when did Cage follow rules?

Kasey called Ted Lunt back and requested he send a man to check out the service stairs. If the guard found anyone there, he was to detain him.

She left Jay's office. Minutes later, she was on the top floor of the six-story parking garage. She would find his car and get the license number, leaving nothing to chance.

Lucas Cage avoided the elevator and took the stairs. This was one time he'd rather not be seen. At least not until after he had made the change.

Halfway to the second floor he heard footsteps on the metal steps two floors above, coming down fast. He paused. In the direction he'd just come from, he heard the metal door open and footsteps now sounded below. He was on the landing between the first and second floor. He couldn't go down. No time. He stood a better chance going up.

He took the steps three at a time, his black Nikes silent on the steps, the footsteps of the two others ringing loudly in his ears.

He quickly unlocked the door on the second floor, and just as he pulled the door closed behind him he caught a glimpse of the dark shoes and blue pant-legs of the security guard coming down. He heard shouting—one guard shouting at the other. He left them to battle it out between themselves.

Cage took a moment to look around the convention area. Except for a porter sifting through the sand-filled ashcans at a bank of telephones, the area was empty. He made his way to the door of the catwalk without meeting another soul.

Inside the clubhouse, the small, stuffy room that Cage had begun to affectionately regard as his home away from home, he opened the nylon bag, removed a brown uniform that the club provided for their maintenance crew, and put it on.

He turned and sat on the large metal toolbox he had brought up to this room his first week on the job. He reached back into the bag and removed a curly blond wig, matching mustache, and a pair of tortoiseshell glasses. He put these on with the aid of a small compact mirror. He clipped a ring of keys to his belt and a laminated ID tag to his pocket. After one more glance in the mirror, he picked up the toolbox and left the room.

He took the service elevator to the lower level, no longer concerned about being seen or running into security. He was just a club maintenance man doing his job.

In the basement he passed employees, both male and female, coming or going from the various rooms in the underground maze. He acknowledged no one as he headed toward the area where a week ago he had killed the maid and left her body for her lover to stumble upon. Foot traffic this far from the building's hub thinned out to nothing. Ahead of him Cage could see the yellow tape cordoning off the crime scene. Just thinking about that afternoon filled him with renewed energy, and he almost went down there to savor the moment again.

Instead, he slowed, took one quick glance over his shoulder to make certain he wasn't being observed, then he let himself into the main mechanical room.

Kasey spotted the Camaro on the second floor. She had walked through four levels looking for it. It was in a place she would never have expected to find it, backed into a slot reserved for the chief of operations, Howard Cummings. Dianne's red Jaguar was parked on one side and Brad's Chevy van on the other. The reserved spaces were near a private door that opened into the reception area of a lounge and meeting room of the club's key personnel. Kasey pulled on the door handle. Locked.

She stared at the car. It had been backed into the space, close enough to the wall to hide the rear license plate. She moved around to the front, peering through the dark tinted windows with little success. The front license plate was filthy. Through splattered layers of mud she made out a Nevada plate, silver on blue. Kasey knelt down and, with the side of her fist, rubbed at the dried mud. MO—she rubbed harder—N—K. A vanity plate. MONK.

To the right of the car, the private door suddenly opened. Kasey quickly ducked down out of sight and moved around to the side of the Camaro. She heard footsteps moving away from her. A moment later she chanced a peek.

Brad King stood behind his midnight blue van, and by the way he glanced around and checked his watch, she suspected he was waiting for someone.

More footsteps. She ducked down again. A moment later, she heard hushed voices, two males conversing. Kasey looked again. Brad stood talking with a man who looked vaguely familiar. It wasn't until she heard Brad say the name *Carne* that Kasey remembered where she'd seen him before. Dan Carne, the mobster that Jay had had thrown out of the club awhile back.

"C'mon," Brad said. "Let's get away from this door."

She heard the sound of footsteps retreating. And before they were out of earshot, Kasey heard the name *Tony Bartona*. What the hell was going on? Bartona was one of Ansel Doyle's men. He was connected with Doyle's Tahoe operation. Mobsters. Rivals. What was Brad mixed up in?

This changed everything. Kasey could no longer keep Brad's involvement a secret from Jay.

She waited a full minute, then quickly headed to the elevator, looking over her shoulder for the two men.

Halfway across the garage, she sensed she was not alone. She slowed, looked around, but saw no one. It couldn't be Brad and Carne; they had gone in the opposite direction and there was no way they could have circled around so quickly. The garage was cool and dim, filled with deep shadows, ominous shapes, and hiding places galore. She glanced back across the garage to Lucas Cage's Camaro. The Monk of Mayhem would soon claim his car, and he was the last person she wanted to run into in a deserted garage.

Several cars ahead, she heard a jarring sound, like a heavy key ring hitting the concrete. The sudden jangling noise startled her. She looked up to see a blond, curly-haired man with tortoiseshell glasses, wearing the hotel maintenance uniform, step out from behind a white van. He started walking toward her.

He moved toward the middle of the lane, forcing Kasey to stay to the side where the cars were parked along the wall. There was something about him that had the hair at the back of Kasey's neck rising slightly. At first, when she realized it was only a hotel maintenance man and not Brad and his companion, she had felt relief.

Relief turned to anxiety again.

The man passed her without slowing.

His black shoes made no sound on the concrete.

Kasey felt a tightness at the base of her spine. She had turned halfway around before she was hit. He slammed into her, drove her down the narrow space between the van and a pickup, crushing her against the wall with such force that the air was knocked out of her. Pain exploded in her shoulder.

She tried to scream but was caught at the throat, the large hand squeezing, making any sound impossible. He was at her back, pressing her face and chest into the wall. His fingers squeezed.

Bright lights burst in her head. She was going to die. He was going to choke her to death.

Through the roaring sound of blood rushing inside her ears,

she heard a metal door clank shut. With what strength she had left in her body, she struggled, kicking at the side of the van, slapping the wall, trying to make herself heard.

"Is someone down there?"

Jay's voice.

Kasey managed to break the hold on her throat. "Jay!" she screamed.

"Brad! This way, Brad!" Jay shouted.

The sound of running footsteps.

She was suddenly released. The man leaped into the bed of the pickup, bounded out the other side, and ran.

Kasey, on her knees, looked up and saw Jay and Brad rushing toward her.

"Follow him," Jay said to Brad. "Don't try to stop him. Find security."

Brad disappeared.

A moment later, Jay was crouched at her side and she was in his arms. He held her tight for an instant, then he was running his hand over her face, throat, and through her hair.

"Kasey. Kasey. Are you hurt? Did he hurt you? Can you talk?"

She nodded, but no sound came out.

"Relax, try to relax," Jay said, pulling her close again. "Take a minute to catch your breath."

Her hand was trembling violently. Jay took it, squeezed it reassuringly, held it steady between their bodies.

When her trembling subsided slightly, she inhaled sharply, deeply, then said quietly, "I'm . . . all right. More shook up than hurt."

Jay put his hand to the side of her face and turned it until she was looking into his eyes. His clear blue eyes seemed to swallow her. She found such comfort in them, comfort in his arms. What was happening to the levelheaded Kasey Atwood, the woman who had no time for romantic fantasies? Here she was on the floor of a parking garage struggling for air, lucky to be alive, and she was thinking about how good it felt to have Jay's arms around her.

The pain in her throat and shoulder hauled her back to reality.

Jay rose to his feet, bringing her with him. He walked her to the front of the van. He held onto her, but moved back a ways to see if she were bleeding or bruised.

"What happened?" He carefully straightened her blouse, smoothed down her skirt, brushed hair from her face.

"He jumped me. He came o . . . out—he jumped me, pushed me back there, then tried to strangle me."

"Was it Cage?"

"I don't know. I don't think so."

"Did he say anything?"

"No."

"It could have been his accomplice."

She nodded.

Footsteps sounded behind them. They turned to see Brad approaching with a security guard.

"Did they get him?" Jay asked, dropping his arm from Kasey's waist.

Brad looked contrite, shook his head. "He gave me the slip. One minute I had him in sight, the next he was gone."

Jay raked fingers through his hair.

"His car is over there." Kasey pointed across the garage. "It's parked in Cummings' space."

Jay instructed the guard to check it out. To Kasey he said, "What's going on? How did you know his car was here?"

In faltering words, her throat sore from her attacker's strong fingers, Kasey explained what had brought her into the garage. She told them that the files were gone but she had a license ID for Cage's car.

"Damnit, Kasey, we have security to do those things. You weren't hired to risk your neck."

"It all happened so fast. I got carried away. I'm sorry."

Brad took her hand. "Kasey, do you need a doctor? Did he hurt you badly?"

"No, Brad, no doctor. Thanks, I'll be okay."

The guard returned. "Sir, there's no car parked in Mr. Cummings' slot. He must have doubled back and driven off without anyone seeing him."

"Shit," Jay said.

"What kind of car?" Brad asked.

"Camaro. Black with tinted windows."

"Haven't seen anything like that," the guard said.

"What's that license number, Kasey?" Brad asked.

"He has a vanity plate." She turned to Jay. "It's Monk. M-O-N-K."

His eyes expressed his incredulity.

"Okay, look, we have to report this," Jay said. "Frank's upstairs with Dianne. I just came down to get some papers from my car. Thank God I chose now to do it. Are you sure you're okay?"

She nodded, rubbed her shoulder, then her throat. "Bruised a little."

"Better come up and talk to Frank."

Kasey decided to go ahead with her plans for an evening with her mother.

Marianne insisted on meeting her at the theater. There was no point, Marianne reasoned, in Kasey's driving all the way out to the ranch to pick her up and take her home when Kasey intended to stay in town again.

Kasey, her blouse buttoned to the top to conceal the bruises on her neck, arrived a few minutes early, bought two tickets, and waited at the door of the twelveplex. Two hours later, mother and daughter, eyes red-rimmed—the movie had been a two-tissue tearjerker—exited the theater and walked to Kasey's car. Once inside the car, Marianne said, "I thought this was supposed to be fun. I haven't bawled this much since Grandma Bane died."

"So pick a fun place for dinner."

"How about fast food?"

"No."

"All right. Chinese. I want Chinese."

"Now you're talking."

Kasey took her mother to the Canton Palace, a place tucked away in the corner of a large strip mall in Sparks. The food was as good as the atmosphere, the decor as tasteful as the house specialty of walnut-glazed shrimp.

The host, Bobby Lee, greeted her with an almost embarrassing display of pomp and ceremony. The year before, Lee had hired Kasey when he suspected that his nephew and one or two other relatives were skimming the profits. After determining that the cash shortage was most likely to occur the day before Lee took the receipts to the bank on Tuesdays and Fridays, Kasey staked out the restaurant after closing time on Monday. She was there to sound the alarm when the culprit entered through the back door, and minutes later the police found the thief elbow-deep into Lee's safe.

The nephew, as well as the ten other family members employed at the restaurant, was innocent. It turned out the culprit had been the previous occupant of that particular mall space. In possession of a back-door key and the combination to the wall safe, which Lee had neglected to change, the man let himself in periodically and helped himself to just enough cash to cause the proprietor to suspect one of the employees.

Bobby Lee, grateful to learn that the theft was not an inside job, placed Kasey, the bearer of the most fortunate news, in a highly revered position.

Inside job?

As Lee seated mother and daughter in a corner booth, Kasey reflected on those words. *Inside job.* Lucas Cage had an accomplice inside. Someone who fed him pertinent information. Someone who had access to the entire club. How else could

Cage come and go so freely and appear one step ahead of them? It wasn't enough to be on the security team.

She had had no chance to be alone with Jay to tell him about Brad. How do you tell someone you suspect their own flesh and blood of conspiring against them? She wouldn't make accusations, just give him the facts and let him put it together.

Bobby Lee took their order himself. Marianne frowned slightly when Kasey ordered a glass of white wine for each of them.

"Relax, Ma. One glass won't kill you."

"It'll just go to waste."

"No, it won't, I'll drink it if you don't."

Her mother's frown deepened. Kasey knew what she was thinking. Like father, like daughter. If Dotus harbored that special gene that made him prone to alcoholism, then it was possible his offspring harbored it as well. At thirty-three, Kasey enjoyed wine or an occasional Bloody Mary, margarita, or brandy, depending upon the circumstances. In fact, she had at least one glass of wine a day, usually with dinner. By no means did that make her a lush, or even close to it. Right? She wondered if her father had felt the same way when he was thirty-three.

They ate with chopsticks, moaning ecstatically with each bite. The chopsticks gave Kasey an excuse to take smaller bites and eat slower. The pain in her throat had eased. It only hurt now when she swallowed.

Yet still her mother noticed. "Gotta sore throat?"

"A little."

"With you it was always the throat. Tonsils, adenoids, the whole enchilada. Other kids got the ear infections, the respiratory ailments, but you always got it in the throat."

A comforting thought. Perhaps that would be her destiny. Death by strangulation. Today she had beat the grim reaper. And though it hadn't really hit her yet—tomorrow maybe, or the next day. No matter, she was determined to see this through.

Every few minutes, Lee showed up at their table with a different dish for them to try—on the house. "Something new. Taste," he'd say. "Tell me if you like."

Kasey and Marianne reached for the soy sauce at the same time, knocking over the salt shaker in the process. In unison, she and her mother grabbed a pinch of salt and tossed it over their respective shoulders.

"Now you've got me doing it," Kasey said, glancing around to see if they'd been observed. "What a sight we must be."

"Once you give into a certain superstition, there's no going back," Marianne said.

"Thanks for telling me."

Over the years Kasey had seen her share of bizarre behavior. Gamblers as a rule were a superstitious lot. But no one could compete with her mother.

At the end of the meal, when the dishes had been cleared, Marianne touched her daughter's hand and asked, "Honey, what is it?"

"What's what, Ma?"

"Something's on your mind. You have a habit of running your hands through your hair when you're worried about something. You're doing it now."

Kasey picked up her wine glass to still her hands. "It's just the job." On the drive over Kasey had told her mother that they thought they had identified the suspect and that she would be spending more time at the club until either the police had arrested the man or until her services were no longer needed. No way would she tell her mother about the attack on her that afternoon. Just thinking about it made Kasey shudder.

"Something else is bothering you, isn't it? Something more personal."

"With all that you have to do, when did you have time to get your degree in psychology?" Kasey asked flippantly.

Undaunted, Marianne replied, "Mothers know these things."

Not prepared at this time to discuss her feelings regarding Jay with her mother, whom she knew would be less than pleased to learn her daughter had fallen for a married man, Kasey again reached for her wineglass, only to find it empty. To her chagrin, she saw her mother had finished every drop of her own wine.

Marianne sighed. "If only Kevin were alive today. The two of you would probably be settled in your own home with a lovely family. I'd be a grandmother and you wouldn't have to be off doing these oddball jobs at all hours of the night."

"Ma, I love my job."

"That's because you don't have anything better to occupy your time. Kevin would've been an established attorney today, making enough money so that you could stay home and raise a family." She sighed again. "Life can be so cruel."

Kasey was spared the burden of continuing this conversation when Bobby Lee, laden with a stack of styrofoam containers filled with leftovers, arrived at their table.

Groaning from too much food, they said goodbye to the doting, hovering Lee clan and left. At ten o'clock, Kasey had her mother back at her car in the theater parking lot, and by ten-thirty, Kasey was inside her room at the hotel.

After calling her mother to make certain she had made it home safely, Kasey reported in to Jay.

Thirty-six

The following day, Det. Frank Loweman picked up Jay King in his unmarked tan Ford Fairlane and headed out of town. On the horizon ahead of them, storm clouds grew as they drove north along Highway 395, past one valley community after another: Sun Valley, Panther Valley, Golden Valley, Lemon Valley, on their way to the valley of Cold Springs.

Despite the approaching storm, or perhaps because of it, the afternoon was hot, muggy, and oppressive. With each mile, the Ford's air conditioner sounded more taxed, whining and squealing until Loweman finally switched it off. He rolled down his window and Jay did the same.

Jay felt a fat raindrop hit the side of his face. A dozen more drops splattered against the windshield, then stopped.

"We know Mr. Lucas Cage didn't work at any of the clubs at the lake that it said on his employee sheet," Loweman said, pulling off his blue paisley necktie and stuffing it in his jacket pocket. "So he probably switched sheets with this Andrews guy. I've got calls into L.A., Vegas, and Florida. If he was a cop in any of those territories, we'll know soon enough."

"L.A. to Miami," Jay mused. "Coast to coast. Frankie, what would influence a cop to play geographical hopscotch like that?"

"Boredom, variety. But most likely he's what the department calls a gypsy cop. That's a cop who's shuffled around in an attempt to cover up something either embarrassing or unsavory."

"Unsavory? Such as?"

"Could be a number of things. Tampering with evidence, a drinking or drug problem, the inability to get along with fellow officers. He may have been swapping favors—sexual or monetary—on the street."

"Taking a bribe?"

Loweman nodded. "On a small scale. Nothing major or he'd get his ass busted along with the rest of the crooks and scumbags. My guess would be unnecessary roughness. Most big-city P.D.s will overlook a cop who once in a while gets a little overzealous in the line of duty. An officer can get away with it for years until one day he maims or kills someone. Someone, that is, with a family who will demand answers. Can't have the whole department looking bad because of some hot-headed shield with a spring-loaded fist."

"His fellow cops just look the other way?"

"To a degree. You don't rat on your own. The *blue wall of silence* is mighty formidable."

"Blue wall of silence?"

"It's an unwritten code. Doctors, lawyers, Indian chiefs, they all adhere to a similar code. There's a simple solution. Transfer the offender. Make him someone else's problem."

"Why would the police force in another state be willing to take this *gypsy* on?"

"Because they usually don't know, or don't care to know. In crime-infested cities like Miami, L.A., Detroit, they don't ask too many questions. They need the manpower and if a couple heads get cracked trying to maintain law and order . . . well, *che serà, serà*. Those are mean streets. Who's gonna miss a pimp who just cut up his lady and threw her out the window or a junkie who just sold his kid to a psycho for smack?" Loweman glanced over at Jay. "The problem is that these bad apples don't limit their brutality to lowlife. Violence becomes a way of life and they get carried away, cross over to the regular folk. A businessman, pulled over for tipping a few too many, gets mouthy, and *bam*. A rebellious teen. *Bam*. A domestic dispute turns into a free-for-all when the law shows up. *Bam. Bam.* You get the picture."

"That profile fits Cage to a tee. The guy was a loose cannon in his twenties. Knew how to use his fists and seemed to derive great pleasure from it. He may have learned to compose himself over the years, but I doubt if he changed much."

"People don't change," Loweman said flatly. He flipped on the right-turn blinker and exited the highway onto Red Rock Road. "What's that address again?"

"Pioneer Trail. Number 6."

"Way the hell out there. If memory serves me, Pioneer butts up against the Peterson Mountain Range. Nothing out there but an occasional trailer or shack and a lot of God's own creatures."

"That fits, too. He was a loner in the service. No one could recall ever seeing him with anyone, male or female."

After a dozen miles or so on Red Rock, Loweman turned onto Pioneer Trail, a gravel road that soon became hard-packed dirt. Very few signs of inhabitants remained. Another mile and the road petered out to loose sand and sagebrush. A hundred feet off the road, to the south, stood a dilapidated house and behind it, a three-sided wood structure, large enough for a car, which stood empty.

"Nobody t'home," Loweman said. "No car, no pickup, no hoss hitched to the post."

Jay felt a sense of relief. He had come along hoping to confront Cage. To be present when Frank questioned him. Loweman had no warrant, no subpoena, no authority to do anything more than ask questions. If Cage refused to talk, there was nothing he could do about it. But now, way out here at the end of the line, miles from anyone, Jay wasn't so sure he was ready to meet up with his nemesis. They were sitting ducks if Cage were inside with a rifle and he chose to use it.

Loweman radioed their position. They left the car and went up to the front door. Loweman rapped on the splintered, peeling wood. Without waiting for an answer, he stepped off the porch and disappeared around the side of the shack. A moment later, having circled the structure, he returned to the front door and turned the knob. The door swung open.

"Keep your eyes peeled," Loweman said and stepped inside.

Jay could see for miles down the road. If anyone came, a plume of dust would mark the course.

A moment later, Loweman was back in the doorway. He stepped off the wooden porch, slapping his hands together as if ridding them of something dirty. "Cleaned out. Well, *cleaned out* might be stretching it. Cleared out. He was here, and not too long ago. There're scraps of food on the table that can't be more than a day or two old."

It was too much for Jay to hope that Lucas Cage had decided to leave town. Cage was deep into the game. For all Jay or anyone knew, Cage had taken up residence at the hotel and was having one helluva good time watching them watch him.

Jay stepped up on the threshold and looked inside. The interior, gray from the pale, dreary light filtering in through small, dirty windows, was littered with fast-food wrappers, pizza boxes, and an assortment of empty booze bottles.

The two men set off toward the ridge. Several hundred feet from the shack, scattered around the base of a massive boulder, Jay saw broken glass and scattered shell casings. He bent and picked up a casing. .44? Rolling it against his fingers, he continued to walk.

He spotted the first body twenty feet away—a tiny, decomposed lump of fur. Ground squirrel. He spotted another and another. All blown to pieces.

Alongside one or two of the brownish-gray bodies was an occasional magpie, the black-and-white winged scavenger of the desert, decomposing as well. Probably picked off while attempting to make a meal of the bounteous feast before them.

"Hey, Frank," Jay called out to his friend, who was poking around some sagebrush with a stick. "Come look at this."

When Loweman joined Jay, both men stood silently, taking in the scene of the carnage.

"More of the same over there," Loweman said, nudging a headless squirrel with the toe of his shoe. "Guess Cage and his neighbors didn't get along too well. They may have outnumbered him, but he was better armed. Not an animal lover, by any means. Unfortunately, it's not against the law to shoot varmints. I can't arrest him for squirrel genocide."

A raindrop hit Jay on the back of his hand. Several more spotted the front of Loweman's light-gray suit.

"C'mon, let's get out of here before the damn sky opens up on us," Loweman said. "Don't want to be caught out here in flash-flood territory."

Jay kept his head down, averting his face from the stinging raindrops as he headed back to the car. The large drops kicked up dust like scattered buckshot. A few feet in front of him, Jay spotted a small white-and-red plastic bottle. He bent down, scooped it up, and dropped it into his pocket before hurrying on.

The skies opened up.

Kasey heard the light ping of what sounded like rain against the window. A moment later, the crack of thunder made an official announcement. She looked up from the newspaper where she had just read her daily horoscope. *Someone is putting you to a test. A day of action. Romance is put on hold.*

"So what else is new?" she murmured under her breath. She stood, went to the large bay window in Jay and Dianne's suite, and looked out. The windows in this room, like all the others in the hotel, were permanently sealed—a deterrent to jumpers. She wished she could open one, if only a crack. She wanted to smell the pungent scent of sage that often preceded a heavy rain storm, particularly a summer storm.

She looked down at the street below, to Victorian Square, and watched tourists scattering about, taking shelter from the rain inside nearby casinos, shops, and the open gazebos in the plaza.

Another clap of thunder, this one louder, like a sonic boom, jarred the windows sharply.

"Jay? Jay!"

Kasey turned away from the window and hurried toward the guest bedroom where Dianne had been napping and was now obviously awake, sounding frightened and confused. Jay had asked Kasey to stay with her while he and Loweman checked out Lucas Cage's residence. Kasey had hoped he would return before Dianne awoke.

Kasey entered the dim room. "It's okay, Dianne. It's only thunder. We're having a long-overdue summer storm. Can I get you something? Something to eat . . . drink?"

Dianne scooted up on the bed until her back rested against the headboard. She swept hair from her face, which was pale and puffy, particularly around her eyes, and reached for a cigarette on the nightstand. Her hands shook so badly, Kasey had to light it.

"Kasey? What are you doing here? Where's Jay?"

"He'll be back any minute. He went with Det. Loweman."

A look of disbelief and dismay came over Dianne's face. Since the attack the night-before-last, she had changed drastically. Her out-of-character behavior surprised Kasey. An average woman might act that way, Kasey told herself, but Dianne was different. Kasey had always thought of her as a *tough cookie,* not one to easily crumble.

That morning Jay had told Kasey that Dianne had stayed up all night again, finally succumbing to sleep in the early morning and sleeping most of the day. Though he didn't say it, Kasey suspected Dianne was drinking during most of those waking hours.

What had that man done to her?

"Went where? Kasey, where did he go?" A note of hysteria crept into her voice.

"He—they . . . they went to question someone who might be a suspect—"

"They think they know who the man is?"

"They have a pretty good idea."

"Oh God," Dianne said, her fingernails clawing at the back of her hand. "What if he kills Jay?"

"I don't think—"

"He's going to try to kill me, too."

"Dianne—"

"How could he leave me alone?"

"You're not alone, Dianne; I'm here. There are men—"

"That . . . that *animal* could be right outside the door now. Right out there waiting to hurt me, to kill me." Her voice was low, gravelly, close to a growl. "What has Jay gotten me into? What, Kasey, what?"

Kasey had no response, no pat answers for Dianne. All she could say was "You're safe here. No one is going to get to you again. There are armed men all around you. He—this man, whoever he is—is not invincible. He'll slip up and the police will get him. Believe me, Dianne." Kasey knelt, took Dianne's hand, and squeezed. "Believe me."

Dianne pulled her hand away. Ashes dropped unnoticed on the bedding. "Could you bring me a drink?" she requested quietly. "Please? I need a drink."

Kasey stood. She nodded with resignation, left the room, and went to the wet bar. An instant later, she heard water running in the bathroom. Dianne was up and moving around at least.

The phone rang. Kasey answered the one on the bar.

"Kasey, it's Brad. Put Jay on. Hurry, it's urgent."

She told him Jay was out and where he had gone.

"We got trouble. Big trouble. Cummings got a call from a man who says he planted a bomb in the main mechanical room."

The mechanical room housed the building's central air-conditioning and heating system. It was in the basement, situated at the core of the entire structure, directly under the hotel and all its rooms.

Kasey remembered the last bomb threat. It had proven to be a false alarm. "Is there anything to it?"

"There's a big metal box down there wedged between some heating units that wasn't there yesterday. Maintenance says it doesn't belong to them."

"Shit," Kasey whispered.

"Yeah."

"Who else knows about this?"

"The chief of maintenance, of course, and LeBarre in security. Cummings called security first."

"What now?" Kasey asked.

"LeBarre says if this is the real thing we have to act fast. The hotel is booked solid. Cummings is calling an emergency meeting with Yanick and Epson. Christ, Kasey . . . *Christ.*"

"Have them meet up here. This is the first place Jay will come."

Kasey called the Sparks P.D. and left a message to have Det. Loweman contact her as soon as possible.

"What about that drink?" Dianne crossed the room, her robe hanging open, the sash trailing on the carpet. "What's wrong? Who was on the phone?"

"Brad . . ." Kasey said, pouring an ample shot of scotch into a rock glass and handing it to Dianne. ". . . I'm afraid we've got more trouble."

Loweman and Jay were on Interstate 80 approaching the Victorian Plaza when two patrol cars sped by, nearly cutting them off at the ramp exit. At the same moment that the dispatcher's voice came over Loweman's car radio, Jay saw a half-dozen emergency vehicles, sans lights or sirens, surrounding the club.

His heart slammed in his chest. What now? Who was it this time? Images of three people—Dianne, Kasey, Brad—flashed in his head like a twirling kaleidoscope.

Loweman stomped down on the accelerator. He ran the red

light at the intersection, narrowly missing a UPS truck before jumping the median to come to an abrupt stop at the main entrance of the club. Both men jumped out and worked their way through a throng of pedestrians on the sidewalk to get inside. Loweman stopped the first uniformed officer he saw.

The policeman took them aside, out of earshot of those around them. "Bomb threat, sir. Lower level. Mechanical room."

"Has the bomb squad been notified?" Loweman asked.

"They're on the way."

Jay scanned the casino, making a quick evaluation of the surroundings. At a little before noon, the club was already crowded and it would continue to fill up as the day progressed.

As quickly as possible they made their way through the mass of tourists to the bank of elevators.

When they reached the elevators, Jay grabbed a courtesy phone on the wall and dialed his suite. "If we have to evacuate," Jay said to Loweman, "I want it done right. I don't want a panic. I don't want people hurt or fright—*Brad,* it's me. What's going on? Who's in charge?"

Brad put LeBarre on the phone.

"Mr. King, this time there's a box. It looks like the real thing."

Thirty-seven

Jay was attacked the instant he entered the suite. Dianne flew at him, pounding on his chest with her fists and shouting accusations.

"Damn you," she hissed, twisting and pulling at his shirt. "How could you? How could you leave me alone when you know the bastard's coming back to get me? You don't care anything about me. You only care about this fucking club. I hope it blows up. I hope it blows into a million goddamn pieces."

"Dianne, please," Jay said under his breath. He caught her wrists and held them.

Loweman had stopped behind him, evidently unsure of what to do.

From the entry hall Jay looked into the living room. Kasey, Brad, and a cluster of men stood staring at them.

Kasey came forward, put an arm around Dianne, and said softly. "You don't mean that, Dianne."

"I mean it. I mean every word of it."

"C'mon, let's let these men do their job."

"No!" she shouted, pulling away from Kasey. "I'm getting out of here. I'm not going to hang around and be blown up. I'm going home."

Jay caught her arm. "Dianne, I'll take you. But first let me find out what's going on."

"I don't want you to take me. I don't want you with me. Don't you understand? I don't want you anywhere near me.

You stay. Stay with your precious club. Stay with your family of executives. Just stay the hell away from me. I'm not safe with you around. He wants you, not me. *Not me."*

She wrenched her arm from Jay's, shoved Loweman aside, flung open the door, and ran out. The door to the adjoining room opened and one of the surveillance men stepped over the threshold just as Dianne charged past.

"Al, get a couple of men and take my wife home," Jay said to the man in the corridor. "No matter what she says, stay with her. I'll be in touch."

Jay felt sick to his stomach. Dianne seemed to be falling to pieces before his very eyes. Dianne, his hard-as-nails wife who liked her sex rough, who had always criticized weakness of any form in others, who could have cared less what he did or where he went as long as she was free to do whatever she wanted. She had to know what he was going through. Not only was he trying to protect those he loved, but also the future of the club—her legacy. Was she so selfish, so self-absorbed that nothing or no one but Dianne Ellen King mattered? He wondered again if she were on the verge of a mental breakdown.

Jay straightened his shirt, absently ran fingers through his hair, and strode into the room. He crossed to the bar, undoing the top three buttons of his shirt. He took a beer from the refrigerator, opened it, swallowed deeply, then said to the watchful group before him, "Talk to me, damnit."

Everyone began to talk at once. Jay pointed at his chief executive. "Howard?"

Howard Cummings straightened. "On the way in this morning I got a call on my car phone. He started right in, calm and cool like, no introduction—nothing. He said, 'Look in the main mechanical room. There's something there I think you'll get a bang out of.' "

"Go on."

"That's it. I called LeBarre, told him to check it out."

Jay turned to LeBarre.

LeBarre bobbed his head excitedly. "Bolin and I found what looked like an ordinary toolbox down there. It was wedged real tight between two heating units. Don't know how he got it in there. There was a red bow tied to the handle."

Cummings said, "When LeBarre apprised me of the situation, I felt I had no choice but to contact the authorities."

Jay looked back at LeBarre.

"In light of the situation, sir, I felt I had to tell him about the threats directed at you and the missus."

Jay nodded. What difference did it make now?

The phone on the bar rang. Cummings answered. He spoke a few words, cupped a hand over the receiver, and turned to Jay. "It's security. He says the bomb squad, FBI, and ATF have arrived. They want to know if you're coming down?"

"Tell them I'll be right there."

Cummings passed along the message, then hung up. "The thing was definitely planted. Now, whether it's volatile or not remains to be seen."

"How big is it? If it goes, how much damage can we expect?"

"That's not for any of us to say," Cummings said. "The experts down there will fill us in."

Andy Bolin, the chief of maintenance, a thin man with a sunken chest, stepped forward. "I can say this, Mr. King, if that thing goes off down there where it is, even if it doesn't do much structural damage, smoke and fumes are going to go straight up that central shaft into just about every room in this building. The hotel rooms in particular. People trying to get out won't be able to see a hand in front of their face. It'll be—well . . . it could be pretty bad."

Jay didn't have to be told how bad it could be. Bolin's nightmare scenario could happen anywhere, at any time. A vision of the blazing Las Vegas MGM Grand with billows of black, choking smoke pouring out of the superstructure, flashed in his mind. As many as eighty lives had been taken in that catastrophe. Most had died from smoke inhalation and some had fallen to their death trying to escape the smoke and flames.

Sheer pandemonium.

The threat of a bomb in the hotel couldn't have happened at a worse time and the bastard knew it. Today was the kick-off day for *Hot August Nights.* Guests had been checking in since last night. King's Club was booked solid. Lodging at every hotel and motel in a sixty-mile radius for this special-event week had been booked in advance a year ago. King's Club had 750 rooms. If an evacuation were called and the hotel shut down for more than eight hours, securing accommodations for its displaced guests would be imperative. Where the hell would they all go?

"It could prove to be nothing more than a ruse," Cummings said. "Like that bomb scare a few years back at the Nugget."

Recalling that incident didn't make Jay feel any better. Not only had the Nugget been forced to close down for nearly twenty-four hours in one of the busiest months of the year, but 6,000 residents, hotel guests, and casino customers for a seven-block radius around the Nugget had been evacuated. It had turned out to be a hoax.

It was a different story in 1980 for Harvey's Resort Hotel in Lake Tahoe when an extortionist's half-ton bomb blasted an enormous hole in the side of the eleven-story building and closed down the resort for nine months.

"And it could be another Harvey's," Jay said. He looked to the foyer where Kasey stood. Their eyes met and held. She knew what he was going through. The compassion and concern on her face made Jay's insides twist. Why couldn't Dianne be more like Kasey? he wondered.

"Did he ask for money? Did he say he'd call again?"

Cummings took a moment to reflect. "Come to think of it, no, he didn't. Just that business about maybe I'd get a bang out of it."

"Start the evacuation," Jay said.

"What?" Mark Epson blurted out.

"Make sure it's done right. No mention of a bomb until everyone's out. I don't want anyone to panic and get hurt."

"No, Jay, not yet," Yanick joined in. "Jesus, what's the hurry? It'll cost the club a small fortune in lost revenue. Why not wait until the bomb squad or the Feds give the order. Hell, it could be a big fat nothing. Everything back to business without a hitch and no one the wiser."

"Bob, if the man who planted that box downstairs is the man I think he is, we have to take him seriously. I know what he's capable of. Evacuate."

Lucas Cage stood at a window on the second floor of the casino across from King's Club and watched a steady flow of people with little more than the clothes on their backs file out onto the street. Police were in the process of cordoning off the building with an endless stretch of yellow crime-scene tape.

He sprayed a quick shot of antihistamine into each nostril, sniffed twice, then chuckled low in his throat.

"Have a good day, Mr. King," he whispered to his own reflection in the window, fogging the glass with his breath. With his finger he made a bull's eye in the misty pane.

In less than an hour, King's Club and the surrounding area resembled condemned property. Deserted. Eerie. Yet, unseen by the curious and the press, like a teeming ant colony deep in the bowels of the earth, a group of experts congregated around a metal toolbox adorned with a bright red bow.

First on the scene was the Bomb Squad with a bomb-sniffing dog. Next came x-ray, neutron radiographic, cryogenic, and fiber optic equipment.

A diner a safe distance down the street became a command post for agents from the FBI, the Bureau of Alcohol, Tobacco and Firearms, and the top executives of the King's Club. Contact by phone between the two sites became constant.

Eight hours after the suspicious object had been sighted, the experts were still uncertain as to its contents and its volatility. Word had it the box contained sticks resembling dynamite and other objects whose size and shape were consistent with explosive devices. Another three hours and the decision to make an attempt to remove the toolbox from the premises was made. Tension mounted. All eyes at the command post remained glued to the twelve-story building.

They were bringing it up and out.

Through radio contact from the bomb site to the diner, a minute-by-minute communique kept Jay and the others informed of the Bomb Squad's laborious progress. The moments of long silence strained everyone's nerves. Whether radio traffic was on line or off, all listened for, anticipated even, the big boom. Jay stood at the window of the diner staring down the street at his small, yet treasured empire, praying that he would not be witness to its sudden, explosive demise.

An hour later, at 11:55 P.M., twelve hours after the bomb had been discovered, news reached the diner that the box had been safely removed from the basement to a special transport vessel waiting outside. It would be taken by truck to a remote area east of Sparks and detonated.

There was no cheering, no applause, no indication whatsoever of joy at the news, only the collective sound of a long, drawn-out sigh.

At 1:30 A.M., the authorities gave the all-clear to reopen the doors of the club. In the thirteen hours since the order to evacuate, nearly all the guests that had not left town had been placed elsewhere and were not likely to return until the following day—if they returned at all.

A handful of people, presumably those who had been gambling and drinking in nearby casinos, began to straggle back once the police cordon was finally lifted. Jay, Kasey, Brad, and the employees who had waited it out, security and main-

tenance mostly, spent the next several hours processing the
returning guests and unlocking rooms that had been secured
to discourage looters.

With only a skeleton crew, the casino, bars, and restaurants
remained closed, not to open again until the arrival of the day
shift employees. At 4:30, Brad walked Kasey to her room and
only half-heartedly made a pass, issued more from habit than
ardor. Jay had gone home to be with Dianne.

Kasey fell asleep instantly and didn't awaken until mid-
afternoon.

Thirty-eight

For the next five days, the club struggled to return to normal. Although the exact contents of the metal box was not disclosed to the general public for reasons of security, the bomb experts had indeed found explosive properties inside. The toolbox contained five highway flares, a bundle of cord, and some wire. The explosives—the "bang" in the box—turned out to be an assortment of fireworks that if detonated at close range could do little more than blow off a finger or put out an eye.

The bomb incident had made national news and for days the local newspaper's main coverage focused heavily on it. In addition to the bomb scare, the media recounted the club's other recent problems: the two homicides; the rash of room burglaries; the fire in the storage room; the computer, switchboard, and elevator failures, and anything else they could dredge up. It was no surprise when words such as *hex* and *jinx* became synonymous with the hotel name. Also no surprise were the cancellations that poured in steadily.

Business, therefore, dropped, with a noted decline in every facet of the club. The bustling crowds were gone. Peak hours—postbomb—were now as quiet as a morning shift during the dead of winter. The weekend following the "incident," much of the hotel staff was kept busy packing and shipping the personal property of registered guests who had had flights to catch before the club reopened or, out of fear or indignation, had refused to reenter the club. The casino staff had the arduous task of paying off winning players of keno and slot machines who were forced to leave before cashing out. Although the advanced slot machines were equipped with a memory chip and a credit meter, thus enabling them to track a player's credits, individual names had to be matched to machines. Full operation for much of the club was days away, perhaps even weeks.

Jay, Kasey, Brad, and the top executives spent those five days in endless meetings with the FBI and other law enforcement agencies. Kasey watched Brad, wondering about his involvement, wondering why she held back going to Jay with her suspicions.

Kasey saw Jay for brief, intermittent periods, and never alone. The FBI sent the toolbox to a forensic lab in Washington, D.C. in the hopes of gleaning a clue to the person or persons responsible. The investigation at the club proceeded. Agents continued to comb the crime scene, field calls, and interview hundreds of potential witnesses and employees.

A surveillance camera in the basement, which photo technicians examined with a fine-toothed comb, had caught on tape a bespectacled, curly-haired blond man in maintenance attire carrying a toolbox out of the service elevator. The I.D. badge clipped on the man's shirt belonged to a graveyard worker named Tully, who claimed it had been stolen at the end of his shift and who had a solid alibi for the time in question. One small footage of tape, a view from the suspect's backside, showed him briefly putting something to his face. Kasey and Jay, who watched it over and over, were sure that what the man had put to his face was a nasal spray, although there was no way to prove it.

Thomas Andrews had been questioned and released. Also wanted for questioning was Lucas Cage, who failed to appear for work on his scheduled shift. His locker had been cleaned out; his uniform was missing.

The days passed quietly. Kasey received surveillance offers

from other sources, but declined, determined to concentrate solely on the job at hand. Jay and Kasey waited it out, the club their private prison, the inaction nerve-racking.

Thirty-nine

She was prettier than Lucas Cage had initially thought. There was a softness, a gentleness, an innocence he hadn't seen in a grown woman in many years. The way his mother had been before his father had beat it out of her.

He watched Sherry Kidd from his room on the second floor as she tended the vegetable garden. A large floppy hat covered her hair and shaded her face and shoulders. She seemed to thrive on the outdoors; she took to nature like the bees behind the orchard took to honey. He could watch her for hours as she played with that big, stupid mutt or picked peaches or sat with the retard reading him poetry or trying to follow along with her own colored square while he made those worthless paper things.

On the few occasions he had tried to talk with her, she'd shied away, which only made him cherish her all the more. Patience, he told himself. Don't push it. This one wasn't like those floozies and whores he was used to.

This one was special.

Early Tuesday evening Kasey took a break from the club to visit her father. For some reason, maybe out of loyalty to her mother, Kasey found it difficult to see both her parents in the same time frame. She hadn't been home to the ranch since before the bomb incident, so it was only natural she gravitate to her father.

It was the third of the month, social-security-check time. Dotus sometimes got carried away when he had a fist full of cash. Kasey often tried to intercept the check. Fifty percent of the time she could talk him into giving her a little of it to hold for him until the end of the month. And ninety percent of the time she ended up giving it back to him around mid-month, along with some of her own cash. Dotus's willpower grew weaker with each passing year.

She found him at home in his basement apartment dead drunk on the floor at the side of his bed, a nearly empty bottle of sour-mash whiskey clutched in his hand. He wore a pink polo shirt—the pocket fat with bookie bets—tan boxer shorts, loafers without socks, and navy twill trousers which were down around his ankles. He had wet himself.

Kasey didn't need this. She wanted to turn around and go out the door without so much as a backward glance. Let him lie in his own booze and body waste. Let him drink himself into the ground. There was nothing she could do to stop it. Nothing.

She went to him, pried the bottle from his hand, and shook him. "Dad? Dad, come on, try to get it together. Hear me? Wake up." She shook him harder. "Did you spend it all? Is there anything left? Dad, answer me."

Dotus moaned, his eyes opening to mere slits. He patted the floor around him, looking for the whiskey bottle.

She tried to get him to his feet.

"G'wan," he muttered, jerking his arm away. "Lemme 'lone."

Kasey went into the bathroom and turned on the shower, using only cold water. She returned to the bedroom and again tried to lift her father.

"Damn you," she said when he rolled onto his stomach, his arms tucked under him, making it impossible for her to get a good hold on him. "Can't you see I'm trying to help you?"

"Get 'way. Go home t'yer mommy. Your stuffy, stuffy ol' mommy. I din't ask for yer help. Where's my bottle? Whad'ya do with it?" He swiveled his head around. "Kasey, darlin', whad'ya do with my bottle? Giv'it to me, girl."

"I threw it out."

"Ohhh, you're killin' me. Don'tcha know you're killin' me?"

"You're killing yourself." She tried one last time to get him up off the floor.

A flash lit up the room. Kasey turned toward the door and was blinded by another bright flash. She held her hand to her eyes.

A figure moved toward her, gave her a firm but gentle push. "Get outta the way, honey. I'll take it from here."

When Kasey's eyes focused again, she saw Sasha, the woman from upstairs, jockeying around between Dotus and her. Another flash.

A camera.

"A picture's worth a thousand words," the woman said. "Your daddy's such a Dapper Dan when he ain't pissed to the gills. I got a feeling he'll be more than a little ashamed when he gets a gander at what he looks like when he loses control."

Dotus groaned and rolled onto his side. She snapped another picture. This one exposed the wet front of her father's shorts.

"That one's a beauty," Sasha said, going into a fit of coughing.

"That's enough," Kasey said. "Help me get him up."

"No. Leave him. You go on. You look like you got more important things to do than waste your time with a fall'n down drunk. He'll be just fine right where he is."

We can't leave him there."

"Why not?"

"Because . . ."

"Because it ain't *dignified?*" Sasha raised her eyebrows. "When he sees these pictures, sees his precious little girl down on her knees trying to lift a lush with his pants twisted 'round his ankles, it's gonna shake him up good. And if it don't, then it don't. There ain't nothing you can do about it, lessen he's ready to face the truth. Till then you're just making yourself miserable. Now go on, get on with your life. I'll take care of him."

"I can't—"

"You ain't helpin' him, honey. You ain't helpin' him at all. You're only holdin' him up, bracin' him for the next fall. Let him fall. Let him try to get up by hisself."

Kasey stood there a moment longer. She didn't know what to say. She suddenly felt an enormous sense of compassion for this woman with the frizzy red hair, smoker's cough, and tough-love tactics.

She thanked the woman with a smile. Then she turned and left the apartment.

That night she went to the Y and gave a class with Peggy. She screamed a little louder than usual.

Jay rang the doorbell. Although it was his own house, the last thing he wanted to do was make Dianne or her three body-guards nervous—or worse yet, trigger-happy. Alan Ginsburg, the surveillance man from the hotel, opened the door.

"Evening, Mr. King," Ginsburg said.

As Jay stepped over the threshold, the mantel clock struck the hour, nine bells. "Evening, Al. How's she doing tonight?"

The man reset the security alarm. He shrugged his shoulders. "Hard to say. She hasn't come out of her room since she took a dip in the pool late this afternoon."

For the past week, up to the bomb threat, Dianne's moods had fluctuated from angry and argumentative to weepy and despondent. Now she was rigid, icy, totally unresponsive. As much as Jay disliked her outbursts, he preferred them to this hostile wall of silence.

"Has she had dinner?"

"The housekeeper took it in to her about a half hour ago."

"Anything I should know about?"

"A couple of suspicious calls this morning. Hang-ups. The

machine ID'd the number as one tied to the central line at the club. No way to get a fix on an exact location, however."

So Cage had been in the hotel that morning. Had he made those calls knowing they couldn't be traced? More than likely he had hoped they would be traced. He wanted them to know he could walk among them undetected, doing whatever he pleased. "Anything else?"

"Naw. Everything's quiet. Mrs. King accidentally tripped the alarm when she went out for a swim, but it's cool now. I don't think she'll forget next time. Chuck's got binoculars on the hillsides and Tob's on rounds. Anybody tries to get within even a hundred feet of this place, we're gonna know it."

Chuck Smith was stationed in the pool house and Tobby Sever was camped out in a special surveillance van across the street. Alan Ginsburg, assigned to watch Dianne full-time, stayed inside the house.

"Sir . . . if I can say something . . ."

"Sure, Al, what is it?"

"Well, we got things pretty well under control here. I don't think your wife has to worry about this creep sneakin' up on her long as we're here."

"I agree."

"It's you, sir, that I worry about. You're taking a helluva chance running back and forth every day by yourself. That clown—the one who's after you—well, he could be anywhere. He knows where you live and he could be waiting out on the highway somewhere, waiting to run you off the road or even take a potshot at you when you're getting in and out of the car."

"I'm aware of that, Al. What do you suggest?"

"Don't make yourself a target. Sit tight somewhere till the cops catch him."

"That could take a long time. I have a business to run."

"Yeah, well—"

"Al, if Cage wants to kill me, he'll have to come out in the open to do it. I won't hole up like a scared rabbit." Jay squeezed Ginsburg's shoulder. "Thanks for the concern. It's appreciated. I'll look in on my wife now."

Ginsburg pressed his lips together and nodded.

Jay found Dianne in the bedroom staring out the window. A ribbon of cigarette smoke rose above her.

"Dianne, come away from the window."

She turned slowly, her arms crossed in front of her. "I'm not safe in my own home with armed guards all around. Is that what you're saying?"

He didn't answer.

"Maybe he'll just shoot me and get it over with," she said.

"Now you're being melodramatic."

"Am I?" She dragged deeply on the cigarette, waved it in the air. "I'm going nuts here. I can't make a move without tripping the alarm or seeing some goon gawking at me."

"You can come back to the club."

"No," she blurted out. "Not back there. All the bodyguards in the world can't protect me from a bomb in a place as public and open as that. At least here there's a measure of security. I have my own bed, the pool, Helga, all the comforts in my own private little prison."

This was the most she'd said in days. "Do you want to go away somewhere?"

She gave him a hard look. "With you?"

"That's up to you. Do you want me with you?"

She dropped her gaze, shook her head. "I don't know yet."

On a table in front of the fireplace, alongside a tray of untouched food, Jay spotted an envelope with the hotel logo. He strode across the room and picked it up. The envelope was addressed to Ms. Dianne King.

"What's this?" Jay asked.

"See for yourself."

Inside he found yet another newspaper clipping. This one was an obituary, a quarter-page in length. The altered headline read *King's Club owner dead at 42.* Below that, also altered, it read *Owner/operator Jay Garner King victim of foul play.*

Jay remembered the original article, written eight years ago for his father, Ralph Gordon King. There were a few changes. A current picture of Jay, also clipped from a previous newspaper article, had been glued over the face of the senior King. The age of the deceased and the subheadline had been crudely inked in with a black marker.

"This came in today's mail?"

She nodded.

"You shouldn't have opened it, Dianne. It could have been a letter bomb."

She paled visibly. She flung her cigarette into the fireplace. "Great, just great. How many more of those have you gotten? How many, damnit, have included me? Tell me, Jay, have you received one with *my* obituary?"

"I'm sorry, Dianne. I wish I knew how to make this easier for you."

"Oh, shit. Shit, shit, shit. Jay, what the hell is happening? It's that stupid club. If you had sold it when you had the chance, we wouldn't be in this mess."

"I can never sell it, Dianne. It belongs to the family."

"Then go back to it," she said, her voice leaden. "Sleep with it. Make love to it. It's what you want. The hotel, not me. Go to it. Get out of here."

"Dianne—"

"Get *out.*"

He stood watching her. Finally he asked, "Dianne, do you want a divorce?"

She turned away, refusing to answer.

Forty

Lucas Cage decided to follow her into town. It was nearly ten o'clock when Sherry Kidd climbed into her old GMC pickup and drove away from the Atwood house.

More than curious about what kept her out so late on certain nights, he had to check for himself. The landlady had mentioned something about a crisis center. She said Sherry worked odd hours at the center, talking on a crisis line. Her work was hush-hush.

As an ex-cop, Cage knew about the work these do-gooders did for the benefit of mankind. He'd followed up his share of dispatch calls from crisis volunteers with their made-up names and calm, comforting voices. Calls to respond to a possible suicide, battered wife, rape. Yeah, it figured. Sherry was the type who'd want to help people, and who'd do it for nothing. Long ago Cage had concluded that most of the nuts who called the center would be doing the world a favor, saving the taxpayers a lot of time and money, if they just bit down on the barrel and pulled the trigger. As far as he was concerned, the only cure for weakness was a chunk of lead.

He had no trouble keeping her in sight. The broken taillight marked her truck from others on the highway. He followed it into the parking garage of a large casino downtown.

Since when did a crisis center use a casino for its headquarters? he wondered.

From across the parking garage he watched her climb down from the truck. She wore a plain cotton top, pants, and leather sandals, and—slung over her shoulder—a huge suede handbag. He followed her inside and kept her in sight until she disappeared into a restroom on the main floor.

Taking up an observation position at the nearest bar, a bar which Cage knew from personal experience encouraged hookers by comping their drinks, the bartenders often acting as pimps, Cage ordered a drink. As he waited, he pondered what she was doing in the club. Probably responding to someone in distress. A friend or acquaintance or someone she'd assisted on the crisis line, someone she felt she could trust. People like Sherry were forever putting themselves out. They had no shortage of friends in need.

Ten minutes later, a stunning woman dressed in a tight green mini-dress and high heels pushed through the door of the restroom. The woman had hair the color of Sherry's. It wasn't the face he recognized first, but the oversized handbag. She headed toward the same bar where Cage stood.

He recovered in time to quickly turn his back to her. She passed without a glance in his direction. After taking a seat at the opposite end of the bar, she reached into her bag and took out a cigarette. The bartender lit it. He leaned toward her, said something to her. She turned her head to look at a man in an expensive blue suit sitting at a table against the wall. The man was playing with a stack of white chips. He smiled at Sherry. She smiled back, slid off the stool, and strolled to his table.

The man stood, put an arm around her waist, and escorted her out of the bar.

Cage gripped his tequila shot in an iron fist. He felt the blood rise to his brain, flooding his senses. The thick shot glass cracked beneath his fingers.

No woman could be trusted. No woman—ever.

At 3:00 A.M., Kasey found herself aimlessly wandering the quiet floors of the hotel. It had been another long day and an even longer night. After her visit with her father earlier that evening, she had driven around for hours. Then, back at the hotel, she had avoided everyone by shutting herself in her room, a room she could no longer stomach.

She had little fear of running into Cage. He was brazen, but not that brazen. Security had been doubled and a few special agents still remained in the club. Any unauthorized person roaming about was immediately stopped and questioned.

She had started for the pool, but memories of being there with Jay turned her away. Her horoscope for the day predicted love and romance. The usual garbage. There was nothing romantic about unrequited love.

She took the elevator to the Skyline Room, a cocktail lounge on the top floor with a sweeping view of the city and mountains. At this time of the morning, even before the recent drop-off in business, she would have it all to herself.

Just as she expected, the lounge was dark, deserted, the bar section closed. Using the lights of the city to guide her, she carefully wound her way through the cluster of tables and plush, padded chairs to stand at the floor-to-ceiling windows.

Beyond the Reno cityscape she watched a track of twinkling lights—sporadic late-night traffic from Tahoe wending down the mountain and into the valley. It was quiet and peaceful here.

She thought of Jay and how harried he had looked since the evacuation. She had caught a glimpse of him that evening leaving for home. Since the afternoon Dianne had stormed out of the suite, refusing to return, Jay had been forced to commute each day.

Kasey couldn't understand Dianne's tempestuous behavior toward Jay. It was common knowledge Dianne was spoiled, selfish, and had a temper; but in the past, she had always displayed a certain measure of respect for her husband. Of course, it was difficult to predict how any one person would react when thrust into the jaws of danger. But Jay was also a victim. Kasey could only hope that she would never have to rely on Dianne in a grave situation.

Kasey felt bad, guilty even, because she could muster no sympathy for Dianne, none whatsoever. Dianne had Jay, yet she didn't seem to realize what she had. Was Dianne that sure of Jay's love and devotion? Or didn't it matter to her? Could she toss him aside so casually in order to protect herself?

Just thinking of Jay, of his ordeal, made Kasey's heart go out to him. He wanted only what was best for the club. Torn between a loyalty to the family business and his beautiful wife—a wife whose only interest in the business was what it could provide her—he now stood to lose both.

Kasey lowered her head, rested it against the cool window pane, and shut her eyes. Behind her closed lids, the twinkling city lights lingered; and then, superimposed on that, Jay's face slowly began to materialize. Jay's face, as it had been that night in the jacuzzi, close to hers, so close she could feel his warm breath lightly caress her cheek. She had wanted so badly to feel his lips on hers. Even now her lips ached for his.

With two fingers, she lightly touched her lips, tracing them. If he kissed her, would he find her lips sensual? Would he compare them to Dianne's? If they made love, would he find her body as attractive as Dianne's? She thought of the scratches and bite marks on his shoulder and wondered if he would expect her to be as wild and wanton as Dianne.

Kasey placed her hand at her throat, then let it glide down across her chest to rest upon one full and aching breast.

How ironic, she thought. Initially, she had been hired to help Jay out. So far, all she had done was to fall in love with him. She couldn't do this anymore. Jay didn't need her. Staying would only further complicate things.

"Don't quit on me, Kasey."

Although the words were spoken softly, Kasey jumped and whirled around.

Rising up from a deep, padded chair, a mere silhouette in the dim room, was Jay King.

Before she could move or speak, he was there, a hand on

each of her arms, squeezing. "You were thinking about quitting. Please don't."

"Jay, I . . ."

He dropped his hands, turned to stare out of the window. "I can read you, Kasey. We're a lot alike, you and I. Right now, we're both doing some heavy soul-searching. Believe me, running away is not the solution."

It's the only solution when I have no willpower where you're concerned, she wanted to say. *When all I can think about is being with you.*

"I can count on you, Kasey. More than I can count on my wife. It appears I'm not welcome in my own home. Just being around me seems to throw terror into her. She blames me for everything that's happened."

Kasey felt a spark of hope, then quickly dismissed it. Nothing has changed, she told herself.

"I came up here for the same reason you did. To think," he went on. "I was thinking about you when you came in. At first, when I saw you enter . . . framed in the light from the corridor, I thought—" He laughed low in his throat. "I thought you weren't real. That I, well, that I'd somehow conjured you out of thin air. But you're real all right. You're so goddamned real it scares the hell out of me. I need something real right now, Kasey. I need . . ." His words died away.

Kasey touched his cheek. He took her hand, pressed her palm to his lips, and closed his eyes.

Her other hand raised up to touch him, stopping inches from his face. Go, she told herself, *get out of here before it's too late.*

"Jay?"

Jay opened his eyes and looked into hers. Again she saw that blend of longing and pain and knew her own eyes reflected the same emotions. He placed her hand flat against his chest, holding it there with his hand. She felt his heart beating powerfully beneath her palm.

His mouth covered hers, silencing her words. His lips were

warm, sweet, sensual. The clean scent of his after-shave swirled around her. Her own heart beat with a force that made her suddenly light-headed.

Their lips, their tongues, moved in perfect sync as though each had been made for the other, as though they had kissed countless times before.

Their bodies came together. They couldn't seem to get close enough. Where his body touched hers, it was warm, charged with a sexual energy, a promise of deep fulfillment. It felt so good, so right. How could anything that felt this incredible not be right? This special man who held her, kissed her, who at this very moment ignited a fiery passion in her, was meant for her. And she was meant for him. All other men in her life paled in comparison.

An image of Kevin burst into her mind. Kevin, with his lost, little-boy look, with his soft brown eyes, his one-sided dimples; Kevin in a groom's tuxedo kissing her at the altar—then it was gone, abruptly cast away, destroyed by the shrill whistle of a speeding train.

Kasey stumbled back. Suddenly she was cold. Jay held onto her; his hands slid down her arms until he held just her fingers.

She shook her head.

"Kasey, I'm falling in—"

"*No.*" She tugged her fingertips out of his grasp. Tears filled her eyes. She backed away.

"We can deny each other for the rest of eternity, but I can't deny the way I feel about you."

She rushed from the Skyline Room with Jay's words ringing in her ears.

Kasey let herself into her room minutes later. She had closed the door behind her and was putting the safety chain in its track when she realized there was something wrong.

Distracted by the episode upstairs with Jay, she was being anything but cautious; she wasn't thinking straight—wasn't thinking at all. A flickering light reflecting upon the door was her first clue that she was not alone.

She heard a loud report, like a gunshot, and her heart leaped into her throat.

She whirled around and saw the candles, at least a dozen of them, burning in various positions around the room.

"Don't be afraid," a voice said. Then Brad, wearing slacks and a dress shirt open to the waist, displaying a smooth, tanned chest, stepped into view holding a foaming champagne bottle. "Do you like Dom Perignon?"

Kasey, with adrenaline racing through her body, wanted to scream, to break down in hysterics, to pound her fist on the wall. Instead, she slumped against the wall and wearily covered her face with her hands.

Brad was at her side in an instant. "Hey, hey, what's this? What's going on? Kasey, what is it? You're not crying are you?"

She drew a deep breath. "Brad, what are you doing here?"

"Hey, I didn't mean to scare you. The last thing I wanted to do was scare or upset you."

"I didn't invite you. I . . ."

"I've been patient, haven't I? Haven't I, Kasey? It's been weeks. How can you get to know me, know the *real* me, if you won't spend some private time with me? Let me show you how gentle I can be. Please, Kasey. I'm not a kid. I'm a man. A man who knows how to treat a woman."

"Oh Brad . . ."

"No, don't start with that 'oh Brad' routine." He lightly fingered the material on the sleeve of her blouse. "One glass of champagne," he said, steering her into the room. "One. What harm in one glass of champagne?"

He eased her down on the end of the bed. "I only wanted to show you I could be a perfect gentleman . . . wine, conversation, a little closeness maybe, without jumping all over you. One glass?"

"Brad, what's going on?"

"I just told you. I'm trying to get to know you—"

She pulled her arm away. "I'm not talking about us," she said, cutting him off. "I want to know what you're up to. I catch you going through Jay's office safe. I see you with Dan Carne the day before the phoney bomb was found. You chase after Cage in the garage, but he conveniently gets away. You're the only one, Brad, who hasn't been threatened or attacked. Would you care to comment on that? Maybe explain what the hell is going on?"

"What do you know about Carne?"

"Damnit, Brad, answer the question. Do you have anything to do with what's happening around here?"

Brad stared at her, the expression on his face changing from playful boyishness to bewilderment, then to something that could only pass for injured pride. A sadness crept into his eyes.

"Christ, Kasey, I can't believe you would think I had anything at all to do with my uncle's problems. I admire him more than any man alive. I love him like a father. I would never, *never,* do anything to hurt him. What kind of a fucking bastard do you think I am?"

Either Brad was a very good liar or Kasey had grossly misjudged him. Could anyone display such hurt and indignation and be faking?

"But you and Carne—"

"Have nothing to do with Jay or the club. Nothing. And for you to even consider that I would . . ." Brad shook his head, stepped to the chair, lifted his jacket, and draped it over his arm. "Good night, Kasey," he said, his voice cracking. "Just forget I was here. That shouldn't be too hard for you."

"Brad, wait." Kasey reached out, touched his arm, felt muscles rigid beneath his shirt sleeve. "Look, I didn't mean . . . It's just that seeing you with . . . with—Oh, shit, I'm sorry. Pour me a glass of that stuff, will you?"

Brad gazed down into her eyes again. The muscles in his

face relaxed. Then he smiled, that slow, sweet smile that reminded her of Kevin.

He dropped his jacket on the chair, picked up the champagne bottle, and filled two glasses. He gave one to Kasey and sat beside her.

Kasey sipped. "Brad, this is not Dom Perignon."

"I didn't say it was. I just asked if you liked it."

She smiled, drank it down, held out her glass for more.

"That bad, huh?" Brad said. He refilled her glass.

She went a little slower this time. "Why were you and Carne—"

"Not now," he said softly, putting two fingers to her lips. "I'll explain everything when the time is right. Trust me."

She looked away, nodded. The last thing she wanted to believe was that Brad was involved. That Brad would want to hurt Jay, or anyone. "How did you get in?"

"With a master." He looked contrite, topped off her glass again. "I wanted to surprise you."

"You did. You really did." She drank, sipping now. She heard soft music, Michael Bolton love songs came from a CD player Brad had brought. She looked around the room. In addition to the candles, there were flowers and bunches of balloons—balloons left over from a slot tournament downstairs that afternoon.

"Where did you get the flowers?" she asked.

"Steak House. From the tables after it closed."

"You went to a lot of trouble."

"You're worth it."

The champagne was going straight to her head. She realized she hadn't eaten since five o'clock, eleven hours ago, between meetings when she'd grabbed a sandwich in the employee kitchen. She was getting high and she didn't care. Again she was reminded of Brad's resemblance to Kevin, and something inside her softened. The dim room, the candles, flowers, soft music, champagne—it was all very soothing. And now Brad was massaging her neck and shoulders. This was a day for love and romance. Her horoscope had said so. The love was upstairs in the Skyline Room. The romance . . . where was the romance?

She leaned into him. "A perfect gentleman, huh?"

"I won't do anything you don't want me to do."

"Don't talk," she said, slipping off her shoes. She turned, stretched out on her stomach, and—with a deep sigh—let Brad massage her back. After an indeterminate amount of time, she felt the zipper at the back of her dress slide down. The clasp of her bra went next. As though in a dream, she lifted herself while Brad painstakingly pulled her clothes down and off. Finally, when he gently coaxed her over onto her back, she was ready for him. Ready to receive his mouth. Ready to receive his naked body next to hers. Ready to receive his hands and mouth at her most intimate places. Ready to receive *him*.

She visualized Jay when he entered her. And a short time later when she reached orgasm, she cried out Jay's name.

Forty-one

Jay tossed and turned in the kingsize bed in the suite's master bedroom. He checked the clock for what seemed the hundredth time since he had fallen into bed several hours earlier, numb from the Jack Daniel's he'd slugged downed after Kasey had run out on him in the lounge.

6:00 A.M. The blackout drapes were drawn. The room was pitch dark.

The alarm on the travel clock began to beep. He groaned. If he had slept at all, he wasn't aware of it. He reached for the light and knocked something off the nightstand. Groping around on the floor, his fingers wrapped around a lightweight object. He switched on the light and squinted at the red-and-white spray bottle.

An antihistamine. It didn't belong to him or Dianne, yet he had seen one like it before, and not long ago.

Suddenly he was wide awake, the bourbon fog instantly gone. He dropped the bottle, leaped from the bed, strode to the window, and yanked open the drapes. Morning light filled the room.

Where was it? What the hell had he done with it? Jay stood naked in the middle of the room, racking his brain. He remembered picking the bottle out of the dirt at Lucas Cage's private shooting range last week with Frank. Jay had dropped it in his pocket and he had forgotten about it. *Where the hell were those pants?*

He found them on the top shelf of the closet in a bag of

clothes to be taken to the cleaners, neatly folded, the cuffs soiled with mud. He shook the pants until the red-and-white plastic bottle slipped out onto the carpet.

With a clothes hanger he turned it over. A neat hole—a bullet hole—obliterated the product's name, but the two bottles were unmistakably the same—a common over-the-counter brand.

Excited, Jay felt certain both belonged to Cage. He recalled the man in the surveillance video at the elevator lobby putting something to his nose. It wouldn't be hard to prove that Cage used—was addicted to?—spray antihistamine. Two identical containers, one found behind Cage's shack and the other found on Dianne's side of the bed. Cage must have dropped it there the night he attacked her.

He had to tell Frank and Kasey. He called Frank at home, told him what he had. Frank promised to stop at the hotel before going to the station.

Jay hung up and dialed Kasey's room. Before it could ring, he disconnected. He had to see her, had to tell her in person. He couldn't let her quit now. They were getting so close. Cage was getting sloppy and soon he would trip himself up. The more evidence they had, the tighter the case against him. As it stood now, the police had nothing really solid to hold him on. But, if one of Cage's fingerprints could be lifted from the bottle on the nightstand, they'd have him deadbang, as Frank was fond of saying. Kasey couldn't quit on him now.

Jay hoped she was still in the hotel. If she were, she was probably asleep. He'd have to take that chance. To wait was to risk missing her.

He pulled on sweats and running shoes, ran his fingers through his hair and over the coarse whiskers on his face, debating whether or not to shave and deciding against it. He left the bottles where they lay in his room and hurried from the suite.

Jay found the floor security guard in the alcove with the ice and vending machines, pulling a Coke from a slot. The guard straightened when he saw him.

"Morning, Mr. King, you're up early. Can I get you something?"

"No thanks. It's Hollise, isn't it?" Jay said.

"Yes, sir. Matt Hollise."

"Matt, do you know a security guard by the name of Lucas Cage?"

"No, Mr. King. Would you like me to try to locate him for you, sir?"

If only you could. "No, it's okay."

"Is Mrs. King doing better?"

"Much better, thank you." Jay lent a hand by holding up the metal lid of the ice machine while the man filled a plastic bucket. He leaned back to look down the corridor and saw the door to Kasey's room open.

Good, he thought, *his timing was perfect. She was just going out.*

But instead of Kasey, it was his nephew who stepped into the hallway, softly closing the door behind him. Brad's hair and shirt were disheveled, the shirt hanging out in back, his jacket slung casually over his shoulder.

The fact that Brad was coming out of Kasey's room at six in the morning spoke volumes. But it was the confident way he squared his shoulders and tossed back a lock of hair from his forehead before turning and sauntering down the corridor that made Jay's stomach twist with an unspeakable force.

"Sir, is there something wrong?" Hollise asked.

Jay returned to his suite without answering.

Kasey awoke at ten that morning in no way ready to face the day. Even though Brad had left her bed at dawn, she stretched out an arm to make certain she was alone.

The night before, Kasey had lain awake listening to Brad's quiet breathing as he slept beside her, unable to close her eyes until the light of morning when she woke him and asked him to leave. Only then was sleep possible for her.

The room was bright. Morning sunlight streamed in through the parted drapes, reflecting off the vanity mirror and into her face. Kasey moaned and rolled onto her stomach. She could hide from the harsh rays of the sun, but she couldn't hide from herself and what she had done the night before. She had opened her arms and body to Brad. Had shared something very intimate with a boy who, in a fragmentary, superficial way, had served as a surrogate lover, temporarily filling a void that only one man could fill.

It wouldn't happen again. She would see to that. Knowing Brad, knowing his type, she believed he would make one or two halfhearted attempts at a relationship before giving up. For him, the real challenge, the thrill of the chase, had ended last night in her bed. If he had heard her call out his uncle's name, he had made no mention of it.

Brad could be very persuasive, very convincing. If she hadn't already been in love with Jay, she might have fallen for his charms, age difference or not, much sooner. Although he'd told her he had nothing to do with the apparent sabotage of King's Club and she had believed him at the time, she now felt a niggling doubt. The next time they met, she would insist he tell her about his association with Dan Carne.

Kasey dressed in slacks and a short-sleeve blouse and quickly packed. The phone rang before she finished. She debated answering it, not eager to talk to either Brad or Jay. But thinking it might be her mother, whom she hadn't touched base with in several days, she picked up the receiver and said a tentative hello.

"Is this Kasey Atwood?" A woman's voice.

"Yes."

"You probably don't remember me. It's Paula . . . Paula Volger."

The maid. The friend of the murdered housekeeper. "Yes,

Paula," Kasey said, trying not to sound too eager, "I remember you."

"Can we talk?"

"Of course."

"Not on the phone. I'm where people can hear me. Can you meet me somewhere tonight?"

"Where?"

"I don't know. Somewhere safe."

"Your place?"

"No. I think he's been watching my house. I haven't been there since . . ." she hesitated. "He'd see us. Know what we were talking about."

"Who?"

"I think you know."

Kasey's excitement rose. "Is it the man who assaulted you in the parking garage?"

"I can't talk now. Look, I feel safer in the hotel than on the street. How 'bout your room tonight at nine o'clock?"

Kasey had planned to check-out that morning. She had left a message with Jay's secretary saying she was no longer on the job and that a bill for services rendered would be sent to the hotel. She would keep the room long enough to rendezvous with Paula.

"Nine then. I'm in room—"

"I know which one. No cops. I'm not ready to go that far yet."

With all her belongings, Kasey called for her car at valet and left the hotel. Since the attack in the garage, she had used valet parking. She had one stop to make before going home.

A few minutes after eleven, she knocked on the door of the King residence.

A plainclothes bodyguard let her in. He directed her to the rear of the house, where he deactivated the alarm, opened the sliding glass door to the patio, and pointed toward the pool.

Kasey spotted Dianne reclining on a chaise lounge at poolside, talking on the phone.

Dianne motioned to Kasey to join her.

"Did they catch that asshole?" Dianne asked flatly, hanging up the phone. "Can I come out of hiding yet?"

"This is hiding?" Kasey scanned the vast grounds, open on three sides. She saw a man perched on a boulder on a high bank above the pool house. He held a pair of binoculars in one hand and a revolver in the other. Another man strolled along the west perimeter of the property.

"And to what do I owe the honor of this visit? Did Jay tell you I sent him away? Did he ask you to come and talk some sense into me?"

Kasey shook her head. "Jay doesn't know I'm here. Although he is the reason I came."

"Oh?"

"Don't you think you're being unfair, Dianne?"

"Unfair? Hardly. Because of his love for that concrete mistress of his, he's put me in jeopardy. Is that fair to me?"

"It wasn't intentional and you know it. He's your husband. The club belongs to you, too."

"What good is it to any of us if we're dead?"

"You're hurting him. He doesn't deserve this. Dianne, he's a good person. Why can't—"

"And I'm not?"

Kasey said nothing.

"Stay out of this, Kasey. I asked you to look into things at the club, that doesn't include our private life." Dianne looked into Kasey's eyes. Her smile was slow, Cheshire cat-like. "Or does it?" she questioned softly. "Are you here to find out if I'm through with him? Did you have in mind to pick up the pieces?" She chuckled. "Oh, don't look so surprised. I'm not blind. I know you've been avoiding him and I know why. Very commendable, but entirely unnecessary. Jay, bless his righteous little heart, is true blue. Not likely to stray. And especially not with someone like you."

Kasey felt the blood rush to her face. "Someone like me?"

"Oh, you're quite pretty . . . in a less-than-classic sense, and you're smart. But I'm afraid you lack that certain— well . . . certain quality that appeals to a man like Jay. A man of his high caliber. Admit it, Kasey: The only men you seem to attract are losers. Drug addicts, boozers, clinging vines, leeches. Men who wouldn't know a backbone from a wishbone. Men like your father, your two husbands. Not men like Jay."

Kasey felt as though she'd been slapped.

The cordless phone on the lounge began to ring. "Excuse me," Dianne said, picking it up. "That's probably Jay now."

Numb, Kasey retraced her steps back the way she had come without being aware of the process. In her car once again, the stifling heat pressing in on her, threatening to suffocate her, she felt a stinging behind her eyelids. She fumbled with her sunglasses and shoved them on, hiding behind their protective shield.

"Well, it's something," Frank Loweman said, studying the two plastic bottles encased in ziplock bags.

Loweman had bagged and marked them. They had located the housekeeper who, in an interview with Loweman in the suite, acknowledged finding the bottle wedged between the bed and nightstand the morning following Dianne's attack.

"But it's not enough," Jay finished for him. He stood behind the wet bar, reached into the refrigerator, brought out a beer and a Coke, and held them up. Loweman, on the other side, took the Coke.

"Probably not. Do you know how many people in this state have allergies? Marlene has used an antihistamine every day for the past ten years. She couldn't breathe if she didn't."

"What about prints?"

"We can always hope. Don't put too much stock in fingerprints, Jay. Not all surfaces are good conductors. And don't forget our boy was wearing gloves at the time he attacked Dianne. At best we'll get a series of smudges. Yours and the maid's included."

"DNA testing? Jesus, the guy stuck it up his nose. That's a body fluid, right?"

"DNA testing is expensive, Jay. A few years back a killer right here in Washoe County was acquitted because the state wouldn't pay for the test. If they had spent the money, they would have found his semen matched the semen found inside the rectum of the dead woman and he wouldn't have been free to rape and nearly kill another young woman."

"Then you'll do it?"

"I can request it, but I doubt the request will be granted. Dianne wasn't murdered. She wasn't even raped. Thank your lucky stars for that. By the way," Loweman added, "I got some feedback on Lucas Cage this morning. Just as I suspected, there was nothing damaging on his sheet in two of the three departments he was hooked up with, but I got a strong impression that the people I talked with knew more than they cared to share."

"That Blue Wall of Silence you spoke of?"

"Exactly. I'm still waiting to hear from Vegas, which we believe was his last official law enforcement attachment. It's possible he screwed up royally there. A cop gets away with so much over the years and he begins to think he's untouchable, beyond the law. There's a saturation point, and Cage may have reached it in Vegas."

"Let's hope so."

"Won't help us much on this case, but it will give us some idea what we're up against—how bad this perp is, shit like that. He was issued a police work card, so he's not a felon."

Jay drank beer from the can. "He's not working alone. Someone has been feeding him information, opening doors, covering his ass."

"Someone inside?"

"Yes."

"Any candidates?"

"Oh, yes."

"Care to share?"

"My guess would be Cummings."

"Your top man?"

Jay nodded.

"You don't trust him?"

"Jesus, I don't know. He's the best CEO we've had. The guy is top-notch. I considered bringing him in, giving him a share of the operation."

"So what's changed?"

"He used to work for Ansel Doyle. So did Cage. Doyle is looking for a piece of the action here in Northern Nevada. He wants King's Club."

"Doyle made you an offer?"

"A generous one. I turned him down. Said the club wasn't for sale. Doyle doesn't like to get turned down. He has a reputation for leaning on people to get what he wants. One of his key men from his lake operation was snooping around awhile back."

"Who's this key man?"

"Tony Bartona."

"I'll check him out." Loweman wrote in his notebook. "And you think Doyle might be behind this?"

"It's crossed my mind."

"But you have no proof about either him or Cummings?"

"No. Just that it was Cummings who received the bomb threat on his car phone. How many people have access to the private line of a casino's chief exec? It was Cummings who sounded the alarm."

"What would Doyle gain by all this?"

"Go downstairs. Take a look around. You could drive the fun train through there without hitting anyone. Local papers, news media, they're having a goddamned field day at the club's expense . . . at my expense. If you were a lender, would you lay out forty million to renovate a joint that you thought might go up in a puff of smoke before you got your money back?"

"Okay, let's say it is Doyle, and that his terrorist tactics are meant to force you to sell out to him. Wouldn't he be sabotaging his own future investment?"

"Not really. The public has a short memory. In a little while, things would get back to normal. Doyle has enough money to ride out the adverse publicity. I don't. No, his main objective would be to scare me into selling. He could accomplish that by keeping me uncertain as to when or where the next strike will come. A fire, another killing, another bomb threat. The fact that the bomb was a hoax leads me to believe it was Doyle. He's not going to do anything that could actually damage the club, only its reputation. No business can survive one attack upon another. I'm not even sure I can make it work now."

"Jay, the club will prosper."

"But will I? Will my family? How far will this go? How far is this bastard willing to take it? Frank, you know this club is my life. But is it *worth* my life or the lives of the people around me?"

Jay thought of those people. Dianne, Brad and Brenda, and most recently Kasey. His love for his niece and nephew was unconditional; they were family. Dianne was his wife. Despite their many differences, he had hoped his feelings for her would remain constant. When this was all over, would he ever be able to overlook her blatant abandonment of him? Could he love her again? He had his doubts. Too much had been lost.

Then there was Kasey.

Kasey, who at this very moment could already be gone from his life. Although she hadn't officially checked out of her room, the clerk at the front desk had seen her passing through the lobby with luggage, and earlier in the day Gail had given him Kasey's message of termination.

Jay wondered who was left. Whom could he trust? His chief executive was a prime suspect. His wife had turned against him. His nephew had spent the night with the woman he loved;

and although that woman had run out on him, too, she was the only person he could trust. Kasey was the only one without a personal stake in the hotel.

As if reading his mind, Loweman asked, "This Kasey Atwood, what part does she play in all this?"

Jay found himself unwilling to meet Loweman's gaze. "She started out as a consultant. Dianne brought her in."

"Interesting." Loweman pulled a handful of change from his pocket and seemed intent on examining it.

Jay looked at his old friend, and saw empathy in the warm brown eyes.

"Does it show?" Jay asked.

"I don't know what you're talking about," Loweman said, returning the coins to his pocket. "If you mean does it show that you like and trust her, yeah . . . yeah, it does. But, shit, I like her, too. She's got a helluva lot going for her. A guy could do a lot worse—for a partner, I mean."

"A partner?"

Loweman clapped Jay on the back. "Gotta go." He went a couple of feet before stopping and turning. "Oh, I'm s'pose to tell you thanks again for lunch last week. Marlene's still talking about it. You're one of her favorite people, y'know? But then, there ain't nobody she don't like," he said with a grin.

"You're a lucky man, Frank."

"Yeah, I know."

After Loweman left the suite, Jay called downstairs to personnel and asked for Kasey Atwood's home address.

Forty-two

Lucas Cage unlocked the box at Reno's main post office and took out the plain white envelope. Although it had no return address, he knew the sender and he guessed the contents. Cage had been expecting the letter.

He tore it open, pulled out the single sheet of cheap note paper. *Do it. NOW!*

He grinned. He could almost smell the desperation in those three short words. Do. It. Now.

Why hurry? he asked himself. He was having too much fun. He wasn't ready to end it just yet. His initial instructions were to get rid of them in a timely manner in any way he chose. He would do it when he chose and how he chose. No one was going to tell the Monk how to do his business. No one. And especially not now, when he had the upper hand.

He folded the envelope and slipped it into his pocket. With long strides, he crossed the parking lot, climbed into Sherry Kidd's old GMC truck, and drove away.

When Kasey arrived home, she spotted her mother walking across the rear yard toward the pasture. Marianne towed a honeycomb box in a Red Flyer wagon, her other arm laden with her beekeeper's tools of the trade—a smoker, bellows, rags for burning, gloves, and veil.

"Ma, wait up!" Kasey called out as she ran to catch up with her. When she reached her mother's side, she helped lessen her load by taking the smoker and bellows. "The Crumbys have a swarm?" The Crumbys were the neighbors to the east.

"Yup. Took a fancy to Cliff's old pickup. Been there a couple days. Crumby waited till they were good an' peeved before giving me a call."

Kasey fell in step beside her mother and clucked her tongue. She knew from experience that in the early stages the swarm was relatively docile. Before taking to the sky, loyal troops of a displaced queen gorge themselves on honey, which makes stinging difficult, if not impossible; but after several days on the move, they become ill-tempered and downright cantankerous.

"Mind if I tag along?"

"Love to have you. I missed you," Marianne said. "It's been almost a week. I thought maybe you would call, y'know, for your horoscope."

"It wasn't necessary; I looked it up myself. You're a bad influence on me, Ma."

Marianne chuckled and nudged Kasey affectionately with her shoulder. "Do you have to get right back? Can you stay for dinner?"

"Lunch, dinner, and probably breakfast in the morning. I quit. I won't be going back to the club."

Marianne gave her daughter a long, hard look. "Why? What's up? It's not like you to quit a job."

Kasey looked away.

Marianne stopped, pulled Kasey around to face her. "What is it, honey? You haven't been the same since you started this job. Whenever I see you, you seem more and more withdrawn. What's wrong? Is it our financial situation?"

"How could it be financial? Yesterday's horoscope said financial worries will soon be a thing of the past. See, nothing to worry about in that department," she said flippantly.

"What then?"

Kasey became somber again. "I don't think you want to know."

"Kasey, honey, you know you can talk to me."

Kasey put down the smoker and bellows and leaned against an old cottonwood tree. She watched a bee buzz around the honeycomb box. "Oh, Ma, I don't know how it happened . . . how I could have let it happen. I'm—I fell in love with someone I have no right to love. The husband of a friend."

"Jay King? You're in love with Jay King?"

Kasey nodded, covered her eyes with her hand.

"Dianne's no friend of yours, but that's not the issue here. Honey, are you sure?"

"Well, I can't eat, sleep, concentrate. I think about him first thing in the morning and last thing at night. He's even in my dreams. What's that sound like to you?"

"How long have you known?"

Kasey picked at the tree bark. "I guess it started years ago. I was attracted to him when I worked at the club. Me and all the other waitresses. He was rich, handsome, charming and kind. He still is, only now he's more mature and even more sensitive. A man with many fine qualities. I might have fantasized, dreamed about marrying someone like him, but that was it. He was beyond my reach." She lowered her head; her hair fell forward around her face. "Until now. Only now it still isn't right."

Marianne tucked Kasey's hair behind her ear, held her cool hands against the side of her face, and gently turned it to gaze into her eyes. "Sweetheart, follow your heart. It doesn't always have to be right."

Jay hardly noticed the picturesque landscape of golden pastures, ponds, the cotton and dogwood trees on both sides of the highway as he left behind the traffic and congestion of the city and entered the valley. He pushed the Lexus above the speed limit, his mind preoccupied with thoughts of Kasey. He had to talk to her. Seeing Brad leave her room that morning had been a hard blow, but what did he expect? He had no claims on her. Granted, he loved her, a love he had no right to possess. But it was his problem, not hers.

She could deny his love, but he refused to let her quit on him. One woman had already done that. He needed Kasey, and the need was deeper, stronger than anything he'd ever experienced before.

In the last few hours he'd come to realize that what he had once thought was so important—his marriage, the club, his position and status in the community—all paled compared to his feelings for Kasey.

The angry swarm had settled in the grill of Cliff Crumby's old truck. Wearing the veil and gloves, Marianne waved the smoker in front of the grill until its smoke gently sedated the displaced bees enough for her to transfer them to the combs in the box.

Kasey stood back a safe distance and watched. This process of gathering bees always fascinated her. Once the queen bee surrendered, allowing herself to be placed in the box, the rest of her army usually came along peacefully. An hour after they arrived, the queen yielded and the renegade bees were making their way to their new home.

"You want these bees, Cliff?" Marianne asked her neighbor, a gangly, stooped man with gray whiskers who stood beside Kasey. "By rights they're yours. They took up residence in your truck."

"Hell no. What would I want 'em for?"

"For the honey, of course."

"You hand over more honey than I know what to do with. Take 'em. Be my guest."

Kasey pulled the red wagon over to the pickup, trying not to jerk or flinch when several bees buzzed near her face. "Ma, maybe you should cut back on the amount of hives you keep. You ran out of storage space for the honey long ago."

"Didn't I tell you? The new boarder is building shelves in the laundry room. He volunteered."

"Really?"

"I think he's doing it more for Sherry than me. He likes to show off his muscles," Marianne added, removing the veil and gloves now that the bees were sedated. "He's quite smitten with our little redhead. Can't keep his eyes off her."

"Isn't Mr. Flynn a bit old for Sherry?"

"Oh, no, not him. Gosh, you're way behind. I decided on the other one. Tom. The one you sent over."

"I sent over?"

"From the club. Tom Andrews."

Tom Andrews. *Thomas Andrews?* Kasey felt as if the ground had been pulled out from under her. She rushed forward, grabbed her mother's arm. "Ma, what's this guy look like?"

"Careful, honey, don't frighten the bees, you'll get stung."

"What's he look like?"

"Tall, balding a little in front. Blue eyes, sort of slanted, Mongolian-like Why? You know what he looks like. He said you told him about the room. You did, didn't you?"

"Where is he?" Kasey said, trying to keep the rising alarm from her voice. She brushed impatiently at a bee that had landed on her arm, felt a sting, but ignored it. "Is he at the house now?"

"No. He went into town to get lumber for the shelves. He took Sherry's rig."

Kasey backed up. "How long ago?"

"Just before you got here."

Kasey took off for home.

"Where are you going? Kasey, what's going on?"

"Later, Ma, later." As she ran through the Crumbys' yard, she heard her mother calling to her.

She reached the house minutes later, breathless, a painful stitch in her side. The truck was nowhere in sight. Kasey felt immense relief, but didn't stop to rest. She ran to the shed and looked through the dusty panes of glass. Inside, like a dark, brooding monster, was the black Camaro.

Damn him. The sonofabitch! He had found out about the vacant room and had used her name to get into her mother's house. Tom Andrews. He had used a name he knew Kasey would recognize, the other security guard at the club whose reports he had switched.

After a quick glance down the deserted driveway, Kasey entered the shed. She was surprised to find the Camaro unlocked. Before she could lose her nerve, she opened the car door and began to go through it. In the glove compartment she found an auto insurance receipt and a registration form made out to a Lucas T. Cage. Also there was a greasy rag, a full bottle of nasal spray, and a hunting knife in a leather sheath.

In the light from the dome she searched the floor. She felt under the front seats, coming up with a dried French fry, dirty beer nuts, and a single pink-and-blue capsule. Kasey raised it to the light and inspected it. It didn't look like an over-the-counter drug. *Amoxil,* she read. An antibiotic, a form of penicillin. The murdered woman in Room 814 had had a purse filled with drugs, the contents of one bottle missing. Had it been an antibiotic? And a week later, a doctor's room had been ransacked, possibly by someone looking for drugs.

Kasey slipped the capsule into the pocket of her pants.

Hurrying now, she popped the trunk. The interior was blanketed with a fine layer of sand. In a corner was a pillowcase crammed with dirty laundry. Kasey poked through the rest of the contents: an empty cardboard beer case; a shotgun and a rifle and a dozen yellow shotgun shells—some spent and others heavy with buckshot; a folding shovel; a first-aid kit, and a green metal box, the kind used for storing important papers. The box was locked.

She slammed the trunk lid, slipped out of the shed, and closed the door.

Snickers came out of nowhere and followed her to the main

house. On the back porch, when she reached for the dog to keep him from bounding into the kitchen, he whined and ducked down, as if dodging a blow.

"What's the matter, Snickers?"

He meekly licked her hand, crouched, and turned away.

Something was wrong with the dog. It wasn't like him to be timid, to cower, she thought, but had no time right now to dwell on it.

She snatched up the kitchen phone, looked up the number for the Sparks Police, dialed, then asked for Det. Loweman. When he came on the line, she told him Lucas Cage was living in her mother's rooming house. Loweman told her to sit tight, that although the Atwood place was out of his jurisdiction, he would call the proper authorities and the feds and meet them there. She was not, he said sternly—repeat—*not* to confront Cage if he turned up before the police arrived.

She climbed the stairs to the second floor. The door to Sherry's room was wide open, the room empty. Behind the closed door of George and Danny Quackenbush, she heard cheering sounds from the TV intermingled with soft snoring. At this time of the day, Danny would be watching a sports event on ESPN while his grandfather napped.

Partially open was the door to Artie's old room, now occupied by Lucas Cage. Kasey felt a renewed wave of anger. How dare the bastard come into her family home, using lies and tricks to lease a room? While she was cooped up in a cramped hotel room wondering where he was, this snake, this animal, was living under her mother's roof in close contact with the people she loved.

Kasey entered the room and quickly went to work, going through the dresser and nightstand drawers. She had no idea what she was looking for or what she hoped to find. Her mother had certain house rules. Except for the bottle of dry sherry kept in the cupboard above the sink for medicinal purposes, alcohol and tobacco products were forbidden in the house. Also prohibited were handguns. With the shotgun and rifle in the trunk of the Camaro and Cage an ex-cop, she suspected he also had at least one handgun.

She found it in a cowboy boot in the closet. She carefully tipped the boot, dumping the revolver onto the bed. Along with the large .44 Magnum, a handful of shells spilled out, several rolling off the bed and onto the floor.

Kasey kneeled down to retrieve the shells.

Outside she heard the sound of Sherry's pickup coming up the drive. A car door slammed.

Quickly coming to her feet, she darted to the window, keeping her body to one side, out of sight. She peered down into the yard, saw Sherry's truck parked behind her own car. Lucas Cage was lifting several wooden planks from the back of the truck.

Kasey raced to the bed, shoved the gun and shells back into the boot and returned it to the closet. The sound of voices outside made her go back to the window.

Cage, still at the pickup, gestured at someone. From Kasey's vantage point, she couldn't see who was down there with him. She hoped it wasn't her mother. She didn't want her mother anywhere near the house until the police arrived.

A moment later Sherry came into view. Sherry, wearing a long T-shirt and knee-high leggings, with her reddish-blonde hair caught in a ponytail, approached slowly, glancing around.

Kasey's heart pounded. What did he want with Sherry? Sherry, with her well-honed *creed detector,* would immediately sense the evil in a man like Cage. And by the way she was behaving—wary, guarded—she had already.

Cage said something to Sherry. Kasey tried to read his lips, but the angle was off. Sherry responded, shifting uneasily, attempting, it seemed, to keep a certain amount of space between them.

Cage reached up, his large hand cupping the back of Sherry's neck. She tried to pull away. He held her.

Kasey stiffened, anger flaring again. The bastard had managed to get a foot into her mother's house, but he sure as hell wasn't going to get away with threatening or intimidating any of them. It suddenly occurred to her why Snickers had cowered when she reached for him. Cage had had five days to terrorize the dog. She glanced at the boot in the closet. She could get the gun and—

Before she could do anything, Cage released Sherry. Sherry said something, then turned and walked away.

When Kasey looked back at Cage, he was looking up toward the window. She ducked out of sight, but not before his eyes locked onto hers.

She moved quickly. He was not going to get back into their house, she told herself. She rushed from the room, down the stairs, through the house to the kitchen. She reached the back door just as Cage, with two planks on his shoulder, opened it.

She barred the way.

Cage looked her in the eye. He grinned. "Find anything interesting in my room, Ms. Atwood?"

"It's not your room anymore," she said evenly, though she was quaking inside. "You're no longer a roomer in this house. The police are on the way, so just turn around and go back down those steps."

She tried to close the door. He pushed on it.

For several moments she managed to hold him off, but she was no match for him. She abruptly let go. The door swung open. He lunged forward, lost his balance, slipping on the step. Kasey drove her arm forward, catching him in the Adam's apple with the heel of her palm, sending him backwards off the porch. She slammed the door and turned the deadbolt.

His face reddened and his blue eyes darkened to black steely pinpoints. With a mighty thrust, he rammed the planks through a pane in the door, shattering it. Glass flew everywhere. Kasey felt the sting of several tiny shards, like bits of burning embers, bite into her throat and upper chest.

He tossed the planks aside, reached an arm through the broken pane, and turned the bolt. The door banged open against the wall.

Kasey turned to run. If she could reach his gun, she could hold him off until the police arrived. And if she had to use it, she would.

She heard barking behind her, and before she knew what was happening, Snickers was there, underfoot. She fell to her knees.

When she looked over her shoulder, Cage was towering above her, reaching for her.

Then he fell back. She saw someone behind him, heard the sound of flesh pounding flesh, and realized that Cage was fending off the blows of Jay King.

Over the commotion of the two fighting men and the large dog bounding among the three of them, Kasey heard the solid punch land on Cage's jaw. Then Cage, with twenty pounds on Jay, charged him, sending him across the room to smash into a utility cart. Jars of jam and honey crashed to the floor. Cage kicked Jay in the side, pulled a hammer from a loop on his belt, and swung it at him, narrowly missing his head. Snickers leaped up and sank his teeth into Cage's arm, and an instant later four uniformed policemen rushed in and quickly put an end to the fight.

Forty-three

Kasey dressed the small cut above Jay's left eye. They sat at the kitchen table, bandages and antiseptic spread out on the table.

After the police and federal agents had taken Lucas Cage away, Marianne had chased everyone out of the kitchen before finally taking herself outside to the garden, giving Kasey and Jay some privacy.

"You should have a doctor look at this," Kasey said, dabbing the cut with peroxide. "It could use a stitch or two."

"It'll be okay. That spot is nothing but scar tissue. In the service when I boxed, it was my Achilles' heel. Some guys had glass jaws, I had a glass brow. A bandage will take care of it."

"Jay." She paused with her fingers pressed lightly to the side of his face. "Thanks."

"For what?"

"For coming when you did. For stopping Cage."

"For *trying* to stop him. The dog's the hero."

"Thanks," she said, ignoring his attempt at modesty.

His eyes met hers. He nodded.

"I don't know why you came out here today, but I'm glad you did."

"I came to apologize for last night . . . in the lounge," Jay said. "I'm not sorry for what I did or said. I'm sorry for dragging you into the middle of my chaotic life, my deteriorating marriage. It's over between me and Dianne. I think it's been over for years now. I wanted you to know that. I can't make any commitments just yet, so if it's Brad you want . . ."

"Brad?"

"When I saw him leaving your room this morning, I . . . well, let's just say I wanted to beat the shit out of him. But then I realized I had no right to be jealous. Brad's single, with no commitments. And he's a good kid. You could do worse."

Kasey felt a knot in her stomach. Jay knew she and Brad had slept together. He thought she wanted Brad.

"We can still work together on this, can't we?" he asked when she remained silent. His eyes met hers. "I need your help. Work with me, please."

"Jay, I want that sonofabitch behind bars as badly as you do," she said. "He's after me, too. All the time the cops were looking for him, he was right here in my mother's house. It makes me sick to think that he was so close to her and the others. These people are family to me. I intend to stop him if it's the last thing I do."

"We'll stop him," Jay said.

Kasey heard footsteps coming down the staircase and across the parquet floor of the entry hall. The screen door at the front of the house creaked open and closed. Several minutes later, she heard Sherry's truck start up, then drive away.

Kasey closed the gash on Jay's brow with a butterfly bandage. "I went through Cage's car and found a prescription capsule of some kind. Loweman said he'd check it out, though he didn't think it was a controlled substance. I also found a very large gun in a boot upstairs."

"Do me a favor: Don't go sticking your neck out again unless I'm there. This guy can be ugly, real ugly. Will you promise me you won't try to confront him alone?"

"I promise."

"Now, we'll get you fixed up," Jay said, gently pushing her into a chair.

He cleaned the tiny wounds where the flying glass had cut her; then he removed the bee stinger on her forearm, which had begun to swell. All through his tender administrations, Kasey was acutely aware of his nearness—the heat from his body, the heady scent of his after-shave, the humming energy that seemed to pass from his fingertips through her skin to touch deep inside her.

Afterward, she gave him a tour of the ranch. They were at the bee boxes at one corner of the property when Marianne called to them that Det. Loweman had phoned and wanted to see both of them at the county jail as soon as possible.

"The capsule you found in Cage's car is an antibiotic, like penicillin." Loweman held it up between thumb and forefinger. "Amoxil. Fairly common, as prescription drugs go."

"Why would he be on antibiotics?" Kasey said.

"I asked him that. He said he wasn't, that he had no need to be. Said he was in perfect health," Loweman said. "Of course he could be lying. If he's got a case of VD, he might not want to advertise it."

"Is it a similar drug to what was missing from the dead woman's purse?" Kasey asked.

"It's the same drug. The same strength."

Kasey and Jay both leaned forward.

"Well, there, doesn't that implicate him in her death?" Jay demanded. "He could have easily gotten into her room, stolen the drugs, and murdered her. We know Cage wouldn't think twice about breaking a finger to get at a diamond ring. He could also have planted the ring in the dishwasher's locker."

"Except he has an alibi for the night she died."

Jay and Kasey looked at each other.

"Not only does he have an alibi for that night, he also has one for the day the bomb was planted. If you recall, a surveillance camera recorded a blond, curly-haired man in maintenance clothes toting a toolbox from the service elevator. The exact time is indicated on the tape; and we know, from specific markings, that the toolbox he was carrying was the same one planted in the mechanical room. As it stands right now, we can't hold him on either charge."

"His alibi, is it valid?"

"Someone, a woman, claims to have been with him on both occasions. In a motel on Lake Street. The motel manager substantiated his alibi."

Kasey and Jay exchanged looks.

"Look, I'm not supposed to do this," Loweman said, "but I think this is something you can help with, Kasey. The source happens to be someone you're acquainted with. And let's just say there's something about this whole thing that don't smell good. In fact, it stinks."

"Who is she?" Kasey thought of Paula Volger. Had Cage threatened her? Was that why she wanted to meet with her that evening?

"She's in the reception area. Go have a word with her."

Kasey rose, left the small office, and went down the hall to the waiting room, fully expecting to confront Paula Volger.

Sherry Kidd paced the empty room, puffing nervously on a cigarette. When she saw Kasey, she quickly looked away.

"Sherry?"

Sherry turned her back to Kasey, stared out the window.

"Sherry, what are you doing here?" Kasey pulled her around to face her. "My God, it can't be true. You can't be that man's alibi?"

"Oh? Why not?"

"He threatened you, didn't he? I saw the two of you talking in the yard. He has something on you. He does, doesn't he?"

"I was with him. What can I say?"

"I don't believe you. There's no way you'd let someone like him touch yo—"

"Oh, c'mon, Kasey. I'm a whore. I let all kinds of men touch me, fuck me. You of all people know what I am."

"Not him. I saw the way you shrank from him today. He put you up to this somehow. You never met Cage until he moved into my mother's house."

"That's not true. He was security at King's Club. He set me up a couple times with men staying there. I owed him, so I took it out in trade."

"You're lying."

"Kasey, drop it," Sherry said angrily, tossing the cigarette out the open window. "You don't know what the fuck you're getting into. Just drop it, okay?"

"It's you who doesn't know what you're getting into. The man is garbage. He's . . . he's probably a killer. Sherry, you can't protect him."

Sherry tried to push past Kasey. Kasey grabbed her by the shoulder and pulled her around. Sherry winced, cried out sharply.

"What? What's wrong? Did he hurt you?" Kasey grabbed the neckline of the large T-shirt and yanked it down in back. She caught only a glimpse, but it was enough. She took Sherry's arm and pulled her the few feet into the ladies' room.

Once inside, Kasey closed and locked the door, bracing her back to it. Sherry struggled, tried to get the door open; but Kasey, more determined than ever to see what Sherry was hiding, quickly pulled the shirt over her head.

Sherry retreated, crossed her arms over her bare breasts, tried to cover herself. But she couldn't hide the hideous marks on her back and shoulders reflected in the mirror behind her.

Kasey wadded the shirt and held it to her face, too stunned to speak. Sherry's entire back was covered with tiny cuts and what appeared to be bite marks and cigarette burns.

Sherry now stood quietly in the corner, her head lowered, eyes closed, breathing heavily through her mouth. Kasey's fingers hovered above the wounds, wanting to give solace, yet not wanting to hurt her further. The injuries looked fresh, no more than a day old. When this had happened, Kasey had not been there to soothe her child-like friend, to make her hot chocolate and gently rock her as on those occasional nights in the past when Sherry had "goofed" and had paid the price.

These wounds, wounds certain to scar, were not merely

marks of abuse, they were marks of calculated torture. And the attacker nothing less than a sadistic monster.

Kasey tenderly folded her arms around Sherry, who leaned into her. They stayed like that for many long moments, with Kasey holding her, neither saying a word.

Then quietly Sherry said, "Drop it, Kasey. Please."

"I can't. He can't get away with this. If he's behind bars, he won't be able to hurt you again."

Sherry's laugh was harsh, ugly. She pushed Kasey away, snatched her shirt and quickly pulled it on. "Drop it. I won't change my story. I was with Lucas Cage on both occasions. I was with Lucas Cage. I was with Lucas . . ."

Kasey went out the door with Sherry's words echoing in her head.

When Kasey told Loweman, he said that he suspected as much but there was nothing they could do unless Sherry decided to come around.

"What about the FBI?"

"They're backing off, too. There was no mention of money in the suspect's telephone conversation to Howard Cummings; therefore, no proof of an extortion attempt."

"Can you arrest him for what he did this afternoon?"

"What did he do?"

"He came after me."

"According to his statement, you attacked him. Chopped him in the throat as he was coming up the back steps with a load of lumber for some shelves he was going to make for your mother. He says he didn't lay a hand on you. Is that so?"

"Well, no, he didn't, but if Jay hadn't shown up when he did—"

"He says you tripped over the dog and fell down. He was only giving you a helping hand." Loweman raised a hand to silence both Kasey and Jay. "I know it's bullshit, but all we got here is a broken window. Jay jumped him from behind before he could lay a hand on you. Neither of you can deny that. He's talking about having the dog put to sleep for biting him and pressing charges against the both of you, Jay in particular. Even if we could prove he intended bodily harm, he'd be out on bail before the day was out."

"I don't want him on my property or anywhere near it. What he did to Sherry was . . . was—He's a sick and very dangerous man. If I have to get a restraining order to keep him away, I will. I'll shoot him if I have to."

"I'll take him back out there to get his car and personal things. I'll make sure he leaves. Go ahead and get that restraining order as an added precaution," Loweman said to Kasey. He looked from Kasey to Jay. "Now, what else do you two have?"

"Meaning what?" Jay asked.

"Meaning, I seem to be a pace behind in this investigation. Are you keeping something from me? Something I should know about?"

Kasey thought of her appointment that evening with Paula Volger. The last thing she wanted to do was tell the police about Paula and have them scare her off. The maid just might prove to be their ace in the hole.

"No, nothing," Kasey said.

It was late afternoon when Jay took Kasey home. Loweman, with Lucas Cage, followed in the detective's unmarked car.

While Loweman waited for Cage to pack his belongings, he talked with Jay outside. He handed Jay a slip of paper with a name and phone number written on it.

"The guy was a cop in Vegas. He was Cage's partner for a while. You might give him a call. He wouldn't give me anything, but he may open up to you. It's worth a shot."

Jay folded the paper, thanked him.

Kasey and Jay stood in the yard as Cage backed the Camaro out of the shed. Looking directly at Kasey, he mouthed the words, "I'll be back." Then, with an ugly smirk on his face, he drove away, Loweman tailing close behind.

Kasey walked Jay to his car.

After settling in behind the wheel, he asked, "Will you be coming back to the club?"

"Yes. Tonight. I'm meeting Paula Volger in my room at the hotel. She called me. I think she has information on Cage."

"The missing maid? When were you going to tell me about this?"

"I don't know. I almost didn't."

Jay looked straight ahead, his fingertips tapped absently on the steering wheel. "Would it be a breach of ethics if we had dinner together first?"

"You can't be there, Jay. I promised her I'd be alone."

"Christ, Kasey, you don't know what you're walking into. I'll be damned if I'll let you do this by yourself."

"I made a promise. I'm sorry."

He sighed heavily and turned his head sharply to look her in the eye. "I'll be in the suite all night. At least let me know when you get to the club. Can you do that?"

"Yes."

Jay inserted the key in the ignition; but before he could turn it, Kasey stopped him with a hand on his shoulder. "Jay, I have something to say. I was going to bring it up tonight, but I think you should know now."

Jay shifted in the seat and draped his arm over the steering wheel, waiting.

"I think Brad is somehow involved in this whole messy affair."

"What?"

She exhaled, looked off toward the orchard. "I caught him going through the safe in your office one night. And last week he had a clandestine meeting with Dan Carne in the parking garage."

"Dan Carne?"

She turned back to him. "The mobster you had thrown out of the club a while back."

"I know who Dan Carne is," he said evenly.

"Brad is about the only one who hasn't been threatened or attacked. He stands to gain the most, Jay, if anything happens to you and Dianne."

Jay stared straight ahead through the windshield. He was silent for many long moments, then he reached over and started the engine. "Brad is not involved." He shifted gears and pulled away.

Kasey watched his car until it disappeared a quarter-mile down the lane beyond the sycamore trees. Weary, her steps leaden, she went to her bungalow and let herself in. The place was hot and stuffy. She opened all the windows and doors.

Her mother had watered the plants and stacked her mail on the kitchen table. Kasey had the feeling her mother had not been the only person inside her house. She went through the drawers. Nothing appeared out of place, yet still she had the distinct feeling her privacy had been violated.

Standing at the bathroom sink, she stared into the medicine cabinet at the assortment of pills and ointments. She lifted a prescription vial, one that had been there for years. A pain-killer, probably, though she couldn't recall what it was for. It was half-full. She opened it, dumped the tablets into the toilet, and flushed.

From there she went into the kitchen and did the same with the food in the refrigerator, dumping everything into the waste-basket. She knew she was being paranoid; but if Cage had come into her private domain as she suspected, she wasn't taking any chances. He was capable of anything.

As she stripped the sheets from her bed and remade it, she listened to the messages on the answering machine. Peggy had called wanting to meet for lunch to discuss her wedding. Two new clients had called with job offers. She was surprised to hear her father's voice; he hated the machine and usually hung up without speaking. Four messages were from Brad; the last said, "Hey, I'm beginning to feel pretty stupid here. What am I, some goddamn one-night-stand? Are you blowing me off?"

She returned all the calls, saving Brad for last. She dreaded talking with him.

"Hey, beautiful, I've been thinking about you all day. Dinner tonight?"

"Look, Brad—"

"I hate it when people start a conversation with 'Look, Brad.' "

"I'm sorry, it's just—"

"Dinner tonight. Meet me in the Steak House. Eight." He paused a beat; then, in a soft tone, he added, "Kasey, we have to talk."

Yes, she thought, as difficult as it would be, they had to talk.

"Eight, then."

Jay sat in the monitor room, the screens glowing as he dialed the number Loweman had given him. It was an Arizona exchange. A man answered. Jay identified himself and asked for Gerald Ordman.

"Yeah, that's me," the man said.

"I'll calling about a man by the name of Lucas Cage."

"What about Cage?" The tone was wary.

"I understand you were partners with him on the police force in Vegas."

"Briefly."

"Yes, briefly. Officer Ordman—"

"You can drop the title. I'm no longer on the force."

"Mr. Ordman, can you give me a few minutes?"

"A Sparks detective called me awhile ago. I told him I didn't have anything to say."

"Look, I'm going to level with you. Cage is harassing me and my family. Hell, it's more than harassment; it's an all out attack, and he's doing some heavy damage. I know about the Blue Wall of Silence and I respect it; but if you could make an exception in this case, it may save a life or two."

There was a long silence on the other end, where Jay thought he had hung up; then, "What is it you want to know?"

"First off, how can I stop him?"

"Get yourself the biggest gun you can lay hands on and blow his fucking brains out."

It took Jay a moment to react. He had expected the man to hem and haw, saying little, offering nothing.

"Cage is bad news," Ordman went on. "What I'm about to tell you goes no further. I'll deny I said it. Understood?"

"Understood."

"We were partners for three months. I asked for a transfer and got it. Cage was the reason for the transfer. He threatened to kill me. If I hadn't left the force and moved to another state, I think he would have done it. A bullet in the back of my head some night while on a call. Friendly fire. Y'know, a little fragging, like in Nam."

"What did you do to piss him off?"

"I laughed at him."

"Laughed at him?"

"That's it. But with him it was enough. No one laughs at Lucas Cage." Ordman shouted at someone to turn down the TV. When he came back on the line he said, "He had this thing about VD. When he was a kid, he watched his granddad die of syphilis. Guess it was pretty bad there at the end, bad enough to make quite an impression on Cage. He had this weird notion that if he took penicillin everyday, he'd build up his immune system. Make it impossible to get it. Someone gave him a dose when he was young, some woman he thought was as pure as the driven snow. I hate to think what he did to her when he found out. Anyway, he used penicillin as a preventative, like vitamin C or something. I don't know a lot about medicine and diseases, but I read about some famous actor or writer back in the fifties who'd done the same thing he was doing. This guy developed an immunity to the drug, taking it when he didn't need it, and guess what? He got syph and ended up dying from it. Ironic, huh?"

"Yes."

"Anyway, Cage seemed like a pretty bright guy, but that was the dumbest thing I'd ever heard. And I told him so. Told him about the guy I'd read about. He said, 'We'll see who's dumb. We'll just see who outlives who, Ordman.' It wasn't so much what he said, as the way he said it. I'd seen enough in those three months as his partner, stuff I won't go into here and now, to be scared. He was like no one I'd ever met before. It was a threat and I damn well took it seriously."

"Where does he get the drug?"

"He didn't say. I suspect he steals it. I wouldn't put anything past him."

None of what Ordman said surprised Jay. He had made the same evaluation nearly twenty years ago in Germany.

"Oh, and if he raped somebody, unless you're doing DNA, forget it. He's a nonsecretor."

"How do you know that?"

"They didn't call him the 'Monk' 'cause he was celibate. And being the macho bully he is, he pretty much took what he wanted. In Vegas, while on the force, he was charged with rape, plus assault and battery. The charges were dropped a short time later when—Guess what?"

"The alleged victim recanted her story."

"Bingo."

Forty-four

Kasey stopped at the YMCA before meeting Brad for dinner. It was the night both Peggy and Artie taught self-defense classes in the gym. She lucked out and caught them between classes.

Artie, in his exuberant way, leaped to his feet and gave her a bear hug when she and Peggy entered the small front office. The big man lifted her off the floor with relative ease.

"Put her down, you big lug," Peggy said. "Can't you see she's dressed for a date? You're going to have her all scroungy and wrinkled."

Artie quickly released her. "Sorry."

"Hey, it's okay," Kasey said, straightening her clothes. She wore all white: skirt, blouse, jacket, and heeled sandals with no hose—her legs were tan from yard work at the ranch. A shell comb held her hair up in back. "And it's not a date—not really."

"Well, you sure look pretty," Artie said.

She smiled at him, then looked from one to the other. "I have a favor to ask."

"More trouble at the house?" Peggy said.

"Not since I talked to you this afternoon. But that's why I'm here. I wondered if you could stay out there for a few days, Artie, in your old room. I'd feel a lot better knowing there was someone looking out for Ma and the others, especially when I'm not there."

"No problem," Peggy and Artie said in unison.

"Are you sure? I hate to split up the lovebirds just before the big day."

"Actually, I was going to suggest it myself," Peggy said. "I have a lot to do to get ready for the wedding; and Artie, as sweet and adorable as he is . . ." Peggy patted his cheek. ". . . has been getting in the way."

Artie gave her a mock look of rejection before turning to Kasey. "I have my last class in a few minutes, then I'll head on out. Is that soon enough?"

"That's great, thanks." Kasey turned to leave, turned back. "I don't think he'll show up; but if he does, don't take any unnecessary chances. Call the police and protect yourself any way you can. You know where Ma's .20 gauge is. He's bad, Artie. Real bad."

Kasey saw Peggy move a little closer to Artie.

As she went out the door, she hoped nothing would come of Cage's parting threat.

At 8:05 Kasey approached the entrance to the Steak House. The reservation desk was empty. She looked around; and instead of spotting the maitre d', she saw Jay standing just inside the door talking with a well-dressed couple. Jay spotted her. As he waited for the woman to finish what she was saying, he stared at Kasey, his expression pensive. A moment later, he excused himself and came up to her. Her pulsed raced. *Oh God,* she thought. *Not now. Not here.*

"You look lovely," he said. "Very lovely."

"Thank you."

"We have to talk."

"Yes. Later. After I've talked with Paula."

"She's meeting you here?"

"No, I'm—"

"Good evening, Mr. King. How are you tonight, sir?" the maitre d' asked, stepping alongside Kasey.

"Fine, Lloyd."

The maitre d' smiled, turned to Kasey. "Ms. Atwood, young Mr. King has already been seated. He asked me to escort you to the table as soon as you arrived."

Kasey glanced at Jay. The expression on his face was impossible to read.

"Thank you, Lloyd." She turned to Jay. "I'll call." Then she moved into the restaurant, leaving Jay standing in the foyer. She had taken only a few steps when she felt fingers grasp her arm.

Jay pulled her to him, whispered in her ear. "More undercover work?"

And before she could react, he abruptly released her and strode off.

Shaken, she was escorted to the back of the Steak House to a booth reserved for hotel VIPs. Brad stood when she approached. She slid into the booth and Brad sat again, sealing off any means of a quick escape.

"You look fantastic in white. I like your hair up like that. You have sexy ears. A sexy neck. Sexy lady."

After the waiter poured champagne—Dom Perignon—and left, Brad took her hand. "Your hand is like ice. Cold hands, warm heart, huh?"

"That's what they say," she said.

"So, where've you been? I swear I've spent the whole afternoon on the phone trying to get hold of you," he said, his voice overly loud. He grinned. "The woman is ruthless. She tosses me out at the crack of dawn; then she manages to ditch me, hiding out all day, ignoring my calls."

"Let's talk about Dan Carne. If you expect me to trust you, you have to tell me why you met with him."

"You want to talk about trust? What about my trust in you? Huh, how 'bout that, Kasey?"

"How much have you had to drink?"

"Not enough." He took a deep swallow of champagne. "Let's talk about you first. Where you went, what you did, who you were with."

"Brad, please, give me a break. It's been one helluva day."

"Yeah?" He stared at her, waiting. "So let's hear about it."

"Look, Brad—"

"There she goes again with the 'Look, Brad . . . ' "

"If you're going to be surly, I don't think I care to stick around."

She started to scoot around the booth to the opening. Brad caught her wrist.

"Sorry. I'm sorry. Look, Kasey—Christ, now you've got me doing it." He took her hand again. "Kasey, I know you didn't want to get physically involved. . . . But, hey, we got involved. What we did last night was kinda intimate, don't you think?"

"It was *very* intimate, Brad."

"Yeah, well, I'd say that makes us sorta—correct me if I'm wrong here—*committed, attached, whatever."*

"You once said it didn't have to be a commitment—between you and me, that is. That you'd settle for raw, unadulterated sex. Remember?"

"Well, I lied. That was before. Now I'd kinda like a commitment. Unless sleeping with guys is something you do a lot and it don't mean shit to you."

"No, it's not something I do a lot. In fact, it—" She cut herself off, took a swallow of water, ignoring the champagne. She brushed at hair on her face that wasn't there, then turned to face him. "Brad, listen to me . . . about last night. It shouldn't have happened. I didn't mean for it to happen. I've been under a lot of pressure lately. I like you, I like you very much, but—"

"But you don't love me like you love my uncle. Is that it?"

Kasey said nothing. What could she say? She refused to lie, and it would serve no purpose to admit it.

"Guess I should have seen it coming, huh? Boy, you've really got this rebound thing down pat."

Don't encourage him, she told herself. He's drunk. Just walk out, leave before things turn ugly.

He drank down the champagne, yanked the bottle out of the

ice bucket, and talked to it as he refilled his glass. "Yeah, if she can't have the one she wants, she goes for the next available sucker. The *rebound* queen. Her husband dies and she remarries before the ink is dry on the death certificate. The ink isn't dry on the marriage certificate when she dumps that poor, miserable bastard. Then she gets the hots for the boss; and when he shines her on, she picks up with the dumbass nephew."

She had told him about her two marriages that night in the monitor room. In confidence. Now he was throwing it up to her. The ugly half of Brad's split personality had reared its head. Last night he had asked her to trust him. How could she trust a man who could turn her words against her in a fit of anger?

When she attempted to leave, he clutched her wrist again. "Just a damn minute. I know he was with you this afternoon. He left your number with Gail. Uncle Jay snaps his fingers and you jump into bed with him and forget what we shared last night. Forget me. How was it, Kasey? Everything you hoped it would be? Hmmm? Bet you didn't make the mistake of calling out *my* name in the heat of passion."

She pulled her arm away and slid around the booth. This time, he didn't try to stop her.

Kasey sat at the downstairs bar drinking a white-wine spritzer. She needed something to take the edge off, yet wanted a clear head for her meeting with Paula Volger.

The bartenders moved up and down the bar, taking money, ringing up sales, making drinks, pocketing tokes. A pile of bills sat in front of her.

Frowning, she spread out the bills. She remembered putting a ten on the bar. When had the bartender taken her money and given her change? How could she have missed that? The art of observation was second nature to her. Or rather, it used to be. She realized that lately her skills had all but deserted her. And she knew when they had departed and why.

Since she had fallen for Jay, what used to come naturally now took a deep concentrated effort. She couldn't see, couldn't do her job because of the distraction. She should have known Lucas Cage would spread his net, encompassing more than the club and the King family. The man knew everything about them, had made a point to find out. He knew about the attraction between Jay and herself. He had gone after Sherry, had hurt her to serve his own means.

Kasey's stomach knotted. She should have known that it was Cage, not an old man with an Irish name, who had moved into her mother's house. She should have asked questions, paid more attention to the signs. Because of her incompetence, Cage had gained a foothold in the Atwood house. There was a good chance Sherry would not be his only victim.

At eight forty-five she went to her room to wait for Paula. Several minutes after nine, the phone rang.

"Meet me on the roof of the parking garage."

"Paula?"

"The roof. Now." Then the line went dead.

Kasey's mind raced. The voice was Paula's. But had she been coerced into calling? Could it be a trap as Jay had suggested? On the roof or in her room—if it were a trap, she was vulnerable either way. She dialed Jay's suite. No one answered. So he had abandoned her, too. Could she blame him?

She opened her clutch bag, checking for her canister of pepper spray. For protection she carried only the spray and her ring of keys. Although she had more than adequate training in self-defense, she prayed she would never have to put it to the test. Earlier today in her mother's kitchen with Lucas Cage, she had chosen to run rather than stand and fight. Time and again Peggy drilled into her students that escape was the ultimate goal. Fight only as a last resort; and then, by God, use everything you have and then some.

Unable to stall any longer, she left.

The elevator came almost immediately. She took it down-stairs to the casino floor, then crossed to another bank of ele-vators that would take her to the roof of the parking garage. She rode the elevator alone to the top floor. Before stepping out into the garage, she took her canister of pepper spray from her purse and held it, her thumb resting on the lever.

Warm, sultry air greeted her along with long and short shad-ows created by the sodium-vapor lights at each corner of the concrete expanse. About two-dozen cars were parked close to the elevators. A few others, probably belonging to employees, were scattered farther out.

"Paula?" Kasey said under her breath. "Paula, it's me, Kasey."

Kasey scanned the parking lot. She expected the woman to exit a car or step out from behind a van or minibus, but it didn't happen.

She waited.

The door to the stairwell opened behind her. She hoped it was Paula, but braced herself in case it was Lucas Cage. An elderly couple exited. Both seemed out of breath. They glanced at Kasey, then walked arm in arm to a nearby car, got in, and drove away.

She paced back and forth in front of the elevators. Although the air was warm, she shivered. Nerves.

Paula wasn't going to show. She would have been here by now, Kasey reasoned. Should have been waiting, in fact. It was crazy of her to come up here alone, unarmed except for a canister of pepper spray. If she had been thinking clearly, she would have refused.

She turned, pressed the button for the elevator, then resumed pacing. After several minutes she pressed the button again and again, impatient now. The elevators were never this slow. She glanced at her watch: 9:18. She had been on the roof nearly ten minutes.

The elevators had to be out. That's why the elderly couple had used the stairs, she told herself. She had two options: Take the stairs or walk the six floors of garage down to the street. Neither option seemed inviting.

She chose the stairs. Once the door closed behind her she listened for someone coming up the metal risers. When she heard nothing, she started down. The light in the stairwell appeared dimmer as she neared the third-floor landing. She soon understood why. The overhead light was out. She continued down, slowing as she left the protective shield of light behind. The second floor was completely dark. One floor to go.

The sound of the main door opening at street level reached her. One floor up, she hesitated on the dark landing. Heavy soles, a single pair, sounded on the iron risers below. Steps too heavy for a woman. Kasey squeezed the canister. Cage had planned all this and she, like a complete idiot, had walked right into it.

She stepped backward, her heel making a hollow echo in the stairwell.

The footsteps below paused. The only sound for Kasey was the blood rushing through her head. The footsteps resumed again, faster now.

Kasey spun around, grabbed the doorknob on the second-floor landing, and twisted. Locked. She twisted, pulled, using both hands, nearly crying out in her frustration. The footsteps were not far away now. Although she couldn't see the man in the darkness, she sensed him, heard him breathing.

She turned, started to climb the steps back to the roof. He was right behind her; his hand touched her back. She fell against the wall, raised the pepper spray canister and was about to press the lever when she heard her name.

Kasey froze instantly.

"Kasey," Jay said, taking hold of her arms. "It's me. It's only me."

She collapsed against him. "Oh God, Jay, I thought you were him. I thought . . ."

"I know. I know. I wanted to call out. But I didn't know if he were with you. If he had you."

"How did you know I was here?"

"When you weren't in your room, I called security. One of the guards had seen you enter the garage elevator."

"The elevators are out."

"Yes, I know. I figured you would take the stairs. I also figured he had set you up, that he would be waiting for you." Jay pulled her to him, buried his face in her hair. "Kasey, what the hell are you trying to do to me? Put me into cardiac arrest?"

"I tried to reach you. Paula called; she changed the meeting place."

"Where is she?" he asked.

"I don't know."

The door below opened. Jay put his fingers to her lips. They waited; and when no one came up the stairs, Jay pulled her gently, urging her to follow. They went down the steps as quietly as possible to street level, Jay in front.

They heard a groan. Paper rustled.

"Who's down there?" Jay called.

Silence.

"Answer or I'll blow your fucking brains out."

A match flared, the glow revealing a street bum sitting under the iron risers.

"Wanna hit?" The bum held out a brown paper bag with the neck of a beer bottle poking out. He dropped the match, cursing.

Jay and Kasey hurriedly passed him.

"Hey, Romeo, get a room," the bum called after them as they went out the door.

Forty-five

Jay and Kasey stepped off the elevator on the twelfth floor just as a security officer rounded the corner from another wing.

Since Dianne had left, taking three of the hotel men with her, Jay had cut security on this floor to one uniformed and one plainclothes guard.

The man stopped. "Evening, Mr. King," he said. "Is everything all right, sir?"

"That remains to be seen, Larry," Jay said. "How's it going up here?"

"Pretty much routine. Got a call earlier about a disturbance in Room 1209. Turned out to be nothing."

"Larry," Kasey said, "did you by any chance see a woman in her thirties, about five-five, with short, blonde hair, coming or going in this wing around nine o'clock? She was supposed to meet me at my room."

He took a moment, pondering. "No, Ms. Atwood. I don't remember seeing anyone like that. Not alone, anyway. Pairs and groups mostly, and I didn't look real close at anyone in particular. But like I said, the last few minutes I was down at the north end."

Jay thanked him. The guard stayed in the area of the elevators as Kasey and Jay went down the corridor to Kasey's room. She wanted to check her room for a message from Paula Volger.

Kasey inserted her keycard in the lock and opened the door. Jay stood behind her.

"If there's no message," Jay asked, "what then?"

"Then I go home. I only came for this meeting with her."

"What about . . ." His words died away. He turned her around, looked into her eyes. "Kasey, we still need to talk. You brought up something today that has to be discussed. At the time I didn't want to hear it—I still don't—but there's a possibility, a remote possibility, you could be right."

"I don't want to be right, Jay. But I thought you should know—"

"Look, let's not discuss it here in the hall. Have you eaten?"

She thought of her confrontation with Brad in the Steak House earlier. She shook her head again. "I'm afraid I don't have much of an appetite."

"Maybe you'll change your mind. Join me, okay?"

"What I could really use is a good, stiff drink."

"Bar is fully stocked. If I don't have it, I'll get it."

She nodded. She opened the door, glanced inside the dark room at the telephone on the nightstand and, when she saw no red message light, she pulled the door closed. "Nothing."

"She'll be in touch. I'll have the front desk transfer your calls to the suite."

"I should call home first," Kasey said, reinserting the card in the lock. "Go on ahead. I'll be right there."

He took her arm. "Call from my place. I'm not leaving you alone."

Kasey and Jay continued down the corridor to the suite. The red light on the security camera above the double doors glowed. Their arrival would not go unnoticed.

Once inside, Jay went directly to the bar and made drinks; scotch and soda for her and straight whiskey for himself. Kasey used the phone on the bar to call home. Her mother told her Artie had arrived minutes ago and that, so far, Lucas Cage was keeping his distance. Not taking any chances, they had brought Snickers inside to warn them if he showed up. Sherry had come and gone again. Her daily horoscope followed. *Something you discover today will help solve a puzzle.*

The capsule in Cage's car? *A dab of contrasts: The day may start favorable and end badly or vice versa.* Kasey thought of her confrontation with Cage and again with Sherry. It could only get better.

Kasey gave her the number of the suite, then hung up.

She sampled the drink, tasting mostly liquor. He had taken her at her word and made it stiff.

Jay picked up the phone, then slipped off his suit jacket as he dialed. Clipped to the front of his belt, in a leather holster, was a small gun. So his threat in the garage had had substance after all.

Jay packing a gun didn't surprise or alarm Kasey in the least. In fact she felt reassured by the sight of it.

"Al, it's me," Jay said. "Would you put Mrs. King on, please." He waited, sipping his drink. Their eyes met and he smiled.

Kasey smiled, then looked away. She felt awkward, wished he had made his call from another room.

"Is she sleeping?" Jay asked. "I see. . . . No, no, that's all right. Thank you, Al. Tell her I called. I'll call tomorrow." He pressed the disconnect lever, dialed again, turned to Kasey, his face expressionless, and said, "Dinner. What would you like?"

She shrugged. "I don't care. Maybe a little soup. And bread."

"Seafood okay?"

She nodded.

He turned away, spoke quietly into the receiver, then hung up. "What do suppose that woman, Paula, wanted to tell you?"

"I'm positive she saw or heard something. After her run-in with Cage a couple of weeks ago in the parking garage, her friend, the maid, was murdered. I'm not implying that the two are tied together in any way, but I know she was afraid of someone. On the phone this morning, she said a man was following her, watching her house. She said I'd know who it was. There's no doubt in my mind she meant Cage." She banged her drink on the bar top. "Damnit, Jay, why didn't she show tonight? Did Cage follow her here? Scare her off?"

"Maybe."

"Jay, what about Dianne? She didn't see her attacker, but she said he spoke to her. I know this is a stretch, but is it possible she could identify him by his voice?"

"I asked Frank that. He said it wasn't enough. Even if she could swear the voice of the man who attacked her belonged to Cage, it'd never stand up in court. I also talked to one of Cage's ex-partners. We can't count on him in court either, but he gave me some interesting information."

"Something we don't know already?"

He nodded. "Cage has an abnormal fear of contracting a venereal disease. His father or grandfather died from one."

"The antibiotics?"

"Yes. He drops them like candy. Some sort of preventative measure. I don't know what, if anything, this information can do for us, but it might come in handy."

Kasey was certain someone had been snooping through her medicine cabinet in her bungalow. She had no antibiotics for Cage to steal, but she remembered finding an empty vial in Jay's medicine cabinet the day she'd packed his things. She told him about it.

For the next half hour they went over everything that had happened. Then they discussed Brad and his possible involvement. What could he have been looking for in Jay's safe? What business could he have with Dan Carne? Did Brad know Cage? Were Brad and Cage accomplices? There was definitely a common link between Cage, Bartona, Carne, and even Cummings. All had worked for Ansel Doyle at one time or another. But where did Brad fit in?

They were interrupted by a knock at the door. "Room service," a voice on the other side called out.

Jay rose. "I believe in my nephew, Kasey. I have an idea what's going on with him. If it's what I think, then it has nothing to do with Cage, sabotage, or the rest of this craziness."

With his hand on the gun at his belt, Jay went to the foyer and, after making certain it was a room-service waiter, he opened the door. He took the cart and sent the waiter away.

He started to wheel the cart to the large round table by the window, but changed his mind midway into the living room. "I'm afraid we'll have to sacrifice view for practicality. This is a meal that requires dexterity and lots of elbow room."

Kasey excused herself to use the bathroom. When she returned she saw an oversized tureen on the narrow top of the marble coffee table. Jay had set out plates and bowls, silverware and wineglasses.

Jay helped Kasey remove her jacket. Her turtleneck silk blouse was sleeveless.

"Good, no sleeves. They tend to get in the way. Sit," he said, indicating the floor on one side of the low table.

Kasey kicked off her heels, hiked up her skirt, and sat on the plush, off-white carpet.

Jay came behind her and tied a bib around her neck, a plastic one with a red lobster on the front. It covered her entire upper torso. The plastic felt cool through the thin fabric of her blouse. He removed the gun and holster from his belt, laid it on the table, rolled up his sleeves, tied on a bib, then sat opposite her.

"Soup?" she asked.

With a flourish, he removed the lid from the tureen. The rich, pungent smells of shellfish, seafood, garlic, wine, and a half-dozen spices wafted upward, enveloping her, making her mouth water. Suddenly she was starved.

"Cioppino."

He nodded. "From the Sea Bar." He filled both bowls, then tossed back the linen from a basket of bread—a huge round of sourdough.

Jay opened a bottle of dry white wine and poured. "Dig in."

She watched him tear into the crusty bread with his hands. She did the same. They began to work at whole mussels, clams, and crab and lobster claws with a small fork made for digging seafood out of the shell. The bread soaked up the rich, red broth like a sponge. Juices ran along their fingers and down the front of their bibs. At one point, their eyes met and they smiled at each other before digging in again. The bandage over his eye gave him a rakish look.

They kept conversation to a minimum. Chitchat mostly, too engrossed in what was in front of them to spoil it with any serious talk. It was the best meal Kasey had had in years. It seemed to go on and on, the *physical* act of eating, the mechanics of it, far more time-consuming than food-consuming. After the shellfish in their bowls disappeared, they plucked choice pieces directly from the tureen, not bothering with formalities or etiquette, selecting what they liked best.

There was something primitive about sitting on the floor eating in this manner. Fingers and mouths in play, sucking, licking, unmindful of running juices and flaking crumbs. She found herself covertly watching Jay's hands and mouth, shiny and moist, deftly at work. And she felt heat rise to her cheeks and chest

"This is decadent," Kasey said softly, sucking on a cracked crab leg.

Jay's only response was a slight, amused smile before returning to the lobster claw in his hand.

She discarded the shell on the small mountain of empty shells and claws between them. Had they really eaten that much? Where in god's name had they put it all?

She dipped a chunk of bread into the broth and, halfway to her mouth, changed her mind. With a moan, she let it fall from her fingers into the bowl, too full to eat another bite.

"I've had my last meal, warden. I'm ready to die," she said, touching a hand to her stomach, closing her eyes and tipping back her head.

"So the way to your heart is through your stomach?"

"Not always," she said, sipping wine, "But in this case, yes."

"I'm glad you liked it. It's my favorite. It's something that should be shared with someone. Not eaten alone."

She understood why. But now that it was over, something would have to be done about the mess. She felt as if she had swum in her dinner rather than eaten it. "What now?" she questioned, holding her hands in the air like a surgeon waiting for sterile gloves after just scrubbing for surgery.

Jay grinned. "Sit tight."

He rose, went to the bar, quickly washed at the sink, pulled off his bib, then wet a bar towel and returned with it to the coffee table.

Kasey reached for it. Jay ignored her outstretched hand, kneeled and began to gently pat at her chin. Next, he took her hands and washed from her elbows to her fingertips. When he was finished, he pulled her to her feet and reached around behind her to unfasten the bib.

"It's knotted," he said, tugging slightly. He brought his other hand up, his arms around her neck. "Your hair, it seems to be tangled in the knot."

Kasey reached up to help. Their hands touched, fingers entwining. When Jay leaned in to see better, she became acutely aware of his nearness. Her pulse picked up, and she felt a tight heaviness in her chest that made breathing difficult.

The bib came free and slid down in front of her. And before it touched the carpet, they were locked in an embrace, kissing.

It hadn't happened suddenly. Everything seemed to move in slow motion, excruciatingly slow, as though their lips would never meet. And when finally they did, it was with a certain desperation. She crushed her mouth to his, wanting to hold him against her forever, wanted his kiss, his touch; she had never wanted anything so much in her life.

Jay broke the kiss, put his mouth to her ear, and whispered, "Kasey, I want you. Nothing else matters—"

"No, nothing else matters," she responded, her voice hoarse with wanting, with passion. Then they were kissing again.

Jay pulled the shell comb from her hair, allowing the soft strands to fall around her face. In the dim light, they undressed slowly, helping each other. Naked, they stretched out on the long sectional. He continued to move in slow motion, caressing, exploring her body—kisses long and drawn out—seeming in no hurry. She was in no hurry either. It was possible this experience would be the only one she would share with him. With only the memory of this glorious moment to last her a lifetime, she willed it to go on and on.

For a brief instant Kasey's mind flashed back to the night in the jacuzzi, to Jay sitting nearby with lovemaking bites and scratches covering his shoulders. If he liked it rough, it wasn't apparent tonight. Jay, right here and now, was the gentlest of lovers. His hands, mouth, and body caressed her like slow-burning oil; and when finally he entered her, she thought she would melt with the wonder of it.

He whispered her name over and over. And this time when Kasey reached orgasm and Jay's name passed her lips, she smiled. The name tasted good in her mouth. The sound of it rang true in the intoxicating air of their lovemaking. A moment later, Jay's body shuddered with his own climax. Long after their pulses slowed and their breathing became shallow again, he held onto her, continuing to kiss and caress her.

They moved into the bedroom, talked for a while of love and sharing, then made love again at the same lingering pace. Before Kasey fell asleep, she thought of the past men in her life. Thought of Dianne and what she had said to her about attracting nothing but weak, helpless men. *Losers.* Jay, although still married, had said he loved her. Jay was not a weak, helpless man. Strong in character, a man in power, a man of means, he was not a loser. But would he ever be hers?

She awoke, felt the weight of an arm across her chest, and it all came rushing back to her. Jay. His suite. The cioppino. Their lovemaking. Pleasing, exciting images, every one. Her day had begun badly, only to end well.

Her mouth and throat were dry from the cioppino, wine, and sex.

She quietly slipped from the bed and made her way to the bathroom. At the door she searched for the light switch and, unable to find it right away, decided to leave it off so as not to disturb Jay. She remembered the layout from the night Dianne had been attacked.

Running her hand along the wall, then the marble sink top, she was well into the room when her bare foot stepped from the cool, dry tiles to something wet and slightly raised. It cracked under her weight. She froze. Glass?

Afraid to go any farther, she gripped the counter for balance. The fingers of one hand slid through something wet, sticky. The other hand felt more shards of glass, also wet and sticky. Suddenly she was aware of a cloying odor in the room, a sharp metallic smell.

In the black windowless room she somehow sensed she was not alone. Someone or something was there with her. She tried to swallow, but her throat was so very dry.

Her fingers groped along the countertop in search of some sort of weapon. She found a large triangle of broken glass. She lifted it and sucked in her breath when a sharp edge sliced into her palm.

"Jay . . ." she whispered, raising the hand that gripped the piece of glass.

The silence answered her, closed in around her, threatened to suffocate her.

"Jay!" This time the single word reverberated throughout the glass-and-tile bathroom, ringing painfully in her head. *"Jay!"*

Forty-six

She heard Jay call her name. Heard him running across the room. Bright lights exploded in her eyes. She closed her eyes and turned her head away.

"Kasey, don't move." Jay said the words softly.

Kasey opened her eyes a little at a time. She saw Jay standing in the doorway, his hand reaching out toward her. On the floor in the corner she saw a pile of female clothes. She turned her head and looked in the plate-glass mirror. Jagged lightning-shaped lines came to a point in a bloody flower pattern. Blood was everywhere. Splattered across the walls and floor, pooling on the counter, in the sink, dripping down from the ceiling and across the frosted shower stall. Blood that erupted into infinity in the splintered shards that mesmerized her by its crimson brightness in the all-white room.

She stared at herself, nude, one hand raised, clutching a bloody triangle of mirror; and beyond her own reflection, in the bathtub, Kasey saw a bare, blood-streaked arm sticking straight up against the tiles.

She dropped the glass, heard it shatter in the basin. Without moving her feet, she twisted around, stared disbelieving at the bathtub. A naked blonde woman, puncture and slash wounds covering most of her pale body, lay sprawled in a thickening pool of blood. There was no question it was Paula Volger. No question that she was dead.

Above the body, scrawled in blood across the tiles, were the words YOU'RE NEXT.

With a towel, Jay swept at the glass on the floor. He threw down the towel and walked on it to reach Kasey. He lifted her into his arms, turned, and carried her out. Blood from her hand, both hers and the dead woman's, smeared across his chest and shoulder.

At 4:10 A.M., for the second time in less than two weeks, Det. Frank Loweman and the CSI went over Jay's suite with a fine-tooth comb. Only this time the victim was not an occupant of the room, and she threw no tantrums.

The victim, Paula Volger, had been dead at least seven hours. While Kasey and Jay were gorging themselves on seafood and wine, while they were making love in both the living room and bedroom, Paula's body was only yards away, cooling, going through the stages of rigor mortis. The thought made Kasey physically sick, and she tried not to dwell on it.

Loweman, Jay, and Kasey sat in the living room. Jay had pulled on a pair of sweats, and Kasey had put on her skirt and blouse. She hadn't bothered with her sandals; there was little point in trying to cover up the fact that she and Jay had been together. After calling the police, Kasey, concerned for Jay's reputation, had started to make up the bed; but Jay had taken her in his arms and stroked her hair. "Leave it," he'd said to her. "It doesn't matter. I've nothing to hide."

As Loweman listened to their account, he stared at the shellfish graveyard on the coffee table and every now and then his eyes flicked toward the bedroom to the unmade bed. If he was surprised, or if he disapproved, he hid it well behind a bland face. A cop's face.

"She probably couldn't make much sound once her trachea had been severed," Loweman said. "But by the vast amount of blood and the long-range splatter points, I'd say she put up a helluva fight until the end. My guess is he took her directly into the bathroom, stripped her and himself down, then killed her. Her clothes showed no signs of being violently removed.

There are traces of blood inside the shower stall and I bet we find more in the area around the drain."

"You mean he disrobed so he wouldn't get blood on his own clothes?" Jay asked. "Then he took the time to shower?"

"Yeah. Appears so. Probably used your shampoo. Maybe even your deodorant and after-shave." Loweman wrote in his notebook. "How long did he have the suite to himself?"

"Half hour, forty-five minutes. No more," Jay said. He turned to Kasey for confirmation.

"That's right. I got the call from Paula just after nine. I was on the roof for about ten minutes. Jay and I met up in the stairwell and then we came back here."

"Straight back?"

"No. The garage elevators were out," Jay said. "It took a couple of minutes to look into it, then we came up. We talked to one of the security officers on this floor for a few minutes before stopping at Kasey's room to check for a message from Paula."

"Jay, were you in the suite right up to the time you went to meet Kasey?"

"No. I was in my office."

"So the killer had how much time here?"

"An hour, ninety minutes."

"But Paula was alive at nine," Kasey said. "She called me."

"It's hard to believe you two didn't pass him in the corridor," Loweman said.

"After leaving here, he may have slipped into another room on this floor and waited until it was all clear," Kasey said. "He may have been waiting in my room. I didn't go inside, just checked for messages at the door, then came down here."

"Makes sense, especially if he has a master," Loweman said, glancing at his watch. "Speaking of security, where the hell's that elevator surveillance tape?"

"Here it is," Barney LeBarre said, crossing the living room with a cassette. "I got here as quickly as I could."

"Was there a tape for the camera at the door of the suite?" Jay asked his head of security.

"No, Mr. King. I was watching that monitor myself. If I'da seen anyone at the door, I woulda recorded it. Nobody went through those doors 'cept you and Ms. Atwood at . . ." He consulted a notepad. ". . . 9:32."

"He got inside somehow."

LeBarre scratched his chin thoughtfully. "At one point I thought someone was heading for your door. I saw you come out around 7:50, Mr. King. Then a little before 9:00, I saw a shadow in the corridor, close to the door, but it didn't get no closer."

"He must have entered through the adjoining room," Jay said to no one in particular.

That was the room the surveillance men had occupied while Dianne was in the hotel, Kasey thought. No one used the room now that Dianne had gone home.

Jay popped the cassette into the VCR and they viewed it. There was no sign of Cage or Paula Volger near any of the elevators, which led Kasey to believe Cage already had Paula before coming upstairs. He probably intercepted her downstairs and brought her up to the suite, where he forced her to call Kasey.

One surprise, however, was seeing Howard Cummings, Jay's chief executive, getting off the elevator at 9:11, about the time the security guard had been dispatched to check out a bogus complaint at the other end of the floor and Kasey was alone on the roof.

"I've already sent for Cummings," Jay said. "He should be here any minute."

One of the crime investigators, holding an evidence bag reading *Biohazard* in gloved hands, approached Loweman. "Frank, we took plenty of blood samples. There's enough broken glass around in there that the killer could have nicked himself."

"I was cut," Kasey said. She opened her hand to reveal a

wad of bloody tissue in her palm. "My blood is on at least one piece of broken mirror. My fingerprints, too."

"We'll get your blood type and prints," Loweman said to Kasey. He turned to Jay. "You?"

"No, I wasn't cut."

"I doubt he left prints. We might get lucky and find a hair or two. And if he raped her, there could be something for the DNA lab. I'll send along those two containers of nasal spray you gave me yesterday, Jay. If we can tie him to the attack on Dianne and again to something in the bathroom tonight, it could be the break we've been looking for." Loweman scribbled in the notebook. "We need everything we can get. Without witnesses, the rest is pretty much circumstantial. This guard you spoke to this evening, did he see or hear anything?"

"Nothing. Lucas Cage managed to send him off in another direction."

"We don't know that it's Cage—"

"It's Cage. And he's got friends in high places within the club. I'd stake my life on it."

"He has friends outside the club, too. His alibi." Loweman turned to Kasey. "Get your friend to recant her statement and we might have something."

A moment later, Howard Cummings joined them. Cummings looked confused; and if Kasey knew anything about reading people, she would swear the chief exec was more than a little nervous.

"Christ, Jay, I heard. I came as soon as I could." Cummings looked from the detective to his boss and back again. "Is there anything I can do?"

Det. Loweman took over. "Mr. Cummings, we have you on video. At a little after nine this evening you were seen coming off the elevator onto this floor. What were you doing here?"

Cummings looked at Jay. "I got a message you wanted to see me. I came right up."

"And?"

"I knocked. No one answered, so I left."

"Did you see anyone else on the floor?" Loweman asked.

"No. Not that I recall."

"Are you sure you didn't knock and, when no one answered, open the door with a master," Jay asked evenly.

"Open with a master? Why would I do something like that?"

"So your man would have no trouble getting in."

"My man? Jay, what the hell are you talking about?"

"Lucas Cage. Are you going to deny knowing a punk by the name of Lucas Cage?"

"Hell, yes, I'm going to deny it. I never heard of this Cage." Cummings puffed himself up. "You don't think—Jesus Christ, Jay, you don't think I had anything to do with the terrible things that have been going on around here? The bomb? The murders?"

"What were you doing here so late tonight? You usually head home before nine."

"I had some business to wind up. I was expecting a call."

"Did the caller tell you to come up here?"

"No. *No*," Cummings said emphatically.

"Have you been in contact with Doyle lately?"

"Doyle? Ansel Doyle?" Gradually, like pages riffling under a thumb, Cumming's face registered complete awareness. "Jay, as God is my witness, I haven't talked to the man since I came to work for you. Look, I won't deny that I didn't wonder about Doyle. I suspected he might have something to do with the things happening here; but Jesus, Jay, I never dreamed you'd think I was in with him."

"Why did the bomber call you? How did he get your private cellular number?"

"I don't know. I don't know."

"As of right now, Howard, you're on leave."

"But—"

"Take a vacation. Take the family to Disneyland."

"What about the club? I have unfinished business—"

"What little business is left, I can handle myself."

"Jay, I wouldn't turn on you. Brad has filled your head with this crap, hasn't he? Your nephew has been out to get me since the first time we butted heads. He's the one you should be interrogating."

"Brad has nothing to do with this. Take some time off, Howard. We'll talk in a couple of weeks."

Cummings opened his mouth to say something and thought better of it. With a solemn expression, he nodded, turned and left the suite.

Jay turned to Loweman. "Why the hell didn't you have someone follow Cage?"

"We did. Two of our best. They tailed him to some dump on Lake Street where he took a room for a month," Loweman said. "He shook 'em."

Forty-seven

At six that morning, Det. Loweman and the CSI finally packed up and vacated the suite, sealing the crime scene. Jay had packed a satchel, and he and Kasey moved down the corridor to her room.

While Kasey showered, Jay ordered coffee from room service, then made some calls. A steaming cup of coffee and an assortment of toiletries sat on the basin counter when she stepped from the shower.

As she dried off, she heard him on the telephone talking to Alan Ginsburg, the chief bodyguard protecting Dianne.

". . . extremely careful. Al, under no circumstances is Dianne to leave the house until I talk with her. That means no swimming, no sunbathing. I should be there by the time she gets out of bed." He left his cellular number and instructed Ginsburg to call if anything the least bit suspicious occurred. A moment later, he was talking to the front desk, leaving a message for Brad to call Kasey's room on the cellular line.

She scrubbed her face of makeup, combed her wet hair straight back, tucking it behind her ears, then put on the same clothes she'd worn the night before.

Leaving the bathroom, she said, "I'm sorry now that I took my things home yesterday. I'm beginning to feel like this outfit is a permanent part of me."

Jay hung up the phone, went to Kasey, and took her in his arms. "Of everything you own, now and forever, this will be my favorite. It'll always have special meaning to me."

She rested her head on his shoulder. They held each other in silence for several long moments.

Kasey stepped back. "Jay, I have to go home. I won't be able to do anything until I see for myself that everyone's okay."

"I'm going with you. No arguments."

"None from me."

He kissed her lightly on the lips and released her. "Give me a sec. Don't open the door to anyone while I'm in the shower."

He went to the satchel on the bed where he came up with a travel bag of toiletries and the rolled-up leather case that held his collection of straight razors. He tossed the holstered gun onto the bed.

He kissed her again as he passed her to go into the bathroom.

Kasey turned and stared into the vanity mirror at herself. She saw a stranger with large dark eyes and, underneath, dark circles to match. From her clutch bag she took out her lipstick, applied it to her lips, and then, using it as a blush, a bit to each of her pale cheeks. The fresh color helped some.

Her day yesterday had begun badly and ended badly. Finding the body of Paula Volger would be forever seared into her brain.

She called home and talked to her mother. So far, no sign of Cage. Artie would stay as long as he was needed.

Water running in the basin told her Jay was out of the shower. She went to the bathroom and stood in the open doorway. Jay, a towel wrapped around his waist, was lathering his face with a shaving brush. She watched in silence as he selected a razor, the one with his father's initials carved in the plain brown handle. She had guessed right on that day she'd packed his things for the move to the hotel—of all the straight razors in the case, Jay used the one belonging to his father. He *was* sentimental, after all.

When he made the first long, deft stroke, Kasey felt her

stomach roll ever so slightly and a feeling of love and affection rushed over her.

Jay saw her in the mirror. He paused with the razor at the side of his face and smiled.

She smiled back.

Everyone was gathered at the kitchen table when Kasey and Jay walked in the back door of the Atwood house. Everyone but Sherry.

Breakfast smells and light conversation filled the air. George buttered a stack of toast. Artie, with an armful of plates and utensils, was setting the table. Marianne transferred an impressive mound of scrambled eggs from frying pan to platter. Even Danny was busy separating and folding sheets of paper toweling to use as napkins.

Kasey and Jay had not eaten breakfast. Neither seemed to have the stomach for it.

"You two're just in time," Marianne said. "Sit. Eat before it's cold."

"Batteries not included," Danny muttered.

"Where's Sherry?"

"She hasn't come down yet. Run up and get her, sweetie. Tell her it's 'Last chance.' " Marianne pushed a coffee mug into Jay's hand.

Kasey turned to Jay.

"Go on, I'll be okay." He sipped the coffee. "Toast looks good. All of a sudden, I'm hungry."

"Mr. King," Marianne said, pulling out a chair for Jay, "if you don't mind my asking, what's your sign?"

As Kasey passed through the dining room, she caught a glimpse of her wedding photograph on the credenza. She quickly looked away. Not from pain or sorrow as she would have in the past. But because Kevin was no longer a part of her current life. Whether or not he would approve of Jay did not matter anymore. Only she, Kasey Atwood, could make that decision.

At the top of the stairs, Kasey knocked lightly on Sherry's door.

"I'm not hungry," Sherry called out.

Kasey opened the door. Sherry was on her side, her ravaged back exposed. When she heard the door creak, she quickly flopped over on her back in an attempt to hide the marks. A look of pain filled her eyes.

"Sherry, you can't stay hidden away forever. You've got to eat. Artie's downstairs. He's come to look out for you and the others."

Sherry turned on her side, pulling her knees to her chest. "Artie is nothing against someone like him."

"Who are you talking about? Lucas Cage?"

"Artie is good. Cage is evil. Good is no match for evil."

Kasey felt an icy chill. Sherry, like Dianne, was usually so strong, levelheaded, and more often than not, tough and cynical. What did that animal do to make mush out of such strong woman? This frightened girl lying in a tight ball, a tangle of strawberry-blonde hair across her face, was no one Kasey knew.

"Sherry . . ."

"Do you think Artie could do to another human being what that monster did to me . . . and laugh afterwards? Do you think Artie could kill without taking a moment to reflect upon it? The man that did this to me has no conscience. No feelings. We might as well be slugs under his shoes for all he cares."

"He's human, Sherry. Cold and heartless, but as human as you or I. Which means he can be stopped. He'll just go on hurting people if he isn't stopped."

Sherry buried her face into her pillow. Her body shook with silent weeping.

"What did he threaten you with? What does he have on you, Sherry? Did he threaten to expose you, to tell what you do at the clubs?"

"Do you think I care about what people think?" The words were muffled by the pillow. After a moment Sherry turned her head toward Kasey, but she kept her eyes closed. "I don't care about me." A tear slipped from beneath her eyelid and rolled across the bridge of her nose.

Kasey sat on the edge of her bed and lifted the hair from her face. "Tell me, Sherry."

"He swore . . . swore he would douse everyone in this house with gasoline and make me watch each of them burn alive. You, your ma, Danny, everyone. He would do it. He would enjoy every minute of it."

A grotesque picture of a fiery body—her mother's body—writhing in agony sprang into Kasey's mind before she could shut it out. That's what he wanted her to see. That's how he got control and used it.

She stroked Sherry's long, silky hair. "Honey, he's going to kill me—try to anyway—whether you speak up or not. He has to kill me; I know too much."

Sherry sat up and grabbed Kasey's hand. "That bastard."

"And if he kills me, think what that would do to Ma." Kasey saw a hardness come into Sherry's eyes. "The only way to stop him is to tell the police that he forced you to lie. Show them what he did to you and why. We can't let dirt like that run our lives. Will you do it? Will you go to the police?"

Sherry squeezed her eyes shut again.

"Will you?"

"Yes. Damnit, yes."

Kasey hugged her; and when she started to rise, she felt something hard beneath the covers.

"What's this?" Kasey questioned, tossing back the sheet. The 20-gauge shotgun, like a wood-and-steel lover, lay alongside Sherry. "I don't think you'll need this." Kasey cracked it open and removed the shells.

On her way out, Kasey paused. "Sherry, did you tell Cage that Ma had a vacant room to rent?"

"Oh, God, no. I never laid eyes on him until after he rented the room. I knew he was shit the moment I met him."

Kasey closed the door. She wondered how he'd known about the room.

Jay was finishing off a triangle of toast smothered in fresh peach jam, trying to concentrate on the daily horoscope Mrs. Atwood was reading to him from the paper, when Kasey come into the kitchen.

". . . and expect the unexpected today," Mrs. Atwood was saying. "Family matters are strained."

He looked at Kasey expectantly. She gave him a thin smile, crossed to the coffeepot behind him, poured a cup, then turned and said quietly, "She's going to do it, Jay. She's going to talk to Loweman."

Jay wanted to hug Kasey, but instead he merely nodded. This was the first real break they'd had.

Without looking at her, Danny tapped Kasey's arm. When she turned, he pressed a white swan-shaped origami into her hand. The paper was lightly smudged with bacon grease.

"Thank you, Danny," she said. "It's beautiful."

The wall phone rang, and Artie Brown, closest to it, answered. He cupped a large hand over the receiver and said, "Mr. King?" He held the receiver out to Jay. "For you."

"It's probably Brad," Jay said to Kasey, rising. He took the receiver. "King, here."

"Hello, Your Majesty. Hey, man, how's it going? Guess you finally found my little surprise last night. Took you long enough."

Jay turned his back to the others. "I found it," he said, as evenly as possible.

"If I know the Atwood household, you're in the kitchen with that screwy bunch staring a hole in you. We need to talk. Take a ride. Get into that fancy silver car of yours with the speaker phone and start to drive. Head back to town. For your own sake don't get the cops involved. At least not until you've heard what I have to say. I'll be in touch." There was a pause, then, "Oh, and make sure Kasey is with you."

"I don't want Kas—" The line went dead, cutting him off.

Jay waited until he heard the dial tone before hanging up. "Business," he said, looking around the room. "I have to go. Mrs. Atwood, thanks for the coffee and toast. And the reading."

Kasey went out with him. At his car he said, "It was Cage. The bastard wanted to know if I'd found his little surprise."

"Jesus." She stopped him before he got into his car. "Is that it?"

"No. He wants to talk. He said to head back to town and he'll call back on the car phone."

"I'm coming with you."

"No, I can't put you in jeopardy, too."

"Damnit, Jay, do you think he's going to just forget about me? Whatever he has to say concerns me as much as it does you."

Jay sighed. She was right; they were in it together now. He felt a sharp stab of contrition for getting her involved in the first place. Because of something that happened twenty years ago, a madman was out to get them all.

He went around the car and opened the passenger door.

"Give me a minute to get out of these clothes," she said.

"No time. Get in."

Forty-eight

Jay drove. They had just reached the main highway when the car phone rang.

"We're on the road, Cage," Jay said, answering the speaker phone. "Go ahead."

Instead of Cage's gruff baritone voice, a weepy, child-like one came through the speaker. "Jay?"

"Dianne?" Jay looked at Kasey. "Dianne, where are you?"

"Jay, please do whatever he says. Don't let him hurt me anymore. Darling, I love you. I don't ever want to be without you again. Please . . ." The connection was filled with static and interference. ". . . please, Jay."

Jay pounded the steering wheel with a fist. "Dianne, what does he—where are you? Is he with you now?"

Jay heard a surprised cry, like a yelp; then, "Yes, I'm with her. We're right here together, cozy as two scorpions in a nest. Why don't you come out and join us? You and that pretty sidekick of yours. I figured you wouldn't mind if your wife stayed with me for a while, since you've been too busy fucking her friend to care about anything else."

"Don't hurt her, Cage."

"Oh, I'm afraid it's too late for that. Some things just can't be helped. She brought it on herself, though. She's a real tiger. I'm not without one or two battle scars myself. But you know what? I think she likes it rough. Don't you, babe? Especially in the sack. Yeah, I think so. We both like it rough. Guess that makes us pretty compatible, doesn't it?

At least in that department. Though we don't seem to see eye to eye on much else."

"What do you want?"

"A trade. You for her. I believe our whirlwind romance is winding down. The fight's all out of her; and, Jesus, whiny broads really get on my nerves. Kasey Atwood will be the mediator. You both come out here—"

"Kasey isn't—"

"Shut up! It's not up for negotiation. *You got that?* The two of you come here. You stay and your wife goes home with your girlfriend. I won't lie to you, Mr. King-of-the-hill; I intend to kill you. But who knows, I might give you a sporting chance. I'll work something out, something that will give me the—how should I put this?—the maximum satisfaction. Yeah, that's it. Maximum satisfaction for having to wait all these years for my payback."

"Where?"

"No hesitation? No argument? Noble." He chuckled. "I must admit I wasn't sure you'd want her back. Thought you might just decide to let me take care of her for you—you know, clear the way for you and the little house dickette. Guess you have some scruples after all."

"You crazy sonofabitch—"

"Watch your mouth, asshole. As long as I have the upper hand, you watch your mouth."

Jay heard a commotion in the background, heard Dianne cry out, then silence.

"Cage!" Jay yelled out.

"Yeah, I'm here. Your wife took a notion to try to leave without permission. Can't have that, now, can we? Not that she'd get very far." Cage chuckled again. "Okay, listen up, I have a place out in Cold Springs at the end of Pioneer Trail. It's a humble abode, nothing like yours. Your wife hasn't warmed to it yet, and somehow I feel she never will. Ah, well." His voice hardened. "Look for my Camaro. I don't have to tell you that if you bring anyone else out here, meaning the law, I'll kill her. And I assure you it won't be a quick death. The main highway is fifteen minutes away. I can see it from here. If I think you're trying to pull a fast one, she gets a taste of the knife again. Only this time it won't be a little initial carving. Fifteen minutes is a long time when . . . well, no matter what your present feelings are toward your wife, somehow I don't think you'll want *that* on your conscience."

Jay heard Dianne scream in the background. More a cry of anger and frustration than one of pain.

"Be right with you, babe." A pause, then, "Oh, King, one more thing. Bring a million dollars in fifties and hundreds. Don't tell me you can't raise that kind of cash on the spot, 'cause I know better. Get it from the club. If you're not out here in sixty minutes—one hour—your wife goes under the knife. And believe me, Kingshit, it won't end there. I'll come after you and Kasey and every last person you both care about. Have I made myself clear?"

"Clear."

Jay disconnected. He quickly dialed his house. The line rang six times before the machine picked up. He listened to his own voice instructing the caller to leave a message, then he identified himself and urged someone, anyone, to pick up. When no one did, Jay disconnected and dialed Dianne's cellular number.

The cellular phone rang once.

Cage sat on the edge of the mattress, pressed the *on* button, and waited until he heard King's voice asking for Dianne before he spoke. In a singsong voice he said, "Time is ticking away, King. Don't waste it on foolish tactics." He looked over at Dianne, who was curled into a tight ball in a corner of the room, just inches from him. Her usually perfect hair was mussed; mascara smeared around her eyes; a drop of blood stood in the corner of her swollen mouth. She was naked, clutching a tattered blanket in front of her.

"I want to talk to her again," Jay said.

Cage rubbed his forehead at a point between his eyes where the pressure was centered. The pain increased by the minute. Lately, the headaches were there when he woke up; and no matter how many pills he took, they seemed to get worse with each passing day. He had little patience for this bullshit.

"Twelve o'clock, King. Don't be late. Every minute past noon will be marked with my trusty knife—like a notch in time—on the flawless face of your lovely wife." Cage stroked Dianne's cheek with the flat side of the blade. She jerked away from him, cursing. He laughed, disconnecting the line and tossing the phone on the bed.

Kasey waited in the car, her nerves on edge, raw. Thirty minutes earlier, Jay had gone into the club to get the ransom money from the main cashier cage. She didn't expect Jay to have a problem getting the money. Cage had done his homework, knowing exactly how much cash the club was required to keep on hand. If someone hit a big payoff before the money could be replaced, Jay was out of business.

She repeatedly glanced at her watch, obsessed with the ticking minutes. The swan origami lay in her lap. Kasey began to nervously work at the folds. When she pulled out a fold, she saw a postage stamp. Curious, she began to carefully unfold it. The swan was in two parts, an envelope and a note sheet. It was addressed to Lucas Cage at a post office box in Reno. The note read, *Do it. Now!*

Kasey jumped with a start when the door suddenly opened. Jay tossed two gray canvas bags into the backseat and climbed into the car.

"I was beginning to worry," she said. "How'd it go?"

"I got as much as I could. It's almost all there. There's a

lot to be said for ready cash. Yanick showed up, demanded to know what was going on. There was no problem once I told him what I was doing and what the money was for. I can trust him to not call the cops."

She handed him the note and envelope. "Does this mean anything to you? Danny must've gotten hold of it somehow while Cage was in the house."

"Someone wants him to do something and they want it done now. With Cage it could mean anything." Jay started the car and drove away, heading for the freeway.

"It was postmarked two days ago. He must have picked it up yesterday while he was still at the ranch."

"Then it's a sure bet it has something to do with us. Me."

Something in the hand-printed note seemed familiar to Kasey. Was it the way the *i* was dotted or the bold slash across the top of the *t* or the shape of the *o?* "Jay, does anything about it look familiar to you? The formation of the letters? The size or spacing?"

Taking his eyes from the road, he glanced at it several times, then shook his head. "No. Does it to you?"

"Yes, something . . ."

"Shit," Jay said, hitting the steering wheel with the palm of his hand. "How did he get Dianne out of the house with three bodyguards and a housekeeper in attendance? How?"

"Try the house again," Kasey said.

Jay dialed. The answering machine picked up on the fourth ring.

"Maybe I should take a quick run by?"

"There's no time."

Jay glanced at the clock on the dash, then accelerated. "You're right. Kasey . . ." He shook his head. "Brad's disappeared. No one at the club has seen him since last night around eight or nine. He didn't sleep in his room."

Kasey remembered how intoxicated Brad had been at dinner. Intoxicated and upset. His disappearance was either an act of defiance directed toward his uncle and Kasey or Brad was deep into the conspiracy. She hoped it was the former.

As they drove toward Cold Springs, Kasey prayed Dianne was still okay.

The surveillance van sat across the street from the house. Frank Loweman remembered it from the last time he was out here. He pulled in the back way and parked beside a Honda Accord in the small graveled lot.

He left his car and went to the rear entrance. The heavy metal gate stood open. He went through, looking for a sign of Dianne or Jay. The first thing he noticed was the absence of any men guarding the property. The pool sweep made swishing, sucking noises as it glided along the stone edge. He cautiously entered through the glass slider, which stood open. The alarm system was not activated. Something was wrong. Dianne couldn't be that rebellious. She had been scared, really scared, since the bomb threat. That much Loweman knew for certain.

Loweman pulled his service pistol and moved warily through the dining room to the kitchen. He found the first body there. The dead man sat at the table, slumped forward, head on the glass top, the murder weapon, a cord from some electrical appliance, still wrapped around his neck.

He backed out, being careful not to touch anything. Moments later, he found the second body in the master bedroom.

After checking the man for vitals and finding none, he hurried back through the house. He had to call this in to the station and report what he'd found. Two dead. Where was Jay and Dianne, he wondered? And where were the third body-guard and the housekeeper?

As if to answer his question, the sound of a car door echoed outside in the driveway. Loweman could see into the kitchen and out through the window above the sink. The housekeeper and a short, blond man, the one named Toby, exited a black four-door sedan. The pair had bags of groceries.

Loweman hurried out to meet them.

Forty-nine

"Shit," Jay said, looking in his rearview mirror. "That's all we need."

Kasey heard the yip of a police siren before she turned and saw the flashing dome lights.

"Do you think Yanick . . ."

"No. He gave me his word," Jay said emphatically. "I trust him."

Jay pulled to the side of the road and stopped, the blue NHP car pulling up behind.

They were at least fifteen minutes from their destination. Kasey glanced at the clock again: 11:41. She looked out the rear window. The cop was taking his sweet time getting to the car.

Gravel crunched on the road. "Afternoon, sir," the patrolman said. "License, registration, and proof of insurance. In a bit of a hurry, are you?" Without waiting for an answer, the patrolman took the papers and returned to his car.

Kasey's heart pounded when she watched him get on the radio. Jay's fingers found hers and squeezed reassuringly.

It took the patrolman five minutes to run a check, write the ticket, and return to the Lexus. Minutes that inched away like the burning fuse on a stick of dynamite. He handed Jay the ticket and his papers, gave him a brief lecture on energy conservation, and finally let them go.

Jay drove off, maintaining the speed limit. When the patrol car behind him took an off-ramp a mile down the road, Jay stomped the pedal to the floor. Kasey kept vigil for additional highway patrol.

He didn't slow once they turned off the highway. For the next agonizing minutes, the Lexus and its occupants took a brutal beating on the unpaved road.

"There it is," Jay said, pointing to the lone house and shed at the end of the remote lane. The black Camaro was parked in the shed.

At precisely 12:02, Jay brought the Lexus to an abrupt halt behind Cage's Camaro. Dust billowed forward, covering both cars, temporarily obscuring the view of the clapboard structure. She opened the door to get out, but stopped when Jay held her back. "Kasey, you don't have to do this. You can leave me here and drive away. Just drive away. This isn't your fight."

"I'm going with you."

"Are you sure—"

"I'm going."

"There's a gun in the satchel in the trunk. I can't chance carrying it; Cage would blow me away if he spots it. If it all falls apart in there, if he reneges and doesn't let you and Dianne go, try to get to it. Okay?"

She nodded.

"I love you," he whispered.

An unbelievable sense of dread came over her, overwhelming her. A premonition? She didn't fear for herself. It was Jay whose life she sensed was in peril. She wanted to pull at him, tell him to run, run and save himself.

He reached into the backseat and grabbed the two canvas bags. They left the car quickly, allowing no more time to think, to stall. They hurried up to the front entrance of the dilapidated shack. Jay eased Kasey behind him as they crossed the threshold and, once inside, stood uncertainly in the doorway, gazing into the dim interior.

"Come on in," Cage called out from the other room. "We don't stand on ceremony here."

Kasey followed Jay through the first room, a room with a

chrome-and-Formica kitchen table, one chair, a wood-burning stove and a stained, sagging couch. They entered the bedroom. She saw Dianne, wearing only a man's wrinkled button-down shirt, sitting on a bare mattress on the floor. Two inch-long cuts, one on each cheek like red teardrops, oozed blood.

The door slammed shut behind them. Kasey whirled around to see Cage standing in the corner, the hunting knife in a sheath at his belt, a menacing grin on his face and an equally menacing revolver in his hand. "You're late," he said. "That's very rude."

Jay looked from Dianne to Cage. "You sadistic bastard."

"Watch your mouth, asshole. You were late. I warned you." He pointed the gun at Jay. "You got the money?"

Jay dropped the bags at Cage's feet.

Cage stepped forward, eased one bag open with the toe of his boot.

Jay turned back to Dianne. "Are you all right?" he asked her.

"Do I look all right?" she returned, her eyes hard and cold.

"Dianne, I'm sorry."

"Yeah, I bet you are."

Cage chuckled. "I see she's getting some of the ol' fighting spirit back." He patted Jay down, looking for a weapon. "Maybe I'll keep her after all."

"Let them go," Jay said. "You've got me, so let them go."

"All in good time. I have a little private score to settle with this one first," Cage said, wrapping his hand around the back of Kasey's neck. He pulled her roughly to him, the long barrel pointed under her chin. "Try any of that Bruce Lee shit on me again and I'll break your neck. And yours won't be the first pretty neck I've broken. My stepmother thought she could fuck with me too, and now the only thing she can do is roll her eyes around. Amazing what a baseball bat can do if one knows where and how to swing it," he said squeezing Kasey's neck until she moaned in pain.

"Back off," Cage shouted when Jay instinctively moved toward him. "I could end it for you right here and now. Shoot you dead. Eliminate the major trouble spot. Is that what you want? You want to go out not knowing what's going to happen to these two fine women of yours?"

Jay dropped his arms.

They were all going to die. Kasey had known it the moment she saw Dianne on the bare mattress, a proud, beautiful woman defaced, demoralized. He had no intention of letting any of them live. He had close to a million dollars, enough money to buy a quick retreat out of the country, enough money to live comfortably anywhere in the world for the rest of his life. He could let them live or kill them; either way, it had no bearing on the outcome. Dead was better. If she knew anything about this man, killing them would give him immense pleasure.

Cage released his hold on Kasey's neck to pat her down as he had done to Jay. His touch was rough and sexually abusive, meant to hurt and humiliate. She wanted to strike out, to disable him, to hurt him as he had hurt Sherry and Dianne, yet she remained passive, waiting for the right moment.

He pushed her. "Dump out that money where I can see it, then put it in that flight bag by the door."

Kasey turned the bags upside down and shook out the bundled stacks of fifties and hundreds. She put them into the flight bag.

"Well, everything looks good. Guess we won't need you anymore," Cage said to Jay, bringing the pistol up to aim at his head. "It's payback time."

"Go ahead and kill me," Jay said. "You're just as dead as I am. In fact, you've been a walking dead man for years."

Cage paused. "Trying to buy a little time, huh? Okay, I'll bite. How do you figure I'm a dead man?"

"You had to take a physical to get the job at the club," Jay said. "The results came in last week. You tested positive for VD. Syphilis to be exact."

Cage chuckled. "It ain't gonna work."

Jay shrugged.

Despite what Cage said, by the skeptical look in his eyes, Kasey thought it might just work. "He's telling the truth," she said. "I saw the report. Extremely advanced. Beyond treatment."

Cage visibly paled; his hand holding the gun began to tremble. "No. You're both lying."

Dianne began to whimper.

The diversion gave Kasey an opportunity and she took it. She brought the flight bag up with all her might, catching Cage in the groin. He doubled over. Kasey rushed in, the heel of her hand aiming for his nose, but this time he was too quick for her. A backhand with the gun barrel sent her flying across the room to crash into the wall.

Jay lunged. A solid right caught Cage on the temple; a left to the solar plexus dropped him to his knees. But not for long. The gun came up, aimed at Jay's chest.

Kasey screamed.

Jay dove straight for Cage, bulldozing him backwards. Both men fell, tumbling onto the mattress alongside Dianne.

Cage rolled over on top of Jay, the gun buried into Jay's side. Jay clutched his wrist, forced the gun away from him.

Kasey crawled across the floor and got a tenuous hold on Cage's boot before a kick from him sent her flying backward again.

"Dianne, the gun!" Kasey shouted. "Get the gun!"

Dianne seemed finally to come out of her self-imposed trance. She moved toward the two men grappling on the mattress, the gun poised in the air between them, and bit into the back of Cage's hand. He howled and released his hold on the gun. She snatched it off the mattress, scooted backwards, waving it in trembling hands, then fired point blank at Cage's back. He stiffened, his body arching, blood gushing from a wound midway down his spine.

Jay pushed at Cage, wriggling out from under him.

Cage tried to get to his feet. His arms flailed about, but his lower body remained still. "My legs . . ." Cage said. "Can't move my legs." He twisted his head around toward Dianne. "You fucking bitch . . . you—"

Holding the gun with both hands, Dianne stretched her arms forward and pressed the muzzle against his cheek, just below one eye. They stared at each other.

"You're a dead woman," he said.

She pulled back the hammer.

"Dianne, no," Jay said. "He's finished. He can't do anything more to you . . . to us."

She squeezed the trigger.

The sound was deafening.

Lucas Cage's entire body jerked. Very little blood seeped from the black hole under his eye, but blood and gray matter splattered over the mattress at the back of his head. He lay still, his eyes and mouth half-open.

Jay rolled off the mattress, stood. He stepped over Cage's body to reach Dianne. He touched her face and said "I'm so sorry, Dianne."

She looked up at him, her expression somber. Then she turned the gun on Jay and fired again.

Kasey cried out as Jay staggered back.

Jay placed a hand to his chest, blood flowing through his fingers. He stood there a moment, a dazed expression on his face, before slowly sinking to his knees.

"Jay!" Kasey crawled on her hands and knees to him. Jay leaned against her, the leaden weight of his body telling her he was unable to remain upright on his own. She lowered him to the floor. "Jay? Jay? Oh, God, don't die. Please don't."

Dianne waved the gun, the barrel going from the body of her captor to her wounded husband. "Bastards," she cried. "Stupid bastards. Can't trust men. Can't trust them. Jay wouldn't sell the club. He was going to risk everything on that expansion. I couldn't let him dig us into a bottomless pit. I just couldn't. It should've been so simple . . . all worked out. They had to die. Jay and Brad. That's why I hired *him*." She kicked Cage's body, sobbing now. "I knew I would be the first one suspected when Jay died, so I brought you in, Kasey. The concerned wife begs her friend to find out who's after her and her husband. You did just what I wanted you to do. You found Cage and his past connection to Jay. But the filthy bastard wanted to play games. Wanted to . . . to do everything his way. Then he turned on me. *Me!* He'd taped our phone conversation and threatened to use it against me if I didn't do what he asked. He didn't care about the lousy twenty grand I offered him. He only wanted to get even with Jay. I fit right into his plan. He wanted to hurt me, humiliate me . . . use me in his scheme to extort *big* money from the club."

She continued to wave the gun.

Kasey felt for Jay's pulse. She found one, erratic and weak, but there.

"And now I have to do it all myself. All myself."

From the corner of her eye, Kasey saw the gun turn toward her. Ducking instinctively, she saw a bright flash from the muzzle, felt a white-hot pain in her shoulder.

Kasey rolled. The next shot went over her head and slammed into the door. Her only chance was to get to the gun in the trunk of the Lexus. As Dianne struggled to her feet, Kasey managed to get the door open. She charged out, dizzy with pain from the bullet in her shoulder, bracing herself for the next round. She fell, got up again and ran, praying she wouldn't pass out before she could reach Jay's car.

Fifty

The Lexus, though right outside the front door, seemed beyond reach. Kasey's shoulder throbbed and blood was everywhere. She left a trail of it behind her. To try to hide from Dianne would be senseless, her own blood would betray her. Her only chance was to get the gun from the trunk of Jay's car and take out Dianne. She had to fight back or die.

Holding her arm tightly to her side, Kasey ran out to the Lexus, skirting around to the passenger side to stay out of the line of fire. As she opened the car door, the window on the driver's side blew out, pelting her with chunks of glass the size of crushed ice.

The keys dangled from the ignition. There was a slim chance she could get into the car and drive away before Dianne could stop her, but that meant leaving Jay behind, alone with her. There was no doubt in Kasey's mind that Dianne would try to finish him off. She was a woman obsessed, a woman driven mad from pain and shock, from a horrendous ordeal of her own making. Kasey had to get Dianne away from Jay. And Jay needed immediate medical attention or he would die—if he weren't dead already.

Keeping her head down, she reached across the seat, grabbed the keys, then the cellular phone. She pressed 911. In a crouch, Kasey inched her way around to the rear of the car. With the keys, she opened the trunk and pulled the satchel toward her, all the while anticipating the next deafening gunshot.

"Police," Kasey whispered to the dispatcher. "Police and ambulance. Hurry!" She quickly gave her location and related what had happened, having to repeat herself several times. While she spoke, she pawed through the bag for the gun. Her fingers touched cool metal. She snatched it out.

It was an automatic, and unloaded.

Kasey yanked the satchel from the trunk and dumped it out onto the ground, kicking at the contents. The ammunition clip lay under Jay's leather shaving kit. Although unfamiliar with an automatic, she'd seen enough movies to go through the motions. She put down the phone, slammed the clip home, moaning from the intense pain the effort caused, and struggled to pull the slide back. It took three attempts before she could inject a shell into firing position.

She rose high enough to see over the trunk of the car toward the house. No sign of Dianne.

Where the hell was she? Why wasn't Dianne coming after her? Dianne wouldn't know about the gun in the trunk, so where was she?

It was important to get Dianne away from the house. If Kasey could only draw her out, allow her to take the car and go, she could tend to Jay. What was Dianne doing?

Cage's .44 was a six-shooter; she remembered looking closely at it when she'd found it in his boot at her mother's house. How many rounds had been fired? How many? She couldn't think. Three inside the house and one at the car? Or was it four inside? How many? Five or six? She thought six. That's why Dianne hadn't fired again. She was out of bullets . . . unless, unless she knew where Cage kept them and was, at this very moment, reloading.

"Dianne, I have Jay's gun. You're out of bullets. Do you hear me? You're out of bullets. Damnit, let's stop all this shit. It's over."

No answer.

Kasey held the gun in her right hand and, again holding her arm close to her side, she ran back to the house. A wave of pain made her weak, temporarily blinded her. *Don't pass out. . . . Please, dear God, don't let me pass out.*

Standing at the threshold, she heard a clicking sound coming from inside. Even in her jumbled state of mind, it took only an instant to realize the clicking was the sound of a gun hammer hitting on an empty chamber. Through the doorway, Kasey saw Jay struggling to get to his feet. Beneath the bandage at his brow, blood flowed down his face. Dianne stood over him, the gun pointed at his head as she pulled the trigger over and over.

"Dianne, it's over. Drop the gun," Kasey yelled.

Dianne glanced at Kasey. Enraged, she screamed, "Bastards. Bastards! Have to do it all myself!" She threw the gun at Kasey.

Kasey ducked, felt it glance off her wounded shoulder. She cried out in agony, falling to her knees. When she looked back into the bedroom, she saw Dianne tugging at the hunting knife in the sheath at Cage's belt. When it was free, Dianne turned back to Jay and raised it high in the air, about to bring it down on his back.

Kasey fired without aiming.

The first round slammed into Dianne's thigh, knocking her against the wall, the second one bore into the wall inches above her head. Dianne shrieked, dropping the knife. She grabbed at it, got hold of the blade near the grip, and tried to stand, shrieking again when her injured leg gave out. She stumbled over Lucas Cage and fell forward, the knife disappearing beneath her. She made a soft exhaling sound, then was still.

Kasey ran to Jay, who had fallen back to the floor. The entire front of his shirt was bright with blood. At first, she found no pulse, no heartbeat. Frantically, she put her ear to his mouth and heard a slight intake of breath. He was alive. Barely.

She sat on the dirty floor and cradled his head in her lap, gently rocking him, blood from the open gash on his eyebrow seeping into the white silk of her skirt.

Hurry, oh please please hurry.

The minutes ticked away along with her own blood. Just before the blackness covered her completely, over the faint buzz of yellow jackets in the eaves outside the window, she heard the steady beat of a rescue helicopter. And off in the distance, coming closer, the sound of sirens.

In her arms, Jay looked at peace.

Fifty-one

Kasey stood under the striped canopy, a gentle afternoon breeze rustling the soft, crinkly material of her skirt and the matching sling, which helped to support her left arm. Although it had been nearly two months since the bullet had gone through her shoulder, fracturing the clavicle, it still ached now and then, especially when she tried to do too much, like today, trying to get everything ready for the wedding.

Kasey had been home only two days. After that fateful afternoon in Cold Springs, she had spent ten days in the hospital. The day following her release, she had left for Seattle to stay with her favorite aunt. Only Marianne, who called her every morning with a horoscope report, knew her whereabouts.

Kasey ignored the dull pain and tried to concentrate on the wedding ceremony taking place before her. From the corner of her eye, she saw Sherry inching her way along the left aisle of folding chairs toward her.

When Sherry reached her, she whispered, "I'm heading over to the buffet table. Your ma's there, getting things ready."

"I'm right behind you. Just want to catch the finale."

As Sherry passed, Kasey followed her with her eyes. She wore a high-collared blouse, one that hid the scars from the wounds Lucas Cage had so brutally inflicted upon her. Whenever Kasey thought of Lucas Cage, and she thought of him often, she felt both anger and sadness. Anger for his evil deeds and sadness for his victims. That animal would never hurt anyone again, but the pain he had doled out while he was alive would live on for a long, long time.

Sherry, it seemed, had already put it behind her, no longer afraid for the people she loved. Her recovery had started when she went to Det. Loweman with the truth about Cage. It was her visit to Loweman that afternoon that had prompted him to go out to the King house where a grim surprise awaited him—the double murder. When Loweman finally tracked down Brad and learned that Jay had taken nearly a million dollars from the cage, he followed a hunch and, with a couple units, headed out to Cage's isolated place in Cold Springs. He'd been almost halfway there when the 911 call from Kasey had come through and, as they say, the rest was history.

Brad's suspicious behavior had hinged on fear and greed. An anonymous someone, probably Cage, had called Brad to inform him his uncle planned to cut Cummings, and possibly Yanick, into the action, thus reducing Brad's interest in the club. In the hopes of getting rid of Howard, Brad had hired Dan Carne to try to set him up, to make it look as if Cummings were working with Ansel Doyle as the insider behind the sabotage to bring King's Club down. The night Kasey had caught him going through Jay's office safe he had been looking for an agreement or a contract, proof that his uncle was planning to give Cummings a share of the club.

A coroner's inquest reported Lucas Cage had died at the hands of Dianne King, who'd acted in self-defense. Dianne had died instantly when the blade of Cage's knife penetrated her chest, puncturing her heart. Manner of death: self-inflicted, accidental. The dishwasher, Juan Ruiz, had been released, all charges against him dropped.

The police had discovered a dried-up well on the Cold Springs property. Hidden inside was enough evidence to implicate Cage and Dianne as co-conspirators in the crimes perpetrated at King's Club. The letters from Dianne, sent to Cage's post office box, and the incriminating cassette setting up the deal between them, were all there. From the beginning Dianne had supplied Cage with inside information, with master keys and schedules. It was Dianne who had informed Cage about the vacancy at the Atwood house. It was doubtful Dianne had had any personal contact with Cage before his assault on her in the suite. At which point she must have realized what she was up against, trapped in the middle, in far too deep to pull out. All this Kasey learned from Frank Loweman within a few days of the deaths of Dianne and her partner in crime, Lucas Cage.

Something bumped Kasey's legs, bringing her back to the present. Snickers dropped an uprooted rosebush at her feet. The dog licked her hand, then flopped down to begin gnawing at the thorny limbs.

"Bad dog," she whispered mechanically.

The ceremony was winding down. From the back of the canopy, Kasey could scarcely hear the minister's words; but when Peggy and Artie exchanged a kiss, she knew the final vows had been spoken. Tears sprang to her eyes and she dabbed at them.

Tears came easy of late.

Kasey waited until the bride and groom had made their descent down the aisle before going off to help her mother and Sherry.

Food and drink for the reception were set out under another canopy. George was already there, popping corks and pouring champagne. Danny sat in the tree swing, his fingers busy with white crepe paper and ribbon, repeating the words, "Caution, explicit sexual content." Snickers abandoned his rosebush to romp happily around the yard, towing children on his back and knocking toddlers off their feet.

Marianne, a basket filled with birdseed wrapped in bright colored net in one hand and a huge bunch of helium-filled balloons in the other, managed to give Kasey a big hug. "What a wonderful day. Having you back home, Artie and Peg's wedding, and Mother Nature—God bless her cotton bloomers—showing up in all her finery." She waved the balloons to indicate the rich, brilliant, red-gold-and-orange autumn landscape.

Her mother handed her the balloons. "Peggy's going to toss the bouquet shortly," she said and quickly moved on.

A moment later, a hundred guests descended upon them. Kasey greeted them, directed them this way and that, and handed out helium-filled balloons.

An hour into the reception, with only one good arm, she soon realized her services were limited, that she was only in the way. She wished the newlyweds well, picked at some food, then went to her bungalow for an aspirin—the dull ache had become a constant throb.

There was a message from her father on the answering machine inviting her to drop by. Had she detected a slight slur in his speech? It was mid-month, the time his funds started to run low. Since that day at his apartment with Sasha, Kasey had made up her mind she would no longer enable her father. When he was ready to make an effort to quit drinking and gambling, she would support him one hundred percent, but until then he was on his own.

For the first time in months, she thought of Kevin. Kevin had been very much like her father. Needy, clinging, weak in spirit. She had loved him, wanted to care for him, wanted him to be happy. She wanted the same for her father. But in the two months away from home she had realized she could not be responsible for anyone's happiness but her own.

There were other messages, business associates and friends, but nothing from the one person who was heavy on her mind.

She thought back to the last time she had seen Jay King. In the hospital, off the critical list, and rapidly improving, he had just been transferred out of ICU to a private room. Heavily sedated those first few weeks, Jay had been unaware of Kasey's daily visits. The day she checked out of the hospital, she had entered his room to find him asleep. Without waking him, she had kissed him lightly on the lips and said goodbye. The following day she'd left town.

Not long after, Jay tried to contact her, leaving one message after another on her answering machine. When he finally called her mother, she told him Kasey had gone away and did not care to be reached at that time.

Kasey took two Advils, then stood at the garden window in her kitchen and looked out over the Bane property, property that would remain in the family for a good while yet. Although Kasey had wanted to be the one to save the ranch—*Perils of Pauline* . . . the heroine herself charging in on the white horse to save the day—it had been George Quackenbush who came to the rescue. With Kasey in the hospital recovering from the bullet wound, Marianne, not knowing where to turn, had disclosed to the boarders her financial status. George had offered to pay off the mortgage in return for assurance that the Atwoods would see to his grandson's welfare in the event he became unable to care for him—a request Marianne, who loved Danny like a son, would have gladly agreed to without any financial consideration.

Kasey left the bungalow and returned to the festivities. The cake had been cut and the folding chairs cleared out of the big canopy where dancing was now in full swing.

She passed in front of a group of women just as Peggy tossed the bridal bouquet. The bouquet hit Kasey's cloth sling and clung for an instant before being snatched away by a young woman in an advanced stage of pregnancy. Kasey caught her mother's eager eye. She held up empty hands, smiled ruefully, and shrugged her one good shoulder. Marianne made a face, then laughed good-naturedly.

Everyone looked so happy, so carefree. There was nothing like a wedding to make one think of good times ahead. Kasey thought of her horoscope: *Exploring long-buried feelings will liberate you. Doubts left over from a previous experience could discourage future happiness. Don't be shackled by the past— reach out.*

She returned to her bungalow for her purse, then headed for her car.

* * *

With the soft, muted shades of dusk at her back, Kasey stepped through the glass doors into a kaleidoscope of flashing lights and ringing bells. She felt an instant rush. For the past eight weeks she had curled herself into an embryonic state in an atmosphere of gentle showers and the lush greens and subtle blues of nature, avoiding stimuli of any kind. The sounds, the colors, now surrounding her were bold and brash, artificial, almost garish. And she had missed them.

She caught sight of Brad King first, walking toward the elevators with another man. Right after the shootings, Brad had come to see her in the hospital, apologizing for his part in the scenario. Their encounter had been somewhat strained in the beginning, but ended well, with Brad kissing her forehead and saying that whenever she was ready for a handsome young man on the rise, she knew where to find him. There would always be a special place in her heart for Brad, she thought, as she watched him and the other man stop to talk.

It took Kasey a moment to realize the man with Brad was Jay.

Jay's movements were slow, careful, his recent injury more than apparent. He held a hand to his chest, rubbing absently at the place where Dianne's bullet had entered. He was much thinner; yet to her relief, he looked stronger, more robust than she would have expected.

As she neared the elevator, Kasey slowed. Her heart did a little jig in her chest. A lot had happened. A lot of time had passed. Would he still want to see her?

Brad moved away and Jay entered the elevator. The doors closed; the lighted numbers above the door stopped at three.

She was tempted to turn and walk away. Instead, she took the elevator to the third floor. She entered the outer office of the executive suite. Gail's desk sat empty. The doors to Jay's office stood open. She went in and, finding that room empty, continued to the open door of the monitor room. She found

Jay standing in the middle of the room staring down at the architect's model. In his hand was her shell comb, the one he had taken from her hair the night they'd made love.

"Hi," she said, her voice scarcely above a whisper.

He turned, saw her in the doorway. The movement, though slow, seemed to cause him pain.

They stood staring at each other. She wanted to go to him, to put her arms around him and hold him. Wanted to feel his arms around her, feel his heart beating against hers.

The moment slipped by and then it was too late.

They both spoke at once, "How are—" They stopped, smiled at each other.

Kasey answered first. "Fine. I'm fine. And you?"

"Can't do fifty laps anymore. Can't even do one. But I feel stronger everyday, so . . ." He let the words die away. He pointed at her sling.

"Oh, this. It's just for support. The doctor wants me to start using the arm. Physical therapy." She adjusted the folds.

"It becomes you. But then you'd look good in a full-body cast."

Kasey smiled. "Business looks good."

"It is. It picked up again. Who would have guessed that the same publicity that threatened to ruin it all is now bringing the people in, curious to see the club where the owner's wife hired a hitman to take out her husband."

She looked down at the architect's model. "I didn't see any construction. Have you postponed it?"

Jay nodded. "Somehow it doesn't seem so vital anymore. It's ironic, isn't it? Dianne was afraid I'd sink everything into the club and there would be nothing left. She hired Cage to kill me and Brad so she could sell it to Ansel Doyle while there was still a hefty profit to be made. And now that she . . . she's gone, the expansion is no longer important to me. Life—being alive—knowing that you and Brad survived, that's the only thing that matters."

Kasey nodded. She felt the same.

"Are you sure you're all right?" he asked. "I mean, emotionally?"

"I have dreams, but . . . well, you know . . ." Kasey had a recurring dream that Jay had died and she had killed Dianne with a bullet to her chest.

This time it was Jay's turn to nod.

"I talked to Frank. He told me about Dianne's hiring Cage. Jay, how did she know to contact Cage?"

"She was in Vegas four years ago with me when I spotted him. She must have overheard me telling Cummings that Cage looked like a guy I knew in the service who had it in for me. When Doyle came to town awhile back and made the offer on the club, she probably saw the newspaper clipping and recognized Cage. It wouldn't have been hard for her to find out who he was, then contact him."

"What about Howard Cummings?"

"He had nothing to do with it—although Brad tried to cash in on a perfect opportunity to make it appear otherwise. It was Dianne all the way."

They stood talking in the dim room with the model and monitors. Neither suggested they go into the office where they could visit in comfort. It was as if moving, even a few feet, might break the spell and one or the other would suddenly vanish.

"Jay, I'm sorry. Sorry about Dianne."

"Yes, so am I."

"I wanted to thank you for paying my medical bills."

"It was the least I could do. You could've been killed trying to save my life. I wish I had never involved you in the first place."

"You didn't; Dianne did. She called me in to divert suspicion from herself. She hoped I would make the connection between you and Cage. That was done, but by then Cage was a loose cannon and I ended up getting in the way. She didn't expect Cage to double-cross her."

"And she didn't expect me to fall for you." Jay's eyes locked on hers. "Just knowing you were on my side made the aftermath that much more bearable. Kasey, why did you run away?"

"To think. To try to put it all together. I'd been running on sheer emotion for so long. I needed time to clear my head and . . ." She paused and looked into his eyes. "And to look into my heart."

"What did you see there?"

"I want to say 'I'm here. . . . That must mean something,' but that wouldn't be entirely right. I'm here because I had to see for myself how you were. How you were doing. I called the hospital every day until you were released. But hearing from some nurse that you were recovering nicely is not the same as seeing with my own eyes."

"What now?"

She shook her head. "I don't know."

Jay stepped up to her. He held out the shell comb, offering it to her.

She took it.

"Maybe we can do it right this time. I've been out of the loop for a while, I'm not sure I remember . . ." he paused.

Reach out.

Kasey reached up and touched his face. Touched the scar at his brow. They moved into each other's arms, slowly, gently, each mindful of the other's frailty. Yet, for Kasey, just this bit of closeness was enough to fill that aching void.

The speaker phone crackled to life, then Gail's voice said, "Jay, they're waiting for you in the boardroom."

She stepped back. "Call me."

Jay leaned over the console, wincing from the soreness in his chest, and switched on the monitors, the ones along Kasey's expected route. Having Kasey reenter his life was worth any pain he had to endure. If anyone could help get his life back in order again, it would be she.

Jay stared at the monitors. He didn't have long to wait.

Kasey, easily recognizable with her left arm in a sling, stepped off the elevator on the main floor into camera view. Another camera picked her up as she strode toward the valet entrance. There was a lightness in her step, and Jay hoped he had something to do with that.

He expected to see her pass through the double doors and disappear, but was surprised when she stopped at the last row of slot machines. She put her purse on the stool and, with the use of only one hand, began to dig around inside. She then inserted three coins in the end machine, pulled the handle, and walked away without waiting for the reels to stop.

Jay zoomed the lens to the reels. Three bars lined up. There was no sound on the monitors, but Jay didn't need sound to know the machine was ringing loud to announce the payoff. Quarters dropped into the tray.

Jay panned back again. Kasey, already ten feet or so from the machine, turned to look back. She seemed surprised, then she smiled. She started back only to stop on the backside of the ringing machine.

Bewildered by her actions, Jay continued to watch. Midway down the same row of slots where Kasey's machine was spitting out the last of its payoff was Agnes JoBeth Snodgrass, age 72, number 1589 in a certain book consisting of casino outcasts. Agnes was the club's most notorious silver-miner.

Kasey had seen her, too.

Kasey tucked her purse under her arm, adjusted her sling, then turned and walked away.

Jay switched off the monitors. The image of Kasey's light-hearted step as she left the club would be enough to carry him through the remainder of the day, and a few days beyond.

About the Author

Carol Davis Luce is the author of many novels including *NIGHT STALKER, NIGHT PREY* and *NIGHT PASSAGE.* Four of her five novels are set in Nevada, from a small mining town to the majestic waters of Lake Tahoe. *NIGHT GAME* is set in the flash and neon of the gaming milieu. She lives with her husband Bob in Sparks, Nevada. Carol enjoys hearing from her readers—write to her c/o Zebra Books. Please include a self-addressed stamped envelope if you wish a response.